Praise for Cindy Nord's
Cutteridge Series

"You'll savor every ounce of passion, adventure, and transformation in Cindy Nord's exquisite debut novel. I didn't want it to end!"
  - *Cynthia Wright, Romantic Times and Affaire de Coeur multiple award winner on No Greater Glory*

"*No Greater Glory* is a powerful, well-crafted Civil War era novel of complex emotions and beautifully drawn characters that explores the inherent risks of falling in love with one's enemy."
  - *Laura Taylor, multiple Romantic Times Award winner*

"The love scenes are steamy yet tender. Recommended for anyone who enjoys historical romance, as well as those who would find appeal in a steamier Gone with the Wind."
  - *Library Journal on No Greater Glory*

"Maybe it is the historical aspect of this novel that made me enjoy it as much as I have or maybe it's the fact that Nord knows how to pen a proper and adventurous western, either way this book is certainly one to read!"
  - *Night Owl Reviews on With Open Arms*

"Nord's *With Open Arms*...has lots of chemistry between Callie and Jackson no matter how much they try to fight it. [...] I look forward to reading the rest of the series when the books come out."
  - *Romance Junkies*

Look for these other titles by Cindy Nord

Now Available:

The Cutteridge Series
No Greater Glory
An Unlikely Hero

Coming Spring, 2018

By Any Means

With Open Arms

Cindy Nord

I love to receive emails from readers who share their 'book thoughts' with me...let's connect! cindy@cindynord.com

This is a work of fiction. Names, characters, businesses, places, events and incidents are either the products of the author's imagination or used in a fictitious manner. Any resemblance to actual persons, living or dead, or actual events is purely coincidental.

With Open Arms
Copyright © 2014 by DCT Associates
Cover by Lyn Taylor
Formatted by Jacob Hammer
Published by DCT Associates

Digital Edition ISBN: 978-0-9976573-4-0
Print Edition ISBN: 978-0-9976573-7-1

First Digital Publication: August 2014
Second Digital Publication: March 2017
First Print Publication: March 2015
Second Print Publication: March 2017

Dedication

To Tom...always and forever, the love of my life. And to Ben and Bill—best brothers ever. ♥

Chapter One

Arizona Territory
March 1866

The warmth of day vanished with remarkable speed, shrouding the desert under a bone-chilling twilight. Murky shadows crept across the Rincons' rocky ridgeline as Jackson Neale slipped into the concealing darkness. Seasoned by four years of war, his body tensed with a caution that defined survival. His fingers folded around the worn, wooden grip of a well-oiled Colt. He could count on one hand the people he'd befriended on the trek westward from Virginia, and knew with absolute certainty the person riding into camp tonight wasn't one of them. Only a fool would enter without hailing first, yet this stranger displayed a boldness that amazed him.

In stony silence, the uninvited guest guided a horse toward the saddlebags by the fire. Small, flickering flames inside the ring of fieldstones washed a glow across the bay's ruddy flank.

His gaze moved upward.

Mexican spurs strapped around the heels of silver-tipped boots caught the fire's glint. Leather chaps encased long legs. And despite the chill, a jacket hung open to reveal a .44-caliber Remington strapped around denim-covered hips. A flat-brimmed hat, its crown encircled with a *concha* band of hammered silver, hid the face of the evening caller.

The visitor dropped to the ground, the rowels on the spurs chinking when they hit the sand. He glanced around, then crouched on a knee beside the saddlebags.

Jackson tightened his lips as all caution evaporated. He knew full well how to deal with bandits, having met a few already on his ride westward. He bolted from the shadows and slammed full-force into the unsuspecting thief. Momentum drove them both to the ground. In an instant, he pinned the fool against the sand. His right hand rose in a tight fist, his left shifting across the cotton plaid shirtfront to seek a firmer grip. In an instant, all the fight, all the pent-up energy, everything inside him dissolved. He'd never be too cold or too tired to forget the lushness of a female breast.

His eyes widened as his arm dropped to his side.

On a sharp breath, he rasped, "You're...you're a woman. I thought you were—"

"Get off me, you stupid son of a..."

The profanity spilled from her mouth with such ease that Jackson swallowed a lungful of air. Indigo eyes blazed up at him like shards of broken glass, and wild wisps of sun-stained hair danced against the curve of her cheek. Swathed beneath layers of trail dust, the hellion's hard edge and tone of voice contrasted sharply with what his eyes told him about the rest of her. His heart responded with an engaging hitch, but he blamed the rush of heat that flushed his face on the nearby campfire, not the comical fact that this frosty little tart had taken him by complete surprise.

He gained control of his emotions. "Why are you riflin' through my gear?"

Leather-gloved hands rose to thump against his chest. "I said get off me. I...can't breathe."

He shifted sideways, pushing against the ground to stand. With a muffled oath, Jackson staggered back another step as she bolted to her feet. She bent to retrieve her hat and slapped it against her thigh. As she did, his gaze raked down the noteworthy curves of her body. Her masculine outfit provided a disguise, yet closer inspection did little to hide her figure. The fringe on her chaps rode both shapely legs, and the sight reminded him of the pleasures a woman could offer— sultry, sexy and full of endless possibilities. In this particular woman, however, all softness appeared to end with the supple leather.

Anger sealed her mouth, and the scowl that creased her features indicated not a shred of sweetness filled her body, either.

An involuntary clench seized his jaw. "Good God, woman, I could've killed you."

She issued an impatient huff. "I live with danger every day, so your words barely register." With a quick flick of her wrist, she twisted her hair into a knot atop her head, then jammed her hat back over the tarnished curls.

Jackson had never expected to see such a raw woman, and the enmity in her bright eyes held all the subtlety of baying hounds. She cursed smoother than a camp-following whore, but she'd die young if she needed to steal from a passerby to survive. He peered into the darkness but heard no other threatening sounds. She obviously rode alone.

His attention drifted back. "Since you're so nicely groomed now, start explaining what you're doing in my camp."

"Your camp?" Her razor-sharp laugh sliced straight through him. "You might think this is your camp, but you're standing on Cutteridge land and I own every damn acre." The heat in her eyes branded him where he stood. "And, I sure don't recall giving you permission to trespass here or anywhere else."

Her statement brought Jackson up short. He'd ridden more than twenty-five miles today, but hadn't figured on reaching Cutteridge property until sometime tomorrow morning. The image on a faded daguerreotype, tucked beside the worn map in his saddlebag, flashed across his mind. The woman's likeness, given to him months ago by his colonel, had been branded into memory. Yet there was barely a whisper of resemblance between the serene beauty reflected in his picture and the foul-mouthed hellion who stood before him now. Somehow, Jackson kept the blistering bile of disappointment from reaching his voice. "Cutteridge land, is it?"

"You heard me clear enough." Her expression hardened as she pressed closer. She brought her point closer still. "All Cutteridge. And all mine."

From somewhere beyond the campfire's light, the forlorn howl of a coyote underscored her words. Smoke curled upward in lazy tendrils. Jackson's nerves constricted as the woman's words slipped around him like a noose. And tightened. He tipped back his head and stared at the wide expanse of stars inundating the ebony canvas above him. "Oh God," he mumbled, the lump in his throat refusing to move. "Please don't let this shrew be Colleen Cutteridge."

A bolt of raw adrenaline shot through Callie when the sound of her given name spilled from the tall, hard-angled man. Her pulse hammered in her chest. She squared her shoulders, her chin jutting higher as his gaze reconnected with hers.

"We've never met," she snapped. "I'd have remembered you." Obviously, he wasn't some cowpoke looking to encroach on her land. Not this one. A red flag rippled inside her, and she pointed to the campfire in an attempt to hide her unease. "I spotted this a half mile away. A fire this bright's a blatant invitation for Apache lookin' to lift a scalp."

Stupid oaf.

A smug smile lifted the man's lips and a slash of white appeared. "I appreciate the warning."

From his chiseled jaw carved straight from granite, to his cool, collected calmness, the man possessed an ease of manner that unnerved Callie, and she didn't appreciate the feeling one damn bit. A stubborn spirit, her companion and strength these past five years, spiked through her. She rubbed her midriff where his thighs had bruised her ribs. And for one disturbing moment, she couldn't help but admire his impressive strength. Granted, he'd bruised her ego more than her body, but—

Callie caught her thoughts and jerked them back into control, exactly where she liked things best. She took a full step backward, the rowel on her boot heel chinking across the tension. "Look, mister, I don't give a squat if the Apache scalp you this night or the next. I just don't want the bloody deed done on my ranch." Her fingers curled around the grip of her revolver as her gaze scanned his belongings, then moved on to his horse waiting in the shadows. "I could shoot you myself for trespassing and spare the Apache the trouble of killin' you. Or…"

her gaze drifted back to lock with his, "...you can gather your gear, saddle that fine Morgan you've got line-tied over there, and get the hell off my land."

Seconds passed like hours before the dark-haired man bent to retrieve his hat.

He straightened slowly, pulling the brim of the sweat-stained Stetson low upon his head. Through dark, cold eyes, he stared at her.

With each thump of her heart, the stranger's unnerving quiet further frayed her nerves. A log from the campfire shifted deeper into the flames, sending a shower of sparks heavenward. The pungent aroma of burning mesquite filled her nostrils and fused with a raw, unspoken awareness that sizzled from the man.

He leaned forward, the brim of his hat bumping against hers. The thinnest hint of amusement lifted his lips. "It appears I won't be riding from your life quite so soon." His words were too soft, too controlling. "And this land isn't just *your land* any longer." Without removing his gaze, he reached into his frock coat. With the speed of a striking rattlesnake, an envelope appeared in his leather-gloved hand, then rose between them until level with her eyes. "The name's Jackson Neale and this makes me your new partner."

Chapter Two

Callie couldn't remember a longer ride back to the ranch, the trip accomplished in stony silence. Who would've thought a day spent tracking a wild stallion would end with this outrageous claimant sitting across from her now? Her foot tapped the rust-colored tiles beneath the desk, and the tick of the mantel clock ricocheted through her as she waited for the man to ease into the opposite chair.

The bulky envelope landed on the desktop in front of her.

He smiled, then added, "Your brother sold me his half of the ranch ten months ago."

Her heart slammed against her ribs as she raked her gaze back to his. The glow from the desk lamp illuminated his face, highlighting years' worth of exposure to nature's elements. Beneath high cheekbones, several days' worth of stubble shadowed a strong jaw, and a dark, full mustache only added rugged masculinity to his handsome face.

He's obviously a liar. And a damn good one, at that.

"My brother wrote many times about remaining east, yet in all our correspondence, he never once mentioned selling off his half of Dos Caballos. In light of what you've just said, I find that extremely odd. Don't you?"

"Given the fact that he was my good friend as well as my commanding officer, yes."

Callie attempted to swallow past a lump of unfamiliar fear rising in the back of her throat. Even as this jackal spoke, she grappled with the horrific possibility that his tale might just be true. Her gaze swept over his shoulders and the unadorned military frockcoat that covered their wide span, the blue wool now faded to gunmetal gray. Dark-blue uniform pants hugged long legs, and black-leather riding boots showed the wear of the trail. Her heart sank further. Good God, could Reece have actually sold his birthright to this…vagrant? The man issued an audible sigh, and the grating sound forced her attention back to his face.

"Why don't you read the letter," he suggested, dropping his hat upon the desk with a loud thud. He raised both hands, then tunneled his fingers through overly long hair.

A chill oozed over her and she dropped her gaze to the envelope. The packet clashed with the rich wood of her mahogany desk. She forbade her fingers to shake as they slid over the parchment. Inhaling deeply, she broke the wax seal, removed the correspondence, then brought the papers to the lamplight to read.

My Dearest Sister,

If you're holding this letter, then you've no doubt met my good friend, Jackson Neale. From my previous posts, you know I've decided to remain in Virginia and marry Emaline. I do believe this was the best way to break the news of your new partnership. I ask your forgiveness for doing so in such a blunt manner. Knowing you, however, any other avenue would have been met with stubborn resistance.

Your new partner hails from Philadelphia with a background in banking. As my second-in-command, my major, during the war, I counted on him heavily. I'm confident you'll be able to do the same. He's intelligent, honest and one of the bravest men you'll ever meet. I trust him implicitly, and in time, you will learn to trust him too. This I promise. He's a good complement for you, Cal; he's strong and able, just like you've had to be these past few years. Give him a chance; he'll become your greatest asset. He was mine.

With much affection,
Reece

Her eyes slipped closed.

The scrawling signature belonged to her brother. Cold fear encased her and she could scarcely breathe. She would have to think of something quickly to divert this newest onslaught of change. She opened her eyes and shifted aside the letter to view a parchment document: the legal deed that sealed the deal. Another wave of despair washed over her. Why would Reece shackle her to a stranger?

And a saddle-worn war veteran, no less!

Callie donned her most menacing expression. From raiders to rustlers, she'd controlled many a situation by presenting just such a formidable show. She glared at the man who lounged before her, yet he didn't flinch or look away. In fact, he appeared not the least bit intimidated by her blistering stare.

"Look—" Her voice propelled across the desk in a righteous fury. "I don't care how agreeable my brother thinks you are, I don't agree to any of this. And I intend to post a missive to him straight away to share my views about this asinine arrangement." A surge of bitterness cracked her voice. "I am fully capable of running this ranch without anyone else, and have done so for years while Reece was off playing soldier. What I don't need is some high-browed stranger ridin' in here thinking he can tell me how to do things differently." She tossed the bundle to the desk and clamped her lips together to keep them from trembling.

The man inhaled, then exhaled with a slow rush of air. "That is certainly not my intention, so let's just calm down. Reece chose to remain in Virginia and I was looking to come west, so this was a sound business arrangement for both of us. But I understand your frustration. Since you obviously didn't know beforehand, this must come as quite a shock."

Callie interlocked her arms across her chest, her sharp laugh anything but welcoming. "Well, you're absolutely right about that." His words set both her teeth and emotions on edge, but she refused to allow the logic that ebbed through his voice to influence her.

He motioned to the papers. "I apologize for the insensitive way this has been delivered. I had no way of knowing he hadn't told you."

An invisible barrier penetrated past muscle and bone to barricade Callie's heart, corralling any warmth that might try to escape. "I don't want a partner,

Mr. Neale."

"I sympathize with you, but the fact remains I've made the purchase and I intend to stake my claim." He reached for his hat and pulled it low over his forehead. "Perhaps you'll feel better about all this tomorrow. Things usually improve in the light of day, and we can talk more about everything then." He gathered the papers and slipped them inside his coat pocket.

Resentment buffeted Callie like grit from a sandstorm, and sent a blazing heat up her neck to settle into two hot spots on her cheeks. "Let's just finish things up now. That way you can be on your way come daylight." She leaned forward. "I'll buy you out. I'll pay you every cent you've paid my brother. With interest, of course."

A smile stacked up at the corner of the man's mouth. "Sorry. I'm not for sale. Besides, I'm beginning to like it here."

She glared at him for a full minute. *An impasse.* Fresh waves inundated her as the pain of her brother's entrapment chiseled wider the hole in her heart. She shoved her chair back, climbing to her feet. They'd get nowhere tonight. "Well, I can assure you, your stay will be short-lived."

"Unlikely," he said, straightening in the chair. "In the meanwhile, though, how about I bunk down in your brother's room, since my purchase also includes half this house." An arrogant gleam brightened his eyes. "With your permission, of course."

Callie bolted around the desk and crossed the room, flinging open the library door. "Pilar!" she bellowed into the darkened hallway.

The sound of shuffling feet filled the candlelit foyer as a short, rotund woman skidded around the corner from the entry hall and shuffled toward her.

"*Sí, señorita?*" The cook's chest rose and fell from the exertion.

"Our visitor will be staying in my brother's room. I'll need you to show him the way."

The woman shot a glance to the man, nodded and then stepped back into the hallway.

Callie pivoted just as Jackson Neale unfolded his large body from the chair.

In three strides, he crossed the room to tower over her.

"Call me a visitor if you want," he said. "But we both know differently, don't we?"

Panic quivered through her, raising her voice. "Until I get the full details from my brother, that's exactly who you are and nothing more." She turned to leave but he braced his arm against the doorframe to block her exit. The intense look he passed over her caused her to step back and bump into the wooden facing. The coolness of the pine nipped through her cotton shirt.

He leaned down and leveled his gaze with hers. "Let's get something straight right now. I didn't ride the width of this country to be run roughshod by a woman wearing britches. So, the sooner you climb down from that high horse you're straddling the better this'll be for both of us." His body eased back a mere fraction. "Now, it's been a long day and I'm damned tired. So if you must continue all this, do so tomorrow morning while I'm looking at our finances. And make sure the ledgers are available to me, because I'm finished with our howdy-dos for tonight."

A moment later, he pushed from the doorframe and swept past her.

Callie threw the pale-blue towel onto the top of her washstand, then twisted her hair into a damp braid. She secured the end with a scrap of leather before she turned away from her mirrored image. Her insides churned. Reece hadn't sold her out for money. They had funds in the coffers to last a lifetime. And he'd always encouraged her to be self-reliant, to be strong and fight for her rightful place in the world. So why the hell had he done this?

Like a caged puma, she turned and paced the room. The chill off the terra-cotta tiles beneath her bare toes seeped upward to settle beside her burning rage. She dropped to the chair, tugged on her cotton socks and then jammed her feet into worn, ankle-high roper boots.

What a conceited vulture.

Jackson Neale presented the self-assurance of one accustomed to getting his way. And, to make matters worse, he wanted to see the record books! Anxiety at the thought of laying the financial status of the ranch before him tightened her chest. Reece had ridden east five years earlier to bury his pain-filled memories of a dead wife under the responsibilities of a Union command. He'd also left full control of the ranch to her. And she'd done her best with the ledgers, but the horses held her interest more. Those she understood. And respected. In fact, she'd spent her entire life surrounded by the wily beasts. But as the months faded into years, a heavy yoke weighed across her shoulders when it came to the juggling finances. The monotony of paying bills on time had become an onerous ordeal. Callie prayed for the day her brother would return to set right the mess she'd made of their books.

But now, that day would never come.

Heaviness pressed across her chest. She knew the sensation well. A weeping sadness clamped hold, digging deep the talons of despair. Onrushing tightness swelled inside her throat.

The death of her parents and her sister-in-law had stripped away the apron strings of her childhood. Her tenth birthday... On every birthday since, the horror resurfaced to reinforce life's bitter lesson. Loving meant losing. To her it always had. And now...her brother was gone.

Another love.

Another painful loss.

Callie stood and balled her hands into tight fists at her sides. Ragged fingernails bit into calloused palms. Like countless times before, she suppressed her sorrow and staunched the flow of tears that time had failed to dissipate. She inhaled deeply, in and out, faster and faster, until she tamped down the grief. As she always had, Callie drew strength in containment, strength in denial, strength in refusing the truth. This house, her land, represented all that remained of her family, and she'd be damned before she'd let her only link to them perish too. To survive the upcoming battle, she would need all her strength to expunge Jackson Neale from Dos Caballos.

Dawn had barely pinked the sky when Callie stepped into the dining room, oblivious to everything except the pungent aroma of coffee. She headed straight for the pot on the sideboard. Surely, the scalding brew would help revive her and ease her past the previous restless night.

"*Buenos dias, Patróna*." Standing near the table, her cook folded small, blue-veined hands before a crisp apron fronting an embroidered Puebla dress.

An answering smile sprang to Callie's lips. "Mornin', Pilar." She accepted the filled-to-the-brim cup the woman held out. From deep in Mexico's core, Pilar represented the true spirit of her people. Earthy and indomitable, she reflected an ancient culture every day through her hearty food servings, the cuisine a true reflection of her heritage. The mother country still pulsed strongly through the old cook's heart.

A sigh of pleasure escaped Callie's lips as the sturdy brew slid down her throat. "Bring on breakfast. I'm starving."

Pilar's eager-to-please wave reflected her excitement about cooking for someone again as she glided through the opening and disappeared into the kitchen. Callie smiled as she palmed the mug, glad she'd hired the cook away from the St. Xavier mission.

Even though Pilar didn't talk much, Callie sure enjoyed her company.

A deep voice resonated from across the room. "I was beginning to wonder if you'd show up."

Thoughts scattered as Callie whirled toward the sound, sloshing liquid over the rim of her cup. Hot coffee met tender skin.

"Sonofabitch!" she rasped. Her gaze connected with Jackson's the exact moment she jammed her fingers into her mouth to suck off the burning mess. The interloper sat at the far end of the trestle table, the same overbearing grin he'd worn last night plastered across his face. She jerked the digits from between her lips and wiped them on her denim-covered hip.

"I don't recall needin' to report to you," she spat.

He raised his cup in a mock salute. Over the rim of china, his gaze locked with hers and he smiled, then took a quick sip before settling the cup upon the table. "I assumed you got early starts around here. Apparently, I was mistaken."

Inside her leather boots, Callie's toes curled so tight her instep cramped.

"Six o'clock is early enough around here, Mr. Neale."

"Call me Jackson. It'll make things easier."

"For whom?" She dropped onto the closest chair, her cup thumping to the table. "You're not wanted here, or have you forgotten that?"

"No, you've made it abundantly clear." He placed his napkin beside his now-empty plate. "But your wishes don't alter the fact I'm staying."

Her breath thinned. "This is a busy place, Neale. The last thing I need underfoot is some worn-out soldier who knows nothin' about horses."

His mouth sunk into a smirk, bringing the haughty glint back to his eyes. "You've no idea my abilities, princess."

The door from the kitchen swung open. Pilar shuffled in with breakfast and deposited the fragrant offering before Callie. The aromatic steam rising from the plate swirled upward in fragrant wisps. Soft bread soaked in egg yolks rested beside the *huevos rancheros,* and the tomato sauce drenching the top of the fried egg caught the morning sunlight and glistened back at her upon its corn tortilla bed. Callie tried to ignore the grumble in her stomach and refocused her thoughts, allowing her frustrations to mount when the cook turned to whisk away the man's empty plate.

His rumbling voice met her ears. "A fine meal, Pilar. And you were right, I was much hungrier than I thought."

The cook's round cheeks lifted with her easy smile. "I glad you eat, *Señor* Neale."

"Yep," he said, leaning back in his chair. "I haven't tasted such hearty fare since before the war."

Pilar's blush deepened. "Well, that's what I do best, *señor*. I cook! Anytime you hungry, you come to me. I make you something." She turned to Callie. "We feed him good here, *sí?*"

Callie narrowed her eyes under the man's steady gaze. "I don't care if he starves to death, Pilar. And I sure as hell don't want you waitin' on him hand and foot." She tried to ignore the gasp that tumbled from the old woman's mouth. Wasn't finagling half ownership of her ranch enough for this smooth-talking vagabond? Now he thought to charm over the cook too? Hell no. And she'd clarify the situation with Pilar at the earliest opportunity.

"She doesn't want me here," he explained, a smirk skirting his mouth. The cook nodded, then scurried back through the swinging door, empty dishes rattling in her arms as she swept from view.

Jackson shot his gaze down the long table and let his resentment build. The situation would have been comical had he not spent good money to purchase this misery. Icy blue eyes glared back at him for a full minute before his new partner dropped her attention to her breakfast.

Jeezus…what an insufferable shrew.

He perused the heaping mounds on her plate, the hearty feast enough to feed half his regiment. No delicate bird, this woman. Apparently, she worked hard and had a hunger to prove it. Nowhere in her controlled appearance could he find the wild-haired waif he had encountered last night. Today, the tart-tongued hellion had curtailed her sun-drenched curls into a tight braid. A dark kerchief wrapped around her slender throat, the ends of the faded cloth stuffed into the V-shaped opening of a full-sleeved white shirt.

The colonel's curvaceous sister was nothing short of a mystery, and the stories Reece had shared about her sharply contrasted with the woman who now sat across from Jackson.

He drained the last succulent drop of coffee. Infused with a soft nutty flavor, the brew was far superior to the bitter ordure he'd been forced to drink during the war. His frustration edged into curiosity as he lowered the cup to the table. *Surely to God there's more to this woman than cursing and insolence.* The bonneted image of the ethereal beauty smiling back at him in his daguerreotype flashed once more across his mind. She wasn't at all what he'd expected and this partnership would not be the easy one he'd anticipated.

Jackson shifted his gaze to the bank of windows on his left. Morning sun filtered through the thin curtains and laid a cozy guise across the room. Adept at ignoring the ache carved out by four years of battle, what he longed for was a new beginning, a halcyon of peace where he could forget the atrocities of war and the responsibilities of command. He'd paid the price and earned it.

His thoughts slipped to the ranch's assets. Taking another fortifying breath, Jackson stood. His new partner swiveled her head upward, and he tried to ignore the ever-present scowl that twisted her comely features. He leaned forward, placed both palms flat upon the wood and stared down the length of pine.

"When you're finished here, join me in the library. We'll go over the financial records together." She shoved a rolled-up tortilla into her mouth and simply glared at him. That she refused to answer further irritated Jackson. He pushed from the table, then strode to the doorway. At the threshold, he glanced over his shoulder. "But don't rush on my account, hellion. You take all the time you need." He slipped from the room, a smirk wrenching his lips sideways when he heard her fork clatter to her plate.

Jackson eased into the leather chair and shook his head in disbelief. He'd spent most of his adulthood before the war pampering the fine ladies of Philadelphia. And he'd had a high time doing so. In fact, most women he'd entertained had been pleased to be in his company. He was quite skilled in taking both their innocence and their hearts.

So what exactly had he gotten himself into here?

Not once had Reece mentioned his sister was such a… Jackson scrambled to think of the perfect word to describe the hellion. Hell's fire, she didn't need or want pampering, and she wouldn't be open to one damn thing he had to offer. Months ago, he'd confided to Reece he was tired of the roguish lifestyle. He wanted nothing more than to find the kind of supportive, tender woman his friend had married.

A groan fell from Jackson's lips as he ran his hands through his hair. When he'd decided against returning to his father's bank, and instead invested in a place of his own, he never dreamed it would turn out like this. He leaned back in the chair, the cool leather dousing the fires of his disappointment. *And I thought to stroll in and take charge with my smooth charms and humor.*

His dry laugh echoed in the room.

Would it have made a difference if Reece had been honest about his sister? Probably not. Hell-bent on riding west, Jackson looked forward to putting distance between himself and bloodstained battlefields back east. Buying half of Dos Caballos gave him the opportunity to do just that, to build again instead of destroy, a solid replacement for the past four years spent wrestling the gods of war.

His thoughts returned to Colleen Cutteridge.

Perhaps he'd been a little too harsh with her. After all, her belligerent behavior was, if not enchanting, at least understandable. No one liked being bushwhacked with bad news, although the thought that he was viewed as such unsettled him. His sigh disturbed the dust motes peppering through the sunbeams that fell across the desk. The air still carried a trace of an old fire mixed around the subtle scent of leather. His unwilling partner's sapphire eyes, blazing brighter than any fire ever could, shimmered back into recall.

"And Reece told me you were such a sweet, young thing," he whispered to the sunshiny streaks in the room. He shoved aside his maddening thoughts. With the restlessness of one accustomed to activity, he pulled his attention back into control.

Before the war, he'd worked in all aspects of the banking environment and had developed a keen eye for finances alongside a fair bit of legal knowledge. As a full partner, he didn't need anyone's damn permission to look at the ledgers.

Jackson slid his gaze past dusty literary volumes on even dustier shelves. Nothing even resembled a financial notebook. His fingers slipped over the brass handles on the desk before him. A loud creak of protest stopped his attempt to open the drawer... The resistance only fueled his determination.

He gave a hard jerk on the knobs and this time, the wood slid free.

The sunbeams splashed across a disorderly collection of papers. Dozens of drafts and notes—IOUs, bank scripts, crumpled and yellowed with age—all shoved into the opening and apparently forgotten. The dust motes swirled around the discovery in a taunting dance as Jackson stared down at what seemed years' worth of disorder.

Good God, is this how the woman keeps the accounts?

He opened the drawer farther, and a handful of paid promissory notes fluttered to the floor beside his boot. *Jeezus.* The hellion cursed like a muleskinner and strutted around in britches like a man, yet acted as if she were the damned Queen of England. The very least she could do was keep their books in order. He could lose his entire investment if she'd left any unpaid bills buried under all this disaster. If creditors foreclosed on her, they'd sure as hell foreclose on him. He'd expected anything but this mess.

Jackson shoved his hands into the interior and raked out endless scraps of pay vouchers, sales slips and bank statements, mounding them into a haphazard pile on the desk. He shook his head.

"This is the first thing I'm changing." A deep growl rolled from his lips and he forced his shoulders to relax. Her highness had shoved her last piece of paper into this desk drawer. Of that, he was certain.

Callie stopped at the closed door and leaned forward, placing both hands against the wood. The smooth surface stood in sharp contrast to the heat roiling through her. She drew a deep breath, struggling to quell the staccato beat of her heart.

Her brother's words filtered up from somewhere deep inside.

Try to act like a lady, Cal.

She shook aside the recollection and reached for the brass handle. The library door eased open. Her gaze fastened on the man sitting at the desk. *Her desk.* Mounded before him lay a huge pile of the transactions and paper receipts she'd paid, then conveniently forgotten.

Embarrassment swept through Callie at her ineptness in record keeping, followed closely by the bewildering pain of his intrusion. She shoved open the door, the groan of hinges and a loud thump when the wood connected with the wall filled the room.

Neale's head rose, his startled gaze changing into a rancorous glare. "Is this what you call managing a ranch?" His hand swept over the mounds of papers.

Callie's lips pulled taut. Her eyes narrowed. Any thought of civility that might've been lingering in her mind flew out the sun-drenched windows. She drove forward, retrieving the gauntlet he'd just thrown. He was right about her poor management skills, but that only stoked the flames of her loathing.

In four strides, she crossed the room.

He shoved to his feet as she rounded the desk. Callie's hand rose, and she pointed toward the door. "Get the hell out of here! No one comes into *my* home and plows through *my* personal papers."

He settled his hand beside the mound of crumpled receipts. "This is unacceptable, woman. My God…a child keeps track of papers better than this."

Callie loomed closer, her cheeks heating.

The nerve of this pompous ass!

"How I store my things aren't nobody's business but mine!" She knocked the receipts sideways, and with a minimal amount of satisfaction watched as they spread out across the desktop. Her gaze recoiled to his, her voice dropping into a harsh whisper. "This is *my* ranch. As long as I draw breath, no one's coming in here to take it away from me." Her hand dropped to the desk for support, her legs nearly buckling from the weight of this man's sudden appearance in her life.

"Rest assured, I want nothing from you," he ground out, his body dwarfing hers in a long shadow. "But, it's imperative we develop some sort of working relationship—"

"The only relationship I want developed is the one between you and your damn horse ridin' off my land."

His jaw clenched; a controlled exchange of air underlined his rage. "Effective today, I'm taking responsibility for the accounts. It's apparent finance is beyond your grasp. You'll need me for—"

"I don't need anyone. Certainly not you." Callie despised being weak almost as much as she despised this man. Her hands rose to his chest and she shoved. Like an unbending oak, he refused to budge.

A heartbeat later, strong hands banded her upper arms, capturing her in a resolute grip. An easy tug raked her up against his chest. She gasped. Through the thin fabric of her blouse, Callie felt the cool outline of the pewter buttons that rode down the front of his shirt.

The brittle sensation of weakness resurfaced.

"Listen to me, you wild hellion," he hissed, his breath stirring the wisps of hair that framed her face. "I'm not the enemy here. Why are you insisting I become one?" She could see the weathered creases that tracked the corners of his eyes, could see too, the sun-nipped strands in his dark hair. A clean-shaven, strong jaw now replaced the bearded stubble from last night.

Her hands rose. She pushed against his chest, frantic to free herself from the intimidating sensations building inside her. "That's exactly what you are." Her heart pummeled her ribs in painful punches. She struggled for breath. "Y-You're stealin' everything I've got left."

An acerbic snort fell from him. "And you're not what I'd hoped would be waiting when I arrived either. Not by a damn long shot."

Like range fire, his words swept through Callie. Engulfing fast. Burning hot. "What did you expect? A jabbering idiot who'd welcome you with open arms? I can scarcely believe this has happened, let alone understand it all." His hold softened, and with it her struggle to breathe.

"Look," he snapped. "I know this is sudden, and I'm sure it's difficult to accept the truth that your brother sold out. But, the fact remains we're snared in this mess together whether we like it or not." His eyes glittered with a strange light and he released his hold. Slower this time, his hand moved over the receipts. "And yes…you do need me more than you realize."

The truth sliced through Callie to sever her rage. She stumbled back, bumping her hip against the desk. Silence hung between them, broken only by the oppressive ticking of the mantel clock above the fireplace.

We're in this together.

Under the magnitude and weight of his words, her throat tightened against further speech. Her mind screamed for distance. And Callie obeyed. With her next heartbeat, she turned and fled the room.

Chapter Three

Standing in front of the window, Jackson shoved his hands into his pockets and shook his head. Drenched in sunshine beneath a turquoise sky, his troublesome partner stalked across the stable yard. With an ease born from repetition, Colleen Cutteridge strapped on her Remingtons in stride.

Jeezus...a woman wearing guns.

The unmistakable sway of her full hips penetrated straight into memory. How could he have mistaken her for a man last night? She was all female, and a feisty one at that.

Feisty? Bullshit. Jackson's mouth tightened as his brows pulled together. She was filled with rage, but what fueled her incredible fury? His presence here was merely the catalyst. He was certain of it. Indeed, he'd seen something reflecting in her eyes just before she fled the room.

Uncertainty?

Fear?

Jackson passed a hand over his jaw and started to step away from the window, then paused when he spotted two men exiting the largest of four outbuildings. The older one, a stocky white man, offered Colleen a greeting before handing her a wide-brimmed hat. The second helper, a scrawny young black man, led her sleek-coated bay by the reins. He bent to tighten the cinch on the gelding's saddle and when he straightened, he too looked toward the house following Colleen's agitated gesture.

Jackson chuckled. No doubt, she was extolling all the grim details about the nefarious mongrel that lurked within. Would she order her men to drag him outside and over to the nearest tree? Moments passed as he watched her rant, her boots scuffing the dirt as she paced back and forth in front of them.

Eventually, the men turned their attentions toward helping her mount her horse, and Jackson released his pent-up breath.

His lynching would obviously wait.

He pushed from the window and crossed to the desk. He had a full day's work ahead of him. Only when he knew the financial status of the ranch could he face what awaited him outdoors.

Out in Colleen Cutteridge's world.

Callie jammed her boot into the stirrup and pulled herself into the saddle. The leather creaked as she settled her weight. She leaned over, accepting Diego's reins from her farrier.

"Now remember, Banner, you don't need to talk to him. I'll still give the orders around here, and nothing will change that."

"Yes'm, I understand. And do ya still want me to go to Tucson for more feed?"

"Yes. And have Bailey at the livery post the bill to my account. I'll settle up with him later."

Banner nodded and then retreated into the barn.

Callie pulled on her work gloves and turned her attention to the hacienda. With understated elegance, the rustic lines of pink adobe glistened in the morning light, but the silent beauty dwarfed beneath the resentment that simmered in her veins. Again, she visualized Neale plundering his way through the bits and pieces of her life.

You do need me more than you realize.

Callie struggled to ignore his compelling presence, and instead drew rein on Diego, clenching the gelding's leads tighter than necessary. She glanced down at her foreman. He looked toward the hacienda, his massive arms folded over his barrel chest.

"I'm riding over to the Angel, Gus. You want to come along with me while

I check on the mares?"

A lopsided smile carved the grooves deeper into his weathered face. "Nope. I think I'll keep an eye on things around here today."

"That's fine, but keep your distance from that jackal. I don't trust him. I'll be back by nightfall." Callie nudged Diego into action and headed toward Angel Creek.

The sun rose on the horizon to bathe the stiff, spiny wands of the ocotillo bush under a rush of warmth. Wildflowers spilled before Callie in a rainbow of colors, tossed across the basin in haphazard abandonment. The usual monotony of her world brightened under early spring's glorious palette. She inhaled the sweet bouquet, then spied an imposing cluster of Saguaro cactus. Dozens of barbed arms soared upward into the robin-egg-blue sky. A lifetime ago, her family had picnicked around the impressive stands and every time she rode past them, her memories rekindled happier times.

But then the Apache came and killed everyone left at home. Family picnics where she plucked wildflowers for Mother and chased desert cottontails with Papa were gone forever.

Callie swallowed back her sadness.

Don't think of those times…just…don't.

Her gaze darted left. From out of the shadows, a mule deer on nimble legs eased into the sunlight. Ever alert, slender ears twitched with apprehension as the buff-colored creature listened for predatory sounds.

Diego snorted when he picked up its scent. Leaning forward, Callie smoothed her hand across the gelding's warm hide. "Easy, fella. You've nothing to fear from that one." Nearby, a lizard scurried over the rocks in search of an insect, only to become the day's first meal for a Harris hawk. The sleek hunter swooped from the sky, devoured the whiptail in a single gulp, then ascended on powerful wings.

Callie stared at the magnificent creature soaring overhead, then cupped her hands around her mouth, and hollered, "If you want to do something constructive, why don't you fly over to the hacienda and snatch up that sonofabitch squattin' back there?" As if mocking her irascible tone, the hawk screeched, yet continued to climb in ever widening circles. "I need a miracle here," she mumbled, dropping her hands to the reins. "And if you won't help me, who will?"

Diego's easy gait rocked her in the saddle and she focused on each hoof sifting through sand. Off to her left, the rising sun arched heavenward, silhouetting the Rincons' craggy peaks. Shimmers of heat radiated off the desert floor just as a shadow slipped past the corner of her peripheral vision. Her gaze lanced eastward and she perused the bushes near a dry wash.

Nothing moved.

I know I saw something.

Callie scanned again slower, then shook her head. The sun was starting its tricks early this morning, she supposed. "Come on, Diego. Time's a-wastin'." With a tap from the spurs strapped around her boots, Callie prodded her gelding into a cantor toward Angel Creek.

In concealed precision, a half-dozen Indians slid unseen through the shadows of the desert willows behind Callie. Clad only in tall buckskin moccasins and breechclouts, they displayed the mark of the hunt, bold streaks of cerulean and black smeared across their sun-bronzed faces. Ever since their spirit-maker, *Usen,* had given the land to the *Chiricahua Apache* at the moment of their creation, this land had belonged to them. Under the leadership of the great warrior Cochise, it would again.

The time had come for them to strike. And this time, they would not fail. They turned their mounts eastward and once more disappeared into the protective embrace of the mountain.

Callie rode into the stable yard; her body slumped in the saddle from exhaustion. Even her fingers ached from gripping rope all day. Keeping the wild horses rounded up in the makeshift corrals was a twenty-four hour job, and she'd hired a dozen *vaqueros* to camp out among the cottonwoods along the Angel for just that purpose. Around noon, everyone had stopped for a serving of lukewarm chili, but the spicy fare had done little to fill the hole in Callie's stomach.

She was more than ready for supper.

She stepped from the stable, glanced skyward at the marvel of stars and then headed toward the house. She'd refused all thoughts of Jackson Neale until now, and a feeling of much-needed control had strengthened her purpose. With any luck, the libertine had grown tired of the ludicrous idea of a *partnership* and had packed up and left for greener pastures. The thought invigorated Callie. Her steps lightened. Despite her weariness, a satisfied grin flitted across her lips. With a carefree toss of her head, she glanced toward the hacienda.

Her euphoria vanished along with her smile.

The unmistakable glow of lamplight shimmered from the library and she caught a glimpse of the broad-shouldered cur through the windowpanes. He still hovered over the record books exactly where she'd left him this morning. She'd had more than enough of this huckster. The kitchen door slammed shut behind Callie as she entered the house. "Has he been in there all day?"

A startled Pilar looked up from the worktable, her hands buried in a mound of dough. A weeks' worth of tortillas, each the size of a dinner plate, were stacked in four precarious columns before her. "*Sí*, Miss Callie. He come out two times to get something to drink. We talk about ranch, about horses. But he not talk long."

Callie pulled off her leather gloves and slapped them against her thigh before tossing them, along with her hat, onto a chair near the door. She unbuckled her holster and draped the pair of Remingtons over the spindle-back.

"Did he say anything about leaving?"

"No, señorita. He say no more." Pilar wiped her hands on her apron. "I have dinner ready soon. I know you hungry after working horses."

"That'll be fine." Callie reached for a tortilla as she passed. Maseca flour powdered the front of her shirt when she crammed the tasty flatbread into her mouth. She paced through the house toward the library, her entire focus now riveted on the door at the end of the long, candlelit corridor.

Jackson tossed the pencil to the desk and tunneled his hands through his hair. Regardless of how many times he added the columns, the same sum appeared. On the tenth day of every month, for the last four years, fifty dollars remained unaccounted for and forty-eight scraps of paper reflected the same clue...a single notation: *F. Miguel.*

Obviously a name.

No other words. No explaining details. Nothing. The thought of a mysterious man in Colleen's life delivered an edgy sensation in the pit of Jackson's stomach. And that awareness unsettled him more than being unable to balance the books.

Whoever this F. Miguel was, he seemed necessary enough to the foul-mouthed shrew to warrant an exorbitant monthly cash withdrawal. Annoyed beyond justification, Jackson shoved the ledger into the pile of stacked receipts. Twelve hours of deciphering had given him a better understanding of the financial status of Dos Caballos, along with a dull headache.

He stood and stretched, then crossed to the door and pulled it open, only to crash headlong into someone entering the room. He grabbed for the slender form to keep them both upright. The scent of horses wafted over him and mingled with the faint trace of soap drifting upward from the woman's hair. The gasp of surprise and the tensed body confirmed her identity.

Besides, he'd held this woman before, and had already burned her curves into memory.

The light from the open doorway behind him illuminated the area with an uneven glow as Jackson settled Colleen upon her feet. His thumb rose with his next heartbeat and impulsively he wiped away a smudge of flour dusting her chin. A brief touch, and so unnecessary, yet the heat summoned by the simple stroke startled him.

"You left a little there," he quipped, a smirk lifting his lips. "And there too." He indicated the dusting of flour across her shirtfront where the lamplight outlined her generous curves in a wash of gold. His gaze rose to lock with hers. "Did you bring me one of Pilar's tortillas too?"

She jerked from his hold and brushed away the flour tracings. "It's not my job to feed the wolves."

Jackson shrugged. "And here I thought you were coming in to announce dinner in that pleasant little way of yours."

"I came to talk to you," she snapped, her hip jutting out in a manner he was beginning to know all too well. Tonight, however, he had more of an understanding of the way things were at the ranch. The last thing he would allow was a repeat performance of their previous encounter.

Besides, he was ravenous.

Jackson pushed past her, determined strides taking him down the corridor. The staccato tapping of boot heels told him she followed close behind.

"Get back here. I'm not finished with you."

He moved on into the entry hall. In a burst of energy, she dashed ahead and blocked his path. "I said I'm not finished with you."

Jackson released a heavy sigh before sidestepping her. She shifted too, and blocked him again.

This time his restraint crumbled. "I've spent a long day cleaning up your financial disaster. And Pilar said anytime I'm hungry, she'll feed me." He leaned down, his nose scant inches from hers. "Well, I'm hungry now, so move." The ledger's unsolved mystery nipped dangerously close to his frustrations.

She pulled into full fighting stance, her hands curling into fists on her hips. "You're through with telling me what I can and cannot do in my own home, mister. And we're going to settle things right now."

Her snarl frayed the last tenuous hold Jackson had on his temper. "Fine. Let's do that…and how about you start by telling me who the hell F. Miguel is?"

Jackson watched her expression run the gamut from anger to surprise to annoyance until she finally stared up at him with her mouth agape.

He leaned forward, his body dwarfing hers under a long shadow. His chest rose and fell as he dragged in quarts of air in an attempt to contain his anger. "That's right, hellion." His finger jammed into her shoulder before dropping back to his side. "Did you think I wouldn't find out? Guess I forgot to tell you

I'm a financial genius. I can find anything, anywhere, and I know you've been paying F. Miguel fifty bucks every month for the past four years." He enunciated each word as if she were an imbecile. "And now since we're chatting so well, you're going to tell me what he means to my ranch." His words carried the same commanding tone, the same unquestionable authority that had seen him through four years of war.

"No." Though barely audible, the raspy reply cleaved the silence between them like the talons of a raptor. On the heels of her one-word whisper, a blistering, unbalanced suspicion crept over Jackson to slice apart his usual logic.

"No?" His brow arched. He stepped closer, the tip of his boot bumping hers. "You're hiding something. What don't you want me to know about him?"

"W-Who…he is…is no concern of yours."

He dwarfed her in his shadow. "Everything about this ranch is my business."

Her shoulders drew back. Her chin rose. "Those fifty dollars come from my half, and what I do with my half of the money is none of your damned business." Her eyes narrowed, spitting malice. Jackson could almost hear her rally the troops. "But, since you're so precise about recordkeeping, Mr. Neale, please see to it that my money is promptly deducted and placed in a sealed envelope the first morning of every month."

She's playing me for some kind of fool.

The high-strung tart infuriated Jackson past the point of rational thought. If she'd been a man, he would've connected a well-aimed fist with her jaw. As it was, he ached to jam soap into her filthy mouth for a good scrubbing.

Jackson disregarded the well-bred code of conduct he'd valued since childhood. He knew better, but standing in the eye of this escalating storm, he gathered his aggravation into a tightly clenched jaw. His whole focus centered now on ousting her royal highness from her haughty throne. He drew himself forward and issued his taunting whisper, thrusting the query into the space between them with a wickedness he rarely used. "Is he your lover, Colleen? Is that it? Is that what you don't want me to know?"

A thunderstorm of emotions rolled across her face.

Her eyes widened.

"My...what?"

"You heard me. Are you paying this F. Miguel for favors each month?" Of course, the thought that even this harpy would need to buy her pleasures seemed ludicrous, yet Jackson knew the exact moment when he'd turned the tables. Her anger dissolved into panic. Throat-clogging fear blossomed in her eyes. When unshed tears shimmered in the blue velvet, his heart winced. *Jeezus, is it true?*

She pushed past him, her boots scuffing the tile.

An unexplained urgency uncoiled somewhere inside Jackson, and his hand snaked out to stop her. He clamped his fingers around her wrist. With an easy pull, he brought her up against him, his breath sending the silken wisps into a wild dance against her temples. An unforeseen stab of possession drowned out common sense. "Are you?" he rasped, his throat constricting around each word.

She glared at him. "How dare you...you vile pig." She jerked free from his hold, and stumbled backward. A heartbeat later, she fled the entry hall, leaving Jackson to watch her disappear around the corner.

"I'll find out who he is," he whispered to the swirling shadows left in her wake. "You can be damned sure of it."

Smoke curled upward in thick plumes and sent the pungent smell of burning mesquite into the night. Wickiups dotted the creek bank for a quarter-mile. Warmed by the glow from a dozen campfires, the walls of the grass shelters reflected the shadows of a hundred warriors.

Weaving in circles in the hazy air, the Apache performed their hallowed dance, a revered ceremony under an audience of celestial stars. Their hypnotic display proclaimed in vivid detail the upcoming clash between the People and the White Man.

A tumultuous shriek permeated the presentation. Murmured voices filtered through the crowd, disrupting the sacred ceremony. Several turned toward the source, then ran to the water's edge, pointing toward the craggy bluff that shadowed the village. Shouts turned to amazement as wonderment filled the multitude.

From the cliff above them, another powerful shriek rent the night and a black stallion cantered into view, then reared backward, stabbing the smoke-filled air with its muscular forelegs.

"The wild beast has returned to taunt us," proclaimed one warrior.

The crowd swelled at the water's edge, watching the stallion prance before them in a splendid show of untamed power and strength. Several voices at once declared, "He is the wind of the desert and the storm of night. We must try again to capture him."

Above the tumult, a determined voice finally rose. The mighty Cochise stepped forward and raised his hands heavenward. "No, my People. This is a sign. The ebony beast is a protector and our spirit-keeper has blessed us with its appearance. This animal is not ours to take. Not yet." The stallion's massive black head tossed in accord with the gifted leader, and an ebony sweep of mane and solid, shimmering hide reflected the firelight and demanded their respect. The warriors slowly nodded in agreement with their leader's words. Yes, this was a sign, a gift they could not ignore.

Minutes passed as they watched in awe.

With one final shriek of defiance, the horse melded back into the night. And at least for now, the stallion, like the People would remain free. With renewed purpose, the Apache returned to their fires and to their quest with the Great Spirit in haunting songs, thanking Him, and seeking His protection in the forthcoming endeavor.

Chapter Four

Since his arrival a week before, Jackson had composed a dozen letters to Reece, but each one ended up in the fire. Every attempt he'd so far made to form a partnership with the colonel's sister curled into oblivion right alongside his correspondence. In the end, Jackson simply sent his friend a note stating he'd arrived safely and found Colleen to be in...robust health.

Amid bites of a spicy frittata, another breakfast between them came and went in silence. Caustic glances punctuated the animosity in the room, nipping deeper than the kick of the chili peppers in the morning's dish. And like the jalapeño that scorched his tongue, Colleen's bitterness overwhelmed Jackson's senses without inflicting any permanent harm.

With the ledgers now balanced, and Colleen's unexplained deductions noted with the letters *F. M.*, he decided to explore the rest of the hacienda.

An hour after mealtime, Jackson leaned against a post on the back veranda and watched his recalcitrant partner ride out, glancing over her shoulder at him as she spurred past. He flicked away the stub of his cheroot, and offered a curt smile, his hand rising to the brim of his hat in a mocking salute.

When she faded from view, Jackson pushed from the weathered wood and headed straight toward the entrance to the stable. His boots crunched across sandy ground and his determined stride ate up the distance.

A dozen horses greeted him when he stepped into the dim interior, the whickering and chuffs underscoring their natural caution. Memories of cavalry life returned full-force and eddied around the familiar smells of manure, hay and well-oiled leather.

An impressive pair of Percherons caught his attention first, sleek ears flicking as they sized up his predator potential. Sensing nothing dangerous, the closest beast stepped to the gate and bobbed its massive head in a request for a scratch beneath its forelock. Jackson smiled and recalled the pair of drafts that had pulled General McClellan's commissary wagons all over Virginia. Whenever Jackson saw them, he'd always slip the beasts a treat, but those animals paled in comparison to this fine pair. Remarkable muscles rippled beneath tight, lustrous hides, and boasted of their ability and strength.

Jackson's attention skipped across the other horses: a half-dozen rugged Morgans, including his, a couple of sturdy mustangs and pintos, and one liver-colored Appaloosa whose spots on the hindquarter were so white they looked like snowflakes.

Every one of the breeds was noteworthy and approval ebbed through Jackson. His gaze centered on a table laden with a motley collection of currycombs, hard-bristled brushes, hoof picks and a shedding blade. On the floor, scraps of damp linen draped the side of a tin bucket. Water droplets that clung to the metal still shimmered in silent testament to the chore already completed.

The stable was the domain of the men Jackson had seen from afar and the place reflected the pride in their work. Swept clean of all debris, the dirt floor was tamped so tightly it appeared at first glance to be wood.

Jackson's smile of appreciation widened. These men weren't slackers, even with a woman at the helm. A scraping sound drew his attention, and curiosity flooded through him. He spotted an open doorway leading to an adjacent room. With senses sharp, he crossed the distance and quietly stepped over the threshold.

The old man he'd seen earlier now sat before a heavy table, the wood scarred from years of wear and tear. The wrangler's white hair would've tumbled to the battered top if not for a leather thong that secured the strands at the nape of his sun-stained neck. His focus was riveted upon a halter strap gripped within large, workworn hands.

Jackson said, "Pilar tells me you're Gus Gilbert."

The wrangler looked up, trying to mask his surprise. A quick scan followed before he dropped his gaze. "Actually, the name's August, after the month I was born. Got me a passel of brothers somewhere named for every other month of the year too." He reached for an awl and pushed the implement into the leather. "Ma kept tryin' for a girl, but never got her wish. December was a bad month for birthin', I guess…'cause she died tryin'." He leaned back and shifted the piece in his hands. "But you're right. Folks just call me Gus."

"Pleased to meet you. I'm—" .

"I know who you are. Callie keeps us well informed."

Jackson leaned against the doorframe. He couldn't stop the chuckle that escaped. "Well, there's no doubt how enlightened you all must be now." A grin stacked up near the corner of the wrangler's mouth, and Jackson felt frustrated by the compulsion that he needed to correct things already muddied by the hellion. "Did she also happen to mention her brother's my good friend, as well as my commander during the war?"

"The friend part she neglected to share, but she did mention the other." Gus placed his tool on the workbench, then looked at Jackson, all trace of humor gone. "Reece has been sorely missed these last few years, and we've supported Callie like he asked us to do. We'll continue to do so, in case you're wondering. But, I'm disappointed to hear he won't be returning."

Gus glanced to the leather again and continued, "His pappy and I fought in the Mexican War together and rode west with the family in '49. Carved Dos Caballos from an untamed wasteland, killin' Injuns and everything else that stood in our way. Still are, for that matter."

Jackson nodded as his gaze surveyed the room. Tack hung from wooden dowels rammed into the low, slanting rafters, and well-crafted saddles lined the far wall across individual bracers. Blankets, bridles and reins draped over sturdy pegs and filled the room with the pleasant smells of leather and wool, the equipment reflecting the excellent care given. Beneath a pair of small, double-paned windows narrow shelves ran the length of the room. They held cruppers and bits, halters and saddlebags. This was the heartbeat of the ranch and it pulsed strongly under the old man's well-organized supervision. But more importantly, it revealed the true character of Gus Gilbert.

Jackson's gaze resettled on the wrangler. Age had etched deep creases into a sun-baked face as hard and battered as the territory he'd conquered. "Well, Gus, I'm Reece's replacement. And I believe you'll find I'm capable. If you know him well, and I'm sure you do, you'll realize he wouldn't have sold me his half of the ranch otherwise."

The blunt words carried a clear message. And several seconds later, the old man dropped his gaze and pushed the leather into a spot clear of tools.

"I reckon that makes sense, Mr. Neale."

"Let's just make it Jackson, all right?"

Gus nodded, and Jackson shifted into a more comfortable position against the doorframe. Relief settled through him, pleased he'd crossed this second hurdle without too much hassle. Winning the proud frontiersman's trust was important, and this initial meeting had gone a hell of a lot smoother than the encounter with the hellion who spewed her animosity with all the force of an Atlantic hurricane.

Surely to God, this man sees her rancor.

"You call her Callie. I've heard Reece refer to her by that name too."

Gus chuckled. "When he was still a pup, Reece announced his baby sister didn't act like nobody named Colleen, so he up and shortened it. Everyone calls her Callie now. The name fits, since she don't cotton to the fanciful."

"So I've noticed."

"And don't be expectin' her to bake you pies or serve up tea. I don't think she even knows how. The girl damn near starved to death before Pilar moved in." His smile widened. "When she was growin' up, she stuck on Reece like she was his shadow. Loved the horses. Always has. Meg tried to teach her girlie ways, but Callie struggled with the lessons." The man's face softened a fraction when he mentioned the other woman.

And Jackson's curiosity won out. "Who's Meg?"

"Margaret Elizabeth. Callie's mother. Killed in a raid years ago. All of 'em.

Meg. Andrew. And Jenny."

"Reece mentioned something about an Indian attack. Andrew was their father?"

Gus nodded. "And a damned good friend." Sadness darkened his eyes. "Apache stole in while most of us was herdin' stock up north. Callie was still a youngster, but she insisted on riding with us that day. And thank God she did, or she'd be gone too." Gus inhaled, then released his breath on a long sigh. "Reece lost Jenny then. They'd been married less than a year."

Jackson nodded. During the war, Reece had shared a bit of the story with him; the heartbreaking loss had torn his friend apart for years. Reece would not allow himself to care about anyone else, but then he fell in love with the courageous Emaline McDaniels during his regiment's occupation of her plantation. He stayed in Virginia afterward and married the spirited widow.

Jackson shoved aside the memory and motioned toward the collection of items on the workbench. "Why don't you show me what you're working on there, Gus?" he asked, pushing from the doorframe.

"Be glad to." Gus pointed sideways. "Pull up that stool over yonder, and I'll show you how I make my bridles." Jackson complied, settling down beside the old wrangler. "See here?" Gus pulled on the strap. "The secret is to soak the leather first, which strengthens the strand."

"And then, you twist the leather, right?"

"That's right."

Jackson's simple questions dissolved forever any lingering tensions as both men moved toward the beginnings of trust and friendship.

The makeshift corrals, a dozen in all, were scattered along Angel Creek in haphazard formations for nearly a quarter-mile. Without the fodder Callie provided, there could be no way to keep the mares contained. With water from the Angel, she only had to bring in food. And Banner, along with several hired vaqueros, had just left with empty wagons for their weekly visit to Tucson.

Callie galloped past the corrals, heading for the last section down by the cottonwoods. Near noon, the heat of the day radiated from the ground. Sweat dampened her face and her tongue slipped out to wet her lips.

The roundup was good this year, and the animals would carry a hefty price tag. For as long as she could remember, the United States Army had bought Cutteridge horses. Most ended up north to supply the territorial forts. During her brother's absence, she'd carried on the tradition without faltering once. Callie refused to consider where Jackson Neale fit into the equation, other than getting her brother's half of the stake now.

As she rounded the bend, Callie spotted the vaqueros gathered near an empty corral. The logs on the far side of the enclosure lay in a splintered mess. *He's back!* She cursed under her breath, and several men ran to her as she dismounted.

"Señorita! He broke the fences again—"

"Anyone hurt?"

"No, señorita, not this time. But we lose thirteen. That stallion wants them back. We could've shot him, but you say no."

Callie stomped to the remnants of the corral, her patience equally as shredded. "That's correct. He is not to be harmed." She kicked at the splintered wood, then swung to face the men. "Which direction did they head?"

"East, señorita. To the mountains," one vaquero answered as several others motioned to the rocky ridgeline stretching along the far horizon.

She pointed to the closest wranglers. "You three saddle up. You're ridin' with me." They nodded and raced toward their mounts tied to a picket line a hundred yards away.

Callie strode to Diego, throwing hurried words over her shoulder. "The rest of you, do your best to rebuild this fence. And double its strength. I'm going to finally capture this sonofabitch if it's the last thing I do."

Jackson scanned the horizon from the shadows of the sloping front porch. Supper had come and gone more than an hour ago, and his reckless partner had yet to return to the ranch.

Callie.

He propped his boot upon the low railing that ran the length of the hacienda and mulled the nickname...Callie Cutteridge, swaggering with harshness and arrogance.

Callie Cutteridge...with beautiful blue eyes.

Jackson couldn't dismiss the truth. She possessed a single-mindedness that drove him mad. He preferred his women exude softness, but she was as hard as nails. He appreciated dewy skin, powdered and perfumed. The scent of horseflesh radiated from Callie. He liked his women willing and easily conquered.

The battle raging between them knew no end.

Jackson took another long drag from his cheroot, then exhaled, watching as the hazy smoke cloud broke apart on the evening breeze.

He issued a thin and knowing smile. Underneath her puffed-up feathers lurked a wounded bird, and all her bravado, all her arrogance, every single drop of animosity hid a broken wing. Jackson had a much better understanding of her past after talking with Gus, and he recognized now that her tough exterior protected an inner frailty. The dogged determination, a traditional man's role, she embraced with unequivocal fervor and made no apologies for doing so.

Jackson sighed.

He'd never known any woman quite like her. Swathed beneath a coat of hostility lurked a vulnerability as soft as her eyes...as near to him as a sigh, yet a million miles away. Would their relationship ever change?

Would she ever be able to allow herself to trust him?

Jackson lowered his leg to the porch. The wood creaked beneath his weight. *Jeezus. Stop this.* Why was he thinking about her this way? They'd not spoken to one another in more than a week. She obviously handled her discomfiture through avoidance. And he abhorred avoidance with every breath he drew.

Jackson raked a hand over his day's stubble, allowing the frustration to penetrate. Again, he surveyed the area spreading out before him in the dying light. Dust devils pirouetted across the desert mere inches above the ground. Kicked up by the warm breeze, they capered among the cacti in untroubled whispers. And somewhere out there amid all the danger rode his willful, sharp-tongued partner—as uncompromising and calloused as her world.

Stop it.

He flicked away the cheroot, then slumped against the post. Filled in on the ranch's schedule, and the upcoming plans to herd the stock to Camp Lowell, he'd spent an enjoyable afternoon with Gus. While they forged iron into horseshoes, the old wrangler had shared the tale of Callie's ongoing struggles with a wild stallion. The unbroken horse continued to damage the corrals in an attempt to reclaim his mares, and Callie's battles with the beast took center stage, overriding all her other concerns.

Jackson rarely worried, but darkness drew near. The woman could handle herself and her ranch. She'd obviously been doing so for years. So why did her absence at dinner fill him with an unnamed disquiet?

Jeezus Christ. Women were supposed to crochet and bake crumpets and attend tea parties, not rove across some desert chasing wild animals. And he damned well knew they shouldn't curse like men and ride astride for hours on end.

A mumbled oath fell from his lips and drifted out into the desert to mingle with the dancing dust. Coddling women had been his hallmark. And every single one he'd ever known had been predictable and easily conquered.

Until Callie.

How exactly did a man deal with someone so headstrong? The direct approach? A tit for a tat? He'd supposed he could try that next. Anything was preferable to this bullshit. For the briefest instant, Jackson recalled wrestling her to the ground, recalled the golden curls spreading across the sand, a curtain of shimmering softness upon a woman as hard as stone.

A sobering thought indeed.

The breeze brushed across Jackson's face, rolling the lush scents of the desert around his tired body. He clamped his hands into fists to stop his tingling fingertips from recalling each one of the hellion's curves.

Jackson refocused on the lengthening shadows. To his left, slipping away on streaks of golden light, the setting sun sizzled from his view.

Concern for his maverick partner returned.

Just when the distant mountains swallowed the day's last rays, Jackson spotted a lone rider guiding her horse across a sandy wash; her lithe, little shoulders hunched forward. Her exhaustion reflected her Achilles' heel, and Jackson's heart hitched a beat as he thumbed up the brim of his hat. At least she was back safe and he could stop worrying.

He pushed away from the wooden post and stepped from the porch.

Straining under the weight of the saddle, Callie pulled the sturdy leather from Diego's back and settled it onto the storage rack. She knocked dried mud from the wooden stirrups, then smoothed her hand over the cantle. This splendid piece freighted all the way from the Hermann Heiser Saddlery in Denver had been her first, presented to her for her ninth birthday.

Supple and solid, the low roper's saddle horn had held many a lassoed horse in place since then. She grimaced as her fingers dropped from the leather. Those were happier times.

Turning, Callie unbuckled her worn chaps and stepped out of the leggings, tossing them onto a nearby table. A few swipes with a stiff-bristled brush removed dust and debris from Diego's coat before Callie led her trusty gelding to his stall and to the bucket of fresh water and food. Gus paid more attention to the horses' comfort than he did his own.

She patted Diego on the rump and left the stall.

Her gloves landed on top of the workbench along with her hat. Inhaling deeply, Callie ran a hand over her head to shove the tangled strands of hair behind her ear. Exhaustion and a full day in the saddle cramped her muscles, but even her exhaustion couldn't dampen the feelings radiating from inside her.

Accompanied by her vaqueros, she'd tracked the wild stallion up into the Rincon Mountains. With each step that brought her closer to the magnificent brute, she marveled at the animal's strength and spirit. At around three this afternoon, they'd finally cornered the ebony beast in the canyon of the needle-eye.

Tears gathered behind her spiky eyelashes. He was a breathtaking creature. So full of life. So resilient to the cruelties of this world. Callie had spent all her strength, and that of the three vaqueros who'd ridden with her, to lasso him and just bring him back to the double-fenced corral at Angel Creek.

A deep voice ricocheted through the stable like a bullet to shatter Callie's thoughts. "Gus told me about the stallion. He still causing you trouble?"

She turned toward the sound. The shadowed image of Jackson Neale stood just inside the doorway, a dark, disturbing mountain of a man who twisted her emotions as nothing else had ever done. The concerned tone in his question rankled against her somersaulting emotions, their last encounter still fresh in her mind.

Jackson moved closer and Callie tensed. A flush of warmth rushed over her cheeks. He came to a stop in front of her, and she drove away the sharp sensation his presence evoked.

"He's been nothin' but trouble these last few weeks," she snapped, fighting to still her pounding heart, tripped even faster by his nearness. A scalding rush of words pushed into the shadows between them. "But I've finally caught the sonofabitch." Her chin rose to convey her victory. "After all this time, I've finally caught him."

"I'd like to see him. If you're free tomorrow, I'd also like to see the rest of the ranch."

Callie barely tolerated breathing the same air with this vagrant outsider. Spending an entire day with him was unthinkable.

"I'll have Gus show you around. I don't have time."

"Make time," he said, stepping closer.

"Look, I have more important things to do than mess with you."

He leaned forward, and his dark gaze nailed hers. "Your rancor's wearing mighty thin."

"Is it?" She tipped her head sideways and glared up into his eyes. "Then I suggest you pack up and ride back east if you're lookin' for a more exemplary style." Callie attempted to push past him but his hand softly wrapped her shoulder to stop her.

Her lips pulled taut and she dampened them, the acrid taste of the desert meeting her tongue. Jackson's scent drifted closer, hinting of leather, horses and the unbridled musk of man.

He leaned over, his lips a hair's breadth from the curve of her ear. "I will be part of this ranch, Callie-girl," he whispered, and the brush of his words sent an immediate wash of tingles down her back. "You don't have to like it, but in time you'll concede. And come tomorrow morning, it'll be you and me riding the length of this property. Don't make me come looking for you."

As smoothly as he'd stopped her, his hand dropped away.

Callie swayed in the darkness.

That he should use her nickname so intimately augmented the chaos pounding through her veins. Seconds later, his steps sounded through the darkness toward the stable entrance before fading off into the night.

Chapter Five

Callie pointed to the craggy peaks that shimmered brownish-pink beneath the wash of morning light. "My land extends north all the way to the Rincon Mountains." She twisted in the saddle, her hand continuing the sweep of Dos Caballos. "It then goes east about fifteen miles toward the San Pedro River over there." She turned, continuing with her outline of the ranch's immense scope. "And then old Fort Buchanan marks the southeastern boundary in that direction. The army moved out when the war started, so the place sits abandoned now." She swiveled and pointed southward. "And then we butt up against the Santa Ritas…that range of gray mountains there in the distance." She darted a quick glance to Jackson. "Not much there but a few deserted mines and dilapidated shacks along Angel Creek. And, before you even ask, the silver's been played out years ago." Callie settled back into her saddle and stared straight ahead. A smirk tightened her lips. "There, that's the ranch, all fifty thousand acres of it."

Jackson scanned the horizon. "An amazing spread."

"Yep. One of the ten largest in the territory. And the Angel winds through most of it to provide water for the mares. Keeps the well filled at the hacienda, too, which makes Pilar happy."

Jackson smiled, pleased with the enormity of his purchase. Before him, a rocky incline tumbled downward, settling into a basin filled with cacti and sagebrush. The flush of springtime flowers brightened the scene. In the far distance, a pale and polished oasis, the hacienda, hovered on the vista. Warmth radiated through Jackson and he recalled the many hours he'd spent listening to Reece describe Dos Caballos. His friend hadn't exaggerated one damn bit. A man could fall in love with the stark beauty of this land.

A bewildering sense of completeness settled over Jackson, paling everything that came before. Again, he renewed his vow to work toward developing a joint venture with this…woman. A bewitching landscape beckoned before him, unlike the nearby hellion who neither welcomed, nor wanted, him here.

He glanced at Callie.

God knows it isn't you compelling me to stay.

He would never have chosen this one to occupy a great portion of his future. His kind of woman entertained guests with a trayful of pastries. She didn't cram them into her mouth with both hands.

Jackson shook off the discomforting image, hoping to keep their conversation flowing. At least they were talking in a civilized tone now. That, in and of itself, was progress. "Must take every inch of the ranch to sustain a herd, since there's so little feed."

Callie nodded. "A hundred acres per head, and more during the dry times." She plucked at the reins in her hand. "The desert doesn't make things easy… for anyone."

"I can see that."

"I provide for the mares we've corralled, but the wild ones, well…they're on their own. Been like this for hundreds of years though, so I'd say they're gettin' by."

"I'm used to the lush pastureland back east; it's hard to imagine where they'd find enough to eat out here." A silent breeze capered between them, lifting the ever-present tendrils of hair escaping Callie's heavy braid. How soft would the rebellious curls feel sliding through his fingers? She turned to face him, and he shifted his gaze back over the desert.

Jeezus, stop looking at her.

"I sell only prime, well-fed stock. Been doing so for years without anyone's damn interference."

Her sharp words fragmented the ludicrous urge to touch her. Yet, somewhere on the perplexing fringes of Jackson's mind, Callie's golden-hued hair…the only amazingly soft thing about her…continued to mesmerize him. If they were to have any chance of this partnership working, then the maturity and patience must come from him.

He straightened, stacking his gloved hands over the saddle's swell. "And you've done an excellent job, I might add. This talent must surge strongly through the Cutteridge veins. Your brother's doing the same thing back east now—raising horses and selling them, I mean."

From the corner of his eye, he noticed her jaw clench, saw her gauntlet-covered hand twist the reins. "Well, he should've come back here to do that," she snapped, anger lacing her words.

Jackson kicked up his lips into a grin, choosing his words carefully now. "Falling in love is a powerful pull…on any man. Your brother is no exception."

Picked up by the breeze, a gilded curl whisked across her face and whispered to him again. Callie pushed the strand behind her ear, then turned to glare at him, her hand flattening over her eyes into a sunshade.

"All love does is hurt people, Mr. Neale."

He stared out across the desert. "Love is what life is all about."

"Well then I guess I must be dead, 'cause I'm real careful not to love anything anymore." She dropped her hand back to the saddle with a smack.

"Well…that's not entirely true," he challenged. "You love your ranch and your horses, don't you? And though you're upset with your brother right now, you still love him." He tipped his head and looked at her. "I'm certain he loves you."

Though only God knows why.

She reached behind her shoulders and jerked her hat into place atop her head. Her eyes brightened with animosity as she threw him a curt glance. "Well now, it looks like you've just got all the answers, doesn't it?" The shadow cast by the wide brim couldn't hide the pain welling into a shimmer across her eyes.

He'd seen it before. *Her protection.*

His gaze dropped to the lanyard spilling down the front of her shirt, the leather strand flowing alongside the soft swell of her breasts. His chest tightened and he issued a terse laugh. "I don't know everything, but I do know there are some things in life worth loving."

"I refuse to continue this pointless conversation when I've got better things to do." Her rush of disgust wrenched apart the mood, leaving only the ribbon of wind to tie them together now. Rocking back in the saddle, she glared at him. "I'm headin' over to the Angel. If you want to see the mares, you'd better keep up." Her mount sidestepped. "I'd *love* nothing better than to leave you behind in my dust."

"Know what I think?" Jackson said, causing her to pull up short on the reins. Her saddle creaked as she turned back to stare at him. His gaze shifted again to the hazy ranch house. "You're terrified of something, though I'm not quite sure yet what that is. Maybe it's me? Could that be it, Callie? Are you afraid of me?"

"Look, Mr. Neale—"

"Jackson." His gaze cut back to hers. "Remember, I asked you to call me Jackson."

"I'm not afraid of one damn thing, *Jackson*. And I'm sure as hell not interested in your opinions on love."

He shook his head, trying to contain a smirk. "You must wake up being difficult. I guess that's it." For a brief moment, Jackson tried to imagine how her laughter might sound. Would it be deep and throaty? Or light? Playful? "You know, hellion, if you'd just relax a bit we might become friends."

With a smothered oath that confirmed he'd hit a raw nerve, Callie dug her spurs into the sides of her horse. The gelding sprang into motion and plunged down the slope, loose shale and rocks tumbling after her.

Jackson pulled his lips so tight even his teeth hurt. He shook his head in frustration as his pounding heart slammed against his chest. The patience reservoir where she was concerned was damn near dry. Good God, why couldn't she have welcomed him into his new life by sitting in the parlor and playing a piano?

And yet, despite their vast differences in manners, or even her association with the mysterious F. Miguel, garnering this irksome shrew's acceptance grew more important by the minute. Another mangled oath tumbled from Jackson's lips. He swept up the reins of his horse, then spurred the Morgan down the incline.

Brawn rippled across the stallion's shoulders and the ebony beast raised a powerful foreleg, slashing the air in defiance. He slammed back to earth, sharp hooves stabbing the ground. The massive head shook, nostrils flaring.

Furious snorts rent the night.

Callie leaned forward on the corral fence and stared awestruck at the animal. His unyielding spirit, his refusal to be broken, humbled her. Her ongoing struggle to tame this beast would end with the rising sun a mere handful of hours away. And yet, her respect had deepened into an almost religious experience, begging her to keep trying, to find some way to spare the beast his fate. A constricting ache tightened her throat.

From out of the darkness, Jackson's voice settled over her misery. "There's another way, you know."

Surprise toppled into irritation as Callie turned to look at him.

Since showing him the ranch boundaries two weeks earlier, they'd skirted one another, speaking a handful of words here, clipped greetings there.

But he never stopped watching her.

For hours on end while she strove to break the stallion, Jackson watched. With a driving determination, made more frustrating by his presence, Callie continued to crawl back atop the hulking beast.

And still Jackson watched.

From morning to dusk locked inside the corral, Callie centered herself on conquering the creature's will, so painful and bruised at night, she would crawl to bed…only to awaken at dawn and head back out ready to face her adversary all over again. Somehow, in her mind, the stallion and the man were one. It was Gus who finally stopped her, insisting she go find her common sense as he jerked the saddle from her hands.

Callie swallowed, her heart now engaged in a war equally as bone crushing.

The beast could not be broken to saddle. She realized that now. Yet here stood this…this man, his boot propped upon the lowest railing, telling her there was another way? If she weren't so damned tired, she'd have thrown him a disdainful laugh.

Instead, she simply stared at him.

Without his usual Stetson, moonlight drenched Jackson's sable strands. The soft breeze teased a stray lock that fell across his forehead. He continued to evaluate the horse and Callie's breathing quickened.

"There's no other way," she whispered, weariness tempering her words. "I've tried everything I know to break him. You should recognize this truth given the fact that you've reveled in my failure."

He shifted, his boot scuffing wood. "I'm not reveling, hellion. In fact, I'm impressed by your amazing resilience. You've not broken a single bone yet." His long fingers wrapped around the railing and he leaned forward. "But horses are smart creatures; this one more than most." He tossed aside a scrap of hay, and allowed his lips to curl into a smile. "And yes, you've done everything you can except…understand him."

Callie straightened, surprised by the statement. Her hands dropped to her sides, then flattened against her thighs. "Understand what?" Even as she spoke, she struggled to locate her anger, but she uncovered a tinge of hope instead. The subtle scent of his tobacco ebbed around her to couple with the anxious energy exuding from the nearby horse. Invisible hands seized Callie, and forced every muscle in her body to tense. Poised on the edge of…*something*, she leaned toward Jackson. She didn't want any part of this new and intoxicating emotion, yet she was helpless to do anything but listen.

"You've assumed he can't be gentled because of his…defiance." His voice commanded attention. Even the drifting stars overhead dropped in closer to hear. "I'm well aware you know horses, and you're good with them. But I know them too. And with this one…" he raised a thumb toward the pacing stallion, "…he won't ever cave to physical control. Not in a month, not in a million years.

What this one needs is to be gentled...and won over."

Callie slid her gaze to the horse. *Gentled?* She tried to swallow, but her throat was dry...more arid than the sand beneath her feet. Exhaustion had blunted her reasoning. There could be no other explanation for the emotions now rippling her otherwise isolated pond.

But...is he right? Could there be another...way?

"Do you think he understands what you want from him?" Jackson continued, his soft, husky question evaporating the last band of irritation inside Callie. She stood awestruck, her mouth agape. Here in the darkness, blanketed under a desert oasis of stars, she realized her animosity toward this man had shifted.

Helplessly, she shook her head, then whispered, "He's...afraid."

"That's right. Fear—it's all you've let him know. He's cornered. And anxious. And completely focused on protecting himself." Jackson slid his palms together into a loose grip in front of him, slowly bobbing them over the corral. "To him, you're just a stranger intent upon changing his world. He's focused all his attention on escaping that one blinding truth. He doesn't really know what he's struggling against, only that it isn't his choice. So...fighting is the only option left." A soothing balm to her battle-weary soul, Jackson's voice melted into her veins, and the muscles in her belly relaxed a tiny fraction more under the compelling pull of his words. "There *is* another way besides breaking his spirit or crippling him."

And then, Callie surrendered to the indefinable pull of this man. Yet still her words contradicted. "He's injured two of my wranglers and thrown me a dozen times or more. Only a fool would face that danger again." She shifted back to the fence, putting distance between them, thankful for the comfortable resentment that again signaled her control. "Regardless of how I feel about driving spikes through his knee joints come daybreak, I'm also rational. If I'm going to use him at stud, then I'm not going to fight to contain him. This horse cannot be broken, Jackson, and if maiming him is all I have left, then so be it." Common sense now ruled, and control felt good. Familiar. "And no matter how much I detest you, I'll not have you getting hurt, either."

His low chuckle skidded over to embrace her. "He's a powerful animal, yes. But he's not mean-spirited. I waited and watched you, hellion. Now it's your turn to watch me move him to my will."

"You'll move him?" Callie scoffed at the words, yet the sparking hope grew larger, dampening her disbelief, which made the ache in her heart more pronounced. "But…if you go in there, all he'll do is trample you. You're not a fool, so don't talk like one." The horse galloped past them again and drew her attention.

"I get one week with him," Jackson said. "If I don't have him gentled… only then will I allow you to maim him."

"You'll…allow?" The question eked from Callie's mouth.

Jackson stepped closer, towering over her by half a foot. Silence stretched around them as she stared up into dark, determined eyes. His hand rose between them, his index finger pointing heavenward in front of his narrowed gaze.

"One week," he ordered. "Do you understand?" His hand slid open to cup her chin, and held. Where his fingers gripped, inexplicable heat penetrated past muscle and bone. His eyes told her not to bother challenging him.

Callie didn't understand any of the heat crashing through her. The words caught deep in her throat, leaving her helpless to do anything but agree.

She nodded.

His hold instantly relaxed. Then, with her next indrawn breath, Jackson traced the pad of his thumb across her bottom lip. The simple act sent an astonishing jolt straight through her. She attempted to speak, but only a faint gasp slipped out. He moved backward, removing his touch, and…as silently as her partner had arrived, he disappeared from view.

Callie reached for the railing, struggling twice before she found support. Her fingers curled around the wood like a lifeline while a tingling sensation vibrated through her all the way to her soul. Her eyelids slipped closed, and with each pounding heartbeat, a raw, unexpected realization emerged…*he controls me so easily.*

She brought her hand upward, pressing shaking fingertips against her lips. An eternity staggered past while she listened to the fading crunch of his footfalls, listened until they too became lost under the stallion's rebellious cry.

Magic.

No other word could describe the scene unfolding before Callie. At Gus's insistence, she had joined him at the main corral after lunch. The half-dozen wranglers she'd brought with her now sat on the top railing opposite them, ready to jump into the arena in case Jackson needed to be rescued from his folly. Instead of throwing a smug *I-told-you-so*, Callie stared, transfixed. She would not be ramming a spike through the stallion's knees today.

Or any other day for that matter.

Sheer joy overshadowed her roiling resentment of the man. The only way she had known to break horses involved spirit-robbing control, hobbles and ropes.

Jackson Neale brought a different technique.

The broad-shouldered miracle-maker walked around the middle of the pen and focused all his attention on every swish of tail, every head toss, every single hoof stomp.

With alert precision, Jackson reacted to every cue. Each shift the creature made held meaning. And a mind-baffling confidence, along with a long black whip, allowed Jackson to strip away the layers of mistrust that emanated from the twelve-hundred-pound beast. With each bite of leather, every caress across its rump, the horse somehow understood what Jackson wanted.

Gus leaned over, his voice cutting through Callie's amazement. "He's good, ain't he?"

She nodded. "I've never seen any wild horse controlled so easily, have you?"

"Nope. It's like he knows Jackson's the boss."

Callie's eyes narrowed on the incredible ballet evolving before her. "But how the hell is he doing this?"

"He's keeping him moving, remember? Like he said he'd do." Gus smiled.

"I've been sittin' here all morning, and I think I've got this whole thing figured out. See…right there. Jackson won't let him stop, not even when the horse wants to rest."

Gus's smile widened as if he alone had shaped this miracle within his hands. "And right there. Did you see the whip nip its hindquarters? That damn horse got a taste of leather 'cause he wasn't movin' the way Jackson wanted him to."

"The poor thing's exhausted."

"Exactly, but until Jackson gives him consent to stop and rest, it ain't happenin'." Gus crossed his arms over his chest and puffed up as proud as a peacock. "Hell's bells. Everything pertaining to stayin' alive in the wild involves movin', be it eatin' or even breeding rights. And that's exactly what's happening here. Jackson's controlling your renegade stallion in that little bitty circle out there just like a herd stud does to his mares in the wild."

Callie blinked. "But why's he standing behind the horse? Why not in front, so he won't chance getting kicked?"

"Don't you see, suga'pie?" Gus unfolded his arms and pointed at the stallion again, allowing a paternal patience to frame his word. Her cheeks heated at the long-ago, little girl nickname he'd given her. "Horses don't like to be pressured from the front, do they? That's what wolves do. Cougars and coyotes too. It's created a natural-born fear in 'em." Sunlight poured over his weathered face and carved the age lines even deeper. "Horses approach each other from the side or the rear. That's how they're comfortable. You know all that. Hell, being watchful is second nature to them. They've needed that instinct just to survive."

An unshakable respect for Jackson Neale had taken root inside the foreman. Callie recognized the admiration as surely as if her beloved Gus stood atop the railing to holler his approval to the vaqueros watching on the other side.

First, my cook. Now…my foreman.

Her gaze slid back to Jackson. He moved the powerful horse like a marionette, plucking the strings of reward and punishment with his ebony whip. He caressed the withers with a soft swish when the beast obeyed—the leather nipping its flank when it didn't.

All the signs became clearer and clearer the longer Callie watched. "I've never seen anything like this before."

"Me neither. And I've seen a hell of a lot of things in my life." Gus's gaze locked with hers and his quick wink followed.

Callie couldn't help herself. She laughed aloud, then glanced toward the vaqueros.

From their nods and excited voices, she could see they, too, were beginning to understand this new method of horse breaking.

Add the hired help to the list.

A newfound respect for her unwanted partner demanded acknowledgment. Jackson Neale had an uncanny power, and instead of being arrogant about his unique method, he had patiently shown her, shown them all, how to create an ally instead of an enemy.

Heat infused Callie's face as her emotions rumbled around inside with the ferocity of a thunderstorm. She lowered her head, realizing she could not stay here another moment without saying something to Jackson.

After all, he had saved the stallion from a fate worse than death.

Sweat trickled down the side of her neck and Callie reached up to swipe it away. She realized Jackson deserved some acknowledgment. Perhaps she'd say something nice to him at dinner tonight. She could manage agreeable, if only for a few short moments.

Right now, however, she needed distance.

Callie swung her legs over the railing, and a moment later, dropped to the ground behind Gus. He glanced at her briefly, before returning his gaze to the corral.

"Where you heading?" he asked.

"I'm going to the stable. Banner should be back anytime with supplies. I'll need to get things ready for him. Besides, I've seen enough to know our visitor will do what he said."

"He saved your stallion, suga'pie. You realize that, don't you?"

Callie wiped her sweaty palms down her hips, then reached behind her shoulders and pulled her hat into place.

"Yeah, I know that. And I don't need you gnawing at me as a reminder. But be sure to give him a big, shiny medal from all of us when he's finished, all right?"

Gus chuckled. His shaking head only frustrated Callie as she tugged her hat brim lower to block the sun. Her gaze tracked through the rails to settle back on her unwanted partner. Under the spill of sunshine, he radiated like some dark-haired, chisel-jawed *savior* moving around the center of their world.

Determination oozed from him, and even where she stood, Callie felt suffocated as she watched the ebb and flow of his persuasive influence. For a fleeting moment, she sympathized with the stallion, even though her gaze remained locked on the horse's master.

Damp with sweat, Jackson's black, dust-covered chambray shirt molded over the contours of his chest. Callie could only stare at the play of power across his shoulders. With shirtsleeves rolled above his elbows, his arm muscles flexed each time he raised and then lowered the whip, always in steady rhythm with the circling, struggling beast. Sweat glistened over the defined forearms dusted with dark hair.

So different from her.

So masculine.

So perfect.

Confliction coursed Callie's veins, and her gaze dipped lower, driven now by some unknown need. *You don't have to look*, whispered the tremulous voice inside her head. Her mouth pressed into a tight line, her lips as parched as her soul. She drank in the long legs encased in dusty denim, the firm buttocks cupped snugly beneath faded blue.

Then, he turned…and rapt now, Callie stared where the stiff straps of his chaps coupled just below his belt buckle. In that split second, she assessed the virility of the man.

Her throat seized closed.

Her breath strained in short puffs. The sun blazed down on Jackson, burning his image into her brain. Every nerve in her body quickened as a heat zipped up her neck to settle into two blistering spots on her cheeks. Her skin tingled, forcing her to roll her fingers into tight fists at her sides. The remembered pressure of his body pinning her to the ground, the texture of his thumb pad as he stroked her lip…all of her memories coalesced at once and lanced through her thoughts. Nothing, not even the stallion's submission, prepared her for the burn that ravaged her veins as she now stared across the corral at the denim-covered bulge of Jackson's maleness.

She swallowed.

Then scrunched her eyes closed as a wellspring of panic crashed over her. A blinding hiss of denial doused the roaring fire of her brief imaginations. Boot heels dug into the hard-packed earth, sending Callie straight for the stable. Her steps gobbled up the distance and as she cleared the threshold, pushing herself into the enveloping coolness, she vowed never to look below the bastard's belt buckle again.

Ever.

Chapter Six

The hacienda nestled in Sabina Canyon under the soft rays of a late-morning sun. Small by standards of most in the area, the pink adobe blushed with a beauty that belied its size. Mexican vaqueros had finished their chores earlier than expected and now lounged in the shade cast by mesquite trellises gracing the southern side of the main house.

Wednesday meant laundry day, a time of relaxation at the ranch. Papago and Pima Indians worked side by side to hang out the owner's wash. Children dashed around the colorful skirts of their mothers while high above their heads in a cloudless sky hawks soared on unseen currents.

The yeasty smell of baking bread filled the air.

Just before noon, the rasping shrieks of "*Pindah-lickoyee!*"—white-eyed enemy—lanced the ears of the unsuspecting inhabitants as fifteen Apache warriors swooped down from the surrounding mountain. Within minutes, all the Anglos, as well as their Mexican and Indian servants, lay dead, their souls carried away on silent winds.

Sweat sheened the copper-skinned warriors while a justified vengeance boiled through their blood. *Usen*—the Creator—had given this land to them, yet the white men—the vile *ndaa*—did not care. Day after day, they violated Mother Earth and all her precious resources. Pushed on by greed, they rerouted water and killed more than they ate; they were the brazen savages here. *Usen* understood the thirst for vengeance, understood why they would not leave consecrated ground where generations had lived and thrived, understood why the white-eyes must die. With pride, the warriors paid homage to their ancestors as the fires left after the bloodbath consumed the white man's world.

Just as quickly as they had arrived, the Apache disappeared into the shadow-filled mountains, leaving behind only their mark of death.

The evening air eddied around Jackson, carrying a pungent promise of rain. He stepped into the stable just as Gus stepped out.

"Whoa, there, didn't see you coming." Jackson moved aside to allow the old man room to pass.

"You finished with the horse for the day?"

Jackson nodded. "I'll start again in the morning, but he's just about broke now. Great animal—I'd sure like to keep him." He pointed over the wrangler's shoulder to the inside stalls. "Been riding that Morgan for several years, and he's been a good horse, but I'm hoping to trade up for the stallion."

Gus chuckled, shoving his hands into the pockets of his denims. "Hell's bells. You broke him. Don't see why you can't keep him." Jackson headed into the tack room, and Gus followed, stopping at the entryway. "I'm taken with your horse sense. Where'd you learn all that?"

"A muleskinner trained me when we were winter encamped around Petersburg in late '64. I became part of Reece's staff after he was promoted to brigade commander, so I had lots of time on my hands." Light shimmered from a lantern on the side table and illuminated the tools and supplies lining the walls. Shadows fell across Callie's saddle, the tooled leather rugged, worn and durable, just like its owner. At least the hellion was home and not out gallivanting around the countryside tonight, not that it mattered one hill of beans to him.

Jackson refocused, tossing the words over his shoulder as he draped the slender whip across the closest peg. "The 'skinner had been tutored by John Rarey; but that Ohio horse trainer's unusual techniques included hobbling one o' the critter's leg with a strap as a means of control. The ol' army 'skinner didn't agree with that particular step, so he up and changed things a bit. I never forgot his routine. Damned if it don't work every time."

"You think you could show us how to do that when we've got more time?

Sure would be easier breaking horses around here. At least we could all stay in one piece."

"I aim to teach everyone." With a loud thump, Jackson dropped the halter used with the stallion onto the workbench. "Except Callie. She wouldn't listen anyway. She's hard-pressed to change, especially where it involves me."

Gus folded thick arms across his chest, then sent a crusty laugh toward him. "She's a lot like that horse out yonder, son. Misunderstood. But she was mighty impressed with your little show this afternoon."

"I'm not sure *impressed* is the right word. More like, she was hoping I'd get trampled to death." Having Callie at the corral had forced Jackson to be even more aware of his work. Her pointed glare cleaved apart his focus, shredding his concentration into tiny slivers. Just knowing she sat there watching unnerved him.

Mocking me better fits the bill.

"Nope. Impressed she was, my friend," Gus continued as if reading his mind. "In fact, she even asked a few questions." The foreman paused and leaned against the doorframe. "Then all of a sudden, she lit outta there like she'd caught a bee in her britches."

"She's the damn bee and her britches should've made a run for it," Jackson retorted. Another chuckle from Gus banked the flare-up that surged through Jackson's veins. "None of her reasoning makes sense. She does things, and to hell with the consequences."

Gus fished in his shirt pocket, pulled out a tobacco wad, and lifted the dried chaw to his mouth, ripping off a generous section. Like crushed autumn leaves, bits of residue drifted to the ground near his boots. "She's quite a handful. You'll get no argument from me on that one."

"A handful? That's a mighty kind word considering that woman. Not once did Reece mention she was such a…" Out of respect for the foreman, Jackson stopped just short of spewing the perfect word. "She's controlling. And always riled up about something."

Gus moved the chaw to the other side of his mouth. "Mule-headed's more like it," he said. "Started when Andrew and Meg died. She's a shadow of the sweet child she used to be." A solemn look darkened his eyes. "I remember a time when her hair was all done up in ringlets and ribbons, her angel smile as bright as the sun. After her folks died and Reece rode east, she became the responsible one. But it's left her with this constant fear that everything will fall apart." He shook his head and chuckled. "So that's why she needs to control things. Of course, she can't, nobody can, but…she can control me. If I let her—which I do, 'cause it makes her feel safe. And that's my job—as her friend. To make her feel safe."

The old man's words settled deep.

"Well, safe or not, she's itchin' for a fight." Jackson surged past him and back into the main stable.

Gus issued a muffled snort. "With you?"

"Maybe." Jackson headed toward the entrance. Whickers from the nearby horses reached out in consoling accord with each of his heavy footfalls.

"That won't help, son."

Heated words pushed from Jackson's mouth. "Maybe not, but it'll make me feel better."

"Sounds like she's starting to get to you."

The ludicrous statement brought Jackson up short. His boot heel dug into dirt as he swerved to face the old man. "I hardly think so. I prefer my women soft and ladylike…and clean."

Jackson turned his back on the man again, and braced both hands on the sides of the rough pine doorframe. He worked to unlock his jaw. "Christ Almighty, what's wrong with a woman just being a woman?" Just beyond the doorway, a steady rain kicked up puffs of dust and carried the scent of dirt and horse manure into his nostrils.

Another soft laugh met Jackson's ears. "With the right fella, she might be willin' to learn." A roll of thunder nearly stole the man's words. The heavens fractured and delivered a full-blown storm.

Swirling wind lifted Jackson's long hair off the nape of his neck.

He contemplated Gus's idealistic remark. Perhaps Callie did need the right man to gentle her, to demonstrate how pleasant womanhood could be, to help her discover all the delicious little secrets of being seduced. Twisted tighter than Dick's hatband, Callie would tumble like a house of cards when she finally found her...*release*. Christ Almighty, he should do it...just to prove to himself how easy the task would be.

Are you out of your damned mind?

The scorching truth coiled in the pit of his stomach and lanced downward to settle into his throbbing groin.

He hadn't pleasured a woman in several months, and what was spearheading this asinine notion dwelled at the opposite spectrum from his brain. Callie Cutteridge was no whore to catch a flipped coin, bury the earnings inside her reticule and scoot out the door with a brightly satisfied, "Thank ye, sir."

Somewhere in the last minute and a half, he had completely lost his mind.

Jackson inhaled and took a full step out into the driving rain.

The water scoured his face and hands. In an instant, his clothes were soaked. His partner might well need a toss in the hay, and by someone who knew exactly how.

He possessed such talent.

Excelled at the job, in fact.

But no matter how long Callie's legs extended beneath those too-tight britches or how firm her breasts swelled under her masculine shirt, he was not a damn bit interested in the shrew.

Sunlight fell in a brilliant wash across the mission nestled in the valley. The cluster of buildings glistened, the pink adobe walls washed clean by last night's rain. Callie eased her horse down the incline and headed toward a mud-brick hut hugging the edge of the compound.

Inside her saddlebag nestled fifty dollars.

She patted the careworn leather for good measure. The corners of her mouth tucked in as she recalled the neatly penned entry of her deduction in the now equally neat ledger. Since their confrontation several weeks before, Jackson had not once mentioned F. Miguel or the money, and when she went to write the draft this morning, she'd found fifty-dollars waiting for her. Exactly as she had instructed, Jackson had deducted the money from her portion.

Her smile deepened at the small victory.

Ten minutes later, Callie reined Diego to a stop before the building. She dismounted just as a wiry man stepped from the doorway of the church to greet her. Swathed from head to toe in brown wool, the priest tightened the robe belt circling his sparse waist. Around his neck, a heavy, filigreed cross dangled from a leather lanyard and caught the glint of the sun's first rays with each step he took toward her. Dark-hued *castellano* heritage etched a gaunt face, yet the padre's small stature belied his hidden reservoir of strength. As he approached, she caught a whiff of tallow from the collection of burning candles in a tray inside the small vestibule of the church. Callie wished she had time to light one. Was it wrong to pray for the day Jackson Neale would drop dead?

Probably.

She draped her saddlebags over her shoulder and met the cleric halfway. "Good morning, Father Miguel," she said, forcing her lips into a smile.

"Señorita Callie! How good to see you again."

"I'm sorry I'm so late this month. I've been getting our horses ready for the move to Camp Lowell. But I wanted to bring you my regular donation for the mission orphanage." She lifted the flap of the saddlebag and reached inside as Father Miguel joined her.

"Your ever-faithful gift keeps food on the table for the children. God will continue to bless you for your generosity, my child."

The priest's cheerfulness tempered Callie's mood. She held out the wad of money, then waited while he issued a blessing over the bills before slipping her donation into the side-pocket of his robe.

Reverence filled her voice. "I'm more than glad to help." She glanced around the mission, her gaze skipping past the outbuildings. "Where are the children this morning?"

"They've just sat down to breakfast. Please. Come. Stay with us and eat. We go join them."

"I'm sorry, I can't this visit. But, do you remember the problems I'd been having with the wild stallion?"

"Ah, yes. I remember well." He motioned toward the courtyard of the compound. Shade trees filled the area, and a water-well occupied its center. They walked into the sheltering relief of a large cottonwood, and Callie rested her shoulder against its white-barked trunk.

"Well, I finally caught him a few weeks back. He's completely broken now."

The padre scanned her from head to toe before returning his gaze to hers. "And you can still walk? I have seen your stiffness from other such occasions."

"I didn't break the horse, Father."

His dark eyebrows swept upward in mild surprise, creasing his tanned forehead. "No?"

"No. My new partner did." The flat statement reflected the strain of the past two months and coalesced into a hard knot in Callie's throat.

"A…partner? This is something new?" he asked.

Callie nodded. "Yes. And not my choosing, I assure you. Reece sent him as his replacement, one of his officer's during the war. His good friend, I'm led to believe." She reached into the saddlebag and withdrew the folded letter. Shoving her brother's missive into the priest's gnarled hands, she said, "This was how he shared the good news. By selling me off to a half-baked easterner like a head of beef."

Squinting against the sun's brightness, the priest scanned the correspondence before handing it back. He clasped his hands behind him and rocked on the balls of sandal-covered feet. "Your brother is a smart man and would not wish you harm. But I sense your unhappiness."

A chill zipped up Callie's spine. She shoved the letter into the leather bag, then pushed off the tree and turned to pace in front of him. "That's putting it mildly." She wasn't sure how to share her feelings with this hallowed messenger of God, and was afraid that once she started she wouldn't be able to stop. Instead, she moved from under the shade of the tree and headed toward her horse. "Well, I better get going. I just wanted to bring the money over early today."

Callie settled the bags into place and then pulled up into the saddle. "I'll be on time next month, Father, I promise. And please tell the children I'll make plans to stay for breakfast then." She reached down and shook his outstretched hand.

"You are an angel sent from heaven," he whispered.

She straightened and gathered the reins. "I don't know about that, Father. I'm afraid there's not much good left in me." She wheeled Diego around and headed westward.

From his position atop the bluff, Jackson watched as his wily partner galloped away from the old mission until distance stole Callie from his view. Earlier this morning, he'd watched her ride out, the fifty dollars buried inside her saddlebag.

Her trail hadn't been hard to follow, not that she tried to cover her path.

Four years with the cavalry had given Jackson some tracking ability... maybe not the intricate skills needed to follow a band of crafty Indians, but certainly enough talent to track someone unaware they were being followed. He intended to have an answer to the burning identity question regarding the mysterious F. Miguel. Callie's lover or not, the answer lay within easy reach now.

Jackson eased the stallion down the incline and headed toward the mission. His lips pulled into a lopsided smirk. Oh yes, the good padre obviously knew something about F. Miguel, and before Jackson was finished charming the priest this morning, Callie's secret would be spilled.

Chapter Seven

"Señorita! Señorita! I have important news." Pilar's voice rang through the hacienda. Callie lifted her head from her reading just as the servant rushed into the room. "I have news of Señor Neale."

Callie tossed aside the manual *European Dressage—A System to Train Horses*. "What kind of news?"

"Well, me and Juanita were talking and..." Pilar paused to shove a black braid over her shoulder to join the other one hanging down her back. "You know Juanita? Señor Eschevon's cook? Like I yours."

Callie issued an impatient nod. "Yes. Yes. I know Juanita. You talked to her this morning. Go on."

"*Sí*, we friends for many years. She just left from a visit, but told me Señor Eschevon is to hold fiesta for Señor Neale." Pilar buried her hands in her apron to still their agitation. "They say he's war hero, *Patróna*, so I thought you want to know."

A war hero...and a party? Callie's stomach muscles tightened. Good God, someone should've offered to throw her a party just for allowing the damn squatter to stay. She drew a calming breath and stood. "Thank you for telling me, Pilar, but I'm afraid I'll not be going to any fiesta. Mr. Neale is no hero of mine."

A deep voice resonated from the doorway. "So you're not planning to attend, then?"

Callie's gaze swept sideways and everything registered at once, from the determined set of Jackson's jaw down to his dusty boots. For one long, static moment, she stared at him before she forced her gaze out the window, settling it on the side of the stable. An orange glow from the late-afternoon sun splashed over the roughhewed walls.

A butterfly flitted past her view. "That's right," she replied. "I'm not going. I've nothing to celebrate." The diminutive creature fluttered away, and Callie wanted to follow.

The sound of rustling paper, however, brought her focus back to Jackson. "The invitation just arrived via messenger." He waved the missive in his outstretched hand as he glanced toward Pilar. The servant smiled, ducked her head and slipped past him from the room. Jackson reconnected his gaze to Callie. "Thought I'd bring this to you."

"Keep it. Parties hold no interest for me." Callie was thankful he could not hear the rush of blood pounding in her ears from the lie.

An amused smile curled Jackson's lips and he stepped into the room. "While I believe a party might do wonders for your disposition, your attendance certainly isn't necessary." He moved closer, the thud of his boot heels heavy across the tiles. "In fact," he continued, tangling her nerves into an even tighter knot, "Gus mentioned Señor Eschevon has recently acquired a fine mare from San Antonio. A Paso Fino, I believe." He stopped in front of her, his gaze wandering over the curls that tumbled past her shoulder in a long, tousled mess. "I'm considering breeding the stallion with his mare, and this party will provide an opportunity to discuss the details."

Callie swallowed. Now he wanted to meet the neighbors. Considering how nosey he was, she was not the least bit surprised. She filled her lungs with a slow inhale, then lifted her chin and offered a strained smile. Having him make inroads with her neighbors might not be in her best interest. "Studding out the wild horse is a waste of time right now. We don't even know if he'll produce, let alone mount."

Jackson's broad shoulders flexed, and he leaned forward. "Any hot-blooded male worth his salt will mount if given the opportunity." The deep chuckle that followed sent a rush of heat across Callie's face. "Besides, he's no longer wild. And like you...I too want to develop a bloodline that captures his special qualities. He needs a partner who will play down his faults—and vice versa. Did I mention, I've decided on his name?"

The heat ramped up another blistering notch. "Oh do let me guess. Satan?" She bestowed upon him her best smirk.

"It'll be Salvaje."

Callie's eyebrow arched. "Ironic, don't you think? Since *salvaje* is Spanish for *wild*." She glared up at him, refusing to blink. This sonofabitch would not get the best of her. War hero or not. "Perhaps I will ride over to the party after all...just to make sure everything with the horses is handled properly."

"Perhaps you should." Something stirred in the smoky depths of his eyes. "We'll want to try and present a united front to our neighbors, don't you think? After all, it's what your brother wanted."

Callie's knees stiffened. "Had he bothered asking me what I wanted, it wouldn't have been you." She tried to ignore the dryness in her mouth left by the remark. "I'm going only to make certain you don't swindle me out of things that are rightfully mine. And any by-blows from that horse are also mine." Her voice lowered just enough to drive home her point. "After all, we're partners." She ended the sentence on a heavy hiss.

Jackson's eyes flickered once, then all emotion faded from his face except for the tight lines that bracketed his mouth. Several moments passed in discomforting silence before he grinned. "This says we're to be there at sundown on Friday. Shall we ride over together?"

"I know where they live. I'll be there." Subtle undertones of tobacco and horseflesh wafted around Callie and brought back the image of the raw-boned man standing under the drenching sunlight in the center of her corral—his gentle power over the horse and his unstinting masculinity. She forced away the recollection.

"Fine." Jackson tossed the request onto the seat of a nearby chair, then tipped his head, scanning her from head to foot. Inside her boots, her toes curled as his blunt gaze reconnected with hers. "Do you even own a dress?"

Callie's spine stiffened. "What I wear—"

"I only ask because I'd like to see the skirt twirl while we're dancing Friday night."

"I don't like to dance." But the heavy thumping his presence had resurrected inside her heart tipped her sanity into another wobbly spin.

"Then it's painfully clear you haven't danced with the right man."

With an abrupt turn, he stalked from the room. A heartbeat later, Callie collapsed into the chair. A well-aimed swipe sent the horse-training manual sailing across the room.

Visible for miles, the lights of the Eschevon hacienda cut through the desert darkness like a beacon across a sea of sand.

Word of Jackson Neale's arrival in the territory had reached as far as the Mexican border. The fiesta had brought Spanish landowners, Anglo military officers and their spouses from miles around. Even the governor would be attending the gala all the way from the territorial capitol in Prescott.

An army band from Camp Lowell provided the musical entertainment for dancing couples swathed in colorful silks and broadcloth. The sound of brass instruments filled the air, and a few Mexican guitars added just enough local flair to please the entire crowd.

The evening was warm and dry, and whiskey and wine flowed through the crowd in unlimited supply. The finely dressed of the territory had turned out accordingly, and everyone wanted to capture a moment with the guest of honor to share a story or invite him to their homes or businesses in the thriving community of Tucson.

Jackson issued a contented sigh as immense pleasure coursed through him. He had grown to adulthood in this type of environment, raised to appreciate the refinement and polish of polite society. His gaze swept the room. Jewel-encrusted *mantilla* combs and lace glistened from the upswept coiffures of the señoritas, and fine cigars and brandy filled the hands of the well-dressed señors. Though the trappings were different, the underlying current of wealth and gaiety oozed over him.

He offered an agreeable nod at the tale told by Charles Cavanaugh, the owner of the local freighting company, then issued a robust laugh at the antics of one of the merchants of Tucson's commercial district. In his element here, Jackson entertained them all, and they accepted and embraced him as their own.

The military officers from Camp Lowell required much of his time. News from back east was scarce, and he updated them about the political reconstruction undertaken by Washington since the war's end. Rebuilding a southland torn asunder demanded troops and money. The locals listened with rapt attention, thrilled to be hearing information other than that of raids by Apaches hell-bent on revenge for imagined transgressions.

Not forgetting the ladies in attendance, Jackson took time to chat about current styles and colorful fashions worn by eastern women. Yet, even as he shared his stories, his gaze returned again and again to the hacienda's entrance. The damnable shrew had yet to arrive, and his irritation mounted with each passing minute.

A wisp of dark-green satin drifted across his wrist and forced his attention away from the front door. His eyes traveled up the petite form of a young white woman in a stunning ball gown. The wide crinoline beneath the silk skirt created the vision of an emerald bell.

He locked his gaze upon a pair of eyes the color of springtime green framed by long, dark lashes that matched the side swept mahogany curls tumbling over the bare shoulders. Alabaster skin radiated with a glossy elegance beneath the candlelight, and Jackson's heart slammed against his ribs.

Hell's fire, woman, where have you been hiding?

"Good evening, Mr. Neale." Her voice was as warm and smooth as the expensive whiskey that swirled in the bottom of his glass. The smoky tones of her voice settled over him like a hot, wet kiss. "I am so sorry no one has yet introduced us. My name is Pamela Talmadge."

Disappointment swamped Jackson. How could such a ravishing beauty be married to the portly post commander at Camp Lowell?

"Well, thank you for the introduction then," he offered, bending toward her extended hand. He placed a light kiss upon her white-gloved fingers, then straightened, leaning closer. "I applaud your husband. Not only for his admirable job in commanding during these troubled times, but for his excellent choice in women."

Her laughter rippled through Jackson like a brook tumbling over shiny stones. "Colonel Talmadge is my father, you silly man." She dropped open the ivory slats of her fan and fluttered the delicate piece with practiced skill. "I'm visiting him from Boston."

"How nice." A broad smile flooded Jackson's face.

"Yes, but I am finding everything here so different. And I've heard the summers can be quite beastly. So hot. So terribly dry."

Jackson guessed her to be nineteen years old, twenty at the most. Just as quickly, their fifteen-year age difference was forgotten. "I can only imagine how difficult it must be for a delicate woman such as you."

"Yes, and so few trees, Mr. Neale." She sighed, her lower lip curving into a practiced pout. "Why, I can't even have a picnic unless it's beside the creek. The only proper stand of trees for miles is the cottonwoods that line it."

"It will take time to adjust."

"Yes, it will." Just as quickly, her sweet smile reappeared, and a charming dimple caressed her cheek. "My father tells me you'll be visiting Camp Lowell soon. Something about horses, I believe?"

"Indeed. We sell horses to the army."

A perfectly plucked eyebrow arched in surprise. "We?"

"My partner Colleen Cutteridge and I."

"Oh. I see." Her fan fluttered once more. "Well then, perhaps I could interest you both in a picnic beneath the cottonwoods the next time you visit."

Callie and this woman lunching? Good God, this delicious little minx had flirting honed to a fine art. Callie, on the other hand, would as soon shoot her as look at her. He stifled a laugh and reveled in his good fortune. "Perhaps, we shall," he assured her. "Perhaps, we shall."

Callie handed Diego's reins to the young Mexican. "Leave him saddled. I won't be here long."

The boy nodded and led her horse toward the stables.

She made her way to the entrance of the Eschevon hacienda, shaking hands with several vaqueros along the way.

Taking a deep breath, she pulled off her leather gloves, shoved them into her leather belt, then stepped across the threshold and into the brightly lit interior.

Above her head an ornate candlelit chandelier suspended from a wooden beam and splashed golden light across the linen-covered ceiling. Seeing the flamboyant piece again reminded Callie of the excitement everyone felt a decade and a half earlier when the Butterfield Stage had delivered it to the Eschevon hacienda.

Edginess settled over her as music spilled into the foyer from the rooms set aside for dancing. The sounds reminded her of the many parties her own parents had given. She had loved every one of them. Callie's chin rose higher as she anchored her smile.

Nodding at people she hadn't seen in months, she scanned the crowd. She rarely ventured into Tucson now, preferring to leave the purchase of supplies to Gus and Banner. Seeing familiar faces reminded her of her chosen isolation.

Callie lifted a glass of wine from a silver tray as a servant passed. The base of the cool goblet nestled in her palm as she wrapped her fingers around the delicate stem.

The glass paused in midair as her gaze found the tall form of her partner. A steel-gray frock coat and trousers covered Jackson's lean body, the crisp linen shirt beneath them the color of drifting snow. His dark hair remained long, but brushed neatly into place. He looked every bit the part of a gentleman.

He could pass as a buyer from back east.

She watched him tip his head down, then smile at something his companion said. A delicate ivory fan tapped him on the arm and Callie's gaze cut sideways, settling upon a breathtaking beauty.

With her next inrushing breath, Callie felt as homely as a pond toad.

Jackson's hand slipped around the woman's tightly corseted waistline as he guided her onto the dance floor. The broad smile plastered across his face suggested things Callie could only imagine. The fan dangled from the tiny wrist and a gloved hand rose toward Jackson.

The image settled like a lead weight in Callie's stomach and she compared the bulky gloves tucked in her waistband to the pristine purity of the one now resting on Jackson's arm. Blood surged through her veins, skittering out of control. She jumped as the high-pitched voice of Carmen Eschevon shattered her thoughts.

"Ahh! Callie. How wonderful to see you again." The hostess pushed her rotund body through the crowd and stood in front of Callie, blocking the view of Jackson and the stunning stranger. "I so afraid you not attend." Mrs. Eschevon clapped her hands in joy, and the generous, caramel-hued swell of her breasts all but spilled from the bodice of her frothy evening gown. "What a joy to meet Señor Neale. He is truly *el hombre guapo!*"

"Yes, very handsome," Callie replied in a monotone, feeling her composure slipping away faster than her patience. She abruptly changed the subject. "I'm sorry for arriving so late, Mrs. Eschevon, but I had a few things to finish at the ranch before riding over."

Callie took another quick sip of wine, then reminded herself to slow down. She'd missed dinner and had eaten only a light meal at noon. But the sweet taste of the wine tingled on her tongue. Impulsively, she swallowed, then sipped again.

"Oh, no worry, we have people in and out all night. Now come along with me and see Roberto. He not talk to you for so long."

Carmen led the way toward a gathering of men.

They parted, offering kind greetings to Callie before they dispersed into the crowd.

A tall, silver-haired Spaniard turned around and her heart warmed. "Señor Eschevon," she said, smiling with genuine affection at the distinguished man. "How nice to see you again." For years, her father and Roberto had been friends.

In fact, the Eschevons had been the first to welcome them to the territory.

"Ah, here's our little Colleen." He bent slightly in a warm greeting. "Still in britches, I see, but lovely just the same." He graced her hand with a whisper of a kiss, and Callie smiled at his subtle scolding of her choice of evening attire. Conversation flowed between them for several minutes, along with several more glasses of wine. And all the while, Callie watched Jackson from the corner of her eye. A restless sensation girdled her hips as he glided his companion around the dance floor to the lilting notes of a beautiful waltz. Strauss's "Beautiful Blue Danube". Unbidden, a childhood memory of smooth piano keys beneath her fingertips forced Callie to tighten her grip on the stemware.

The wineglass rose to her lips, and she took a bigger gulp.

They made a striking couple as they moved with elegant grace to the haunting melody. Jackson so tall and confident and so much in his element tonight. And his radiant dance partner, a total stranger, resting oh-so-cozy in his strong and guiding embrace.

Callie nodded as Carmen twittered on about the latest endeavors of the Tucsonian Women's Guild, but an unexplainable longing engulfed Callie. Her mind retraced the years since she'd last danced. A half-dozen? Maybe more. For a brief moment, she recalled a silk ball gown, her first. The berthe of the exquisite dress a brilliant cerise over a full chemisette of lace. Callie's eyes slipped closed as she gathered her emotions under invisible wings of despair.

Those were happier times.

Her gaze lifted and she glanced again at Jackson. He now had the woman pulled up against his body. Sweet laughter spilled from his dewy-skinned companion and spread across the room to slam full-force into Callie's bewildering irritation.

She damn well knew enough about what occurred between a man and a woman to know what would come next for those two. But, to display it so boldly to a roomful of people, their own neighbors for God's sake, in such a suggestive manner was unacceptable. People might behave that way in Philadelphia, but she'd be damned if her new partner would fondle the willing woman right in front of every single resident of the territory.

Downing another glass of wine, Callie pulled her attention back to the smiling hostess.

"Excuse me, Señora Eschevon, but I must go talk to Mr. Neale." She deposited the empty wineglass upon another passing tray, then coursed straight onto the dance floor. Impatience heated her steps as she moved through the shifting crowd, bumping into one couple, pushing past several more without so much as an apology. By the time she stepped into her partner's line of vision her simmering disapproval had bubbled over into a rolling boil.

Jackson's eyes widened upon seeing her, and he stopped dancing and guided the stranger to the side of the dance floor.

He then turned to face Callie, and quipped, "I see you've finally arrived." He scanned her from head to toe as he shook his head in disapproval.

"I've been here long enough to see things I don't like." Callie contained the desire to haul off and kick him in the shin.

Jackson turned to his companion. "Miss Talmadge, allow me to introduce Colleen Cutteridge, my errant partner."

The eastern beauty scanned Callie from the single braid hanging down her back to her scuffed-up riding boots. Clothed in black slacks and a white cotton shirt, Callie realized she appeared more outfitted to brand horses than attend any type of social gathering, and would have much preferred doing so to standing in front of this socialite.

The woman offered a tiny smile and extended her gloved hand. "I've heard so much about you, Miss Cutteridge. It's a pleasure to meet you at last."

"Yes, thank you." Callie touched the tiny hand, then dismissed the woman as her gaze locked on to Jackson's heated glare. "We need to talk," she snapped.

His voice thinned. "I'm with Miss Talmadge right now."

"I can see that, as can everyone else in the room."

He compressed his lips, glanced at his companion, and then back to Callie. "Whatever you need to say will wait." He smiled at the curious bystanders and nodded before lancing his gaze back. "Lower your voice," he rasped. "You're making a scene."

Instead, Callie's tone rose even louder. "Come with me right this minute." She made a full pivot and pushed back through the crowd. Behind her, Jackson offered a hasty apology to Miss Talmadge, then the deep thumping sound of his boot heels rose above the music.

She headed straight down a hallway, around a corner and into the summer kitchen, where several Indians looked up from their food preparations. Callie scanned the room and spotted an open door, a supply closet in the far corner. Moments later, she skittered inside. A lantern suspended from the ceiling by a rope illuminated the small area.

The smells of ground coffee and cinnamon infused the air. She braced her hand against the wall for support, attempting to stop the swirling sensation caused by too much wine and too little understanding of her anger. Hot on her heels, Jackson stepped in behind her and slammed the door.

"What in the Sam hell do you think you're doing?" His voice boomed over her and Callie whirled to face him, dwarfed by his formidable size.

"Me? What about you?" She blew out her breath. Like a bitter pill, she tasted her unbalanced fury. Her hand slid down the wall and ended in a tight fist at her side.

"I *was* dancing," he snapped.

"Dancing? That's not what I'd call it, mister." Callie refused to point out the sordid details of what his penchant for groping women might do to her sterling reputation.

He loomed closer. "What the hell are you talking about?"

She raised her right arm and pointed toward the closed door, her index finger wagging furiously. "Out there…on the dance floor is what I'm talking about. You and Miss…" Callie struggled to remember the name and failed. So she settled for, "…Prim and Proper!" She swayed again and rammed her back straighter.

An agonizing moment ticked past as his gaze seared hers. Finally, his voice boomed with scorn, "Good God, woman, is that what this madness is about?" A lock of dark hair fell over his forehead and he reared back, his eyes crushing into slits. "You've been drinking."

"A few glasses of wine. And don't even bother changing the subject."

Jackson braced his hand upon the rough wall behind her, then leaned forward, closing the distance between them to mere inches. "Why do you care what I do?"

"Because you can't do *that* here. You damn polecat, *people talk.*"

Three more beats of her heart passed before he whispered, "It's not acceptable for me to dance with a beautiful woman?"

"I'm not talking about dancing, and you damn well know it." Her chin rose in a blatant challenge. "I didn't realize you were planning on seducing women tonight. Had I known, I wouldn't have bothered riding over." Her cheeks burned in frustration. "I clearly remember you saying you were coming to this party tonight to talk about horses!"

"I already spoke to Señor Eschevon," he ground out behind clenched teeth, his features tightening into a mask of stone. "Had you been here earlier, like you should have been, you would have known."

The faraway notes of a guitar underscored the momentary pause. Callie grasped for the closest thought. "Well?"

"Well what?"

"Are you going to breed her or not?"

Jackson leaned closer, pushing his lips into a sideways grin. "Who, darlin'? The horse or Miss Talmadge?" The damnable chuckle that followed pommelled Callie like a scorching wind. "And seduction is a mighty strong word for simply enjoying the charismatic allure of a woman." The sultry smell of him, all citrusy and spicy and so unbearably male, embedded deep inside her brain. "At least she appreciates being a woman, which is far more than I can say for lonely little you."

Callie shoved him away and lurched sideways, bumping into a shelf. Glass jars of pickles and preserves and ruby-red tomatoes rattled together, silent onlookers watching her squirm under his stinging words. "I am not lonely, you onerous toad. And a corseted waistline will do nothing to make the tart you crave be strong enough to survive in my country. If creamy skin and *décolletage* are the only things you're after, then you won't last long at my ranch either."

A dangerous glint flashed in Jackson's eyes and his features grew rigid. He pushed closer still, wrapping her inside his shadow. "Men like softness and kindness in a woman. Qualities I now know even you possess, but are too damned afraid to show."

"I'm not afraid of one damn thing." The lie forced her scalp to tingle as her breathing tripped in and out. She lost track of time and place as the absolute truth of her weaknesses now twisted everything into knots inside her.

"Bullshit. You're terrified of responding to anything, let alone a man. And God only knows what or who it'll be to break through that armored wall you've erected around yourself."

"Well I can say with absolute certainty it won't be you."

"You're damned right." Soaked in sarcasm now, his voice deepened as the glint in his eyes darkened. "I'll always choose softness and sensuality, both things you're not."

A wild tremble rolled through Callie with the force of some unknown demon. Her right hand curled into a tight ball and a second later, she drove her fist full-force into Jackson's midsection. A resounding *oomph* resonated as he nearly doubled over from the unexpected blow.

She went rigid with shock as he straightened.

Her gaze locked on his flushed face.

On a slow push of air, he released his breath. A muscle twitched in his cheek. His eyes burned with something Callie could not comprehend. She panicked, but before she could slide away, Jackson's hand jammed into the hair at the base of her braid. He cupped her head, his face looming so close now she could see the flecks of gold embedded in the depths of his dark eyes. He pushed her up against the wall, knocking over a bucket and a broom in the process.

Her heart banged against her chest and a peculiar sound sputtered out. Had it come from her? Or him? Heat drained from her face as her eyes widened.

He dipped his head.

Surely to God he wouldn't dare.

The empty cavern of her lungs flooded with air as she tried to scream. The sound never materialized. Jackson slammed his mouth down upon hers, capturing her lips in a fierce, hot possession. A hellish, mind-spinning burn that yearned for release swept aside her icy wrath of moments before. The frisson of fear coalesced through Callie's veins into an all-consuming rush of heat.

Strong arms wrapped her waist. Then lifted her.

Jackson filled every part of her senses…his taste, his smell, his strength. His presence burned high and hot and strange guttural sounds consumed her. She fought to dislodge him. He tightened his hold, crushing her breasts against his body. She could not get rid of him, so she scrambled to push him from her mind. With a maddening will of its own, however, her mind refused to listen. The hard nubs of her nipples rasped against the cotton camisole beneath her shirt. Her hand slipped over Jackson's shoulders, her fingers digging into the bunched muscles that strained against expensive wool. A wave of tightness spiraled down to settle into her most intimate place. The only thing dominating her now was the pressure of Jackson's lips and his hand…and the intoxicating smell and taste of him. Richly caramelized. Oaken.

Bewitching beyond belief.

When had the nameless feeling become her master, careening through her like some living, breathing beast?

Desire aroused a slumbering demon.

All too soon, the pressure against her lips lessened. The release was now as upsetting as the unexpected kiss had been. Callie's breath caught in her throat when the warmth of his mouth lifted.

Their gazes locked.

His breath rushed out hot and fast, and in the subdued light, the tight line of his cheek appeared cut from chiseled stone.

Seconds crawled past as raspy, panting sounds escaped her throat.

And then, with unbearable achievement, Jackson's mouth returned to the same mocking smirk. His gaze never left hers as he reached sideways for the door. A second later, he twisted the knob and the sounds of music and laughter and rattling pots and pans spilled inward. Without another word, he stepped from the small room.

Callie's whole body jerked when the door slammed shut.

Her hands rose, and she spread trembling fingers across her mouth. Her tongue slipped out, wetting her lips…but all she tasted was him. The ache inside her chest swelled, her muscles paralyzed. Unable to breathe now, and as hard as she tried, Callie could not deny the all-encompassing need Jackson had just brought to life inside her.

Chapter Eight

Jackson nodded at one man's statement, smiled at another's, but cared little about what was being said.

First, we're screaming at each other.

And then I'm kissing her?

He brought the whiskey to his lips. In one long pull, Jackson emptied the tumbler. These Spanish landowners adored Callie. In fact, they'd spent the better part of the evening extolling over and over all her extraordinary qualities to him.

Jackson had nowhere to escape.

And all around him, conversation droned on. He drove a hand through his hair. The shocking news discovered from his visit with Father Miguel further perplexed Jackson. Callie's magnanimous support of the local orphanage proved that somewhere beneath her caustic exterior breathed a warm and benevolent angel.

Why would she pretend otherwise?

"Are you all right, Señor Neale?" Eschevon whispered beside him.

Jackson refocused, plastering a practiced smile into place. How could he tell his amiable host that he'd just come from ravaging Callie Cutteridge in Eschevon's well-stocked supply closet? "Yes, I'm fine." He chuckled, raising his glass in a mocking salute. "I just need to go slower with your fine whiskey." Roberto laughed, reached for a decanter from a passing tray and refilled the cut-crystal tumbler clutched in Jackson's hand.

"We are holding this fiesta in your honor, señor…so it is permissible to drink your fill tonight."

As the amber liquid rose to the rim, Jackson slid his gaze across a sea of faces. On the opposite side of the room, Pamela Talmadge leaned upon the arm of a young lieutenant. Her bright smile quenched Jackson's wounded pride, as well. The woman radiated charm and abruptly altered his thoughts. She was the type of female he understood. Indeed, Callie could never hope to match the well-honed *naiveté* of the Miss Talmadges of this world.

And the lieutenant?

A minor inconvenience, nothing more. Jackson's gaze narrowed as a smile tugged his mouth. When he wanted something, nothing stood in his way. And yet, scouring the darkened corridors of his mind, Callie's innocent surrender sunk in with teeth and claws and sent a sheen of sweat across his brow.

He hadn't expected her enigmatic response, fueled with some volatile fire that frightened the hell out of him. Jackson knew from her silent reaction, Callie also had been shaken by the kiss.

A grimace dissolved Jackson's smirk. There had to be a reason for the mess that shredded the layers of his self-control. As hard as he searched his brain, however, he couldn't quite find one.

Shouts brought his attention back to the fiesta and to the cluster of guests milling around him. Several men approached the group, and the mundane flow of conversation abruptly stopped. Jackson stepped sideways into the shadows to allow the new arrivals more room.

Two Papago Indians, enemy of the Apache as he'd discovered earlier this evening, walked behind a lanky cowboy, and their travel-worn appearance implied urgency. The young Anglo removed his hat, and long brown hair draped over his dust-covered shoulders.

He directed blunt words toward Roberto Eschevon. "There's been another raid." Behind the man, the Indians pressed forward, speaking gibberish. The interpreter nodded, then continued. "A small ranch in Sabina Canyon. Near Dragoon Springs Station. Everyone's dead, including women and children." He angled his thumb over his shoulder toward his comrades. "Some of the victims were Papago servants, and their tribes are demanding retribution from the authorities. They say the Apache must pay for this."

Murmurs filled the room as news of the massacre spread through the crowd. Music and dancing stopped as people pressed closer. John Noble Goodwin, governor of the territory, entered the circle of men. Standing barely five feet five, the Maine native's mild appearance, thinning hairline and spectacles were at odds with the strength in his voice. "Is this the same band that killed the superintendent of the Patagonia mines last month?"

The Indians nodded at the translated question, their response thrown toward the governor in a rush of unfamiliar words.

"Yes. Definitely Cochise and his warriors," the interpreter delivered. "They say the Papago and Pima trade wheat with the Anglos, and work in their homes. They demand justice for the murders of their people."

Colonel Thaddeus Talmadge, commander of the garrison at Camp Lowell, stepped forward, his voice booming above the Indians. "This is exactly what I've been trying to tell you, John. The Apache slip out of the mountains, strike quickly, then disappear before we can even find their trail." The interpreter translated the words for the Indians in a low, rushed voice. "I've sent couriers to General Stoneman's headquarters at Drum Barracks, with news of the recent uprisings. But he says I'm to do nothing at this time. He states the Apache have peaceful intentions, that the government is gathering them toward reservations."

William Oury, a wiry-framed, hot-tempered Virginian who'd fought in the Texas War for Independence as had been pointed out to Jackson several times tonight, glared at the governor. "These murdering bastards ain't goin' to no reservations, John. This is exactly why we need that local militia." His gaze slid to the colonel. "To fend off attacks the army is unwilling to even try and stop."

"I resent that, sir," Talmadge protested. "I've every intention of protecting the citizens of the territory, but I must have more manpower to do so."

The governor raised both hands to silence them as the crowd continued to shove inward. Lacy fans waved around fearful whispers, and cigar smoke wafted through the room in a cloudy haze. "I understand what you are saying, and I'm authorizing your request for a local militia at least until I can arrange for territory-wide militia staffing. I promise you all, I'll talk to Washington about this matter. But right now I need someone who's willing to step forward and lead this local project." He glanced around the sea of onlookers until his gaze fell upon Jackson. "I need someone like you, Neale, recently from the war. You'd be the perfect choice."

Cheers filled the room as everyone agreed with the governor's selection for their new militia leader. Jackson's stomach somersaulted. All he wanted to do after the war was ride westward, drink whiskey, smoke cheroots and bed big-breasted señoritas.

Inside his boots, Jackson's toes clenched.

Damnation.

His now-empty glass thumped to a nearby table and Jackson stepped forward into the circle of men. He'd already had his bellyful of fighting. He would decline with grace. "It takes more than words to create a militia of qualified soldiers, Governor. And, it is certainly not something that can be thrown together." He met every eye before reconnecting his gaze with Goodwin's. "I'm deeply honored you thought of me, but I believe this task should be handled by the military. Perhaps the colonel might want to appoint a soldier to fill the leadership position in the interim."

Talmadge countered, shaking his head. "I can't afford even one soldier absent from my ranks, Neale. We're stretched thin as it is protecting the supply trains and providing escorts for the freighting wagons. Washington refuses me reinforcements, though I write daily for more soldiers to fill the roster." He glanced to the governor. "Since the military is stalled where this is concerned, I'm in complete agreement with you. Neale is an excellent choice. In fact, Cutteridge wrote me, stating Neale was twice commended for bravery during the war." The colonel scanned the crowd, his words reassuring the worried mass, rising higher so everyone could hear. "And according to Reece…" his gaze slipped back to Jackson, "…a more qualified man, you're not likely to find."

Sonofabitch.

"Those commendations, sir, came upon the heels of me simply fighting for survival. The war created many heroes in four years, and everyone who rode with me that day deserved recognition." He'd obviously have to try another tactic, since this was going nowhere. "Besides, I've just recently arrived in the territory."

"All the more reason why you're the perfect choice. You still have the freshness of battle in your blood."

A rueful smile tightened Jackson's lips. "I hardly think freshness conveys the horrors of war, Colonel."

Talmadge gestured wide. "Look around you, Neale. Who else has your experience?"

Jackson scanned the crowd of onlookers composed of both Spanish and Anglo. Most were elderly businessmen and their families. A few hotheads, such as Oury, were famous for their fiery tempers, but the man was no leader. In fact, stories of two recent duels involving the Texan had entertained the gossiping crowd all evening.

The local freighting company owner Charles Cavanaugh spoke up. "I'll be glad to supply foodstuffs to the militia when it's riding in search of Apache, Neale. Surely that'll be a weight off your mind." Cavanaugh glanced at the governor, who acknowledged the offer with a quick nod.

"That's very generous of you, Charles," Goodwin said. Then the governor settled his attention back upon Jackson. "You see, Neale, we're all in need of your skills. I can't say enough what a service you'd be providing the local citizenry."

Jackson drew in a heavy breath.

Dammit, Reece.

Several long moments pulled at the edges of Jackson's sanity. He knew he could no more turn and walk away from this new responsibility than he could have walked away from staff assignment after Reece was promoted. Resentment simmered in a hot push through his veins as he glanced at the governor.

"Fine," he snapped. "But if I agree to this, I want every man trained accordingly. I'll not have them riding off shooting at everything that moves in these mountains." He paused to look at Oury, and then slid his glance over the nodding mass. "And the volunteers must come to Dos Caballos for training. I won't leave my partner alone during all this."

From the back of the room someone yelled, "Callie takes care of herself, Neale."

Another added, "She's been doing fine for years. Don't think she needs you or anyone else protectin' her."

"That's right, Neale. This country made her grow up fast and mean. The Apache know to steer clear of that hellcat," another proclaimed.

Jackson laughed with the rest of the crowd. "I'm finding that out right quick, but the only way I'll accept the position is if training is done at my ranch."

Everyone agreed, and Jackson instructed those wishing to join up to meet at Dos Caballos in two days. He glanced at the Indians, then over to their interpreter. "Ask if I can count on them to assist in tracking down their enemy."

The man translated the request, and both Indians nodded. Jackson shook their hands before settling his attention back upon the scout. His hair was the same dark color as the close-cut beard, and the blue eyes that stared back at Jackson looked like twin seas. "You got a name?"

"Reed. Dillon Reed."

"Can I count on you to translate for me, Mr. Reed?"

"You can."

Jackson looked toward the entrance of the room, and his chest tightened. Callie stood just inside the doorway, staring at him. A grim expression darkened her features. He wasn't sure whether his agreement to lead the militia or the memory of his kiss moved the storm cloud across her face. All he knew was where his hand had earlier plunged into the base of her braid, blonde hair now spilled over her shoulder in a soft-as-silk wave.

The haste with which Callie turned and crossed the foyer to the entrance of the hacienda surprised him and instantly dissolved any momentary desire to bed Pamela Talmadge tonight.

Jackson muttered a hasty goodbye, then shouldered past the scout. He didn't know what the hell he'd say to Callie, but somewhere inside him lurked an apology. The disheveled brat was maddening to say the least, but nowhere near as maddening as…*him kissing her*. In his raucous past, he'd been slapped by a myriad of debutantes too numerous to count. Why had Callie's lone punch driven him to the point of retaliation?

And for what? Reminding him of his rudeness?

She'd had every right to land the blow. Schooled in society's rules, Jackson knew he'd been out of line. She'd been out of line too…*Christ almighty, miles out of line*…but that was in her nature; it certainly wasn't in his.

A heavy hand clamped around Jackson's upper arm to stop him. Oury's face twisted into a scowl, his lips drawing thin. "I suppose you'll want us to bring our own rifles?"

Jackson narrowed his eyes. Already he didn't like this bastard. Dillon stepped forward, and the Texan dropped his hold. "I'll go check with the colonel about weapons if you'd like, sir?"

Thankful for the intervention, Jackson slid his attention to the scout. A quick smile followed. "I'd appreciate that. And while you're at it, Reed, ask him about additional ammunition."

"Yes, sir. I will."

"In the meantime…" Jackson's gaze lanced back to Oury's, "…let's plan on using our own weapons until we hear differently." The scowling Texan nodded, then melted back into the crowd, grumbling his displeasure.

Jackson turned in time to see Callie slip from sight out the front entrance of the hacienda. A heartbeat later, he surged toward the doorway to follow her.

Chapter Nine

Callie scrunched her forehead. If Jackson thought to unravel her by kissing her, he was sorely mistaken.

She had complete control of her emotions.

Didn't she?

She compressed her lips and tried to refocus her thoughts. Each attempt smacked into the strong wall of Jackson's chest, his warmth, his overwhelming presence. Even his scent lingered on her shirt. Everything she'd worked so hard to attain…her chosen isolation, her self-protection, the detachment from others… now seemed altered.

All because of this damn jackass.

Her thigh muscles clenched against the leather, the saddle beneath her molding to the contours of her body as Diego plodded through the night. At least the animal's steady gait felt comforting and familiar.

Callie's hands tightened on the reins.

As hard as she tried, she couldn't quite muster the bitter animosity she'd relished before Jackson melded his body against hers. And that fact alone disturbed her far more than his bold and bracing kiss.

When she had finally composed herself enough to stumble from the closet, she'd encountered a cheering crowd and the discovery that her partner would be organizing a local militia. He'd been here less than two months, yet the entire population of the territory now stood poised and eager to please the bastard.

Was there nothing the man couldn't do?

The thrumming pulse in her throat squeezed tighter. Why hadn't she heard before now of the recognition he'd received in battle? Good God, even the commander at Camp Lowell knew.

An hour passed in a maddened haze before Callie could force herself to relax. Jackson would be at the party for hours, no doubt. With militia plans to make, as well as a beguiling coquette to *entertain*, hell, he'd most likely be gone all night. If she never spoke to him again, it would be too soon.

The arrogant toad.

A bone-deep weariness settled over Callie. She hadn't needed him in her life before now, so what difference did it make if he slept with all the women in Tucson?

He'd be gone soon enough anyway.

No one ever stayed.

Callie sighed. Thread by angry thread, she allowed her wrath to fray. Her horse continued an ambling gait and Callie leaned forward, stroking the animal's sleek neck. Even blindfolded, the trusty sorrel could find the way home.

Her grip on Diego's reins loosened.

In silent purity, the moon skipped across the top of the mountains while she gazed at the craggy peaks. Silhouetted under a silver wash, the earthen giant more resembled a fortress whose shadowy ramparts loomed over her life.

Just like Jackson.

She tipped her head back and stared at the wash of stars, her throat constricting under a fresh surge of tears. Amid the whirlwind of such conflicting thoughts, Callie felt small and lost.

The pounding cadence of a galloping horse split the solitude. She stiffened her spine and then swiveled in the saddle to peer over her shoulder into the darkness. The thudding hooves confirmed one rider, and she was as sure as springtime the horseman wasn't Apache. No Indian would gallop through the darkness with such reckless abandon.

Her gaze swept past moon-drenched cacti for any identifying signs. Within seconds, she spotted the unmistakable gleam of a white shirt, the horse beneath the rider as black as night. Her eyes widened.

A flush blistered her cheeks.

Jackson!

Swerving around, Callie fastened her gaze upon the Rincons. The blood in her veins bubbled, and then burst with...what? Anxiety? Delight?

Sonofabitch.

She didn't want to confront this man so soon after his kiss. The impulse to outrun the stallion flashed through her mind before she shoved away the foolish idea.

Jackson would easily catch her.

A half minute later, he reined Salvaje alongside. The horse blew hard, shaking its massive head. The halter chain on the beast's headstall jangled.

"Racing through the dark like that is a sure-fire way to get you or your mount killed," Callie ground out, staring straight ahead. "Any hole in the ground and you'd have both gone down."

"Why did you leave?" His voice was curt.

"Why do you care? You had Miss Peaches and Cream for company." Her racing heart roughened her words.

"Let's just leave Miss Talmadge out of this, and tell me why you left."

Because your kiss scared the hell out of me...how 'bout that, you jackass?

Warmth welled over her at the remembered pressure of his lips. The knot in her throat increased as a chill collected in her lungs. "Let's just say I was finished with partying."

Jackson sighed. "Look, I allowed things to get out of hand back there...in the closet. And when you punched me, I lost my temper. For that, I apologize. Frightening you was not my intention, Callie. I was out of line, and it won't happen again."

For a thread-thin moment, disappointment zipped up her spine as the remembered taste of his kiss eased dangerously close to the hole in her heart left by her parents' death. Callie turned to stare at him. The sincerity of his words twined around her anxiety. Her gaze dropped to the molded perfection of his mouth and the kiss replayed in her mind...the sharp bite of whiskey, his mellow cheroot, the tantalizing tang of something more. "I'm your partner, Jackson," she said in her coldest tone. "Not some...dalliance."

He, on the other hand, looked strangely pleased. "Nine weeks ago, you'd barely acknowledge me. Now, you're proclaiming we're partners. A colossal turn of events, don't you think?" His smile widened, and a row of perfect teeth gleamed in the pale, polished light.

"Only because there's nothing I can do about it."

"You've heard back from Reece, then?"

"Yes." The single word, tasting odd and empty in her mouth, would get no further embellishment.

They rode in silence for several minutes until he again broke the quiet. "Why didn't you tell me about the orphanage?"

Her breath caught as she reined Diego to an abrupt halt. Turning in the saddle again, she glared at Jackson. "How did you find out?" Her jaw tightened in childish petulance.

"I followed you."

"That was a private meeting. You had no right to—"

"What you're doing is admirable."

"I'm not doing it for admiration." But his unexpected kindness already had squeezed aside her resentment.

"That's what I mean. You're not forced to support them. You just do. It's compassionate." His gaze met hers and held, and the penetrating intensity she'd seen back in the supply closet returned. "You should've told me about Father Miguel when I asked you. There must be no secrets between us."

Callie's stomach dipped.

Her gaze fell to his mouth, his shoulders and the wide expanse of his chest before rolling back to the mountains. "You mean like the secret concerning your battle awards?"

His deep chuckle splashed another bucketful of warmth across her heart, allowing the unwanted thaw to continue. "They're called commendations, Callie. Not battle awards. And you never asked or I would've told you."

"Well, I'm asking now," she snapped, staring back at him. As quickly as her anger rose, however, it ebbed. How could she fight such a charismatic smile? *Damn devil.*

"All right," he said. His words were as solemn as a sigh, and the saddle beneath him creaked as he shifted his weight. "I received the first commendation for leading an assault on the Confederate left flank during the Fredericksburg Campaign in December of '62. Your brother had been promoted to temporary brigade commander, so I assumed control of the regiment." His shirtsleeves billowed in the breeze as he readjusted the dark jacket laid over the saddle in front of him. "While the others were engaged in drawing the rebs with a frontal assault, I led our regiment around the side and swept into their trenches." He paused to stare into the darkness. "And the other one I received for helping capture General A.P. Hill and his staff outside Petersburg in April of last year." His fingers curled around the leather reins as brusqueness filled his voice. "All my men deserved commendations, not just me. But that's not the way of war."

Callie studied his profile, her heart thrumming. The war had taken her brother away from her, yet bewildering pride crept over her, inch by tenacious inch, until she finally sputtered, "The colonel says you're a war hero."

Another deep laugh embraced her.

"Not of my choosing, hellion, I assure you. A man does what he must to survive in battle. That's why this militia I've been corralled into leading is so important, to help protect everyone from these Indian raids."

The sudden memory of her family's death displaced the warmth. Callie's chest rose and fell as suffocating remorse followed. Her lips parted on a rush of air. "Well, my folks are already dead, so your militia comes a dozen years too late to make a damn bit of difference to me." She forced all her attention back upon the mountain and covered the remainder of the ride in stony silence.

Chapter Ten

Dawn barely pinked the sky when a wagon rolled past the low adobe wall surrounding Dos Caballos. Jackson watched as Dillon Reed brought the four-horse team to a halt, slamming the brake bar into place. The scout hoisted himself over the side of the vehicle, then dropped to the ground in front of Jackson.

"Colonel Talmadge sent along a wall tent and some wedges, and a few other supplies," Dillon said, motioning to the pile of tarpaulin-covered lumpy mounds heaped inside the wagon's bed. "He also said to choose what mounts you want from your herd and send him the bill." After reaching into the pocket of his canvas duster, the scout handed over a crumpled dispatch. "Here's the official order."

Jackson scanned the document, then shoved the requisition letter into his back pocket. "Good. And thanks for showing up so early. I appreciate your help."

"No problem. Anybody else here yet?" Dillon asked as they carried the folded canvas toward the adobe wall. With a heavy thud, the tent met the ground.

"Nope." Jackson pulled on a pair of leather gloves. "I don't expect folks to begin arriving until later this morning, after their chores are finished and all."

"How many you figuring on?"

Jackson shrugged as he headed back to the wagon. "Maybe fifty. Depends on how fast word spread after the Eschevons' fiesta."

The scout gathered up a pile of iron tent stakes, and with a loud clank, dropped them into a metal bucket. "Well, someone's already posted banners in every storefront in Tucson."

Jackson laughed. "Then we better push that count up to seventy."

Gus walked toward them from the bunkhouse, pulling up his suspenders. His faded green shirt and denim trousers had seen a dozen years of wear. "Don't this fool know the birds ain't even up yet?" He chuckled, stretching over the side of the wagon to extend his hand. "Name's Gus Gilbert."

Dillon smiled and slipped a palm into the man's clasp. "Dillon Reed. Pleased to meet

you."

"You the scout?"

"Yep."

"Well, I've heard stories about how you tracked down that renegade who killed those army teamsters last month."

Dillon nodded. "The colonel brought me in from San Antonio specifically for that one. Just doing my job."

"Your job? Hell, son, you tracked that sonofabitch halfway to El Paso from a stone-cold trail."

The corners of the scout's mouth kicked up. "Got lucky, that's all."

Jackson reached over and pulled out a few tent poles from the back of the wagon. "You two going to stand there gabbing all morning like a couple of hens?"

The other two laughed, then joined him, and within an hour, they had the wagon nearly emptied and the beginnings of a camp marked off. At the end of the double-row of wedge tents stood the ten-by-twelve-foot wall tent. The canvas structure would serve as headquarters while their local militia trained.

Jackson tightened the last strand of rope, then straightened in time to see Callie step from the doorway of the hacienda and onto the front porch. Her sudden appearance coalesced into a hard shove against his heart.

She leaned against a post of the overhang, her full-sleeved white shirt tucked into the waistband of her pants. A black leather belt cinched her waist. Jackson looked away, wishing he could shut her out of his mind. A now-familiar tightness settled in the pit of his stomach and forced his gaze back to her.

Good God, her pants were too damned tight, exposing long, denim-encased legs that seemed to stretch into next week. He nearly groaned aloud. Would he ever become accustomed to seeing a woman dressed like this? Their gazes locked just as the soft sound of the scout's low whistle slid up Jackson's already taut spine.

"Who's the girl?" Dillon asked, sidling up to stand beside him. "Never seen her before. 'Course, I ain't been in these parts long."

"She's my partner."

"Well, shit. Ain't you the lucky one."

Jackson's voice chilled. "That all depends on how you look at it."

"Well, from where I'm standing things look pretty damn good." Dillon chuckled as he moved toward Gus, who was busy settling an iron tripod over the campfire.

Jackson's leg muscles tightened as he watched Callie step into the sunlight.

Just why she felt it necessary to move closer to him, Callie couldn't quite say. What needed telling could've been hollered across the clearing. She came to a stop in front of Jackson and waited while he raised his foot to the hub of the wagon's wheel and leaned forward.

"Morning, Callie," Jackson said.

"Morning," she quipped. "I'm expecting Banner back from Tucson this afternoon. I'll be needin' Gus by then to help him unload supplies."

Jackson didn't move. He didn't even blink, yet somehow she knew he'd tensed. "Hey, Gus," he hollered over his shoulder in a sarcastic tone. "You think we'll have this wagon emptied by this afternoon?"

Callie glanced to the wagon's bed. The only item left inside was a wooden folding chair. Her gaze cut to Jackson's again. A heavy silence followed. Gus ambled over, his boots scuffling along the sandy soil to sever the mounting tension.

"Mornin', suga'pie," he said, wiping his sweaty brow with a faded, blue-

and-white checked handkerchief.

She nodded, but her gaze remained locked upon Jackson.

The old wrangler stepped between them and peered into the wagon. "Well, looks like we won't need a passel of time to figure that one out, will we?" He pulled the remaining chair toward him. "There. All emptied." He braced it on the ground, then sighed, shaking his head as his gaze shifted back and forth between them. "You know, if you two young'uns just learned to get along, things would be a hell of a lot easier around here." He pivoted on his heel, then sauntered back to the fire, carrying the chair with him.

Jackson leaned toward Callie, his voice dropping to a whisper. "Aren't you tired of looking for trouble?"

His ruggedness wafted around her, kicking her already thumping heartbeat into a chaotic stampede. "I'm not looking for trouble. I was simply letting you know Gus won't be able to play militia with you this afternoon."

His brow arched. "*Play* militia? You think we're *playing* at protecting everyone?"

"I don't need anyone to pro—"

"Don't even say it," he snapped. His gloved finger pointed at her, the leather nearly scraping the tip of her nose. "I'm sick of hearing it."

Callie's mouth dropped open just as Pilar's cheery voice rang across the clearing.

"Everyone. Come. Breakfast ready."

Jackson lowered his foot from the wagon, then thumbed up the brim of his hat, his expression softening. He hollered toward the cook. "You got coffee ready, ladybug?"

"*Sí*, señor. Come. Come, everyone."

"Gentlemen." He directed his words to the two men walking toward him. "Let's do as the lady bids." He glanced at Callie, then swept his arm outward. "Shall we?"

Wordlessly, she turned and retraced her steps, a dull despair rolling around inside her.

Conversation had been sparse during the few meals Callie and Jackson had actually shared. Now, however, she had a feeling all was about to change with Gus and the tall, dark-haired newcomer joining them. Pent-up annoyance simmered inside her.

Control me, will he?

Jackson took his usual spot at the head of the table, and the other men chose chairs flanking him. She lowered herself into the seat at the opposite end. Heaping bowls of food covered the linen tablecloth: tortillas, mashed beans, and slabs of fried beef and eggs, potatoes and gravy. Curly-cues of steam rose from each dish, infusing the air with tangy aroma and clashing with her ever-growing frustration.

Gus reached for the closest bowl, but his hand paused in midair when Callie cleared her throat.

"I would like to say a blessing before we eat. I trust no one objects."

The bowl thudded back to the tabletop as Gus nodded in agreement.

Callie bowed her head. "For the bounty we are about to receive, Lord, I thank you. And as always, I beseech your help and strength to endure this partnership. Amen."

She raised her head, and reached for her napkin, unfurling the burgundy cloth with a flourish. She laid the material across her lap, then looked up at her dining companions.

They stared at her.

She smiled, motioning toward the food. "Gentlemen, please. Begin." Her gaze settled on Jackson. If his eyes had been twin fires, they would have seared her to the bone. A frown creased his brow and stayed there even as Gus handed him a bowl of potatoes.

Callie refused to blink. Her heart, however, was pounding so loudly she wanted to cover her ears. He deserved that, she reminded herself. After all, hadn't he kissed her without permission?

"Nice to eat on a real china plate, miss," the newcomer said, pulling her attention from Jackson's grim expression.

"Why, yes. Thank you. It's Havilland china. A rare pattern that was shipped all the way from Limoges, France—a gift from my father to mother for their wedding. I still own every single piece belonging to the original set of eighteen place settings."

The young visitor offered a bewildered smile as he took a bowl of potatoes from Jackson's outstretched hand.

"And I apologize," she continued. "I'm afraid Mr. Neale hasn't the manners to introduce us. With whom am I sharing my meal this morning?"

Jackson's sigh reached her ears.

The young man wiped his hands on the napkin and looked at Jackson before offering her another lopsided grin. "Name's Dillon, ma'am. Dillon Reed. I'm a scout out of Camp Lowell. I sure appreciate the invite to breakfast. Beats dried beef any day of the week."

Callie glanced at his plate. Mounds of food covered the entire surface of her mother's periwinkle pattern.

"Well, Pilar's the best damn cook in the territory," Gus said as he placed a generous portion of fried beef upon his own plate. "Yes, just the best ever." He then handed the serving platter to Jackson, who simply passed it on to the scout.

"You're not eating this morning, Jackson?" Callie tipped her head sideways as her brows rose. "Aren't you feeling well?"

"I've never felt better." The bite in his words nipped at her all the way down the table.

Gus pushed another bowl of food his way, the wrangler's voice now straightforward and matter-of-fact. "You just better let this go, and eat something. You've got lots of important things to do today."

Pilar bustled in, a coffeepot in her hands. "Who needs coffee?" she asked.

Jackson abruptly raised his cup.

The cook moved around the table and filled his china mug. Then she slipped back into the kitchen.

Inhaling deeply, Jackson lowered his coffee to the tabletop and exhaled a long, acquiescing breath. He reached for a bowl and stoically began loading his plate with food. "We're expecting around seventy or so men to show up for training today," he said, turning toward Gus.

The wrangler nodded. "That's a good number. Folks've wanted this militia for a while now. Had things been organized months ago, maybe they could've stopped some of the killings."

Jackson reached for a tortilla and sopped up some gravy. "I'm going to divide everyone into companies, like my command structure during the war. But with our numbers here, I'll probably only need two or three."

"Makes sense to me," Dillon agreed, shoving a forkful of beef into his mouth.

"I'm glad to hear that. Because I've also decided you're going to be in charge of one of them."

Dillon's jaw tensed. "You sure? I usually just scout and interpret."

Jackson pointed with his fork. "I need someone I can trust, and I believe you're that man."

"But I thought the militia had to elect leaders."

"Well, usually they do, but since I'm in charge, I'm electing you right now."

The scout shrugged. "That's fine, I'll do it. But who's going to interpret?"

"You're going to do that too." Jackson smiled. "I'll leave the other captain's positions open for the others to vote on."

Callie listened to their plans, her gaze drawn to her partner. He was ignoring her now, and she struggled to pretend it didn't hurt. Conversations between the men flowed for another twenty minutes while Pilar refilled cups and cleared away their empty plates.

"Hell, you two make me wish I was young again." Gus chuckled, swallowing the last swig of his coffee.

Jackson finally looked at Callie, though he directed his comments to the wrangler. "Even though I could use your skills, Gus, you realize I'll need you to stay here and keep things running smoothly." His mouth quirked sideways. "And though God and everyone else in this damn territory thinks she doesn't need anyone..." he paused and lifted his napkin, "...keep an eye on her anyway."

Her eyes narrowed as Jackson swiped at his lips, then dropped the cloth beside his plate.

He shot another easy smile her way and her throat constricted. This man radiated a frightening power over her emotions, and as infuriating as he was, she no longer could muster the skills needed to deflect the sensations building inside her.

Jackson leaned sideways, picking his hat off the floor. Settling the Stetson upon his head, he stood, then said, "By the way, Callie. I enjoyed the story of your mother's wedding china a great deal. Thank you for sharing it this morning."

He turned and crossed to the door.

Right behind him tramped the other two men, leaving her all alone with a plateful of cold food and a burning, bewildering confusion.

Chapter Eleven

The militia consisted of Mexicans, Spanish, Indian and Anglo ranging in ages from sixteen to sixty. For five days, Jackson worked hard the sixty-five eager-to-please citizens into some semblance of an army. Though he damn well knew these men were nowhere near ready to face their enemy.

With the election of officers completed on the first day, Jackson turned his attention to organizing and drilling his troops. He allowed no alcohol. And if the fine merchants of Tucson, the hacienda owners or the farmers fought among themselves, he forgave them once. If sparring happened a second time, Jackson thanked the perpetrators for their time, then dismissed them from the ranks. Just as he expected, Oury was the first to be escorted from Dos Caballos. Jackson was not sad to see the hothead go. For the most part, the remaining volunteers wanted to learn and worked hard to prove it.

"Are you going to allow them any time off?" Dillon asked on the fifth night as he settled into a chair near the campfire beside Jackson.

"Nope. I've got two days left with these men, and I intend to use every bit of time I've got." He tossed the remaining cold coffee from his cup into the campfire, then glanced at his new comrade. "Their life, or the lives of their families, may one day depend on the skills they're learning here. I want to work on their tracking abilities tomorrow. Think you can come up with something they can follow?"

The scout laughed. "Now you're talking my language."

Jackson nodded and swept his gaze across camp. Several men remained awake, some cleaning weapons. Others talked. He inhaled, allowing the pungent smoke of burning mesquite to curl into his lungs. For nearly a half decade, he'd lived this nomadic lifestyle, and the aromas and ambience of camp life brought him comfort.

But not tonight.

Tonight, even these things could not help him relax—not when a real bed waited for him just across the clearing. He was bone-tired, and the previous nights' sleep on a hard cot made for a restless mind. But Jackson knew he would never choose the comforts of inside when his men were sleeping on the ground. Even as he tried to refocus his wandering mind upon a training agenda for tomorrow, Jackson's thoughts returned to Callie.

Each sunrise, he watched her gallop away from the ranch, and concern for her safety began. Throughout the day, his worries escalated, until he finally saw her riding back at dusk. The more he refused the disquiet, the stronger his concerns for the maverick grew.

Ever since that reckless kiss.

Good God, what demon possessed him that night? He chafed, resettled his hat, then glanced toward the hacienda. A light glowed from her bedroom window. Was she asleep? Hell, she probably wore a chastity belt to bed secured by an iron lock. With such ease, the hellion sealed away her womanhood. The sexy image of a willing Colleen, swathed in translucent batiste and spreading long legs wide for him to crawl between, dispersed across his mind.

With a muffled curse, Jackson thrust aside the annoying reflection and rammed his feet against the ring of stones around the fire.

What the woman wore to bed was no concern of his. She was his partner, nothing more, but the heart-pounding frustration escalated when seconds later, the hacienda's front door opened. Illuminated by the fire's glow, Callie walked straight toward camp. And with each step, the restlessness inside Jackson billowed thicker than any fogbank rolling in off Virginia's Rappahannock River. His heart slugged hard against his chest as she eased down onto a chair on the other side of the campfire from him. Above the flickering flames, her gaze met his, then darted away.

Jackson never expected to see her tonight, and he looked her over, a habit he'd long ago perfected in order to control any uncomfortable situation. No longer captured in the restraining braid, her hair fell around her shoulders in a thick wave, shimmering in the fire's glow like a candle's wick touched by flame.

A convoluted truth chiseled past Jackson's anger.

She's so beautiful.

He could no longer pretend otherwise. With a few choice words, this golden-haired shrew could blister the skin off any man, yet none around her seemed to mind. The few volunteers still awake moved closer, eager to share details of their day with her. Callie smiled and nodded, listening to every story with rapt attention.

Jackson's jaw wound tighter the longer he watched.

What the hell are you up to now?

She'd made her lack of interest in the militia obvious by her refusal to support him. And not once, in the entire time he'd been here, had they so much as shared a decent conversation. Yet here she sat, exuding more radiance than the damned campfire between them.

The ineffectual, uncomfortable stirrings of envy enveloped Jackson. With each laugh she issued, with each nod she gave, the discomfort inside him spiraled.

His lips thinned as an awkward and unforeseen jealousy grew.

She had no business sitting here with this motley collection of men, not at night and certainly not looking as fine as she did right now. A thousand times more dangerous than a bottle of whiskey, a lone woman flirting among a group of men promised nothing but trouble.

With the decision to remove her from his camp made, Jackson climbed to his feet, drawing a half a dozen stares, including Callie's. His heart hammered his ribs as he skirted the campfire in a couple of long strides. The volunteers scooted backward, allowing him into the circle.

He reached her side and leaned down, leveling his mouth near her ear. "I'd like to speak with you in private, please."

"I'm busy." She dismissed Jackson with a twist of her head, turning her attention to a young Spaniard sitting nearby. A small Stauffer guitar rested across the man's lap and the brass tuning gears on the curved headstock caught the firelight, reflecting a taunting glint.

Jackson slipped his hand to the back of Callie's chair and thumped the hard pine. "Let's go. Now."

Callie braced her foot against the fieldstones. "Need I remind you, Jackson, you don't own me? I'll do what I damn well please, and right now I'm going to listen to a song Jose has written."

Jackson glanced at the young man, who abruptly dipped his head in embarrassment and plunked the bottom string of the instrument. The tremulous note vibrated against Jackson's last nerve. His fingers dug into the soft flesh of Callie's upper arm as he pulled her to her feet, the chair beneath her collapsing to the ground in a dull rattle.

"Not tonight, you aren't," he growled.

Callie stopped just short of making a scene. She allowed Jackson to pull her away from the campfire and out into the shadows. Despite her protesting struggles and balking steps, however, he kept right on walking, hauling her along with him toward the house. Several moments later, he ushered her back inside and slammed the door behind them to close out the rest of the world.

She whirled to face him, at last jerking free from his hold. "How dare you embarrass me like that, you…you bastard."

"Listen to me carefully." He towered over her by half a foot, glaring into her eyes. "I've a militia to organize. And the safety of each man, as well as their trust in me as their leader, allows no room for your coquetting."

"I've done absolutely nothing wrong." She leaned toward him on tiptoes, coming so close to him their noses nearly touched. "You reek of vulgarity."

"That's clearly a pot calling the kettle black."

"You cannot control me." Her arms interlocked across her chest as she issued a wafer-thin smile. "I'll speak to whomever I choose, whenever I choose."

"Then it's obvious you know nothing about men."

Consternation carved a crease between her brows. "I know all I need to know."

Jackson shifted, blocking the firelight filtering through the window. "If you did, then you'd know women do not visit men in camp at night with their hair unbound like this." He lifted a curl from her shoulder. "Unless they're selling. And while you are indeed many things, you are not a whore, as you so clearly stated once before. So I'll not allow you to act like one."

Her mouth dropped open, then closed in a tight-lipped seam. The clock in the nearby room cleaved the silence that followed with unbearably slow ticks. When Callie had brushed her hair in preparation for bed, the idea to enter Jackson's camp in a justified show of bravado seemed so perfect. She'd show him no man could restrain her. She'd stroll into camp, the same camp that was on her property and even allowed to be there by her unvoiced permission. How in God's name had things backfired so quickly? Her fist curled at her side, then rose toward him in an overwhelming need to strike out at…something.

Jackson deflected the blow. "Not this time," he stated flatly, his dark eyes glaring through tiny slits as he held her fist in a vise-like grip. His other arm swept around her waist with the vengeance of a storm, slamming her body against his with all the force of a wave crashing upon a granite shoreline. "I was caught off guard once by your damn temper. It's not likely to happen twice. You can carve that guarantee in stone."

Callie struggled to shove from his embrace, but he held firm.

"Or what? You'll kiss me again?" she huffed above the muted strumming of a guitar coming from beyond the closed door. "Suffice to say, I've already had a sampling, and I'm not one bit interested in a repeat." The turmoil in her stomach had little to do with her escalating rage and everything to do with the delicious taste of the man.

His gaze dropped to her mouth as his jaw clenched, revealing she'd hit a nerve. Callie flexed her free hand, bunching the fabric of his shirt beneath her fingers. Soft material contrasted sharply with hard-muscled perfection under the layers of dark cotton.

Jackson's lips drew sideways and forced her focus back to his eyes. "That's the frightened child inside you talking, for you've yet to be truly kissed by me."

He released her fist, and then tunneled his hand into her hair. Long fingers slid through the strands until only one wispy curl remained between his thumb and forefinger. When the ringlet met his bottom lip, something flickered in his eyes.

Her trembling lips parted, but panic stole her breath as the curl feathered from his hand back to her shoulder.

Jackson released her. "Don't enter my camp again with your hair unbound unless I've invited you into my bed."

"You are the last man on earth I'd crawl into bed with," she hissed as he turned away. When the door opened, a tangerine glow outlined his profile, carving out sharp angles and a chiseled jaw. The scent of burning mesquite swirled in to join with her animosity.

Jackson swept through the opening and slammed the heavy pine behind him. As he crossed the planked wood on the front porch, the boards creaked beneath his weight.

Callie stared at the doorknob as something dark and dangerous heaved inside. Before she could stop herself, she flung open the door and dashed after Jackson.

"Come back here, you sonofabitch," she shouted toward his broad back as he strode across the clearing toward the encampment.

Jackson spun to face her.

Firelight outlined the incredible span of his shoulders as he stalked back. He stopped directly in front of her, and she faltered back a step, her head pounding with such intense rage she was nearly blinded.

With a squinting glare, Jackson pinned her in place. "Lower your voice and get back inside."

"First thing tomorrow," she hissed, trying to hide her escalating anxiety behind short, stabbing gasps of air, "I'm…ridin' into town to secure a lawyer. I'll get this partnership dissolved if it's the last thing I do."

Jackson loomed so close she felt the heat emanating from his body. "Dammit, I'm not leaving. Not now. Not ever."

The blunt declaration severed her last thread of strength. She wanted him gone...yet, she longed to believe him. In a nauseous rush, horror stung her throat. His face blurred before her eyes. *Dear God. No.* She blinked rapidly in an attempt to stop the tears, but they slipped out anyway, cascading over her cheeks. She struggled to swallow, struggled to stop her lower lip from trembling, struggled even to draw her next breath. The mortifying signs of weakness fell faster than she could sweep them away, all of them so unfair, all of them uncloaking everything she had worked for years to deny. Grief finally broke the surface, her breath a shredded series of pants now.

"You miserable liar." The raspy words flowed outward from some agonizing place inside her soul. "You'll leave me too. You'll see. Sooner or later...just like everybody else."

The fury in Jackson's eyes dissolved into something new...and Callie saw it smoldering in that fraction of a second between him not understanding her anger and a total comprehension of her fear.

Her hand clamped across her mouth to hold back the grief-stricken sobs. She shuffled sideways, then swiveled on her heel, bolting past him and heading straight for the stable. She wouldn't wait for tomorrow to ride into town.

Not now, not after what she'd just revealed. *Run, Callie, run.*

But as fast as she flew across the clearing, she couldn't quite escape the crunching sounds of Jackson's rapid footfalls behind her.

Chapter Twelve

A galloping horse stopped Jackson in his tracks just as Callie slammed the stable door behind her. He looked toward camp, where a lone rider dismounted beside Dillon.

Long strides took Jackson to them.

"There's been another massacre outside Patagonia this afternoon," Dillon said as Jackson came to a stop. "A small ranch. Four killed."

"How many in the raiding party?"

"About a dozen, and the same group of Apache."

The volunteers gathered closer as the news spread through camp.

Jackson glanced toward the stable just as Gus stepped out and headed in his direction. The concern etched across the old man's face meant Callie had already crossed his path. As much as Jackson needed to talk to her, he didn't have time to deal with her temper tantrum right now.

His gaze shifted back to Dillon. "Send someone to Camp Lowell with the news, then muster the men. We're riding out in five minutes, but first I'm going to bring Gus up to date on a few things."

Three hours later, the inability to sleep suffocated Callie. She kicked back the sheet, left the bed and crossed to the open window, her footfalls slapping against the tiles.

Her fingers wrapped the windowsill and she leaned forward. Beyond the veranda, the moon struggled to hold on to night, spilling a hazy, silver-hued wash across the now-empty militia camp.

Callie's mind raced as a coyote's desperate, faraway cries nipped at her. She had agreed to stay at the ranch tonight instead of riding into Tucson only because Gus begged her not to leave.

Her hands plunged through her unbound hair and jagged fingernails dug into her scalp. The earlier encounter with Jackson still chased through her mind, the ache left behind in the aftermath raw and disturbing. Gasps rattled deep in her throat as she struggled to deny freedom to the torment Jackson somehow had summoned back to life.

You've yet to be truly kissed.

His words rolled through her like the thunder did in the approaching storm hugging the horizon's edge. The size of him. The mere presence of him in her life. The entire personification of disorder he'd wrought inside her world. Everything was unraveling at a rapid rate inside Callie's mind.

"I don't want you here," she shouted to the thickening black clouds. "Do you hear me, Jackson? I don't want you." Rushing puffs of air fell from her mouth and lifted the wispy strands of hair brushing her face. Like some living, breathing creature, fear surged down her body and into her legs.

I...can't...care.

She dropped to her knees as a wracking sob broke apart her lips, but the sound whisked away on the pre-dawn, rain-slicked wind.

Rust-colored buttes surrounded the smoldering ruins of the hacienda below as Jackson swept his field glasses to the right. Smoke coiled upward from charred remains, the intricate pattern stark against the turquoise sky. Pulsing anger climbed from his gut as he studied the carnage and death left in the wake of the attack. He'd seen just such grisly sights across a hundred different battlefields back east. Beside him, astride a black-and-white paint, Dillon waited in silence.

"Mr. Reed?" Jackson asked, his tone flat with impatience. "Folks keep reminding me you're the best damn scout in the territory."

"Yes, sir, I am."

"Well, I'm in desperate need of knowing which way these sonsofbitches went." Jackson lowered the field glasses and locked his gaze on Dillon. "And I need the information soon."

"I'll find 'em."

"Take the Second Squad and when you locate a solid trail, send someone back for us." Jackson slid his field glasses into the black leather case hanging from his saddle.

This time, his enemy didn't wear Confederate gray. There were no battle lines, no flags flapping above the advancing rebs. His adversary today was an unseen foe shifting soundlessly over the land. Behind him, a Papago Indian spoke soft, garbled words to Dillon, pointing west toward a gathering of black clouds just above the early morning horizon.

Dillon replied and nodded, then directed his words back to Jackson. "Let's hope they didn't head in that direction. Apache are damn good at hiding their tracks, but rain'll wipe out what little they've left me to follow."

"Do what you can," Jackson said. "In the meantime, the rest of us will muster down here and start burials."

The scout nodded and reined his paint around, then headed back toward the militia. Several minutes later, he and a dozen other riders galloped down the slope and out of view.

Jackson spotted the Apache as soon as he crested the hill. Ten Indians, their blue-and-cerulean-streaked bodies visible even from across the valley, drove a herd of three dozen cattle and horses southward.

"See where the creek spreads out beyond those rocks?" Jackson pointed to the right and Dillon nodded. In the distance, red boulders shimmered through swirling dust kicked up by a strong, prevailing wind. "I want to engage them right there, before they have time to cross. We haven't been spotted yet, and I want to keep it that way."

"Good plan. They're heading the stolen herd for water anyway."

"Once we contain them, they'll be trapped in this valley." Salvaje shifted sideways, and Jackson drew the reins tight. "Take a squad and circle around them. I want you on their right flank while I bring the rest of the men up from behind. You may start the engagement whenever you're in position." Thunder rolled overhead and lifted Jackson's gaze. They had stayed ahead of the storm all afternoon, but the roiling black clouds finally caught up with them. A few heavy raindrops pelted the brim of Jackson's hat. "Come on, let's get moving."

Twenty minutes later, the first rifle fire echoed across the valley and an Apache tumbled from his horse.

Another shot, and a second Indian fell.

Then, the clouds released their ravaging storm. Around deafening rolls of thunder, shots resounded off the canyon walls. Cattle and horses scattered into a frenzied scramble as the skirmish intensified.

Soaked to the skin, Jackson shouted above another crack of thunder. "Third Squad, move to the left and hold that area. Don't let anything past." He dug his spurs into Salvaje's flanks and the powerful stallion plunged forward, kicking up water and sand with each strong stride. Behind Jackson, the column of men split. One group followed his orders as the second followed him. On his left, a rider cried in pain, then slumped from the saddle. Under a hail of Indian bullets, half a dozen men panicked and reined their mounts away from the main line toward cover.

Jackson sighted his Colt and pulled the trigger. Another Indian fell, but Mother Nature and his inexperienced militia had more to say about the outcome of this day than he did. The storm ensnared everyone inside a torrential fury. Jackson's frustration grew as he watched an easy victory wash away before him. Horses surged past in a wild stampede as more and more militiamen panicked and ran.

"Hold steady, men," he roared. "Take aim before shooting." However, though well delivered to his men, his words no longer held weight. Fear now scattered the volunteers.

Several minutes later, above the gusting wind, Jackson heard the scout's voice. "The Apache have escaped across the creek." Dillon reined in beside him. "I tried to follow, but the water's too high and fast to cross now. It'll take hours to recede and by then the bastards will be long gone."

"We should've had them," Jackson growled.

"I agree, but my men broke rank and ran for cover behind the rocks as soon as I started firing."

Jackson sighed. "Mine too. Rain and panic never make for good soldiers, especially with an untried army." He turned back to the chaotic battlefield. Horses and cattle darted between frantic militiamen. "We'll do better next time." As the rain fell, Jackson scanned the area for dead volunteers, but saw none. Despite the mayhem of the past few minutes, relief filled him. "Looks like we've only got minor wounds."

"And don't forget, we took out several Indians and recaptured their spoils of war."

Jackson urged Salvaje forward, hollering over his shoulder above another roll of thunder. "Let's gather up the wounded. Give the task of herding the stock to the fort to all those who broke rank."

By dusk the rain had ended and a soggy militia rode northward in two long columns, heading back to Dos Caballos. Horse hooves mashed against soggy ground and the sound sluiced against Jackson's building dilemma. The militia would never become a coherent fighting force without more training. He flicked the stub of his cheroot into a nearby puddle.

"You know, I rode out here thinking I was finished with all this bullshit."

"What do you mean?" Riding beside him, Dillon led the second column of volunteers.

"With war. And command. I've had a bellyful of these things already. When I came west, my plan was simply to seduce pretty señoritas, smoke cigars and raise a few horses."

"Well, that's a nice idea…for someone else."

The scout's irksome words underscored Jackson's vexations. He resettled his hat over long, sodden hair. "I'm finding out you can't run from a damn thing. That millstone called responsibility always finds you, and it'll roll straight over your ass when you're not watching."

"You just saw how these people need you, right? You're good at organizing and command, Jackson. You can't outrun those facts."

"I'd damn well like to keep trying."

"Bullshit. I ain't known you long, pal, but even I know you're not cut from a coward's cloth. 'Sides, there's no law that says you can't raise some pretty señorita's skirt while you're being responsible, is there? Hell, even I find time to wrap a woman around me every now and then." He laughed, then reached for his canteen and took a swig of water.

Jackson offered a clipped laugh. "Perhaps, you're right, my friend. But I've still got a hell of a lot of decisions to make between here and Dos Caballos."

Callie knew the exact moment Jackson entered the house. She lowered herself to the bed and waited, nausea swelling inside her like some torturous fire from hell. For a full day, she had paced the house waiting for this man's return, but as soon as he headed for the back door, she ran to her room like a frightened child.

Would he dare to confront her so soon after arriving?

An hour before, she'd watched from the window of the front room as the waterlogged militia rode back into the stable yard, watched them break apart camp, watched as Jackson dismissed the weary volunteers to return to their own families earlier than he'd planned.

Her spine stiffened as the thud of his boot heels registered in the hallway. Callie's breath caught, her fingers digging into the blue-and-white counterpane when he came to a stop before her closed door. Her gaze cut to the wood the exact moment her bare toes dug into the looped rug beneath her feet.

Did the knob turn?

Callie's eyes burned, yet she didn't dare blink.

Unfathomable yearning spilled through her veins and she bit her lower lip to stop the trembling...and again tasted Jackson. Tears pricked the back of her eyes. She'd spent the past five years facing danger head-on and riding roughshod over anyone or anything that stood in her way, but now her courage unraveled like a battered rope. She quivered like some frightened doe facing an intimidating wolf.

Her hands rose to her chest, fingers splaying wide. She pressed inward. What if Jackson heard her frenzied heartbeat? Would he kick open the door and provoke her again?

Do I want him to?

Yes... No!

The maddened scramble for answers ended when a heavy sigh came from the other side of the door. A heartbeat later, the sound of his footfalls continued down the hallway.

Callie's whole body jerked when Jackson slammed his bedroom door. A long sob snaked out from her lungs as she fell backward across the coverlet, staring at the linen-covered ceiling. Tears pushed steadily upward.

Jackson pulled the chair out from under the desk and slumped onto the sturdy pine. His breath unfurled from his chest like the passing clouds and draped a deep moan into the room. Saddle-weary from head to toe, he rolled his shoulders and tried to work out the ache. Lamplight spilled over him in rippling waves, yet the heaviness inside his heart refused to budge.

An overwhelming urge to see the colonel's daughter undulated through Jackson. He would do everything he could to escalate the process of breaking the mares and getting them ready for their move to Camp Lowell.

His pride had nipped at him all the way home this evening, and after the scalding encounter with Callie the night before, the eastern beauty was exactly what Jackson needed to regulate his mood. Besides, Miss Pamela Talmadge smelled of rosewater and unadulterated woman, not the nerve-wracking vulgarity and horse sweat Callie stacked around herself like some damned rampart.

Jackson wanted sweet and docile for a change. Something he could control. He leaned sideways and jerked a clean sheet of paper off a desk shelf, then slid the inkwell in front of him, removing the crystal stopper. The weight rolled heavy in the palm of his hand. He stared at the piece for a moment before laying the decanter top aside. Drained, and unwilling to think beyond this moment, he straightened his shoulders, then reached for a pen. The carved ivory implement rolled between his thumb and forefinger. This had belonged to Reece and reflected his friend's good taste. Refined. Orderly.

So unlike your sister.

The truth was a quick-moving shadow across his heart. His sigh became a drawn-out moan as he raised his head and stared at the ceiling. He wished he could talk things over with Reece. But times were different now, and his friend was on the other side of the country…and far enough away from receiving Jackson's hard-driven fist in his gut for even introducing him to such misery.

Relief warred with churning disappointment as Jackson lowered his chin.

The situation loomed much larger than just he and Callie, regardless of how much he tried to deny it. The citizens of the area needed protection, the young scout was right about that…and he was good at what he did.

Jackson dipped the pen into the ink and swirled the indigo liquid several times. Would time away from Callie help their situation? Probably not. No two people on earth were more opposite on every level that mattered. She was a damn hellcat who required daily mouth scrubbings. And he? The left side of Jackson's mouth sunk into a halfhearted smirk. Well, he was a tired old soldier who knew nothing about running a horse ranch. Considering the circumstances, there was no other recourse at the moment. Before Jackson could change his mind, he leaned forward, put pen to paper and began to write.

Governor Goodwin,

I have enclosed a full report of a recent skirmish near Patagonia between the hostiles and my local militia. The Apache are indeed much more determined than I ever expected. After personally witnessing the horror inflicted upon our citizens, I now realize the safety of the many far outweigh any selfish desire that I, as an individual, may possess. After much consideration, I believe your plan to form a territorial militia is vital. Should Washington approve your proposal, I volunteer my services as commander of this force. Dos Caballos' doors are open wide for you anytime you are in the area, or I will come to the territorial capitol if you would like to discuss this matter in further detail. On a final note, I also suggest that you consider the territorial militia be organized and trained at Camp Lowell in Tucson, rather than Fort Whipple near Prescott as this will put them much closer to the raiding Apache.

Until I hear from you again, I await your direction and remain your obedient servant,

—Jackson Neale

Chapter Thirteen

Dos Caballos

Three weeks later

Callie stopped just short of putting her foot in the stirrup when Gus entered the stable.

"Hold up, gal," he said. "Have you talked with Jackson this mornin'?"

"No." Her foot lowered to the hard-packed earth. "Haven't seen him in a couple of days. He's been spending his time out at the Angel with the vaqueros. Why?"

The wrangler headed across the stable to the closest stall, then lifted a gloved hand to scratch behind the ear of an eager Appaloosa. "He's making plans to drive the mares to Camp Lowell."

Callie's jaw dropped open. "What?"

"Yep. He's actually been in Tucson for a couple of days. Just got back last night and told me to get things ready. He's going to move the herd out tomorrow."

Her mouth went dry. "He can't do that without consulting me first." Her eyes narrowed into slits. "Last I looked he wasn't the damn king around here. Nothing happens without my approval, Gus, you know that. Everyone knows that." She glared at the wrangler as he shuffled toward a nearby pitchfork.

"He said he was hopin' to talk with you about this at breakfast today." Gus buried the tines into a mound of hay piled high in the corner. Chaff danced in a shaft of sunlight that streamed through the window as sharp, grassy aroma swirled around Callie.

She planted her hands on her hips. "Well, I wasn't at breakfast 'cause I was busy."

"Doin' what?" His patronizing chuckle floated toward her, causing her face to flush hot.

"None of your damned business, that's what."

Gus lifted the hay-filled pitchfork over the side of a wagon and dropped the load into the bed. "I'm thinkin' your *busy-ness* has a heap more to do with steerin' clear of Neale than anything else."

Callie stretched the reins taut in her hands as she rasped, "What the hell's that suppose to mean?"

Gus kept on shoveling. "Like right now. You know the herd is long past ready to sell, yet here you are getting all riled up again 'cause Jackson made a smart decision." He turned and buried the tines into the hay again.

Callie stared at the man's back. Faded blue cotton pulled taut across sweat-stained, sloping shoulders. The only thing missing was the word *traitor* stamped in black ink across the material. Her anger thinned as a lump climbed her throat. Her hands clenched around the reins as she snorted, "Fine, we'll take 'em over then. Just because he's deciding doesn't mean a damn thing anyway." She shoved her foot into the stirrup and pulled up. A split-second later, Callie plopped in the saddle, then regretted taking out her frustrations on poor Diego. But, she needed to put distance between Gus's knowing chuckle and her own asinine desire to spill the conflicted feelings she had about Jackson with him.

Without another word, she nudged Diego's flank and swept past the wide-open double doors.

Thirty minutes later, Callie arrived at the corrals along Angel Creek, spotting Jackson's horse seconds before seeing the man standing with her vaqueros. Taller than the others, Jackson cut a daunting figure, but his boldness in taking matters into his own hands still grated across raw and frazzled nerves.

Worse…now she'd have to talk to him.

Several vaqueros waved, forcing Callie to nod back. After dismounting, she headed straight to the supply wagon. Her fingers wrapped the handle of a battered tin pot as she sloshed coffee into a nearby cup. She raised the mug to her lips and sipped. The acrid brew bit her tongue and she propped a foot atop one of the rocks that ringed the campfire.

Jackson bee-lined toward her and a moment later, his shadow fell across her face.

"Morning, Callie." His straight-forward demeanor clashed with her erratic heartbeat. "Waited for you at breakfast, but you never showed."

"I was busy." She continued to stare across the clearing at the horses.

"I rode into Tucson the other day and made arrangements to move the herd to Camp Lowell tomorrow."

She issued a harsh laugh. "So I heard."

"Once the horses are delivered, Colonel Talmadge will transfer payment into our account at the bank."

"Well perfect," she rasped, her words an ominous whisper. "Looks like you've just taken care of everything." Pressing the hot tin against her lips, she took another quick sip. "We've got nothing left to say."

Jackson issued an indignant huff, then shuffled the stones beneath his boots. "This bickering gets us nowhere, and you know it." His arms crossed his chest. "And I can think of several things still left to discuss."

"Not with me, that's quite obvious." Her entire body stretched taut as she glared up at him. She brought the mug to her lips and took a full swallow. The liquid slammed against the back of her throat in a scalding rush, yet she refused to grimace.

A deep furrow creased Jackson's forehead as his eyes glittered back, their dark depths taunting her beneath a miasma of emotions. His nostrils flared. "Good God, must you always be so contrary?"

His breath wafted across her heated face. "Look, I'm done talkin' with you."

"I'll tell you the problem here, and it's got nothing to do with moving the stock to Tucson and everything to do with your damn attitude."

"*My* attitude?" Her eyes narrowed under the rebuking tone of his voice.

"Ever since you arrived here, you've schemed to work things your way. First with my household staff and my finances, then with the way I break horses, and now with my hired hands and my decision-making." Exhaustion enveloped her.

Jackson stepped closer, crowding in on her unbalanced resentment. His dark eyes glinted coldly. "Every day we wait to sell this herd costs us money in supplies, food for the horses and wages for the men. Now if you think otherwise, enlighten me."

He was right…he was always right and the thought rankled. She compensated the irritation by tossing the coffee to the ground near his boots. "I'm not an idiot or a child and I don't want you to treat me as such." The tin cup followed with a clatter upon the stones.

A tight smile flattened Jackson's lips. "I'd like to treat you like a valued partner, if you'd let me."

Her head whipped up and she stared at him, his statement a screeching fingernail across her anger. Her gaze cut back to the Angel. Clear water tumbled over small stones, reflecting sunlight back at her.

A powerful awareness breathed to life inside Callie. The familiar aromas of burning wood and horses and boiling coffee teased her. Yet above all these, Jackson's scent, his cool briskness and seductive spice, slammed against her steaming unease.

She inhaled, and drew his unique scent deeper into her lungs.

Jackson's silence forced her gaze back to his face. She scanned his features, pausing on his mouth. The mustache rode above his lips, full and neat. Her mouth parted as her bottom lip pulled inward, inexplicably bringing the taste of him to her tongue once more.

The left side of his mouth lifted into a knowing smile, which just as quickly disappeared when the crunch of footsteps registered.

A small-framed Mexican stepped beside them, and Callie angled her gaze back to the creek. When Jackson turned to face the vaquero, she resettled her attention back to her partner.

"We separated yearlings from mares as you request, Señor Neale."

"Good job, Ramero. Make sure the horses we're keeping get branded while we're gone?"

"*Sí*, señor."

"And one more thing, Gus'll be out later this afternoon with a wagonload of hay. See that the herd gets a double helping before we head out tomorrow."

The vaquero nodded, then turned and walked back to the corrals. That he would defer to Jackson instead of her forced Callie to tighten her lips again. For a moment, however, she could not help but recognize Jackson's leadership qualities. These vaqueros trusted him… Again, she found herself fighting an overwhelming desire to relax and express her gratitude for the way he eased her everyday burdens. Callie shifted her gaze sideways when Jackson turned back to her.

He picked up where he'd left off. "And that arrogance you keep strapping on like a gun has lost a bit of its bite since I've seen your vulnerable side…so here's my advice, whether you want it or not." He stepped closer and brought his crisp, clean fragrance closer still. "Let's move past what happened that night three weeks ago. We've got a job to do. During the drive to Camp Lowell, I don't want these men to see us at odds."

She scrambled to control her wobbling emotions. "What they see is irrelevant to me."

Jackson's brows drew together, dark wings over equally dark eyes. "Well it's relevant to me, hellion, and that's all that matters now." A storm cloud of confusion rolled in but could not sweep away her ever-increasing and mystifying wonderment of this man.

Their gazes held for several more seconds, until he abruptly turned and crossed the clearing to his horse. Shoving his boot into the stirrup, he mounted, then settled into the saddle. A moment later, he and the magnificent Salvaje disappeared from view.

Chapter Fourteen

Callie rode point position on the herd, leading them ever northward. Thirty-five miles of unforgiving desert lay between her and Camp Lowell. Dry this time of year, the Tanque Verde corridor served as the natural passageway to Tucson. Scoured from stone by centuries of swirling waters, the dusty creek bed ran for miles. Sun-bleached boulders littered the ground around clumps of brittlebush and cactus. On both sides of the natural ravine, spiny wands of ocotillo plant hugged the banks and arched over blood-red stands of mesquite. High atop the ridgeline, multi-armed saguaros stood like sentinels, ready to inflict their spines on anyone foolish enough to stumble into their embrace.

Callie glanced up at the rocky crest where a pair of coyotes moved alongside her at a steady pace. The cunning little hunters probably would shadow them for miles in hopes the caravan might scare a jackrabbit or two out of hiding. Callie admired the tenacity of the grayish-brown pair whose sole focus in life centered on their ongoing struggle to survive.

Just like me.

Her gaze dropped. In the far distance, she could just make out the canvas-topped supply wagon lumbering at a steady pace along the old trail. In charge of the two-Percherons team pulling the vehicle, Gus knew every inch of this Tanque Verde corridor along the foothills of the mountain, and he'd always blazed the way. By the time they arrived at the midway point near the colossal cave high in the sandstone, he'd have the camp set up and dinner ready. Her stomach rumbled at the thought of the delicious stew Gus would prepare tonight. She clapped a hand across her belly, and lifted her gaze to the hard flatness of the afternoon sky.

So blue. So unbelievably beautiful. How could constant danger lurk around such a magnificent day? Diego snorted, stepping sideways, and Callie dropped her gaze in time to encounter a gray streak darting from behind a large boulder. Several horses behind her also nickered at the sudden movement.

"I didn't mean to scare you, little fella," she said as the javelina announced his displeasure with a sharp squeal. The animal darted up the rocky slope, small stones and sand tumbling behind him. Giving a final grunt, the pig-like peccary vanished into a tangle of mesquite to continue foraging for food. "Prickly pear is your favorite," she hollered, a smile lingering on her lips. For years, only the wild creatures of the desert had heard her woes. She knew them and their habits well.

Callie turned in the saddle and looked behind her at the herd. They moved in hypnotic symphony, heavy dust roiling over brown, black, white and chestnut in a vacillating display of shadows. Hooves struck rocky ground in rhythmic strides while reassuring words from the drovers kept the beasts calm.

Warmth filled Callie's soul as a recollection of riding beside her brother on her first drive returned, their conversation years ago rolling into recall.

"They're so beautiful," she whispered.

"And damn temperamental," Reece snapped. "Anything can cause a stampede. You should've stayed home like Father insisted."

Callie fired him a petulant glower. "Pa wants me to learn to cook and be a lady, but I want to be like you."

"Little girls shouldn't straddle a horse."

"I'm not little. I'm nearly ten."

"Ten or not, you should learn how to take care of men folk, not sweat alongside them."

"But y'all have more fun."

Her gaze locked with his, and a smile finally creased his face. She knew he couldn't stay mad long. A wink from his dark brown eyes followed. "Yep, that we do." He chuckled. "I suppose it's all right for you to come along. Just listen and learn."

"I'll do everything you say."

"I'm holding you to that promise. We've got a couple more miles before we reach the switchback. There's a natural spring below the cave in the rock that'll provide us water." Her brother glanced at the herd behind them. "We've been at this all morning and by the look of 'em, they're in bad need of a drink."

Callie pushed back the oversized Stetson and pointed westward. "Well, why don't we just light out that way? Seems a lot quicker to me."

"Quicker? Yes. But safer? No. This is the only route with a mid-point of water year round. We'll always come this way."

Callie's thoughts returned to the present as she uncorked her canteen and took a long swig. Metallic-tasting and warm, the water slid down her throat to quench her thirst. The lessons she'd learned under Reece's tutelage guided her onward now.

Water waited for them at Maricopa Wells, and that was exactly where she headed the herd today, just as Reece had instructed those many years ago. With dozens of trail drives under her belt since then, she never again questioned her brother's wisdom.

Until Jackson Neale arrived.

She turned and scanned past the slow-moving animals and vaqueros. Her gaze settled on the lone rider at the rear of the herd.

Her brother's replacement.

Visible even from this distance, Jackson moved the powerful Salvaje in an ever-steady arch. Responsible for the stragglers, he stayed in constant motion to keep the herd together. And just like her brother, this man too displayed a strong confidence and a natural-born leader's ability. Rugged, reddish-brown chaps covered his denims, and a pale blue shirt protected his upper body from the harsh sun. Pulled low over his eyes, a slouch hat threw his face into shadows, the lower half-hidden behind a faded bandana to keep out the dust.

Callie squinted, trying to see the expression in his eyes, but he was too far away. Her partner now rode at the extreme edge of civilization—this Tanque Verde corridor a far cry from those rolling pasturelands back east.

She shook her head in amazement. Somehow, the man had endured the desert elements without complaint, and having him share this drive with her forced Callie to see him in a new light. Before she could corral the sensation, a frisson of excitement shot through her.

Exasperation tightened her lips.

Sonofabitch, here I go admiring him again.

Yet, three hours later, Callie shoved a steaming bowl of stew against the flat plane of his belly. "Eat this," she ordered.

Startled by her sudden appearance, Jackson stepped back and dropped Salvaje's saddle beside the others on the ground.

"Thanks," he said, reaching for the bowl.

"You've got to keep up your strength," she said, shuffling backward several steps. "Won't do to have you falling off your horse back there." She turned and headed toward the supply wagon as Jackson shouted at her retreating form.

"You picking me up if I do?" A dismissive wave was all he got as she kept walking. He chuckled, joining the other drovers already eating.

"Everyone did a great job today," he said around a mouthful of cooked carrots. "Don't believe we lost a single head."

The vaqueros nodded, some scraping their bowls, others acknowledging the compliment as they lounged against saddlebags. These men had elected to take second shift in guarding the herd, so they had settled in for a much-needed rest.

Jackson finished his serving, then said, "That was just a starter. I'm going for seconds." He headed toward an iron pot suspended from a tripod over the fire. Dropping onto a campstool beside Callie, he watched her shove a piece of cornbread into her mouth.

"Mighty tasty," he proclaimed, smacking his lips. Leaning over, he scooped another generous helping of stew into his bowl, then shot her a grin. "Don't mind if I do." Settling into a more comfortable position to eat, Jackson glanced toward the supply wagon. The backend of the conveyance lay open into a makeshift table suspended by iron chains. "You know, Gus," he announced as he lifted another tasty spoonful. "If you sold this grub, you could make one hell of a small fortune."

The wrangler laughed as he reached for a Dutch oven. "Glad you like it. I've spent years on the trail perfectin' it." He picked up a knife with one hand. With the other, he reached into a blue ceramic bowl. A split-second later, a shiny red apple appeared and he tossed it into the air several times, before slicing the fruit into the pot.

"What're you working on there?" Jackson shoved another spoonful into his mouth at the same time Gus dropped a handful of flour on top of the fruit.

"Cobbler," he said as a glob of butter followed. "Figured y'all might want something sweet to end your day."

Jackson's gaze slid to Callie. "Yum, that'll be tasty."

She nodded, crumpling the last bit of cornbread into her stew.

Jackson finished eating, placed his bowl and spoon on the ground, and then scanned the nearby vaqueros. Their muted conversations flowed around him. With a full belly now, he relaxed. A satisfied sense of belonging filled his soul. Unlike Callie, he didn't like being alone, and here was all the companionship of his war years—without any of the killing. He felt damn good tonight and had done the work to earn it.

Soft whickering from the dry creek bed carried to his ears. This was exactly what he needed, this kind of life. He enjoyed the outdoors. Always had. If only he could reclaim those banking years he'd wasted. A final argument with his father, and the bloody division of the country, had pointed him in a different direction. And now, thanks to Reece Cutteridge, he had a little piece of heaven to call his own.

His gaze slid to Callie.

Well…almost his own.

Over her right shoulder, the ragged edge of daylight squeezed right up against the onslaught of night. Jackson settled his attention on the impressive spread of color. No sunset back east could rival the fusion of purple, orange and red flooding the sky tonight. The scraping sound of Callie's spoon against metal pulled his thoughts back.

"Nice time of evening, isn't it?"

She glanced at the setting sun and then back to her now-empty bowl. "Yep."

Jackson grabbed a tin cup and poured himself some coffee from a battered pot sitting next to the fire. Leaning back, he took a full swallow, enjoying the rich flavor that coursed down his throat. "I figure we'll get to Camp Lowell sometime late afternoon. That sound about right to you?"

Her dish dropped to the ground, the spoon rattling inside the bowl.

"Most likely," she said, wiping her mouth on her sleeve. Leaning sideways, she retrieved her coffee cup from the ground. Before the tin met her lips she said, "Nobody likes riding drag on the herd, Jackson, but you kept 'em together, nice and tight. Good job."

Her unexpected praise startled him, and a shadow of a smile skirted her lips.

"What?" He chuckled. "Did I just hear a compliment?"

This time she laughed aloud. "Don't push it." She took another sip of coffee, and for several minutes they sat in companionable silence watching Gus. Firelight flickered against the sides of the wagon's canvas top, highlighting years of wear and tear. Gus pulled the Dutch oven off the back of the wagon and headed toward the campfire.

Squatting down opposite them, he nestled the heavy iron cauldron into the smoldering coals. Embers popped and sent sparks heavenward. Using a small hand shovel, Gus scooped additional coals onto the pot's wide lid, smoothing all the way to the raised edge. He lifted his head and smiled at his attentive audience. "Now that'll need thirty minutes or so to bake. Too bad we ain't got some of that ice cream they serve back east."

"Last time I had some was in '62," Jackson added. "We were stationed near Washington, and I'd accompanied Reece to a fancy dinner party honoring the president." He smacked his lips, tipping his head. "Umm boy, best tasting thing

I ever put in my mouth."

"Years ago," Callie said, "I remember going with my folks somewhere over near the Rio Grande. We made snow ice cream along the way." She paused and looked at Gus. "Where'd we go? I forgot."

The old man separated out more coals from the fire with a metal rod, then placed a pot of clean water on the embers.

"Y'all went to several forts over there." He glanced at Jackson. "Andrew was visiting the New Mexico forts to sell 'em horses. At the time, Lowell wasn't much more than a *presidio*—"

"That's right," Callie interjected, excitement filling her voice. "Fort Filmore, I remember now."

Jackson's gaze cut to hers. Sapphire eyes sparkled in the glow of the campfire as a wide grin covered her face. "On the way we went through one particular mountain pass, and I'll never forget the snowdrifts. Knee-deep in some places. Papa made us snow ice cream that very afternoon. 'Member me telling you about that when we got back home, Gus?" She leaned forward and poked the man's shoulder while he shifted pots into better position on the fire.

"First thing outta your mouth, as I recall," he said with a laugh.

"Now let's see if I remember this correctly…" Her hand rose and she counted her fingers. "There's sugar. And vanilla. And an egg. Oh, and canned milk. Is that right?" Her eyes twinkled when Gus nodded. "I knew it. And it tasted so good I ate five bowls right then and there." She glanced at Jackson, a rosy blush coloring her cheeks. The smile pushed higher across her face. "We get snow here on the Santa Catalinas sometime, but I haven't tasted snow ice cream since then."

Jackson stared at her transformation from a full-grown sullen shrew to a sweeter-than-sugar little girl, his mouth agape. *Good God, why do you hide such incredible charm?* He scrambled to find his voice, not wanting the hypnotic glimmer to fade from her eyes just yet. "Well, how about we make some?" His gaze shot to the wrangler shuffling back to the wagon. "What do you say, Gus? If it snows in the mountains, should we go make our Callie-girl here some of that homemade ice cream this winter?"

"Sounds good to me," Gus replied, his voice fading off as he disappeared into the darkness on the opposite side of the wagon.

Jackson's gaze drifted back to Callie and he smiled. "I've never known a place where weather could be so different," he continued, hoping to keep the amiable mood alive. "I mean, I can be standing in a pool of sweat and yet lift my eyes to see snowcapped peaks in the distance."

Callie stared into the fire, a soft, subtle grin lingering near the edge of her mouth. "My mother said we wouldn't be staying here long, you know. But the moment we arrived I knew we would."

Jackson stretched out his legs and stacked his boots. A twig snapped in the fire, sending up sparks to draw his gaze. Smoke wafted in thin, ghostly tendrils around the legs of the tripod and draped the best part of camp life around him. "Reece said you're all from St. Louis."

She nodded. "I was just a little one when we left. Papa had a shipping business along the Mississippi, but all I remember about those times were the dang mosquitoes." She flashed him a grin and the simple display drove a mesmerizing tingle straight down Jackson's spine.

He chuckled. "Around here, Gus told me to watch out for diamondbacks and scorpions."

"And maybe gila monsters and black widow spiders the size of boulders," she added. The languid tones of her soft laughter bounced between them. "They won't hurt you though if you don't provoke 'em. And don't forget to sleep with your boots on." Her voice dropped lower, weaving around the buttery scent of cooked apples. "Tell me what she's like?"

Jackson's brow lifted. "Who?"

"My brother's wife. Emaline. You've met her, is she nice?"

Jackson recalled the raven-haired beauty who'd captured his friend's heart. "Yes. She's very nice and has a caring nature about her. I believe you'd like her." He took another swig of coffee, choosing his words carefully. "We commandeered her plantation for winter encampment. Reece tried not to fall in love, but…his heart didn't listen." Jackson's smile deepened as he recalled the many fights between his friend and the spirited widow.

"I'm glad," Callie whispered. "He deserves happiness. He was so sad when he rode east."

The evening breeze settled around her, bringing the murmurs of vaqueros and the soft, reedy notes of a harmonica to her ears.

A fine finish to a long day, yet she wasn't nearly as tired as she thought she'd be. Maybe it was the excitement of finding they hadn't lost a single horse yet.

Or maybe it was something more. She locked her gaze on Jackson's profile. The amber light lessened the lines that bracketed his mouth. "How old are you, anyway?"

His dark eyes narrowed as he stared into the flames. "Last count…thirty-four." He took a sip from his cup and swallowed. "You?"

"Twenty-five. An old maid."

"Nah," he countered, his gaze meeting hers. Firelight flickered golden across his handsome face. "You don't look a day over nineteen."

Callie released a throaty, embarrassed laugh. She didn't even like this man, which made their agreeable little interlude now so enchanting. Her usual animosity toward him had somehow wandered off into the darkness and forgot to return.

Callie tipped back, peering into the moonless sky. A million stars twinkled overhead, so pretty and bright and awe-inspiring she wanted to pluck one from the ebony night and hand it to him as her way of saying thanks for the flattering remark. "We've reached a milestone this evening," she said as the sparkling trail of a falling star caught her eye.

"How so?"

The drifting redolence of cinnamon swirled around her as his voice rolled warm into her ears. "Well…" She dropped her chin and looked at him again. "We've somehow managed to sit here together and have our first civil conversation." Her right foot rotated in a small circle working out the tightness from hours spent inside a stirrup.

The spur on her boot heel glinted back at Jackson.

"Yep. Kinda nice, isn't it?" The corner of his mouth tipped upward. "And it's only taken three months, twenty-five days..." He dipped his hand into a vest pocket and pulled out his watch, then glanced at it. "Nine hours and fifteen minutes to get here. Amazing." He palmed the watch and sent her a quick wink. "Maybe you realize I'm not so bad after all, *pahhdner.*"

"Maybe you are...then again, maybe you're not." An unsettling warmth shimmered through her more luminous than the embers beneath the baking cobbler. She climbed to her feet, and without another word headed into the darkness, her spurs chinking hard against the ground to hide her soft humming.

Morning wove lavender wisps through the lingering ribbons of night as the Dos Caballos entourage pushed on toward Tucson. Callie turned in her saddle, searching for Jackson through the dim light. His silhouette at the back of the herd, even from this distance, caused her breath to catch. Their conversation last night still simmered warm inside her.

Just go tell him.

Before she could change her mind again, Callie nudged Diego toward the edge of the herd, nodding as she passed several vaqueros. Guiding her gelding around them, she headed to the rear of the wide column. A few minutes later, Callie pulled up alongside Jackson. The faded blue bandana still covered the lower half of his face to keep out the choking dust.

"Howdy," he said, his words muffled beneath the filthy cotton. "Nice surprise."

She slipped her hand across an extra canteen draped around her saddle horn. Earlier, she'd filled the container with fresh water from the barrel strapped to the side of the wagon.

"Here," she said, shoving the wool-covered bull's eye toward Jackson. "Got you some fresh water. It's a hell of a lot tastier than that brackish stuff you've been chuggin' down."

His eyes widened as he accepted her gift. A second later, he yanked down the bandana.

"Thanks. Don't mind if I do." He pulled the cork, then tipped the canteen until the pewter spout met his lips. Closing his eyes, Jackson gulped, his throat muscles working to down the revitalizing liquid. Several droplets escaped the sides of his mouth and fell to darken the front of his shirt.

She couldn't ignore the well-defined contours of his chest, apparent even beneath the grubby layer of chambray.

He cleared his throat, and their gazes reconnected. A broad smile brightened his face as he jammed the canteen's cork into place. "Mighty refreshing," he said, dragging a sleeve across his chin. "I appreciate your thoughtfulness."

Callie shifted her attention to the rump of the closest mare. If she had to have a partner, she supposed she could've done worse. "Glad you liked it…" She paused, searching for her next words. "Um…after our chat last night…" She took a deep breath, shoving all thoughts of his well-muscled form from her mind. "Well…it's like this, Jackson. I'm thinkin' maybe you're not so bad after all."

There…I've said it. The words weren't as elegant as she'd practiced, but at least she'd gotten her point across. Callie flipped the ends of the reins against her hand, trying to ignore the growing frenzy in her pulse.

"That's high praise," he said, draping the canteen strap around his saddle horn. "How about you and I make a pact to chat more often then? What do you say?"

"I suppose we could manage that." The staccato echoes of her drumming heartbeat flooded her ears.

"And for the record," he added, "you're starting to spoil me, so I'm liking this side of you too."

Callie's gaze swept to his face. Despite her best efforts to contain a giggle, the damn thing spilled out onto the dusty wind. "Exactly which side of me are you referrin' to? The one who doesn't want you to die of thirst during your first trail drive?"

He cast her a sidelong glance and grinned, which deepened the soft squint lines around his eyes. "Yeah, that one."

Sunlight slipped over the canyon's rim and enfolded Callie inside a warm embrace. By noon, the unforgiving ball of fire would scorch them all with hellish heat. But for now, the indulgent rays proved refreshing. Truth be told, she found this side of Jackson refreshing, too.

"I'll have you know," she said with a chuckle, "I don't share my spare canteen with just anybody."

"Well then, the water's even sweeter…knowing you don't mind my mouth touching where yours usually does." Jackson winked, then flicked a glance to her lips.

The warmth creeping across her cheeks carried all the burn of a bonfire. Where had the logical side of her brain gone? No doubt smothered under his damnable charms. Her gaze landed once more on the chestnut mare's rump while her mind made a different journey, returning to the Eschevons' supply closet and the pressure of Jackson's mouth on hers. Whiskey caramelized his breath. Her traitorous body so easily responded to his raw masculinity…frightening, yet mesmerizing. She nearly groaned aloud.

Say something, you idiot. Anything.

Callie pulled her hat brim lower to shade her eyes from the rising sun. "So, what do you really think about our southwestern landscape?" *What the hell?* The landscape was the only subject she could conjure? She stifled the urge to roll her eyes at her own rattled foolishness.

"It's a far cry from the bustle of Philadelphia and its sultry summers, that's for sure."

"Gus said we live in one of the hottest deserts on earth." She pointed to a large stand of saguaro cactus jutting from the side of the rocky ravine. "And those only grow here, by the way." She cleared her throat, straightening her shoulders. The words, now allowed to flow, tumbled out in a rush. "And our earliest settlers were Spanish. Father Miguel teaches the children at the orphanage how the Catholic Jesuits established missions here in the 1500s. The friendlier tribes, like the old Hohokam and Pimas, welcomed them."

Jackson's smile widened. "I enjoy learning about the history of our place."

Our place? More than just the sun's warmth spread through Callie. The truth of his powerful statement wrapped around her. "Me too," she said. "History was my favorite subject in school. Especially the history of the land and the wildlife." The swirling in her belly grew. No one had managed to fluster her the way this man did, and yet Callie found she enjoyed their banter. Nervous laughter slipped from her lips as she attempted to quell the perplexing unquiet inside. "The poppies and desert lupines bloomed before you arrived. I'm sorry you missed them. They were beautiful."

"I'll look forward to seeing them next spring. But since I've no idea what lupines look like, you'll have to point 'em out." He sent her another damnably charming grin.

"Sure," she said, laughing. Apprehension's knot loosened, the ends slipping away on the warm tendrils of wind. "Lupines are easy to spot, though. They're sort of pinkish-purple and grow on a vertical spike nearly a foot tall." A wisp of hair whipped across her face, and Callie scraped the roguish curl behind her ear. "The O'odham Indian name for lupines means sun-hand, 'cause their leaves move to face the sun's path, then fold up at night. In years when the rainfall is generous, they'll carpet the desert as far as the eye can see, but this season's been drier than most. We're due for a real gully-washer soon; we get one every couple years."

Jackson angled a thumb over his shoulder toward the copse of saguaros. "Dry or not, I like it here, even though she's chock full of barbs that jab straight to the bone." He dropped his hand to his reins, and his saddle creaked as he redistributed his weight. Another comfortable laugh followed. "Yes, ma'am, I'm quickly learning how to give her a wide berth."

Callie glanced at him. Again he sent her a wink, the softness reflected in his eyes kicking her already thumping pulse higher. As she struggled to find her next words, a tumbleweed captured by the ever-present breeze bounced across the clearing and hit the hip of the mare directly in front of her.

The animal snorted and sidestepped, bumping into a nearby Appaloosa.

Like a building tempest, other horses snorted and stomped, their agitations contagious. Two more mares threw back their heads, their dark manes whipping in the wind. Squealing and kicking at their closest neighbors, the horses clustered tighter.

A shiver spiked through Callie. Her eyes went wide as a half-dozen horses broke from the herd and thundered past Jackson. Immediately, he turned Salvaje, spurring the beast into a chase after the runaways. His solid body leaned forward. His strong legs tightened, gripping hard against the stallion's side. And this oh-so-impressive partner ripping through the cyclone of dust knew exactly what to do.

A split-second later, common sense yanked her focus back to the danger.

"*Estampida*," she yelled toward the vaqueros before yanking Diego's head around and gigging him with her spurs. The little sorrel leapt to block the path of the stampeding mares before their panic could encompass the entire herd. If she and Jackson could turn the leaders around, the following horses would naturally bond together.

"Over there," Jackson shouted, pointing toward a break in the dust. Nodding, Callie leaned low in her saddle and angled Diego through the roiling cloud.

"Behind you," she shrieked in return, darting to cut off three of the runaways.

"On it," he hollered, maneuvering Salvaje into position to block the other mares.

Excitement thundered up Callie's spine. Drifting dust, whipped into a churning, chalky veil by the frenzied rush of the horses, smothered her and nearly stole her breath. Still she pushed on, following Jackson's lead.

"Turn the Appaloosa now," he roared.

And she obeyed, a broad smile pulling across her face. She edged Diego in closer, and then closer still, until her mount brushed against the spooked animal. The heat of the mare's damp hide penetrated her denim-covered leg.

Callie chanced a quick glance sideways. Jackson leaned low over Salvaje, his broad-shouldered form formidable atop the black stallion. He angled his horse in closer too, gaining control of the lead mare. "I think it's working," she yelled. Had he even heard her? Her parched throat, coated with powdery dust, muffled her words.

His laughter rang above the chaos. "You're doing great, Cal."

"You too!" Tingling pride flooded through her. He really did know what to do in a crisis. Waving her arm, she helped Jackson move the beasts into an even tighter circle. And finally, the panic which had earlier driven the horses evaporated under her partner's calming influence.

The mares eased back into the main column.

Callie guided Diego in beside Salvaje, reining the gelding into a slow gait. Euphoria flushed through her and she drew in a lungful of air. She truly liked working with this man. "Now that was fun," she said, laughing as the sweetness of accomplishment enveloped her.

Jackson's voice was raspy with dust. "More so because we worked together."

A peculiar awareness rumbled through Callie. She stared at the wide set of his shoulders, his chest rising and falling in patchy breaths. Even coated in trail dust, he looked good. Damn good. The heat suffusing her face spread farther. He was so handsome. And happy.

And right.

As swiftly as the truth arrived, Callie shoved it from her mind. What the hell was she thinking? He was just a man, like any other…wasn't he?

Her shaky breath eased out. "Well, at least we averted disaster."

"That we did, partner," he said. "That we did."

She shuddered and glanced forward, trying to pinpoint the bliss now messing up her well-ordered life. Yet, the harder she searched, the more fearful she became of the revelation. Her chest compressed. Along with her lips. Dust sat as acrid as lye on her tongue.

"Well…" She paused, struggling to regain control. She sure as hell didn't have time to dwell on such tripe. "Guess I better get back up front." Her gaze flicked to Jackson once more. "Anyway, I just wanted to say thanks for being here."

She spurred Diego into a canter away from Jackson, but his deep words penetrated her ears, tangling with the twisted mass that had become her heartstrings.

"I'll always be here for you, hellion. Come back anytime you'd like."

Chapter Fifteen

They hadn't lost one horse. Not one. Which was something Callie had never been able to accomplish in all the years she'd been *partnerless*. Two hundred and fifty-nine animals thundered past her into the corrals at Camp Lowell. Visible through the dust across the clearing, Colonel Talmadge shook hands with Jackson.

Sold.

Regardless how she felt about this man, he excelled at the taking charge *part* of their partnership. The tendril of pride once more shimmied through her. She swallowed an impulsive grin. Jackson had played a colossal role to ensure their profits. Happiness eddied alongside Callie's discomfort.

Payday again.

Now Gus could buy his new wagon, and she could get the building supplies Father Miguel needed to add an extension onto the orphanage. And even after the vaqueros were paid, she'd still have plenty of money to buy a new saddle.

Jackson's laughter reached her ears and she narrowed her gaze. Oh yes... he'd also be getting half—this man who'd ridden drag all the way here. The same one whose kiss had forced her to feel things she'd been trying like hell to forget ever since...the very same man who promised to make her snow ice cream come winter.

A tingle sputtered through her and her smile widened. From the corner of her eye, Callie watched Gus step from the livery and walk toward her, a wad of bills clutched in his hand.

She pointed to the greenbacks. "Looks like you've made quite a killin' on the sale of your horseshoes."

"Yep." He waved the money in front of her like a fan. "I offered to share this with Jackson since he helped me make 'em up, but he declined and told me to just buy him a couple of them fancy cigars, instead."

Ah, yes...Jackson, again.

"I'm headin' over to the sutler now." He shoved the bills into his pocket. "Wanna come along?"

"Nope...I'm waitin' on Jackson. He's wrapping up details with the colonel."

Gus nodded. "Well, I'm glad he said we'd stick around here a few more days. I've got money to spend now, and I promised I'd pick up a few things for Pilar too." He resettled his battered hat. "Well, suga'pie, guess I'll be seein' you at supper, then." His laugh trailed off as he headed toward the closest merchant.

Her gaze swept the area and stopped on a brand new, two-story wooden building...no adobe for this newest addition to the military post. Painted white, the structure served as both headquarters and hospital. A fine row of cottonwoods shaded the wide, dusty lane out front, and to the left of the trees, huge clumps of prickly pears clustered beside the parade ground.

A flagpole stood smack dab in the center of the field. Several years ago, her brother helped bring the sixty-foot Ponderosa Pine mast in by mule-team from the Mogollon Rim country up north. At the top, a United States flag fluttered in the breeze, and even where Callie stood, she could hear the rippling snap of fabric.

A soft, feminine voice reached her ears and Callie pivoted in time to see a woman glide across the stable area toward the men. A tiny parasol held aloft tilted ever-so-properly to keep the sun at bay. Rows of turquoise ruffles edged the imbecilic contraption, fluttering in the breeze like diaphanous butterflies.

Her eyes narrowed into slits as she stared. Jackson had danced with this woman at the Eschevons' party last month. Callie scrambled to remember a name.

Patricia?

Petunia?

No...Pamela.

Pamela Talmadge—visiting for the summer.

More festooned for strolling the main streets of Boston than an army post, the woman nonetheless swished her elaborately draped Peterson walking dress through the dust with incredible elegance. Atop her bell-shaped skirt made with yards of turquoise taffeta ruffles and pleated frills, the form-fitting and boned bodice fit like a second skin. Tight and long, the sleeves drew the eye to a high, square neckline, and each step the eastern beauty took toward Reece oozed tribute to a pampered lifestyle.

As Jackson bent, brushing a light kiss over the woman's outstretched hand, Callie's curled into hard knots at her side. Ragged nails nipped into calloused palms when the woman slipped her hand up Jackson's forearm.

A stiff huff blew past Callie's clenched teeth as she turned, refusing to give a name to the green-eyed monster squeezing her heartstrings. Long strides carried her in the opposite direction toward town. She would probably be expected to dine with them later, but, if Callie had anything to say about it, she would find herself busy doing something else.

The next morning, however, found Callie stepping into the Talmadges' adobe dwelling on officer's row after all. Frustration simmered inside her. She had far better things to do than waste time like this.

Callie peeled her hat from her head, then tossed the Stetson onto a side table near the entrance. "Miss Talmadge? Are you in here?" A rush of impatience sharpened her voice as she shoved her heavy braid over her shoulder. An eloquent note requesting this visit, delivered by courier to her hotel room earlier today, landed on the side table beside her hat. *Miss Prim and Proper* wanted to share an idea with Callie. But just exactly what the idea was, the invitation revealed no clue.

"Miss Talmadge?" Callie repeated, annoyance driving her to the closest door. She peered inside, and her eyes abruptly widened.

A magnificent square piano monopolized the center of the room. Massive and elegant and shined to a high polish, the mahogany looked more like plate-glass than wood. Elegant, carved legs supported the Steinway, and scrollwork decorated its front and sides. Raised and braced, the lid beckoned her inward.

Callie stepped across the threshold. Moving past horsehair stuffed chairs and a matching burgundy settee, she headed straight for the instrument. Lifting her hand, she smoothed it along the intricate scrollwork. And a moment later, she lowered her hand, then tapped her fingernail upon the closest ivory key.

A single, crystalline note floated from the piano.

Callie glanced over her shoulder, making sure she was still alone, then peered inside the Steinway. She pressed again, then watched the coordinating metal strand vibrate. She pressed once more.

And another note filled the room.

Like water soaking into sand, her soul drank in the sound. Widow King's parlor in St. Louis appeared before her and she visualized the frail woman swathed in mourning bombazine, lemon verbena drifting through the corridors of Callie's mind.

"Curve your fingers, dearest. Like so." Her teacher guided the eight-year-old Callie through the afternoon's lesson. "Now we will try again." A blue-veined hand rose to the music sheet, and she pointed. "Start right here."

Ever the dutiful pupil, Callie began…and this time, she finished the musical score without error.

An hour later, with an oatmeal cookie clutched in one hand and a cup of peppermint tea in the other, Callie said, "I like playing the piano, Mrs. King."

"And I like teaching you," the widow whispered, her words a soft embrace. "You're one of my best students, Miss Colleen. One of my best, indeed." At the corner of her faded blue eyes, crepe skin draped like curtains.

As her thoughts returned to the present, the lump in Callie's throat thickened. The untold hours she'd kept pace with the widow's quavering instructions, the steady cadence of a metronome, everything from her early childhood leapt to the forefront of her mind.

Callie jerked her hand back, a snort tumbling from her lips. "What's a damn piano doing in this God-forsaken place?" she mumbled. Her hand brushed down her hip.

You know you want to play.

Again, she pressed the key. This time, her lips shifted into a smile.

What the hell…why not?

Callie dropped to the piano stool, being careful not to nick the scrolled legs with her spurs. A few minutes wouldn't hurt one bit. After all, she was obviously alone in the house anyway.

Stopping before the keyboard, she lifted her hands and spread her fingers into proper position. She pressed down, and the heavenly chord breathed life into Callie's long forgotten and little girl passion. She glanced over her shoulder. *Still alone.*

Callie giggled, her smile widening as the musical score from a childhood recital skittered into recall. She envisioned the sheet music. Resembling tiny ants scurrying across a page, the notes of Beethoven's "Fur Elise" materialized. She began to play as her foot found the pedals beneath the piano. She worked them with ease, the instrument perfectly tuned. Giggles became laughter as she struggled through the piece, her hands stumbling over the ivories, a missed note here…another there. Callie's eyes slipped closed.

She visualized her mother listening to her play. And when the last note faded, Callie settled her hands into her lap, allowing another contented smile. She inhaled, imagining the unforgettable fragrance of her mother. *Roses.*

Several moments later, Callie opened her eyes…and her gaze settled directly on Jackson Neale.

Chapter Sixteen

Jackson leaned against the doorframe, his slouch hat held loosely in his hands. A black serge jacket nearly hid the holstered Colt strapped low around his hips. He looked relaxed and pleased, and for several numbing seconds Callie stared at the buckle that held the gun belt in place. Her gaze rose and met his, mortification burning her cheeks.

A soft smile tucked into the corner of his mouth. "Beautifully played," he said.

Callie shoved back the piano stool and climbed to her feet. "I haven't bothered with one of these things in years," she said, scrambling for composure. "I've forgotten how silly they are."

Jackson straightened. "Yes, they can be, for folks with no talent." He stepped over the threshold and dropped his hat onto the side table.

An apprehensive thread twisted around Callie's embarrassment. She still hadn't forgiven him for coddling up to Pamela yesterday. "I was waiting for Miss Talmadge. She asked me to meet her here."

"I see," he said. "And while you waited, you were able to entertain yourself. How nice."

He stepped closer, and Callie turned in the opposite direction and headed to the open window. The burn across her cheeks refused to subside. If she ignored Jackson maybe he would go away, then she could pretend he hadn't heard her play.

He followed, nonetheless, and a moment later, he stopped behind her. Every muscle in Callie's body tightened when he leaned forward and whispered,

"You've got lots of little secrets locked away inside, don't you, Cal?"

His breath brushed her neck and sent a scorching flush down her shoulders. Gone was their amiable bonding on the trail drive over here. Callie sucked in a lungful of air and focused on the soldiers outside on the parade ground. They drilled in perfect formation, a blatant contrast to the tumbling disorder inside her.

"Everyone has secrets," she said, angry with him for drawing closer—angrier with herself for caring. "Even you."

"True," he said with a chuckle. "But now I know another one of yours."

Her eyes slipped closed as the tingling inside prickled clear down to her fingertips.

A crisp, swishing sound accompanied Pamela's entrance into the room. "I am so sorry to be late." Her cheery voice fractured the tension. "Can you believe I was detained by the laundress, of all people? These locals are so difficult to understand. The language slurs something fierce."

Callie separated herself from Jackson by a wide step, then turned to face the newcomer. Copper-colored taffeta rustled with each step Pamela took toward her. A light-brown chip bonnet ruched with ivory silk covered the woman's curls, and silk rosettes sprinkled across a matching ivory underbrim further brightened her youthful, symmetrical face.

Callie swallowed. "You wanted to see me?" She took another sideways step.

"Yes." Pamela smiled, opening her arms. "I wanted to see you both." A charming dimple puckered her cheek as her gaze lingered upon Jackson a trifle longer than necessary. "And thank you for waiting, Major Neale. I know how busy you must be with all your horse duties."

Callie's breath stalled as the nip of jealousy returned. She felt like an outcast, her nose scrunched against the glass as she peered at something she'd rather not watch unfold before her.

"And speaking of horses," Pamela said. "I was visiting the stables this morning and could not help but notice your own strong mount. I believe you call him Salvaje?"

Jackson nodded, chuckling. "The name in Spanish means wild, much like my partner hiding over there in the corner."

Callie pinched her lips, holding back a curse. She wasn't wild and she sure as hell wasn't hiding. She took a small step closer just to prove him wrong.

Pamela pressed an embroidered hankie to her throat, just above a delicate, gold-rimmed cameo. "Well yes…" She hesitated, glancing at Callie. "I see what you mean." She scanned the dusty denims and faded blue shirt, then cleared her throat with a quiet cough before turning her attention back to Jackson. "Anyway, as I was saying, while I was in the stable, I conceived the wonderful notion of organizing a horse race. I mean, wouldn't you like to know who owns the fastest mount in the territory?" Excitement bubbled through her voice as her hands, gloved in expensive ivory leather, clapped together in muffled enthusiasm. "Now, tell me quick. What do you think of my idea?"

I think your corset's laced around your damn brain.

Callie crossed chambray-covered arms over her chest and asked, "A horse race?"

Pamela turned to face her again, the taffeta shimmering under a beam of late-morning sunshine that spilled through the narrow bank of windows. "Yes, sweetest. Everyone is so serious now with the Indian uprisings and all. I thought a competition might be just the answer for cheering everyone up." Capricious charm illuminated her face as she fluttered a hankie in front of her. "Why, we could even have racing colors for each contestant."

Callie stared. This woman oozed a well-honed innocence that could force grown men to their knees with desire.

I'm a waddling duck next to this swan.

The truth of her shortcomings stung. She unfolded her arms and her hand rose, skimming over cheeks she knew were sun-darkened. Struggling with her own inadequacies, she shoved back a strand of hair, then snapped, "What an incredible waste of time."

"But, Callie dearest, this will be so enjoyable, and we haven't had any enjoyment since the Eschevons' party. Why, we could invite people from miles around. And of course, you could assist me with planning the soiree if you'd like."

Callie's forehead tightened, her eyes narrowing. "I'm real busy, but thanks anyway."

The coquette slid her attention back to Jackson, her head tipping into a flirtatious tilt. A raven curl peeked from beneath the skirt of her bonnet. "But I'm most interested in knowing what you think, Major Neale."

Talons of possessiveness sank deeper into Callie's heart. It took every ounce of strength she had not to stake a claim. *But to what? A man I don't even want?*

Pamela continued, "From the splendid qualities I see in Salvaje, I'm most certain your mount would win." Her eyes widened. "And I just had a daring thought. Do you suppose I might bestow a kiss upon the champion?"

The smile amplified across her face and Jackson chuckled at the woman's ploy. Having grasped this game years ago, he knew the rules well. Unfortunately, the anticipated arousal he'd ridden over thirty-five miles to experience had yet to develop.

With renewed focus, Jackson forced himself to play the role he'd mastered in a hundred parlor rooms back east. Despite his lack of interest, he nonetheless skimmed Pamela with a knowing eye, then cupped his chin, stroking his finger over his mustache in contemplation.

A full five seconds passed before he anchored a grin. "My dear Miss Talmadge, how can I resist such a passionate entreaty? The anticipation of winning such a prize is the icing on a most delectable cake." His hand folded around hers in a light clasp as he bent forward. He dusted a kiss across the creamy leather glove. "Of course, I agree with you," he said as he straightened.

His added wink sealed the deal, and he heard Callie snort her displeasure.

Pamela, however, giggled just as he expected, dipping her head as she rested her hand upon his arm. Her fingers squeezed the black cloth. "How wonderful, Major Neale. Then that settles things. I knew I could count on you. Now, I must search out Father and inform him of our plans."

A bronzed belle, Pamela turned and sailed out the door, yards of taffeta swishing softly behind her to toll her exit. For less than a millisecond, a suffocating silence filled the room before his partner's voice careened toward him.

"What the hell's going on here?"

His smile faded as he turned, his gaze reconnecting with Callie. "I've agreed to have a good time."

"A good time?" She stiffened. "We're here to sell horses, collect our money and leave…that's all."

Mockery clung to the corners of his mouth. "Well, I've just changed our plans."

Her partner's words skewed deep, reminding Callie she could sooner harness the wind than she could control this man. His insufferable flirtation with the colonel's daughter rammed against a raw nerve. "We don't have time for this idiocy."

"Why?" His eyebrows slanted over the bridge of his nose. "Oh, I forgot. You discount interaction with people."

She took a step closer, her chin jutting. "I fail to see how racing around a horse track constitutes companionship with others."

He walked across the room and peered down into her face, his gaze direct and unblinking. "Since you haven't enjoyed living for quite some time, how could you possibly know?"

"My idea of merriment may not match yours, but then again I don't feel the need to seek pleasure from a bag of wind that preens around like a damn peacock." Building anxiety pressed heavy upon her chest. "I've had enough of this nonsense. I'm going home."

She attempted to step around him, but he blocked her path, then eased back, his eyes narrowing. "You're bothered over my continued affinity with Miss Talmadge, aren't you?"

"Absolutely not." The words grated into the space between them, and she blinked fast, staring at the steady pulse in the hollow of his sun-darkened throat.

"In fact, you're perfectly suited to each other. You talk alike, yet your words are filled with innuendo and senseless—"

"So you'd rather I not talk to her at all then, is that it?"

"I don't give a damn what you do with her. But if you're foolish enough to be lured in by that scrap of lace—"

She gasped when Jackson slid his hand around the back of her neck. Where his palm cupped, heat swelled. She struggled to draw breath, her knees locking to hold her upright.

"We're only talking, Callie." The pad of his thumb stroked the sensitive skin beneath her ear. "I promise not to bed her just yet."

She closed her eyes and scrambled for her anger, a heart-wrenching lifeline now. Fighting was such an integral part of her world—for so long and so many reasons. She opened her eyes into his, but his mocking grin had disappeared.

Instead, his features softened. "I saw comfort on your face when you played the piano, but long ago you crawled inside your parents' death and never came out."

Callie stared at him, struggling to swallow the growing lump in her throat. The truth in his words had opened a pathway back to the little girl place in her heart where she'd shoved all her needs and her wants.

"You enjoyed playing the piano again whether you choose to admit it or not." His thumb caressed the curve of her cheek. "Refusing to enjoy life won't bring your parents back or change what's happened. You're allowed to keep on living, Callie. Don't fight so hard against this truth."

Her lower lip quivered as Jackson peered down at her, sympathy and understanding radiating from the depths of his eyes. She refused to cry in front of him.

He squeezed the back of her neck, then a split-second later, his hand slid away, taking the warmth with him. He turned slowly and headed across the room. When he passed the piano, his fingers raked the ivory keys and the sound underscored the chaos swelling inside her. A tear spilled down her cheek to chill her face. Another tear followed. Then another.

At the doorway, Jackson paused and retrieved his hat, settling it over his long brown locks. A crooked smile lifted his lips as he looked at her. "Now I'm going to participate in that race. I'd sure like for you to stay and cheer me on."

A moment later, he disappeared, and Callie stared at the doorway, fighting an incredible emptiness that eddied in his wake.

Word of the horse race reached the citizenry in record time and on the day of the event, Camp Lowell played host to more than a thousand visitors. Not a single cloud marred the endless, azure canopy stretching above their heads.

As fast as soldiers erected stands, spectators arrived to fill them, eager to place wagers on the horses of their choice. Camp Lowell's brass band offered pre-race entertainment, while trios of Mexican guitarists strummed festive tunes among the milling crowd. Several sutler tents decorated the parade ground as merchants hawked goods to the multitude. Contestants in the race ran the gamut from young to old, selecting mounts from strapping, broad-backed mules to nimble mustangs to the mighty stallion Salvaje.

The lace-paneled curtain dropped back into place as Callie stepped away from the hotel's window. She checked herself in a mirror above the washstand, took a deep breath and then settled her hat into place. A slow smile lifted her lips.

Oh yes, she would win this horserace if only to save Jackson Neale from his folly. The idea of entering had nipped at her heels for two days, the thought solidifying after she'd seen him strolling arm in arm with Pamela under the cottonwoods last night.

I promise not to bed her just yet.

Callie's smile faded.

Not ever, if I have my way.

Obviously smitten with the colonel's daughter, Jackson could not think straight. And that, of course, would not bode well for Dos Caballos. Why, he might even do something so asinine as to fall in love and insist on bringing the woman back to the ranch!

Callie pinched her mouth into a thin line and stared at her reflection.

Her hand rose to her lips, fingers pressing against the sensitive flesh. The image of Jackson kissing Pamela bounced up each nerve in her spine.

Would it feel the same? Christ Almighty...stop thinking about that!

She reached for her holster, swung the leather around her hips and buckled the gun into place. And twenty minutes later, she pushed through the crowd toward Jackson.

"So you decided to come wish me luck after all?" Jackson's lips swept into a broad smile.

"You're going to need all the luck you can get." She reached into her back pocket and withdrew a cotton sash. The material fluttered in the cool breeze before Callie slipped the cloth over her head and settled it into place across her body. She looked up, a goading smile lighting her features. "Luck's the only hope you've got now, since I'm your competition."

Jackson dropped his gaze. Stretched from her left shoulder to her right waist, the racing banner presented a blood-red statement against the white cotton. His eyes reconnected with hers and narrowed.

"Callie, women don't race." He clipped each word as he tried to squelch his surprise.

Her smile widened. "They do now."

Jackson stepped closer, his voice plummeting into a harsh whisper. "Now look, this isn't funny. You can't do this."

Callie planted a gloved hand across his shoulder, then squeezed. "You're the one who told me to have a good time, partner. Remember? Well that's just what I'm doing."

"I only wanted you to stay and watch the race, I didn't mean for you to enter. Dammit, you could get hurt here."

"Hurt? Please. You're just worried I'll win—which of course I will—and you'll be denied your victory kiss from *Miss All-Things-Perfect* over there."

Her naive assumption sent a surprising cascade of warmth through Jackson, and a genuine laugh fell from his lips.

Now I see what's happening here.

He leaned forward, tucked a finger beneath her racing banner, then pulled her to him. A soft whoosh left her lips when their bellies bumped. She smelled like sunshine and fresh air and Jackson felt an odd stirring down below. "If I wanted a kiss from Miss Talmadge, your winning this race wouldn't stop me."

The booming voice of Colonel Talmadge powered above the sea of droning voices as his words outlined the race for all seventeen contestants. "Around the seven flags, then back to the starting point, a furlong between each turn. The first to cross the finish line wins."

Loud cheering filled the air around them as Jackson continued, his breath sending her ash-colored tendrils adrift. "My horse is faster than yours."

"Mine is swift and sure-footed."

"Mine is completely under my control."

Callie turned, scanned the crowd, then pushed even closer, staring deep into his eyes. The soft, perfect feel of her breasts outlined against him seared the image into Jackson's brain.

"And you like that, don't you?" she asked. "Having people under your control."

He chuckled. "Almost as much as you do."

"I aim to win."

"And take away all hope for me getting a congratulatory kiss." A smile filled his face as his index finger slid free from her sash.

She stepped back and resettled her banner. "You're such an arrogant ass." She laughed.

"I couldn't agree with you more," he said. Their gazes reconnected and lingered before she turned and pushed through the crowd to the waiting line of horses. With each subtle sway of her hips, Jackson's mouth tightened. Son of a damn bitch, he was beginning to like those denims after all.

He moved to the starting line and reached for Salvaje's reins. A soldier surrendered the leather leads and then shook Jackson's hand for good measure.

He'd be lining up next to Diego. His stallion dwarfed Callie's little gelding.

As he straightened, Jackson glanced toward the platform where Pamela Talmadge stood beside her father. Ever so slowly, she raised an emerald swatch and waved his color toward him. He knew she wanted him.

Damn shame too...since I'm not one bit interested in you any longer.

The truth stung like a blistering burn, but with a nod in her direction, Jackson pulled up into the saddle. Easing into place, he shot a glance toward Callie. She shook hands with the soldier holding Diego's reins.

And it's all your fault, you wild hellion.

His gaze shifted down the row of other contestants, then over to the huge gathering of spectators. A rainbow of colors fluttered against the sky as the crowd waved their cotton swatches. Surprisingly, more than a few waved Callie's colors.

A smile pulled across his lips.

He inhaled, and his nostrils flared from the smells of horses and barbecue as he resettled his gaze on his partner. The brim of her hat now leveled with her eyes. He leaned sideways and offered his hand.

"Good luck, partner," he said above the clamoring excitement.

Callie extended hers and their fingers touched, then slid together into a firm shake. Happiness brightened her flushed face and she gifted him with another one of her incredible smiles.

"You too, partner," she said. Breathtaking softness warmed her eyes and caused Jackson's heart to thud in his chest.

Colonel Talmadge boomed above the growing din. "*READY...*"

Jackson struggled to rally his emotions. "You realize I'll win," he calmly stated. An uncertainty rumbled through him and surprisingly, however, he found himself not wanting her to be disappointed. Still, there wasn't one other woman in this race. Not one. Good God, why couldn't she be as predictable as the vacuous Miss Talmadge?

"*SET...*"

Anticipation danced across Callie's mesmerizing blue eyes. With her gaze still locked on his, she leaned low across her saddle. She looked so young and so alive.

And in that exact moment, Jackson realized he did not want her to lose.

"*GO...*"

The sound of the starting pistol shattered the air.

Chapter Seventeen

Horses surged from the starting point in an explosive rush and the dust cloud raised by the thundering hooves nearly choked Jackson. He leaned forward and gave Salvaje free rein, the beast's powerful stride pushing them forward into the first turn. Jackson veered sideways and clipped past the first marker. His shoulder brushed the wooden staff, before Salvaje shot off across the open field toward the second white flag fluttering in the breeze an eighth of a mile away.

"Come on, boy," he urged, leaning even lower across the saddle to cut the wind. "Let's make our move." At the third marker, Salvaje claimed the lead, galloping past a bay gelding and a plucky little mustang that faltered in the turn. Jackson glanced over his shoulder and spotted Diego, now in second place but still a full length behind.

Finally. Come on, Callie…move it.

He tightened his grip on Salvaje's reins and flew past the fourth and fifth guidons with ease. The pommel pressed against the base of his ribs and the animal's silky mane whipped his chin, prickling his face. He chanced another backward glance as he applied slight pressure to the steel bit inside Salvaje's mouth. The beast snorted and tossed its massive head, fighting the subtle command to slow. "Easy, boy." Jackson issued yet another slight draw on the reins. "I'm taking over now."

With crimson cloth fluttering above her saddle, Callie edged alongside Jackson; the sound of their horses' hooves pounding against the earth rumbled between them. Neck and neck, they battled for the lead down the home stretch.

Mere seconds from winning, Jackson again tightened his grip. "Let 'er go," he whispered to his stallion. Callie swept past them as Diego barreled across the finish line. Only then did Jackson release the restraining pressure on Salvaje's reins, allowing the horse to blaze across the line a moment later.

He let me win!

The crowd rushed forward, oblivious to the confusion resonating through Callie. Before she could stop them, the spectators pulled her from Diego's saddle and hoisted her to the shoulder of the closest man. All around her, in a tempest of crimson, her racing color whipped in the hands of the multitude chanting her name. "*Callie...Callie...Callie...*"

Perspiration ran in rivulets down her face.

But this isn't right. He...let me win.

The crowd headed to the winner's stand. From her perch atop a brawny shoulder, Callie scanned the sea of faces in a maddened search to locate her perplexing partner.

With her heartbeat hammering in her ears, she finally spotted Jackson near a crowd of supporters. Surrounding him, they shook his hand and pummeled him on the back.

With a quick swipe of her tongue, she moistened her dry lips and tasted acrid dust. But no words formed—he was unlikely to hear them anyway. She passed from shoulder to shoulder in a steady move toward the winner's platform, yet her gaze remained fastened on her partner.

He threw the race.

But why?

Then his gaze locked on hers. His lips shifted upward into an indisputable smile. He winked, and the simple gesture penetrated every corner of Callie's confused heart.

Jackson touched the brim of his hat and his partner's lips lifted ever so slightly in return. That tentative smile validated his decision to let her win.

This feels good. Damn good.

He surrendered Salvaje to a waiting soldier who also held tight to Diego's reins. After scanning the crowd, he turned and followed them as they carried Callie atop their shoulders toward the winner's stand. An easy lift by a burly sergeant placed her on the platform in front of Pamela Talmadge who held high a carved statuette of a running horse.

Near the stage, Jackson came to a stop beside Gus. The old man nodded and clapped a palm against Jackson's shoulder in good-natured camaraderie.

"Hell of a race, son," he said.

"I gave it my best shot."

"Um-hum." Gus chuckled, sliding thick arms across his barrel chest. "I'm sure you did."

Before Jackson could reply, the booming voice of Colonel Talmadge drew everyone's attention. "Settle down, folks." He gestured with his hands. "Settle down. My daughter has a few things she'd like to say, so listen up."

Pamela nodded and offered a bright smile. "Thank you, Father," she said, turning to face the crowd. "Indeed, we offer our congratulations to Miss Callie Cutteridge who ran a most exciting race. Although Major Neale gave her a run for her money, Diego crossed the finish line the victor." She faced Callie and held out the prize. "Cheers to a fine win, darling."

The crowd applauded, their shouts deafening.

Callie hesitated before accepting the trophy. Her voice rose above the din. "Thank you, everyone. Yes. Thank you. But, please listen to me…listen all of you." The crowd politely quieted. "I appreciate your support, but I must share this win with Jackson Neale, for his horse is also one of the territory's fastest." Her gaze cut to her partner. "It was he who allowed this exciting and entertaining finish for you."

Pamela smiled. "Yes, I agree…Major Neale, please join us up here." The colonel's daughter extended a white-gloved hand, summoning him up the stairs with a wiggle of her fingers.

The crowd cheered. "*Jackson…Jackson…Jackson…*"

Jackson raised his hands in mock surrender and aided by a light shove from Gus, he took the stairs two at a time. Another few steps brought him to Callie's side. He waved to the crowd, causing yet another round of applause to erupt. Emerald swatches now joined the twirl of crimson as the spectators brandished their racing colors high.

He glanced down at Callie. Her hat had fallen from her head and now dangled down her back by its leather lanyard. As always, wayward strands escaped her braid in a disheveled cascade around her face. High on her right cheek, dirt smudged golden skin.

She looked a radiant mess.

Strange warmth penetrated Jackson as he turned to face the crowd. "Rumor has it the winner is entitled to a congratulatory kiss from Miss Talmadge," he hollered, glancing at Pamela. "With the colonel's permission, of course." Uproarious laughter erupted from the multitude as Jackson's gaze shifted back to Callie. Her eyes widened. "Since Miss Talmadge obviously won't be lavishing such a valued prize on our girl here…"

Callie took a full step backward, bumping into Colonel Talmadge.

Jackson flashed a quick grin to the crowd before fixing his gaze back upon his bedraggled partner. "I would be honored to serve in Miss Talmadge's stead."

Applause burst around him. Before Callie could refuse, he swept her into a tight embrace. The crowd pushed forward chanting, "Kiss her…kiss her…kiss her." The gasp from a startled Miss Talmadge and the clearing of the colonel's throat barely registered inside Jackson. Kissing this woman in front of half the population of the territory might not make her a damn bit happy. At this precise moment, however, he didn't care. An urge he'd not once felt for the properly predictable Miss Talmadge blistered through him to settle in his groin.

Ever so slowly, Jackson leaned Callie backward, nestling her body against his. The hard swell inside his denims fit nicely at the juncture of her legs.

His gaze froze hers. Perspiration beaded his forehead. He tasted her rasping breath as it slid across his lips. His nostrils flared as he took in her unforgettable scent. A white cotton shirt clung to her skin and somewhere deep inside, Jackson conjured the image of her naked body clinging instead to him. Pausing just above her lips, he whispered, "With her permission, of course."

And a heartbeat later, he covered her mouth with his.

Callie hadn't expected him to let her win the race—much less foresee this kiss. A wave of heat exploded inside her, shooting down both legs. She trembled, nearly collapsing in his embrace. This was not the punishing kiss he'd delivered at the Eschevons' party. Where his body pressed against hers, disorder now ruled. Nerve-endings sparked into life as the pressure between her legs built into a roil that left her wobbling where she stood, even while an explosion of disbelief choked her brain. Awareness bounced up her spine to splash into a hot rage across her face as she scrambled for control of her emotions. This damn jackass was humiliating her in front of everyone.

Everyone!

She wasn't some parasol-twirling ninny, who swooned at the mere sight of him. As soon as Jackson straightened, Callie curled her hand into a knot and buried her fist in his abdomen.

The crowd erupted with laughter. "Give him what for, Callie… Give it to him good!"

She wrenched free of his embrace and with each foot stomp across the platform, her pounding heart nearly stole her breath. Clutching her wooden statuette in shaking hands, Callie descended the stage in two great steps, then shoved her prize against Gus's chest.

"That was one hell of a congratulatory kiss, wasn't it, suga'pie?" he hollered. His fingers gripped around the trophy as Callie stormed past. She pushed herself into the rollicking crowd, ignoring their affable slaps on her back.

Callie jerked a dry saddle blanket from a wooden peg. "But, Gus…he kissed me! And right in front of everyone." Diego swished a silky tail against the old man's shoulder.

"Neale was just havin' a little fun. Ain't no reason to head for home."

She lowered the Mexican blanket; the striped wool covered her boot tops in a pool of reds and yellows. "Don't you realize what that sonofabitch did to me?"

"He kissed you. So what? That's still no reason to leave before the barbecue."

"Gus," she screeched. "I don't want to be kissed."

"Oh for God's sake, kissin' won't hurt you none."

"You're missing the point."

"What point?" He stepped closer. "That you were kissed or that Neale did the kissin'?"

She glared at him, her eyes narrowing. "People are going to talk."

"About what?" He pulled the blanket from her gloved hands. "A harmless little kiss?"

"It's not harmless." She paced before the man, her hands flinging wide. "You saw him, sauntering up there as bold as you please in that obnoxious way of his. Making the asinine assumption I'd be delighted by his...his..."

"Kiss?" Gus said.

She whirled to face him. "No. His assault! He's so insufferably arrogant." Callie stared at the man's back as he led Diego back into a nearby stall. "Like I'm some addle-brained Pamela who swoons each time he draws near." She snorted, crossing her arms over her chest.

"Of course you aren't," he agreed, his voice monotone as he closed the gate of the horse stall. "Not one damn bit."

Her chin jutted. "I'm certainly not all slop-eyed over him like she is."

"Absolutely not," he said, bending to grab the saddle off the ground. He heaved the leather across the stall and turned back.

"And he shouldn't think I would be, either," Callie groused, flinging her arms wide. Of course, she chose to omit Jackson had kissed her once before, which also involved a sound punch to his midsection.

Gus chuckled. "Oh I'm sure he realizes how things work with you by now. Besides, Neale's a man. And we men don't think clearly at times."

"I had a right to punch him."

"Um-hum," Gus murmured, looping the tack over the top of the railing near his elbow.

Her cheeks burned. "Nobody takes advantage of me."

"That's exactly right," he repeated.

She re-crossed her arms. "And—there's something else." Her voice spiraled down into a rasping hiss. "I think…he let me win."

The man retrieved the leather traces from the ground, then straightened, looking genuinely puzzled. "How's that?"

Callie dug her fingers into her upper arms, her breath a tight exchange of air. "He pulled up short on the final stretch and gave Diego the win."

"You saw that?"

"Yes. Though subtle, he pulled back on Salvaje's bit. I swear it."

A smile inched across the man's face as he wound the leather ribbons into his hand. "Now why do you 'spose he'd do a thing like that?"

Again she splayed her arms wide. "Hell, I don't know. I didn't ask him to, that's for damn sure." She paced in front of him. "I only mentioned I was going to win to keep him from kissin' Miss Talmadge."

The wrangler's snowy white brows shot up. "He wants to kiss the colonel's daughter too?"

He dropped the reins on a nearby table as Callie's frustrated sigh fell between them.

"I don't know if he wants to kiss her or not. But if he won the race, then she'd be kissin' him that's for damn sure. I mean, she was all but pantin' for him. This whole race was her idea to begin with, just so she could lock her mouth on Neale's."

Gus leaned against the stall, crossing his arms over his chest. His smile widened. "But then he kissed you instead, right? And in front of everyone else, to boot."

Callie nodded.

"Yep," he continued. "I'm beginning to see how things might be frustratin' for you."

Her fists clenched at her sides as she resumed her pacing. Why in God's name did she feel like crying? No worse, she wanted to vomit. Right here, on the brand new boots Gus had purchased this morning from sutler row.

The wrangler nodded, cupping his chin. His discerning eyes never left hers. "So why do you think Miss Talmadge wants to kiss Neale?"

"I guess she sees him as the most wonderful catch this side of the Mississippi. Hell's fire, her corset's laced so damn tight she's delusional."

"And you don't want that happenin'? Her layin' claim to Neale, I mean."

"Hell no, I don't want that to happen." Callie stepped up, staring him dead in the eyes. "If she did, then the imbecile would marry her and bring her back to the ranch."

"Oh...I see," Gus said. This time a broad smile illuminated his features. "If he wanted that kiss, then why'd he let you win?"

Her shoulders slumped as her heart pounded so hard it actually hurt. "That's what I've been trying to tell you, Gus. I don't know why he threw the race. He was clearly in the lead and moments away from that silken windbag's mouth." Callie's insides churned.

Gus pulled in another breath, then stretched out his arm, gently resting a gloved hand on top of her shoulder. He leaned down, leveling his face with hers. "Because he wanted you to win, darlin'."

She stared into his sagacious old eyes. "But...why?" she whispered.

He squeezed her shoulder. "Well, I 'spose you need to go ask him. And when you're askin', don't bite his head off. Go about it all soft and ladylike. He'll probably tell you why, then." Gus slowly straightened. "Now come on, let's go grab some barbeque. I'm starvin' near to death." He tightened his one-armed embrace and pulled her toward the exit.

Go talk to Neale? That was his big answer?

Callie's heart lurched. Gus made things sound so damn simple. How could she approach Jackson with this new conundrum when their friendship was still so...tentative?

The wrangler led her through the double doors and out into the sunshine. Blinding light enveloped her and she narrowed her eyes. A swirl of afternoon wind kicked up a dust cloud as a breeze blasted warm across her face.

She licked her dry lips and scanned the crowd for her partner. Jackson was nowhere in sight. Callie swallowed the great lump in her throat, her gaze faltering as she released a breathy grunt. Talking to that…man again wouldn't hurt anything, she supposed. Then, a rush of panic seized her. She didn't know one damn thing about how to be *soft and ladylike*.

Callie groaned aloud. Gus had stressed the point so obviously being coy and flirtatious was important for a man like Neale.

Damnation.

She only knew how to manage horses and run a ranch—neither of which required one shred of softness or the worthless folderol of being a lady.

Dread pitted her stomach, then a moment later a bizarre thought took form in her mind. *Soft and ladylike, huh?* She pursed her lips. *Fine.* She knew someone who lived and breathed those exacting, inane qualities.

Well, two can play this damn game.

Callie pushed from Gus and stood on tiptoes, searching across the throng of people for Miss Talmadge's idiotic, peach-colored parasol.

Chapter Eighteen

Deep within the Dragoon Mountains' granite labyrinth, Cochise's eldest son, Taza, slowed his nimble buckskin into a walk as he headed toward the secret entrance. A band of sixteen warriors followed closely behind. A series of sharp chirps drew his attention to a rocky outcropping where several of his clansmen stood atop massive boulders, their broad smiles welcoming the warriors home.

Taza's answering whistle rose on the summer breeze. As he rode into the secluded valley, the small, pollen-filled leather pouch suspended around his neck thumped against his chest. The sacred amulet had served him well, providing strength and protection.

The warriors galloped through beargrass and around thick stands of ancient Yucca, their victory cries swirling on the wind. Cattle and mules loped along behind, their hooves clattering across the rocky soil.

A few battle-weary warriors kept the herd moving at a steady pace toward camp.

On Taza's left, astride a brown-and-white pony, rode his younger brother Naiche. With each triumphant shout, the boy of twelve winters shook a bloodstained lance high above his head. Fresh scalps, Taza's trophies of war, dangled from leather strips at the end of the long spear, testimony to Taza's courage in avenging the scalps bounty hunters had ripped from the People's heads a full moon before.

Taza smiled, knowing his father would be proud. This hunt of fifteen days had been a good one and being able to outsmart those who profaned Mother Earth was a source of great pride. He'd led the warriors westward to the Rio San

Pedro and attacked a supply caravan bound for Yuma. With their booty of guns and ammunition, livestock, grain, and several dozen bolts of cotton and wool strapped to the backs of the mules, they turned and headed for home. Along the way, they attacked a settlement and killed the inhabitants, adding much-needed flour, cheese and fresh fruit to their cache. More importantly, they seized a dozen cattle and managed to herd them up the Dragoons' rocky slopes without losing a single, bawling beast.

High above Taza's head, an eagle soared on the wind. The majestic bird had served well as his eyes in the sky. But this time, they'd been followed back to their mountain stronghold.

This time, *ndaa*, the *white-eyes* drew closer.

Shrill cries from the golden bird heralded the warriors' return to camp. Villagers poured from their wickiups in jubilation. Soon, Taza would wrap his young wife Nah-dos-te in his arms, and together they'd enjoy the juice of the sotol. The fermented elixir burned the mouth yet gave him the words he would need to describe this latest adventure and his growing concerns.

From the farthest dwelling, Cochise stepped into the waning sunlight. Six feet tall and broad across the shoulders, Taza's father stretched his arms wide to welcome Taza home.

Tonight, they would celebrate.

There would be much dancing. Naiche had done well on his first successful raid. Everything they did depended on faith and prayer, and the Gift Giver had been kind, bringing glory to them all.

Yes—tonight they would reap the rewards.

Jackson hollered across the livery at the dismounting scout. "What did you find out?"

Dillon handed the reins of his paint to the farrier, then pulled the worn saddlebags from the horse and tossed the leather over his shoulder as he scuffed toward Jackson. "I was right. The same band that attacked the Butterfield day before yesterday also killed those settlers outside Dos Nogales."

Jackson resettled his slouch hat, then tugged low the wide brim to shadow his eyes. "It's damn frustrating, I tell you. These bastards seem to appear out of thin air."

Dillon nodded. "And the settlers along the border are sittin' ducks. They haven't even organized a local force down there." Both men angled toward headquarters as the scout continued, "But the governor finally got his funding for a territorial militia."

The long-ago letter he'd sent, promising to command the militia at Governor Goodwin's request, flashed into recall. Jackson tensed but kept walking. "You sure?"

"Yep. The adjutant confirmed the news. Even better, the military agreed to send additional cavalry companies to the territory to reinforce the existing garrisons."

It wouldn't take long for the organization to begin. Jackson tensed again. "That'll surely make a difference." *Especially since I'm not a damn bit interested in leaving the ranch now.*

"I followed the war party all the way to the Dragoons this time," the scout added, "but lost their trail inside those slot canyons. They're up there somewhere, and I aim to find 'em." Boot heels crunched over rocky ground. "Driving cattle slowed 'em down a bit, but the crafty sonsofbitches split the group, sending small parties along several paths, then they kept doubling back on their tracks." Dillon straightened his shoulders and sniffed the air. "Hell's fire. Did I miss the barbeque too?"

Jackson shook his head. "They've just started serving."

"Good, 'cause that dried jerky I ate this morning barely filled my gut." The scout pulled off his gauntlets and crumpled them in his hand. "I assume you won the race, right?"

"No. Callie did."

Dillon scraped to a stop, his spurs chinking in the sand as he turned to stare at Jackson. "What the hell did she ride?"

"Her horse—Diego."

"And that little thing outran Salvaje?" Dark brows slanted inward. "I find that hard to believe."

"Well, she won." Jackson resumed walking. "Let's just leave it at that."

Dillon caught up and slapped the gauntlets against Jackson's upper arm. "With a little help from you, I'm sure." When they reached headquarters, the scout paused. "Tell you what…let me turn in my report to the colonel, then we'll get something to eat while you share why you threw the race. How 'bout that?" Without waiting for a reply, he tromped across the planked walkway and disappeared inside.

Jackson shoved his hands into the pockets of his denims, then leaned against the nearest cottonwood. Images tumbled around one another in his mind: The determination stamped across Callie's face as she leaned forward in the saddle seconds before the race. Her tentative smile afterward.

And…the kiss.

Well damnation. The governor probably hadn't forgotten about wanting him to lead the militia. But where did that leave Callie—*who already believed everyone leaves?* Heat rolled down Jackson's chest to war with his churning gut.

The Territorial Army needed his leadership skills, and yet…

Things had now shifted between him and his little hellion.

The spicy aroma of gingerbread wafted around Callie as she balanced the teacup on her denim-clad knee. A yard of bird's eye linen draped her other leg. Over-stitching in gold-colored silk secured a half-inch fringe trimming the border of the napery. The corner closest to her elbow bore an embroidered flower bouquet stitched from the same elegant fibers.

Who would wipe their mouth on such a frivolous item? She surely wouldn't— not when a shirt sleeve worked as well.

In the hallway beyond, the longcase clock ticked in a steady rhythm. Sweat slid in vexing prickles between Callie's cambric-covered breasts while she waited for Miss Talmadge to arrange herself in the opposite chair.

By comparison, the young coquette looked as tranquil as an early spring day in her Paris-made afternoon tea dress. The cool swish of silk sliced through

Callie's unsettled nerves. The bright blue outfit was decorated with matching braid and a green tint fringe, also in silk. And a ribbon belt with its two long decorative blue-ruched panels rested upon the front of the skirt. The woman resembled a peahen, albeit a breathtakingly composed peahen—and silent remorse grated against Callie's earlier decision to endure the torture of becoming a lady.

The image of a lumbering cow trapped in the middle of a china shop suddenly came to mind.

Pamela smiled. "Now remember, darling, one neither clanks her spoon against the porcelain nor guzzles from the cup as if it were a tankard filled with demon potations." A fawn-colored brow arched as she shot Callie a glance. "We are ladies. We are not Boston dock workers."

A melodic chime from the hallway tolled the quarter hour to emphasize her words.

Good God, the woman even has her timepiece whipped into servitude. In dutiful acknowledgement, Callie nodded, though her lips pressed into a hard line of uncertainty.

"And remember, valuable is the gift of speech." Pamela lowered her cup to the saucer. "We must converse in gentle tones during our evening gathering. We say only kind and pleasant things while entertaining guests. Ladies never act in anger."

Callie longed to lean forward and flip the cup's contents into the debutante's napkin-draped lap, but the woman's sincere enthusiasm eased the desire and bit off another chunk of the humiliation oozing through her.

"All right, Miss Talmadge. I promise not to slug it out with anyone again." *More specifically Jackson, though he fully deserved the blow this morning for assuming I wanted his kiss.*

"It's Pamela, dearest. Please call me by my given name now that we're such close friends."

Callie ran a ragged fingernail around the cup's flared rim. "All right, Pamela. So where does my spoon go when I've finished stirring in the sugar?"

"That is an excellent question." A benevolent smile flooded her face. "Most prefer to rest it thusly." She tucked the demi-spoon along the saucer's gilded edge. "But we mustn't rattle the utensil into place. No. No. Doing so would draw notice, and a lady must never draw attention to herself this way. Now, watch while I demonstrate how to elevate the teacup."

Pamela raised the china. Rose-painted porcelain met coral-tinted lips. She sipped, emitting no sound.

"Now you try, my sweet. And remember, we always sip. We never slurp. Your objective is to produce no sound. More than any other activity, that displays true gentility. Well, other than knowing how to eat with manners and how to use the utensils, and a few other things. But we'll work on all those later. Now go on." She nodded. "Sip."

Callie tightened her finger around the teacup's thread-thin handle. With Herculean effort, she emulated the process.

The beverage slid down her throat in complete silence.

Oh my gawd…I…I did it!

Her heart soared along with Pamela's encouraging words.

"There! You see. You sipped perfectly. I'm so proud of you for—"

"I'll do it again…I mean, if you want me to," Callie interrupted.

"Absolutely. A lady can never practice enough."

This time Callie held out her pinkie, emulating what she'd seen her mother do so many times in the past. Another sip followed with equal perfection.

"Well done, dearest. Well done. I've scored you one hundred percent." Pamela giggled as she placed her teacup and saucer on the side table. "Let's move on to the dessert, shall we?" She reached for a small plate. "Now…about table manners." She inhaled, then eased out a soft sigh. "We all face challenges, but I'm confident you will master this part too. And no matter how *recherché* or sumptuous your *carte du jour*, if your guests are not suited to each other, your responsibility as hostess is to steer conversation toward more favorable topics." She reached for a silver server, lifted a wedge of gingerbread, then placed it on the closest tiny plate. "When we are finished here, we must begin your preparations and clothing choices for tonight. After all, a woman is never a lady unless properly corseted."

A corset? Hell no. "I don't think we need to go that far."

"Nonsense. If we're going to all this work, we might as well see it through to the finish, don't you think?" She returned the server to the cake and repeated the process. "And don't you worry one bit, either. I have all the underpinnings and outerwear you'll need to acquire the correct appearance."

Pamela settled a square of gingerbread upon the second plate. Callie frowned at the miniscule serving. Jeezus, she could eat the damn thing in one bite.

"Besides, correct attitude comes with the correct curves," her mentor chirred. "And of course, lessons on comportment, hygiene and presentation will follow later this afternoon." She passed the gingerbread to Callie. "I am thrilled you came to me for help, darling. Truth be told, I've been so bored until now, and helping you become soft and ladylike will be my...my *joie de vivre. Indeed, the highlight of my* summer." She caught Callie's gaze. "Please allow me the privilege to dress you. It would be such an honor."

But...a corset?

Sonofabitch.

Callie dropped her gaze to the plate, then raised it back to Pamela's face. Sincerity glowed bright in the woman's eyes. On one hand, Callie was mortified to be a fully-grown woman so unsure of her own femininity, yet on the other hand, how could she deny such a plea?

Oh, what the hell...

"Fine," she sighed. "Work your magic." Anyway, traipsing down the rose-strewn path to gentility, if even for a little while, might not be so deplorable. Her fingers closed around the fork. For a fleeting moment, she became that little girl in St. Louis again, long before tragedy had buried her under many years of sadness.

"I promise we shall have a delightful time," Pamela whispered.

Callie shoved a forkful of gingerbread into her mouth. The cake was moist and delicious. Around the food, she mumbled, "Whatever it takes to learn. I'm ready." She scraped the plate, twisting the tines of the fork back and forth to capture each crumb. "Damn this tastes good."

Pamela's head tipped sideways and she issued a reprimanding glare.

"What?" Callie said, laughing. "It does."

Her mentor shook her head and then laughed. "Yes, it does. And I suppose now is as good a time as any to learn how a proper lady consumes her food. Now, hold out your plate and I'll serve another piece."

Callie nodded and shoved the dish forward.

Forty-five minutes later, and to Pamela's satisfaction, Callie had completed lessons on how to eat like a lady, how to hold the utensils, how to sit and stand, and the expected comportment while entertaining in the parlor.

Now she stood naked and alone in the woman's shade-darkened bedroom. Before Callie, curlicues of steam rose from the water inside a massive copper hip tub three Navaho servants had filled earlier.

Rose-scented oil coalesced on top in a glistening sheet.

Taking a real bath in the colonel's home wasn't anywhere on Callie's list of things that needed doing, but Pamela had glared at her and insisted she strip from her filthy duds. Callie's thoughts replayed the scene that had brought her to this incommodious moment.

"You will have a half hour to bathe," Pamela instructed. "And use the soap in lavish abandon to scrub away the embedded dirt and grime." She pointed to Callie's fingernails, then swept her gaze upward. "And I want you to unbraid your hair and scrub your scalp with equal fervor. Use beneficial friction when drying to send a glow over your entire body." She stepped forward, narrowing her eyes. "And do not force me to re-bathe you like I'm some scullery maid, Miss Cutteridge. I would find that detestable." Stepping back, her smile returned. "Now, I'll just go write our invitations for this evening."

Click…the door had closed behind her.

A lady's body is supposed to glow?

Callie shuddered. She'd already lost valuable minutes unbraiding her hair, stripping and staring at the damn water. She inched toward the tub. The contraption looked comfortable enough, what with its high back and all. But she hadn't slid into a full bath, *naked*, in years. She preferred standing on the oilcloth and splashing water from her washbasin. As far as she was concerned, that process worked just fine. And every now and again, especially during her monthly flow, she included a brisk dip in the Angel. Nobody had complained thus far.

'Sides, Gus smells worse than I do.

On the other hand, Pamela smelled like roses, and Jackson obviously liked women to smell that way. Therefore, if something as absurd as taking a full bath would get him to talk about why he threw the race, Callie could wallow in the water for a little while.

She gripped the side of the metal, lifted her right foot off the floor and brought her leg over the tub's edge. When her toe touched the water, a tingle zipped straight through her body to settle on her scalp.

She plunged her foot to the bottom. The scent of roses coiled upward, floating into her nostrils. Callie inhaled, drawing the fragrance deeper. A heartbeat later, she slid into the center of the heavenly oasis. An exaggerated sigh escaped as she leaned against the metal.

I forgot how good this feels.

Her eyelids closed as the water enveloped her within a slick cocoon. She reveled in the sensation for long minutes, losing track of time. Liquid pooled across her stomach. She rose and lowered her fingers, tapping the shiny surface. The past several days had evoked a cyclone of unwanted sensations, and the combination of events proved once more how unstable she was when it came to confronting her emotions.

Callie lifted her hands and stared as water droplets formed on her fingertips. Each prism glistened in the light that spilled from the lamp on a side table near the bed. She slowly brought her finger upward and smoothed the silky liquid across her lower lip. An instantaneous ache pulsed through her as she recalled the heat of Jackson's mouth.

Warmth billowed across her chest and past her stomach like a hot wind. Her thoughts spun on a cyclone of imagination. Naked in body and mind, Callie dropped her emotional barrier. Willingly, she allowed the image of her broad-shouldered partner to enter the bedchamber of her mind.

He gently raised her leg out of the tub and rested the sole of her foot against his bare chest. Water darkened his hair into a mat beside his dusky nipple and then sluiced downward to soak the waistband of his pants. The air vibrated around her. A deep moan caught in her throat as his hand stroked the limb's length, working ever upward, moving closer and closer to…

A knock on the door startled Callie. She swooshed upward with such force the water cascaded over the sides of the tub. Her spine stiffened.

"Y-Yes?" she rasped, struggling to quell the erratic beat of her heart. Her breath came in deep pants. *Bloody hell. I'm thinking about him again!* Her body still hummed with anticipated pleasure, and a strange flip-flop fluttered deep in her belly…and below.

From the other side of the door Pamela's muffled voice reached out to her. "Did you find the soap, darling?"

Callie swept the area around the tub in a maddened search, looking for the lye bar. Her gaze fell on a nearby chair. Several flower-shaped soaps rested atop the toweling.

"Y-Yes," she stammered, wrapping her fingers around a silky rosette. "I found them." She plunged the diminutive piece into the water beside her right hip. "I'm latherin' up right now."

"Good. Now just enjoy your bath and I'll be back in a few minutes."

Enjoy my bath? While becoming a lady, I must've lost my damn mind. Callie shoved aside the all-too-vivid image of her half-naked partner. Her head felt ready to burst from the pressure blossoming behind her right eye. But the ache in her head could not quite equal the ache still nestling…down there.

She bent her knees and slipped down the back of the tub until her head completely submerged. Seconds later she surfaced, sputtering as she brought the soap to her tresses and lathered her hair. Her fingers dug into her scalp in an effort to wash away the prior image. The bubbles built. The glorious fragrance swirled around her again. Callie slowed her efforts and allowed the richness of the suds to slick through her fingers. The unwanted reflection of Jackson was not going to make her rush through this event.

The rich, creamy soap amazed her.

She immersed herself again and rinsed, then sat upright, wiping the water from her eyes. Laughing, she gripped the little rosette tighter between her palms and quickly rubbed to produce another foamy cloud. The suds weren't harsh, certainly not as abrasive as the lye soap she used back home. In fact, her skin wasn't irritated one bit.

I've got to get me some of this.

Moments later, she glided her hands over her arms and legs, around her breasts and hips and down farther into her secret place. Not only did she wash away the grime and sweat, but also any lingering resistance. Aside from the momentary loss of sanity in dreaming about Jackson, so far nothing had surprised her more than her enjoyment of this bath. But the lessons weren't over, and there was little time to waste. Callie glanced at the door. Pamela would return any moment.

Cupping her hands, she scooped water over her shoulders and then climbed to her feet. She stepped from the tub and reached for the towel, her fingers folding into the long nap of thick, soft cotton. Was this a Turkish towel? She'd seen advertisements in an occasional periodical, but she'd never actually touched one. Regardless, a splendid item like this would soon replace the scrap of huckaback linen she ordinarily used.

She dried off until her body tingled. Surely that was the expected glow.

A moment later, a knock upon the door preceded Pamela's announcement. "I'm going to enter now, so do not be startled."

Callie wrapped the towel around her and tucked it into place over her breasts, then turned to face her mentor. "I did as you asked," she announced as a part of her heart rejoiced. "I scrubbed away all the grime. See?" She extended her hands for Pamela's inspection.

A quick survey later, the woman proclaimed, "Wonderful, my pet! Now let's keep going, for there's much left to do." Pamela moved toward an armoire nestled against the far wall and opened wide the mahogany doors.

A wardrobe full of silks and satins greeted Callie.

A sidestep later, Pamela tossed back the lids on three steamer trunks to reveal a mysterious collection of items made of cotton and linen. Callie had no clue what they were. All she knew was *soft...and ladylike* beckoned.

Gone was her earlier unease. She now stood with bated breath, her hands clasped, her heart lodged in her throat.

In one outstretched hand, Pamela fluttered a pair of ivory lace stockings, and in the other hand, two matching grosgrain ribbons. "Now sit there and draw these on, then tie them just above your knees." Callie obeyed. The stockings slipped up her legs in a whisper of silk. A quick twist secured them. Pamela handed her a pair of silky split-crouch under drawers and a long chemise. Callie dropped her bath towel and then donned the items, marveling when the smooth textiles caressed her skin. These underthings were so different from the usual cotton drawers and battered camisoles she wore, and a quick glance toward the pile of dirty laundry crumpled in a heap near the tub revealed the extreme difference. Embarrassment blazed across her cheeks, but a rustling sound brought her gaze back to her teacher.

Pamela held out an exquisite slip. "Underskirts, even those of fine muslin, should always be gored. Any gathers about the hips spoil the effect." She shook the item, and the lamplight caught the embroidery's sheen.

The only reference to goring Callie knew involved animals, horns and tusks, but willingly she accepted the garment. Coolness whisked up her stockinged legs as she settled the cloth on her hips and secured the ribbon.

"It is *broderie anglaise,*" Pamela stated matter-of-factly, yet Callie only saw the beauty of the needlework. A repeated eyelet pattern scampered around row upon row of white satin-stitched hollyhocks dancing merrily around the material.

Why would anyone cover up such a breathtaking garment? She whirled in a circle before the standing mirror. Underwear or not, she could wear this to any damn tea party and feel just like a princess.

A giggle escaped Callie's lips as the soft clearing of Pamela's throat met her ears. Her gaze darted back to her teacher.

The woman held out a corset.

Oh, no...not that. Already her chest hurt. She'd seen the contraptions before in myriad catalogs and at the mercantile in Tucson, but she had never considered donning one. How could she work the horses when such a device forbade the lungs to expand, robbing her of life-giving air?

Pamela jiggled the item and narrowed her eyes. "This is designed to enhance our female figure, reshaping us into a more fashionable silhouette. A lady should never be without this article of clothing."

"If I put that thing on, it'll probably kill me."

"Nonsense," Pamela said. Before Callie could draw her next breath, she was wrapped inside a silken sheath. The steel basque up the front of the piece pushed her breasts upward into mounds of surprising lushness.

Good Lord... what if they flop out onto Jackson's gingerbread?

Callie burst out laughing, but abruptly stopped when Pamela jerked the laces that crisscrossed her back. Breathing became a series of short inhales and exhales, but a few moments later, Callie surprised herself by adjusting to the change.

Stepping sideways, she glanced at her reflection. Twisting in both directions, Callie marveled at the transformation. She didn't possess an ounce of excess weight, yet the garment did enhance her figure.

With a rattling sound, Pamela collapsed an apparatus onto the floor beside her. "Now step in the middle here, darling." She pointed to the small opening in the set of graduated steel hoops, six rings held together by cotton tabbing. "Pull it over your hips and into place around your waist, then tie off the casing strings. And make a bow or we'll be here forever getting the knot untied. This is the newest Boulevard-style crinoline. It's flatter in the front and is a vast improvement over those full balmorals we wore during the war."

Callie had no idea what any of that meant, but she nonetheless nodded and dutifully obeyed. Despite its extreme size, the contraption was light, not at all cumbersome, and swayed as she rocked from side to side.

"Good heavens, Callie. Stand still," Pamela chided, wrapping her hands around the corset-covered waist to stop her movement. "A lady must never swing her crinolines, and when she walks she must glide across the floor."

"I—I'm sorry. I promise not to do that ever again." Her mentor smiled and squeezed her waist, but as soon as her back was turned, Callie swayed three more times, resembling the bell inside the church tower at Father Miguel's orphanage.

She stifled another giggle.

Seconds later, Pamela returned with a corset cover and overslip and dropped them over Callie's head into their proper place. Awed, Callie stared at the stitching on the camisole…so delicate. So unlike her. Dressing up as a lady took a long time…yet for some bewildering reason, she didn't mind. Besides, this entire afternoon had proved to be enjoyable—not that she wanted to do this daily, but for right now…she could endure.

A rustling whisper caught her attention. Pamela carried an evening gown toward her from the armoire. "I've chosen this one for your debut tonight. It's a John Redfern creation, and other than Charles Worth, I usually prefer this British designer's dresses. The color will transform your pale hair into spun gold. You'll see." She reverently lifted the garment over Callie's head, and all sixteen yards of emerald silk damask drifted down her body.

As Pamela settled the material around the crinoline, Callie stared at her reflection. The décolleté bodice dipped low and accentuated her breasts.

Who is this stunning person? Surely not me.

Her hair, though dry now after her bath, tumbled down her shoulders in a tangled wave, but somehow Pamela had transformed her body from a vaquero into…a woman.

"Now, come here and sit. I'll address your hair."

Callie didn't move. She stared into the mirror.

"Come along, dearest. Our guests will be arriving soon. We mustn't keep them waiting." Pamela patted the stool that occupied the space before her dressing table, then gently pulled Callie's arm to guide her onto the bench.

A rush of warmth crept up Callie's neck. *I wish Mother could see me now.* She stared in the small mirror as her mentor worked the tangled mass of curls into place.

"I'm going to suggest you wear a chignon low on your neck tonight," Pamela said. "The waterfall coiffure is no longer in vogue, but I believe the Marie Antoinette style will be perfect for you. And I'll also crepe your hair. It's the trend back east." With a flick of her wrist here, a tug of an unruly lock there and the application of a heated iron implement later, Pamela drew the disorderly curls into a stunning display.

A half hour later, she finally pronounced her work of art complete.

"Oh, Pamela." Callie's hands rose to her mouth. She mumbled around her fingers. "Just look at what you've done."

"Yes." The woman stepped back and smiled, admiring her handiwork. "You look radiant."

Callie shifted her gaze, staring into the twinkling-eyed reflection of her mentor. "This is so much more than radiant, woman. Christ Almighty, y-you've made me into a whole new person."

With hairbrush in hand, Pamela leaned against Callie and squeezed her shoulders. "Nonsense, darling. You simply forgot how to be a woman. That is all."

A strange yet refreshing bond somehow had been forged this afternoon. Callie reached up and patted the hand still resting on her shoulder. A dimple flashed in the Boston beauty's cheek. They lived completely different lifestyles, were worlds apart in their thoughts and beliefs, yet now they shared a friendship.

Callie stood and glided over to the oval mirror again. Her lips kicked up into a huge grin. Indeed, this was exactly what she wanted. *Soft and ladylike.*

On the outside.

Her smile widened. How perfect. She dipped into a faultless curtsy.

Oh yes...she was now more than ready to look that broad-shouldered, kiss-stealin', sonofabitch partner of hers straight in the eyes and demand he tell her exactly why he threw the race.

Chapter Nineteen

Renaldo's Cantina occupied a prime location near the entrance to Camp Lowell. Each time thirsty patrons entered and exited, the batwing doors thumped behind Jackson. An easy breeze swept the planked boardwalk beneath the building's overhanging roof and brought welcome relief from the afternoon's heat.

With an unlit cheroot dangling from his lips, Jackson tipped back in a chair and elevated his legs upon the railing that ran the length of the cantina. At the moment, no horses obscured his view of Santa Catalina's ghostly gray peaks shimmering in the distance.

He appreciated this country more and more with every passing day.

Dillon sat to his left in much the same fashion and looked equally as comfortable—an empty dinner plate near his elbow the only evidence of the barbeque he'd wolfed down earlier.

"I knew I'd find you boys here," Gus said, shuffling into view from the side. "Miss Talmadge gave me strict instructions to give y'all this invite to a get-together back at her place later on." The old man waved an envelope in the air before him. Jackson tucked the cheroot back into his shirt pocket, then thumbed up his hat.

"A get-together?" He took the elegantly scripted item from Gus's outstretched hand. Memories of social gatherings back east crammed his mind as he broke the wax seal and withdrew the formal request. He scanned the paper before handing the invitation to the scout.

"Yep," Gus said, leaning against the railing. "Miss Talmadge proclaimed it was high time for Low Tea right here in the middle of the desert." He cocked a thumb over his shoulder, pointing to the row of dusty storefronts next to the cantina. "Saw her over yonder at the mercantile not a half hour ago. She was buying ribbons and other gewgaws. Told me to make sure I brought y'all back to her place by five o'clock sharp." He straightened and rocked on the balls of his feet, humor lighting his eyes. "She also sends her apologies for not allowing the usual two weeks' notice."

Jackson brought a half-empty whiskey glass to his lips, then paused. "Well, I'm no longer interested in sampling any of her...tea. Besides, I'm going to turn in early since we're heading back home tomorrow. You be sure to give her my regrets."

"Mine too," Dillon said. He dropped the invitation to the table, and wrapped his hand around the neck of a nearby bottle. "I don't do teas or any other high society bullshit." He poured another shot into his glass. "And from everything y'all have told me about this woman, she already exhausts me."

Gus propped his foot on a stone mounting block and waited while a couple of drunken miners wobbled down the dusty street in front of them. "Trust me, boys. This here's one tea party you don't wanna miss."

Jackson elevated a brow. "Why's that?"

The man shifted his gaze to the scout, then back to Jackson before sliding a tobacco wad to the other side of his mouth. A wide grin broke the leathery surface of his face. "Well, for starters, Callie's gonna be there."

"Callie?" Jackson's chair hit the ground. Since his bold kiss this morning, he'd bet a shiny silver dollar the woman's anger still ran deep. "What's she aiming to do? Poison the tea?"

Dillon snorted, shoving the cork into the bottle's small opening.

"Don't know the details," Gus said, leaning forward to rest his arms on the smooth wood. "All Miss Talmadge said was Callie's gonna be lookin' mighty fine and that it was vitally important y'all showed up."

What the hell you up to now, you little hellion? Jackson glanced at the scout, who immediately narrowed his eyes and shook his head.

"Forget it," Dillon growled. "I ain't going anywhere near her place."

"What kind of friend are you?" Jackson glowered at the man. "If the roles were reversed, I'd damn well go and watch your back."

"Christ a'mighty. Fine," Dillon groused. "If you're so damned determined to go, then I'll tag along if only to make certain the hen doesn't peck you to death."

Jackson smiled, then glanced at Gus. "We'll be there. And since the invitation said I could bring guests, you're coming along too, so forget about bowing out on us."

The old man widened his eyes, spit into the sandy soil near the walkway, then glanced heavenward. "Lord, give me the strength to endure." His gaze locked with Jackson's. "Me at some fancy folderol makes no sense a'tall." Gus pulled out an empty chair and plunked down beside them. "But since we've still got nearly an hour 'til tea time, how 'bout you sharing some of that fortifying elixir you've got sittin' over there? I feel I'm gonna need it to face the madness."

"Here. Use mine." Dillon shoved his now-empty glass in the man's direction.

"I'll pour." Jackson sloshed in the tawny liquid. "And if you drink fast enough, you'll have time for several more rounds to lend you strength." He settled back in the chair and slipped his fingers around his glass.

A buckboard filled with revelers rumbled past, stirring up dust. Like tattered butterfly wings, racing banners fluttered along behind them. The bacchanalian crowd spotted Jackson and hollered its congratulations.

He raised his glass in a good-natured salute before turning to his companions. "By the way, do either of you know a merchant in town who'll place a special order for me?"

"Cavanaugh can get anything you might need," Dillon said. "But he no longer guarantees on-time deliveries since the Apache attacks. What're you ordering?"

Jackson tossed back the whiskey, then issued a soft hiss as the liquid settled. "Something we don't have at the ranch."

"What might that be?" Gus asked, curiosity shining in his eyes.

Jackson reached for the bottle and refilled his glass before reconnecting his gaze to the old man's. "Well now, my friend—you'll just have to wait and see."

A little over an hour later, Jackson stood alongside his friends in the entryway of the colonel's home, hats dutifully in hand. The spicy aromas of cinnamon and ginger wafted around them.

"Gentlemen, do come in." Miss Talmadge swept him with a disapproving glare. "I'm so glad you could attend." She led the way into the parlor where a glow from oil lamps illuminated the room. A few chairs had been arranged into a circle for conversation, so obviously the guest list was small. Relief flooded Jackson, because he'd broken the cardinal rule of appropriate garb. He'd stopped by the hotel on his way over to change his shirt, but his cutaway jacket and dress trousers remained in his duffle, along with his desire to keep pretending eastern society's rules mattered out here.

And his errant partner figured largely in his redesigned outlook. Jackson's thoughts returned to Callie, a state that was becoming more and more frequent of late. He thumped his fingers against the Stetson's felt brim, matching the heartbeat that banged inside his chest. When exactly had he come to accept her hard-boiled approach to life? When he'd discovered her support of the orphanage...or her skill with the horses? Or was it when he'd sampled the sweetness of her lips?

He forced his hands to calm and met Miss Talmadge's gaze. Another icy scan told him she had noticed his breech in etiquette. "I wanted to host a little soiree to help celebrate Callie's win," she said, recovering nicely. "Please. Sit. All of you."

Jackson settled upon a spindle-backed chair beside the piano, leaving the wingback for Gus. Dillon slid onto the nearby settee.

Their hostess turned a softer smile upon the old wrangler. "And thank you for locating the others, Mr. Gilbert. I trust you found what you needed at the mercantile?"

"Yes, ma'am. Bought me a shirt to go along with my brand new boots here." He lifted his foot, then hiked a pants leg to reveal well-crafted black leather. "A Berringer-Shumway & Company original brought in from Philadelphia." His leg angled to better display the heel and wooden-pegged sole, the topstitching on the geometric cutouts, and the puckers that rode the top of the rounded toe. "And this ain't no Wellington either." He tapped the leather. "This here's the genuine thing worn back east."

A grin tugged at Jackson's mouth. Before the war, he'd owned several boots made by the same designer, who probably had no idea when constructing the fanciful footwear that they'd be put to such extreme tests in the climes of the southwestern desert. Seeing them on Gus's feet now, the boots looked out of place. His gaze swept the room again, disappointment swelling inside. *No cart. No china cups. And no partner. Had she changed her mind about attending?*

"Well that's just wonderful, Mr. Gilbert. They are indeed works of art." The hostess glided toward the settee. "And it's Mr. Reed, isn't it?"

"Yes, ma'am. I work for your father...for the army, I mean."

"Yes, I remember him telling me about your bravery and excellent tracking skills. He also mentioned something about hound-dog determination, I believe."

"Did he now?" Dillon laughed. "I'll have to thank—"

"Where's Callie?" Jackson interrupted, plopping his hat upon the piano. Pressure built inside his chest and he swallowed hard. *What if she decided not to show up?*

"Oh, she'll be along in a moment, Major. She's just finishing up in the other room."

Relief rolled through him, but each tick of the hallway clock increased the anxiety hammering at his gut. "Finishing up with what? Plans for my demise?"

Dillon snorted as Pamela settled on the settee. "Now, Major," she scolded, arranging her dress to avoid the trail dust that clung to the scout. "You're being silly. She has no intentions of harming you tonight."

Jackson leaned back in the chair. "I wouldn't put it past her."

"You got what you deserved, son, catchin' her off-kilter this mornin' with that brazen kiss." Gus pulled a cigar from his breast pocket and rolled the fat cylinder between his thumb and forefinger. "Mind if I smoke, ma'am?"

"Not at all."

Dillon's words rolled across the room. "You kissed her?"

Jackson ignored the scout's question. "What's she finishing up with, Miss Talmadge?"

The clock marked the passing seconds in steady *tick-tick-tick*s as the woman met his unwavering gaze. Vixenish humor illuminated her eyes as she tipped her head, then offered a coy smile. "Why, Major Neale…she's finishing up for you."

Her words settled over Jackson like a sultry night, reminding him of summers spent in the forests of northern Pennsylvania—and she was a sprite cavorting in the understory of his impatience.

A stream of smoke from Gus's exhale curled in a fragrant haze across the room. Curiosity coursed the length of Jackson. "I thought we were here for tea." Amusement was fast dissolving under an unbridled annoyance.

"We are, Major. Callie will be serving."

Callie?

Jackson leaned forward, locking his gaze upon the woman. Whatever was happening here, he'd bet his half of the ranch this little Lorelei was behind it. "Miss Talmadge, Callie serves no one. She barely serves herself." *If I'm not poisoned by midnight, it'll be a damned miracle.*

Gus puffed out another aromatic curl. "Now this oughta be good," he said and Jackson cut the man a scathing glance. The wrangler simply shrugged, but the mirth sparkling in his old eyes compounded Jackson's frustration. "Now don't go lookin' at me like that, son; I'm only here for tea. I don't know a damn thing 'bout what's going on." Gus issued an apologetic glance at their hostess. "Pardon my cursing, ma'am."

Miss Talmadge smiled and nodded.

The cotton wick inside the lamp flickered, and ripples of light scampered up the walls.

Across the room, the door swung wide.

Jackson drove his gaze toward the opening, and his heart vaulted up against his ribs.

Callie stood in the doorway holding a tray. Lamplight caught in the folds of emerald silk, wrapping her in an evocative display of light and shadows, curves and sensuality—the embodiment of pure elegance.

His breath locked up deep inside. If he had known what to expect this evening, he would have been better prepared. If he had known this woman would lay claim to an enormous chunk of his heart, he would have been better prepared. If he had known his life would never be the same after tonight, he would have been better prepared.

And yet...had he known, Jackson realized, he never could have prepared himself for the exotic goddess who stood in the doorway now.

"Good evening, everyone," Callie said. "I am terribly sorry to be late, but I wanted the water hot for our tea this evening." Rustling silk whispered to Jackson as she passed. He stared, transfixed. She glided with an angel's grace and placed the tray on the side table.

Jackson tightened his throat muscles as he searched for anything to center his world. He swallowed, releasing his breath in a silent, shallow exhale.

"We were having a little chat about you, darling." Pamela rose from the settee and moved toward Callie, patting her hand. "Now I've changed my mind. This is your celebration, so you go sit and let me serve your guests."

"At least allow me to help," Callie insisted, then accepted the spoons and napkins. She spread them across the table. "You were all talking about me?" She looked at Jackson. Wickedly delicious—in body and manners, her infinite blue eyes bewitched him. A diminutive smile lifted her lips before her gaze flicked away.

His heart ramped into his throat.

"We were just wonderin' where you were," Gus said with a chuckle. He laid his cigar in a nearby ashtray, then took the teacup she offered. "And you look real nice tonight, suga'pie. Yes indeed, real nice."

"Why thank you, Gus."

"I—I've never seen you in a dress before, ma'am," Dillon stammered. "You do look real nice."

Jackson sucked in much-needed air. *Real nice?* The words came nowhere close to describing the enchantress standing before him. In all of his thirty-four years, he'd never seen any woman more beautiful. Not even Michelangelo could have painted such a provocative smile; her lips displayed such sweetness he nearly begged her for another taste.

"And thank you, too, Mr. Reed." A becoming blush stained her high cheekbones. "I'm so pleased you were able to attend this evening what with your scouting duties and all."

Jeezus Christ…who is this glorious angel?

Ringlets of spun gold called to Jackson, begging him to sink his fingers into her resplendent curls. He flexed his hands against the pulsing ache, then pushed his gaze down the column of her neck. Diamond earbobs brushed against sheer perfection, sending a twinkling glint his way in silent invitation.

His gaze halted, caught on the unbelievable luxuriance of this ethereal vision he never knew existed. Then, his eyes dipped lower. And again, he failed to breathe. Lush, sumptuous curves above the bodice of Callie's evening gown drove a stiffness between his legs the likes of which he'd never known.

Mother of God…she's wearing a corset!

Heat flushed his face as blood surged in waves through him. Employing enormous effort, he dragged his gaze away from her voluptuous form. Confusion warred with desire. Nowhere in the flawless beauty holding court before him could he find his hellion.

Why in God's name have you been covering up such amazing splendor beneath bravado and faded denims?

Sweat gathered on his brow. If she had indeed poisoned his tea, at this precise moment he could think of no sweeter death. Jackson crossed his arms over his chest, reining in his damned libido.

Shit, even his palms were sweating.

Do I still even own a voice?

He cleared his throat, offered her a slow nod and then finally managed to say, "Good evening, Callie."

"Good evening, Jackson." She retrieved a teacup and saucer from Pamela, then bent so low before him her breasts nearly spilled from the lace-edged bodice.

He centered his gaze upon them and prayed they would.

"Would you care for tea?" she asked.

Tea?

His nerve-endings frayed. *Good God.* All he wanted to do was bury his face against her breasts and stay there for the remainder of his days. Somehow, he managed to drag his gaze back to hers. Blazing bright eyes burned him to the core.

Her lips lifted into an ever-so-soft smile.

"I don't drink tea," he said. The calmness in his voice belied his internal chaos as the ungodly pressure inside his groin built into a pikestaff, begging him to drink any damn thing this goddess offered.

Her mouth tipped downward into a kittenish pout. "But I made mine sweet and delectable—just for you. How disappointing you won't even sample what I offer."

A fresh wave of heat rolled through him. "Frankly, I'm surprised you'd even offer at all."

"Whatever do you mean?" She straightened and slid his cup onto the piano, then seated herself opposite him. Her gaze remained locked upon his as Pamela handed her another full teacup.

Stifling the urge to drag her from the chair and up against him, Jackson uncrossed his arms and swept a hand in a long wave in front of her. "I mean this. I'm somewhat puzzled you'd find interest in all this."

"Well now you know another secret of mine." Her cup rose and the coral-tinted bud of her mouth drew his gaze. Flawlessly, she elevated her pinkie and sipped.

Arousal flared within Jackson's depths. For a moment, he was swept back to parties at his family's manor where a gaggle of debutantes waited at his beck and call. None of them had managed to capture his interest. Not one. Tonight, however, the roles were reversed. He was the one now craving the angel that sat across from him in Miss Talmadge's parlor.

The scent of cinnamon swirled around him and he inhaled, refocusing on her statement. A grin tugged at the corner of his mouth. "No, now I know four secrets."

"Four?" A perfectly sculpted brow arched and her laugh twisted Jackson's quixotic emotions into a knot. The pressure inside his pants grew. He envisioned her naked beneath him, her long, coltish legs wrapped tight in a lover's squeeze around his waist. A sliver of sweat slid down his neck.

God help me, I want her.

He shot a glance to the cup and saucer on the piano. "You make and serve tea. That's one." His hand slid along the Steinway, thankful for the coolness beneath his fingers. "Two…you play this instrument with remarkable skill." He motioned toward her green damask evening gown. "Three. You do know how to wear a dress." He then rested his elbows on the arms of the chair, and steepled his fingers in an outward show of control. Inside, however, his blood still churned. "And four…" Jackson paused to slide his gaze in a deliberate, self-indulgent sweep over the curve of her breasts before reconnecting with her now-widened eyes. "You're an incredibly beautiful woman."

"But, Major Neale," Pamela interjected, draping a snow-colored napkin across her lap. "Beautiful women hold many secrets."

"Now that's the damned truth," Gus declared, rattling his cup in the saucer. He caught the curse word a bit too late and cast a sheepish glance in Miss Talmadge's direction. "Again, ma'am, pardon my language."

Pamela nodded.

Callie should have felt embarrassed by the carnal sweep of Jackson's eyes. Fury should be roiling through her veins right now at his blatant and vulgar appraisal of her…womanly blessings. Instead, however, excitement pulsed through her—a living, breathing animal, vital and raw. Consuming her.

She stared at him. *My God, his face is…flushing!* Her brain grew dizzy. Heat scaled her cheeks in an instant response. The corset's metal stays dug into her ribs as she pulled in each ragged breath. Her nerves unraveled in agonizingly slow degrees beneath the smoldering heat that radiated back at her from his eyes.

Restless fingers threaded and rethreaded the handle of her teacup, a useless attempt to stop her hand from shaking. How in the world could she steer the conversation toward today's race?

Redirecting hadn't been part of her lessons.

"I raise my cup and salute the winner," Dillon said. The scout's words broke the mesmerizing hold Jackson had over her and drew Callie's immediate and thankful gaze. "Here's to an exciting race, Miss Cutteridge, even though I missed the entire thing."

"Th-Thank you, Mr. Reed," she sputtered, corralling her wild emotions. *All right, here's the opening I need. Now focus!* "I-I had no idea I would win. Especially since Salvaje was clearly in the lead."

Her gaze drifted back to Jackson's, but he said nothing. He simply continued to stare at her with those disarmingly dark eyes. The silent message of desire Callie saw wreaked havoc with her emotions, and she ached to curb the calamity he incited inside her. The entire purpose of tonight's escapade was shredding into comical little pieces beneath this man's unnerving control over her.

"Yep," Gus said. "We couldn't have asked for a finer finish."

Conversation rolled on around her between Gus and Dillon and Pamela, while Callie sipped her tea and fragmented further beneath the fire flash of her partner's stare. The warmth in the room enveloped her. Her head felt heavy. His gaze swept her body. Perspiration heated her face.

No, no…don't think about his kiss!

Callie swallowed and dropped her gaze to his mouth. Twice she'd been assaulted by those lips.

And both times they carved a hole in my heart.

Inconceivable craving for Jackson oozed through her veins. She tightened…everywhere, the passion coursed stronger and stronger. The image of him working Salvaje in the corral that long-ago afternoon, his chaps hugging his body like a second skin, everything flashed into recall. Her hand rose to her lips in a maddening need to stop their tremble.

She forgot about the cup balanced on her lap.

Forgot, too, the spoon resting in its oh-so-proper place. She bumped the utensil and sent honey-laced Darjeeling over the side of the china. As if in slow motion, the liquid slipped past the saucer's gold-rimmed edge and puddled upon her lap. In less than a heartbeat, the scalding liquid penetrated the fashionable trappings to reach her skin.

Callie bolted upright with an explosive rustle of green silk. The rose-patterned teacup and saucer propelled skyward in a somersaulting display.

"Sonofabitch," she shrieked, smacking at the blistering spot.

A heartbeat later, the dishes struck her dress, whooshing downward. With a juggler's attempt, she splayed her hands wide, trying to catch each piece.

She failed. Disastrously. Delicate china crashed onto the weathered floorboards. Her mouth dropped open and she stared at the tiny porcelain icebergs amidst an amber sea. Adding insult to her insufferable misery, her demi-spoon clattered into the center.

The longcase clock in the hallway chimed the hour, underscoring her torment. Heat razed her cheeks.

Callie widened her eyes. She jerked her head upward, locking her gaze to Jackson's.

Her breath caught in her chest with an agonizing squeeze.

He didn't speak.

Nor did he bend forward to help.

In fact, he hadn't even unsteepled his fingers. His gaze bored into hers. Amid his cool expression, his eyes exuded an intensity that unnerved her.

And then…his lips lifted on a smidgen of a smile.

Tears burned at the backs of her eyes, yet she refused to allow a single mortifying drop to fall in front of this man. Her jaw clenched even as her legs trembled. The earlier fabricated image of him stroking her limb while she bathed reappeared in her mind.

Every muscle tightened. On a gravelly rush, Callie released her trapped breath and hiked the heavy skirt to her knees. She didn't give a damn if God or His entire Heavenly Host saw her under drawers. She only knew she must put distance between herself and this insufferable man.

She hurtled over the mess, then headed straight across the room. Each footfall swayed her hoops with such force that had she been a bell she would've fractured wider than Old Liberty. With a final, humiliating smack of crinoline against the doorframe, she swept from the parlor.

A quiet discomfort settled over the room.

Jackson eased out his breath in a slow push of air, then folded his fingers into tightened fists. Callie's unexpected sensuality had ripped a hole in him, shredding layer upon layer of his self-control. He smothered the truth beneath a rush of anger.

You're not some damn schoolboy.

But he felt like one…and it had been an eternity since he'd grappled with such feelings. Disbelief rolled in undulating waves through him as each heartbeat rammed home the gritty truth that he actually wanted this woman.

"Oh dear," Pamela whispered.

Dillon dropped to a knee beside the glistening mess. "I'll get this cleaned up."

Gus slipped from his chair to join him. "Here, son, let me help."

"Thank you, gentlemen," Pamela said, laying aside her cup and napkin. "I—I'll just go see if she's all right."

"Sit down." Jackson's voice emanated with such force the woman stopped in mid-rise. "I'll go."

With eyes as wide as saucers, she nodded, then sank to the sofa. "I—I'm sure she's in my room…down the hallway on the left."

"I'll find her." Jackson turned and headed for the parlor door.

Chapter Twenty

The bedroom door opened with a creak, yet Callie remained slumped in the chair, staring through the window into the pinpricks of light across the camp.

"I told you it would never work," she whispered, her voice cracking. A soft thump closed out the faraway sound of dishes clanking in the parlor. "I—I'm so sorry, Pamela. There's just no way to make a lady out of me."

Jackson's deep voice rolled across the room to splinter her melancholy. "And why, exactly, is that important?"

She sucked in a breath and bolted to her feet, swiveling to face him. "Wh-What the hell are you doing in here?"

He crossed the rug, decisive footsteps muffled by the thick, woolen weave beneath his boots. Scrambling to tamp down a rush of panic, Callie angled the chair between them.

He came to a stop on the other side, his legs bumping against the tufted brocade seat. "I've come to collect some answers."

He pushed the tension through the air ahead of him and it smacked into Callie. She flicked her gaze down his imposing form. "Why don't you just mind your own damn business and get out of here."

His lips lifted into a smirk. "You are my business, remember? So start telling me why you're doing all this."

Her muscles went rigid. Here was her chance to ask him why he'd thrown the race. But somehow the reason didn't matter anymore. Instead, Callie squared her shoulders and snapped, "Doing what?"

"This fancy bullshit." Leaning forward across the seat, Jackson folded his fingers over the wooden top. With a hard shove, he thrust aside the chair and stepped closer. When the rush of his warm breath met her face, tingles registered.

She swallowed, then speared him with a piercing look. "Well—why not? You've been harping at me to wear a damn dress ever since you got here." Her chin rose. "Now I have, so you can shut the hell up about it."

Their gazes locked, and an agonizing second later a scowl thinned his lips. "I thought you had more gumption than to kowtow to someone else's expectations."

"By someone else's, you mean yours." Anger pulsed through her, accompanied by an unnerving excitement, something she dared not revisit.

"Yes," he said. A shadow darkened his eyes. "Mine."

"You said we were supposed to get along."

"But we aren't getting along." An odd sharpness gleamed in his gaze. "Instead, you're changing."

"I am not changing. I'm…expanding my perspective."

"Perspective, my ass." Jackson inched closer. She refused to back down. Cool stucco met her back and chilled her as his hands propped against the wall on both sides of her body, corralling her inside his arms. A tight laugh fell from his lips. "You've no idea the power you hold, do you?" His dark lashes swept downward, his gaze spilling over her breasts before reconnecting with hers. "This isn't the tough-as-grit girl I've come to know…and respect."

Another rush of heat spread through Callie, and her heart missed a beat. Surely to God she wasn't falling for this bigger-than-life beast. Was she?

"Y-You don't know me at all," she stammered, angry at him for flinging the stupid dress-up exhibition in her face, angrier at herself for the catch in her voice.

"I know you enough to know you don't know what the hell you're doing tonight."

"What's that supposed to mean?" She was cold to the bone, yet she burned to the core. The raw reflection she'd seen in his eyes in the parlor returned. Her heartbeat, rapid and high in her throat, nearly strangled her.

"Let's see...what did you say? Ah yes...you made this sweet and delectable, just for me. Then you were disappointed I wouldn't sample what you offered." He loomed nearer. "Never utter something suggestive if you're not prepared to follow through with it."

The low-burning lamp across the room spilled shadows across his face and the strong line of his jaw tensed. She bit her lower lip to stop its tremble and prayed he would just go away. But the glint flickered behind his eyes and brought an unexplained burst of anxiety inside her to the surface. Callie surged right in a rustle of silk, but his arm lowered, blocking her exit.

She pitched left.

Again, he blocked her way.

Her hands rose and pushed against his chest. How could she have forgotten she could sooner move a tree?

The room closed in on her as her fingers curled into soft, faded cambric. In rapid-fire puffs, her breathing rushed in and out. She stared at the hard planes and angles of his face.

His eyes were mysterious pools.

Something pulsed, then leapt to life inside...sweeping downward. The frantic madness that had careened through Callie in the parlor seized her once more. She tugged on his shirt, ripping a seam at his shoulder. She knew she should scream...she needed to scream.

But, she couldn't scream.

His hand rose between them. The pads of two fingers caressed the curve of her cheek. Each stroke summoned rippling waves from deep inside her as if a stone had been tossed into the murkiness of her empty life. Jackson opened his palm, then sank his hand into the hair at the nape of her neck.

Pins scattered...along with her futile resistance.

Her elegant chignon uncoiled.

Tresses tumbled down.

When he wrapped his hand in her curls and gently pulled, Callie gasped. He brought her face upward. Her gaze tumbled into his. She was hopelessly lost in the hunger that radiated from their smoldering depths.

Jackson leaned closer and the faint trace of whiskey enveloped her. In a breathless tone, he rasped, "What you search for has nothing to do with dressing up or tea parties and everything to do with finding your way back to this—" With all the force of a life-altering storm, his mouth came down upon hers. Before she could protest, he pulled her up against him in a breath-stealing embrace.

The burn of his kiss robbed her of all logic.

Yearning flared inside her, unbelievable and exhilarating. Her mind reeled. She knew only one blinding need—how best to answer his questing lips.

With a will of their own, her hands coursed up his chest, then over his shoulders in a desperate dash. His mouth shifted across hers—demanding and nipping and wild. Hers answered with equal fervor, softening, then parting for more.

A rap on the bedroom door resonated somewhere in the recesses of her mind. A moment after that Jackson released her and Callie stumbled back against the wall.

Another knock and he spun to face the door.

Pamela swept into the room. "Is everything all right in here?" the coquette asked, her gaze skimming from Jackson to settle upon her. Callie swept back curls tumbling across bare shoulders. Instant awareness widened the eyes of her mentor. "Oh my, I'm...so sorry to have intruded."

Gus cleared his throat as he stepped from behind the woman. "My Dejarlin's gettin' cold, suga'dumplin'," he mumbled around the cigar clinched between his teeth. His gaze traced Callie from head to toe, and savvy old eyes brightened with understanding. From behind the old wrangler, Dillon's tall form darkened the doorway. "I'm still mighty thirsty, ma'am," the young scout said. "How 'bout you come back out to the parlor and pour me some more of that tea."

Mortification blistered Callie's cheeks. Her gaze lanced back to Jackson and she saw a flicker of understanding in the dark depths of his eyes. He stepped in front of her as if to shield her from the others, but Gus just laughed.

"Too late to hide things now, son." A wide smile flooded his face.

Humor replaced the concern in Jackson's eyes and he stepped sideways. "You're too damn nosey for your own good, Gus."

Pamela's gasp, Dillon's laughter and the old man's knowing smile all sent Callie's emotions spinning. With more charm than should be allowed, Jackson leaned from the waist and swept wide his arm. "After you, partner," he said with a wink.

A bewildering ache seized Callie and with a push of her hands, she straightened from the wall. The corset dug into her ribs, a maddening reminder of her foolishness. Her chin rose and without another word, she swept past them all and glided straight out the bedroom door.

Chapter Twenty-One

The faraway sound of thunder rolled over Callie, interrupting her contemplation. She drew back on Diego's reins and glanced toward the Rincons. An angry gloom draped the craggy palisade, mixing with the late-afternoon light.

A sudden wind drove pinpricks of hot sand against her face and the aroma of piñon and sagebrush overwhelmed her. Saltbush seemed to grab out at her legs with its splintered branches as Diego pushed past the shrubs. Dried fruit pods still clung to them and rattled like paper lanterns.

A second gust nearly lifted her hat from her head. Callie grabbed the felt brim and tightened the lanyard, anchoring the slouch into place.

Her gaze skimmed the serrated mountains. Gunmetal gray clouds piled high, building in thickness and intensity all along the peaks. Twisting in the saddle, she looked west toward Tucson. A reddish-brown, dust-laden haze marred the sun's majestic streaks.

Gus and Jackson were a couple of hours behind her, longer if they'd stopped to rest the team. The moon had still owned the sky when she'd climbed atop Diego and pointed her gelding toward home. Had Gus found the message she'd left him? Would he understand her need to leave before everyone else?

A shudder that had nothing to do with the wind whipped through Callie. Truth be told, she wasn't ready to face Jackson so soon after last night's kiss. She needed time to think.

And yet, hours later, she found herself in the same asinine quandary. Her belly quivered as an undeniable heat simmered inside. She wanted Jackson, and all that unfamiliar want frightened her.

She issued a defiant snort, pointing her index finger toward the hazy horizon behind her where he and Gus by now probably rode. "But I sure as hell don't need you. Do you hear me, partner? I don't *need* you one damn bit." The words had trouble getting around the wad of misery lodged in her throat. She tried to swallow, but the lump refused to budge.

Callie swiveled and faced east. Before her gut twisted any tighter, she gathered the reins and nudged Diego's flanks.

The gelding opened up into a strong gallop.

Fifty minutes later, and under a bank of ominous clouds, she rode into the side yard of Dos Caballos. A flash of red, Pilar's billowing Mexican skirt, drew Callie's gaze to the washhouse. The cook struggled against a pounding wind to remove clothing from the line, her head averted from the striking sand.

Callie reined Diego to a halt near the stables. The corrals were empty. Where the hell was Banner? And what about the mares they'd left penned along the Angel, the ones they chose to keep? Had her farrier, or the other vaqueros, thought to bring them closer to the ranch?

"Pilar," she hollered, but the wind threw the word back at her. A small dust cyclone spun nearby as Diego paced in a tight circle. Callie cupped her hands around her mouth and shouted again. "Pilar!"

The cook turned and waved. "Señorita!" She shifted the clothes to her other arm and pointed toward the house. "I so glad you're home. Storm's nearly here. Hurry, let's go inside."

Raindrops splattered Callie's hat brim. She stole an upward glance. This was no summer shower. This was a driving desert demon. An angry wall of tumbling sand and ebony clouds rushed to engulf the ranch. Before she could worry about herself, she must make certain the mares were safe.

"Not yet," she shouted, settling back into the saddle. She gathered the reins, then pulled them taut to stop Diego's pacing. "I've got to ride to the Angel corrals and make sure the horses are safe. Gus and the others are a couple of hours behind me. I'll be back soon."

She dug her spurs deep and her horse sprinted forward.

A thunderclap swallowed Pilar's response.

Callie had no time to spare. She leaned low in the saddle and gave Diego free rein. Another boom opened wide the sky. And a moment after that, the torrential rains began.

"What do you mean she's not here?" Jackson yelled above the storm as he reined Salvaje to a stop before Banner. "Where the hell is she?"

"Pilar said she rode out to da Angel to bring in da mares." Banner stepped back into the stable to avoid the slicing rain. The lamplight inside outlined him in a ghostly halo. "She don't know we'd moved 'em to da Dos Llamos corrals yesterday."

Water sluiced down Jackson's military slicker and reflected the gleam of lightning around them. His gaze cut sideways as Gus reined the Percherons to a stop.

"What's wrong?" the old man bellowed above the wind as he shifted on the wagon's bench to face them. They'd ridden hard to get back to the ranch, and weariness reflected in his face.

"Callie rode back out in this mess." Rain soaked the collar of Jackson's shirt.

Gus rammed home the side brake with his foot. "*Jeezus*…why would she do that?"

"She thought da mares were still out by da Angel," Banner hollered from the open doorway. "But we moved 'em to higher ground while y'all was gone."

Jackson stared down at the black man. "How long has she been gone?"

"A couple of hours. Maybe more."

"A couple of hours?" Jackson rasped. His pulse thrummed inside his veins.

"She knows better than to be out in the dark after the creeks flood," Gus yelled above another clap of thunder.

The statement hit Jackson hard. Why in God's name had she sneaked out and ridden back ahead of them?

His throat tightened. *You knew why.*

He gripped the reins until the soaked leather stretched taut. A premonition as powerful as the storm's fury rumbled through him. "Something's wrong, Gus."

He pulled Salvaje's reins to the left, but the wrangler reached out and gripped Jackson's arm. "Hold up, son. I'm sure the bridge across the Angel's washed away by now. You'll have to go through the pass, if it's still open."

Jackson nodded as his stomach cramped. Callie *was* in trouble. He felt it clear to his bones, and in that moment his heart lurched, followed by a reeling stab in his chest. *Jeezus*, how long had the truth been there? Taunting him... riding beneath the confusion and anger and every other emotion Callie had ever evoked from him?

The admission clamored louder than any thunderclap: *My God...I love her.*

The weight crushed him. What was so baffling a moment ago now became inescapably clear. Damn, a blind man could've seen it...why in the hell hadn't he?

"Do you want me to ride with you?" Gus yelled.

Water poured from Jackson's hat as he stared down at the ground beneath the team.

I do...I—actually love her.

"I said do you want me to come too?" Gus screamed again.

Jackson swallowed, then lanced his gaze to the wrangler's. Worry carved across the old man's leathery face, trenching lines in his forehead and around his mouth. "No... Just take care of the supplies. I'll find her."

Without another word, Jackson set spurs to Salvaje. Hard and fast, they galloped from the stable yard.

Leaning over the saddle, he demanded more speed. And the stalwart stallion obeyed, thundering over the ground with all the fury of the wind.

The desert could no longer absorb the monster storm. Angel Creek already had crested its boulder-strewn banks, channeling the flood into the Rincons' sandstone labyrinth. Ancient corridors filled with roiling water, flooding into slot canyons, and building in intensity, swirling, accelerating through a hundred narrow passages. An unstoppable, unrelenting beast on a churning rampage of destruction. Rain coursed in rivulets down Callie's face, soaking her saddle and leathers. Her clothes stuck to her like a second skin and her boots filled with water. She barely had any feeling left in her feet. She was shivering and bone-tired from battling against the sand and driving wind.

"Come on," she begged, urging Diego toward the closest incline. "We're almost there. Come on." She dug her spurs into the gelding's flanks, demanding more strength from the already exhausted animal. The horse neighed and balked, fighting to get footing in the saturated soil.

An ungodly rumble startled Callie. She glanced over her shoulder in the direction of the roar. A frothy wall of water tore around the bend in the corridor and bore straight down upon them. A bolt of lightning cracked the sky, reflecting branches and debris churning inside the mud-colored, on-rushing demon. The raging torrent caromed off the canyon walls, moving faster than any horse and rider ever could. Callie's stomach heaved.

"Move it," she screamed above another roll of thunder, but she knew they had little time left. Fear drove the gelding up the incline, but he slipped, losing precious time in a frantic search for quarter among the ever-shifting shale.

Leaning low, Callie jerked the coiled rope from the saddle. She looped one end of the lariat over the leather horn. The other, she knotted around her waist.

Closer and closer the horrific howl grew.

Precious seconds were all she could offer the horse before the rope tightened.

"Go with me, God," she mumbled. Before she could change her mind, Callie shoved over the cantle of the saddle, then off the back of the animal. She hit the ground hard, boot heels slipping against the shale.

"Move it," she shrieked, slapping Diego on the rump. The gelding bolted, throwing sand and loose rock as it clambered upward.

Would there be enough time to drag her up the embankment and out of the torrent's grip? Would the force of the water snap the line?

The rope zipped through Callie's gloved hands as she scrambled, lost her footing, then scrambled again.

Free of a rider's weight, her horse's stride lengthened, then the rope pulled taut. Callie jerked forward onto her hands and knees. Jagged stones ground into her denims. Water slapped her thighs, then wrapped her belly and chest, encasing her inside an ice-cold tomb.

The bitter taste of fear gagged her, yet still Diego climbed. Callie dug her hands into the earth to right herself, but the water rose too fast, up her neck to clog her throat. Tears coursed her cheeks, mixing with the rain and debris, robbing her of sight.

Jackson's image filled her thoughts, followed by a mind-shattering truth. If only she could have one more moment with him to say...to tell him...she loved him.

"Jackson," she rasped, rounding his name into a brittle, broken sob. "Please, God—let me live long enough to—"

The wall of water slammed into her, sweeping her inside a roiling hell.

Chapter Twenty-Two

Jackson glanced skyward. Rain pummeled his face, drenching him. Irritation stretched further the thinning thread of his patience. There wasn't a damn thing he could do to stop Mother Nature's wrath.

The stinging wind buffeted him as he pulled Salvaje's reins up tight. He swiped his face against his shoulder to wipe away the water running in his eyes, then scanned the area where the corrals once stood. Fence posts had snapped in half, and splintered railings littered the ground like a wagonload of scattered lucifer matches.

High water had taken out the bridge, as well.

The musty stench of creosote bushes and saturated earth filled his nostrils, penetrating deep into his throat. He could almost taste the desert.

He certainly tasted fear.

For more than an hour he'd searched for Callie, and his worry pressed heavy on him now. He inhaled, then heaved a weighty sigh. Impulsive and reckless, both words perfectly described her. And there was nothing he could do to alter her independent ways, either.

His gloved hand rose. Another swipe across his face removed more rain. He had so many conflicting things drumming through his mind, but his next breath stopped the confliction. He didn't want Callie to change. Not now. Not ever. He admired her strength, her courage, her dogged determination. All he wanted to do now was find her and tell her so.

The horses, the ranch, nothing mattered to Jackson without her. She *was* Dos Caballos, and that truth penetrated even deeper than the biting wind.

He again swiped his face, then roared, "Callie." Still no reply. He nudged Salvaje toward a lone cabin perched on the nearby hill.

Waterfalls gushed down the small incline and cut several streams through the trail leading to the old mining shack. Void of any overhang, the knotty, rough-hewn building glistened a mottled gray beneath the eerie light.

Please, God, let her be inside.

Jackson slid from the saddle, then splashed to the door, leading the stallion by the reins. Rusty hinges groaned as he shoved open the flimsy panel and peered inside. Through the solitary window, lightning illuminated the room. He could make out an empty bed, a stack of firewood on the hearth, a cold grate, but no Callie.

"Sonofabitch," he hissed, turning back to stare through the driving rain. The worn step beneath his Wellingtons creaked. Inside his boots, damp toes tightened. He pressed his free hand against the doorframe, gauntlet-covered fingers digging into the weathered pine. *Where are you, my wild little hellion?*

His gaze cut in the direction of the sandstone corridors, the worst possible place to cross the Angel.

And the only place left to search.

Oh God, no.

The rush of blood in his ears overrode the storm's fury. He turned, vaulted into the saddle, then pulled the reins sideways to turn his horse.

Jackson reached the ravine and urged Salvaje along its rocky edge. Desperation gripped his chest, twisting his gut into a knot. His saddle creaked as he leaned over the precipice and peered into the blackness. Water poured in rivulets from his hat brim.

"Callie!" he bellowed again.

Salvaje stopped and issued a full-blown neigh. Jackson tightened his legs around the stallion and urged him onward, but the animal still balked, tossing his head in protest. The long, sodden mane slapped against Jackson's wrist.

"Keep moving, dammit," he ordered, jaw muscles clenching around his gritted teeth. But the beast held firm, snorting and pawing the ground. Then, from out of the darkness came the answering neigh of another horse.

Hope swelled inside Jackson. "Callie," he yelled just as a slash of light outlined the other animal.

Riderless.

Jackson's veins constricted. Urging his horse forward, he closed the gap. He swung his leg over the saddle and dropped to the ground, boot heels sinking.

When he reached for Diego's headstall, the gelding flinched and jerked his head away.

"Whoa, there...that's my boy." Jackson smoothed his hand down the horse's neck, then chest, then farther down the leg past the cannon. He found no injuries.

Had Callie been thrown? He straightened, his gaze lancing to the askewed saddle and the rope looped around the horn. The hemp trailed over the animal's rump, before snaking down into the ravine.

What the hell? He pulled on the lariat, but it didn't budge. And then, a horrifying realization punched into the pit of his stomach.

Jackson dropped to his knees, then flattened onto his belly, sliding his hand down the taut line as far as he could reach. "Oh my God..." He scooted closer to the rim, the stones beneath him digging into his stomach. His hands cupped around his mouth and he yelled, "Hold on, Cal. I'm here." The back of his throat burned as his strained voice sliced into the churning darkness below.

He surged to his feet and maneuvered Salvaje to the edge, looping one end of his own rope around the swell on his saddle. He threw the other end into the crevasse. The stallion snorted and sidestepped.

"Hold firm," Jackson demanded, jerking on the rope. He maneuvered into position alongside Callie's lifeline and stretched out his right hand, gripping her taut cord.

Slowly, he worked his way over the rocky lip. Loose rock pressed against the soles of his boots, skidding beneath his feet. He paused, carefully planted his foot and started again.

Inch by inch he descended.

Shale tumbled toward the deafening torrent. Rain drenched his shirt, ran into his mouth, poured from his hat. Yet still Jackson pushed on. The slick ropes cut through his sodden gloves, but one false step would send him plummeting down the hill. Lightning speared the sky, sending forth a bolt as jagged and raw as his patience.

"Hold on, hellion," he whispered. Another footstep, and then another. Finally, Jackson touched something other than rock. His tight hold on his emotions slipped, catapulting him to the edge of terror as he peered into the angry black void.

"I need some damn light," he bellowed. As if the heavens heard his hoarse petition, another streak of lightning cleaved the sky.

Jackson's breath halted deep in his throat. Turbulent water swept over Callie's partially submerged body, smacking against her shoulders in cresting whitecaps. The leather lanyard around her neck had secured her hat, but the slouch bobbed wildly in the current. Wet hair veiled her upturned face.

She wasn't moving.

A sharp pain tore through his heart, rivaling the bolt of lightning that had ripped open the heavens. *Dear God...I'm too late.*

Jackson yanked on her rope, struggling to pull Callie's limp form away from the outcropping of granite.

She didn't budge.

Fear spiked through him as he slid his hand down the line. His fingers bunched the material of her shirt into a cambric wad, allowing him a firmer hold. Shoulder and arm muscles tightened under his frantic pull. Twice more he tugged, but to no avail. A third pull caused the fabric to rip under his effort, and his raspy demand met the rain-soaked night. "Let go of her, you sonofabitch." He leaned closer, his body now hip-deep in the churning water. Another hard jerk finally freed Callie from the boulder's death grip.

Her body swung free, but the current tore her from his clasp. Desperate to catch her, Jackson scuffled sideways, slapping and flaying the water. He slipped, banging his hip against the rock. Lunging once more, he snagged the rope—

pulled her from the undertow and up against his chest.

"I'm here, Cal," he whispered, cradling her in his arms. His lips grazed her icy face. *Please, God, she can't be dead. Not now. Not when I've finally found her.*

His hold tightened.

And Callie stirred.

He stared down into her pale face. Had he imagined her movement? Rain drummed against his hat and shoulders as the seconds ticked away in agonizing torment. The wind drove deep the truth: Nobody had a command over his emotions like this woman. Nobody.

Stay with me, hellion.

Ever so slightly, she moved again. Hope shot through Jackson's veins. With his sharp exhale, sanity returned. He had to get her out of this mess. *Now.* He yanked on his rope, sending an order up the incline to Salvaje.

"Pull," he bellowed. "Pull." Callie's groan met his ear when he shifted her into a more secure position across his shoulder.

More shale gave way beneath his feet. Why wasn't the horse moving? Jackson sidestepped, and fell sideways against the boulder. Using his foot as leverage he pushed off the rock, jerking harder on the tether. "Move, Salvaje!"

This time, the horse responded. Jackson lurched upward, fighting to stay erect. Thigh muscles tightened beneath each step and seconds passed in wretched agony. Hip joints strained against the climb. Cautiously, he planted each foot.

Jackson clenched his teeth to stop his body from shivering, to stop the cold dread from seeping into his bones.

At last he crested the edge and toppled over the stony lip, dragging Callie with him. She fell onto her back with a shallow groan, her arms splayed wide.

Gasping for breath, he rolled to his side and faced her. He smoothed the wet strands of hair off her face. "I'm so sorry. I should've found you sooner." She struggled to lift an arm as another moan slipped past her trembling lips. "No, no...lie still," he whispered. "Let me untie the ropes first."

He undid the knot around her waist, then climbed to his feet. Looping his arms under her shoulders, he pulled her farther from the edge.

His lips brushed the curve of her ear. "I'll be right back. I'm going to get the horses."

Pent-up energy weakened him as he coiled the ropes, stowing them on the saddles before tightening the cinches. Ribs ached from the drubbing force of his heartbeat. He focused on his words to corral his frayed emotions. "Good boy, Salvaje. Good, Diego. You helped save her."

Callie's will to live ran strong. And now, he might just have a shot at the happiness he hadn't even known he'd wanted until he'd almost lost her. Of course, convincing her to feel the same way about him might prove to be a different set of challenges. But he'd worry about all that later. Jackson bit back a snort, knotted Diego's reins through a ring on his saddle, then led Salvaje back to his partner.

She would ride with him. Any hope of getting back to the ranch tonight had vanished. The abandoned shack would have to do.

He gathered Callie into his arms and then hoisted himself into the saddle. The McClellan creaked as he settled into place. His lips pressed against her clammy forehead.

I came so close to losing you. If he didn't warm her soon, he still might.

Callie trembled against him. He drew her closer, his chest constricting. His devotion to her had been growing for months—he just hadn't realized how much. He imagined her fear as she'd dangled in the water, imagined her losing hope as she waited, imagined her believing no one knew of her fate. She issued another shallow groan and turned her face toward him, nestling closer. Long hanks of hair had escaped her braid and lay in a wet tangle across his arm. Wisps clung to her cheek. Jackson resisted the urge to brush his lips against hers. Instead he set spurs, and Salvaje took off in a hard canter toward the cabin.

Chapter Twenty-Three

Cradling Callie in his arms, Jackson heaved a shoulder against the cabin door. The wooden barrier flew open and smacked the wall with a bang. He carried his shivering bundle inside and headed toward the solitary bed set against the back wall, floorboards creaking with each step he took.

To avoid soaking the mattress with her wet clothes, Jackson nestled Callie on the floor near the iron headboard. After pulling the threadbare coverlet from the bed, he draped it over her, then spun on his boot heel and headed back outside.

With an economy of motion he hadn't used since the war, he tethered the horses inside the shack's attached lean-to, then stripped them of their saddles and tack, placing the equipment on nearby pegs. A moment later, he snatched up his saddlebags and bedroll and then headed back to the cabin at the double-quick.

Slamming the door behind him, Jackson closed out the stormy night. At the fireplace, he dropped the gear and sank to a knee upon the hearth. He scooped a handful of wood shavings from the kindling box and tossed them onto the grate. Leather scraped across uneven pine as he pulled his saddlebags closer. One hand lifted the flap, the other rummaged inside until his fingers closed around a tin of lucifers. He struck the match and welcoming light nipped the darkness. The stench of sulfur wafted upward, and a moment later, a fire crackled into life.

Jackson stood and fed several logs to the flames, then turned and shucked his hat, gloves and poncho, tossing them onto the table. He scanned the room.

In one corner, cobwebs hung in gossamer drapes from the rafters, but the roof was sound, the walls and floor dry.

Heat permeated the cabin and stirred the silken webs into an eerie dance. Scooping up the bedroll, Jackson retraced his steps to Callie.

An amber glow embraced the tight ball into which she'd curled and her braid lay like a sodden snake over one shoulder. Caught between her teeth, her bottom lip trembled.

Jackson lowered to a knee beside her and untied the leather strap on his gum blanket. The rubberized canvas bedroll unfurled across the floor, brass grommets embedded in the corners catching the firelight. He lifted free a blanket and shook open the wool. A stale scent of past campfires met his nostrils as the letters *U.S.*, embroidered on the far corner, flashed and then disappeared into the woolen folds.

Another blanket followed, devoid of insignia. Jackson dropped both beside Callie's huddled form, then leaned over and touched her shoulder. "We need to get you out of your wet clothes."

She didn't reply. He didn't expect her to. Exhaustion had taken its toll. Jackson glanced at her shirtfront and sucked in a quick breath. Rain had soaked the thin material. She wore no undergarments. Her curves held him spellbound, but this was not the time to marvel. He swallowed, wetting a mouth suddenly gone dry, and tamped down a desire that rose unbidden.

After ridding her of boots and socks, he raised her from the floor and pulled her against him. A low groan fell from her lips.

Working quickly, Jackson fumbled his stiff fingers over the tin buttons running down the front of her torn shirt. As he pushed the wet cambric off her shoulders, his breath lodged deep in his throat. Flawless perfection drove a spike of heat straight into his loins.

Soft light glistened across honey-hued breasts, illuminating dusky aureole and nipples puckered from the cold. His gaze lingered a trifle longer, then rose to the hollow of her throat. The pulse nestled there matched the unrequited throb in his groin. Jackson pulled in another lungful of air, clamping his lips tight.

How many months had it been since he'd touched a woman? *Too damn many.* He gritted his teeth and refocused on the task at hand.

Carefully, he lifted Callie and placed her on the bed. The dark fan of her lashes fluttered, yet her eyes remained closed. She hurt from her horrific ordeal, but he now ached for a far different reason.

Jackson spread the cavalry blanket over her. After slipping his hands under the wool, he unfastened the buttons of her denims, then stripped away the wet britches and tossed them over a rickety chair in the shadows.

Callie lay naked beneath the coverlet. Jackson eased out a lengthy sigh, trying to calm his pounding heart. Muscles knotted with tension as he leaned over and jammed the edges of the blanket beneath her to form a cocoon.

The action both frustrated and offered satisfaction, knowing he'd created a sufficient barrier between his partner and his nerve-wracking need.

He mustered his thoughts under control and draped the second blanket over her before turning his attention to his own soggy clothes.

Lowering to the floor several feet from Callie's tempting form, Jackson pulled off his boots and tossed them aside. His wet socks joined the pile of garments.

With arm muscles bunching, he climbed to his feet and peeled off his shirt and pants, leaving on his cotton under drawers.

Jackson fed several more logs to the fire, then stared into the flames, the radiating heat warming his bare chest. A cynical chuckle followed. Alone in a remote cabin with a naked woman—the old Jackson would've found the situation enticing. But the old Jackson had never been in love.

His lips ground together.

Callie captured him in ways no other woman ever had, and his concern for her far outweighed his own selfish needs. The fragility she'd tried to hide behind her fearless façade now lay exposed before him.

He flexed his hands, turning his palms upward. A splotchy line of dried blood marked the cuts made by the ropes. His fingers shook, not from the superficial wounds, but from the thought of nearly losing Callie.

Jackson jammed his hands into his hair, tunneling his fingers through the damp hanks that waved to his shoulders. Shoving the length off his face, he glanced back at her.

His breath caught in his throat.

From under soft brows, Callie stared at him, her eyes opened wide enough to catch the fire's glow. Rain pounded the roof in a steady rhythm as their gazes held. Desire shimmered in the mesmerizing blue of her eyes.

Jackson's body hardened, pulsing in hungry reply. Air gusted from his lungs and his gaze slid away, only to return to hers. He'd seen that look before, reflected in the eyes of a multitude of past lovers...women who wanted him, women who plotted for more, women who'd mattered little beyond mere physical satisfaction. But Callie wasn't one of those sultry temptresses. She was an uncontrollable innocent.

Untamed and unmatched.

His stare dropped to her lips, and his own pursed tightly. He wanted another taste of her, craved the length of her body against his. Tension raked through him. Unbeknownst to her, she now held all the power.

Jackson exerted every ounce of control he possessed to keep from responding. He probably imagined the beckoning glint, anyway—a trick of his own desires amidst the vacillating, gold-limned shadows. Instead, his words snaked out in a raw, guttural whisper, "You're safe now, hellion."

The light in Callie's eyes dimmed, a slight nod moving her head a fraction of an inch.

And yet, her cheeks flushed when he stepped closer.

Jackson steadied his breath and cleared his throat, choosing his next words with care. "I'm going to lie down beside you and hold you so you'll warm up faster. Don't be afraid."

Another nod. This time her eyes held no captivating shimmer, only exhaustion and acceptance and relief.

He skimmed the blankets, his mind swirling in a conflicted whirlpool of need. Jeezus, how could he simply hold her when he wanted so much more?

Then Callie's eyes drifted closed and she shivered, sending the gray wool into a rippling eddy.

In a heartbeat his foolishness vanished, and he stripped from his damp under drawers. The bed creaked as he climbed in beside her, pulling the second blanket over them both. He rolled her onto her side facing away from him, and then slipped his arm around her waist. His biceps flexed as he pulled her closer, spooning her into his warmth.

Her raspy breathing knotted his heartstrings. His own became a muffled groan that washed past parted lips. She felt so small, so tiny in his arms—for once, so helpless.

Does she feel my heartbeat?

He felt hers. His hand splayed across her belly, fingers flexing against the suppleness he found there. For months, his struggles with her had equaled breaking his wild stallion. She'd fought hard against his ropes. But he'd uncovered her secrets anyway—the orphanage, her loneliness and fear. She'd gifted him Salvaje, yet still they fought: she, with her jealousy over Miss Talmadge, he, with a heart still in denial. Their volatile kisses had lit a simmering fuse. She'd played dress-up to prove her control of him, and failed miserably in the attempt.

All those moments—and a million more—somehow had melded them, transforming his recalcitrant little mustang into a glorious Pegasus who now soared magnificently through his veins.

Wisps of drying blonde curls feathered against his face, and his buttocks tightened in response. Callie moaned, settling closer. His stomach clenched. He breathed in her scent and tightened his arm around her.

She slid closer still, tucking herself into him.

Jackson's entire body corded with need.

He forced his eyes closed, forced himself to focus on the rain drumming against the roof, on the fire's crackling hiss, on the long, rolling echo of faraway thunder—on anything besides the desire blazing a path to his loins.

A sharp clap of thunder penetrated Callie's dream, dashing the sunbeams that danced through the velvety-red roses. She fought to hold on to the image, but consciousness beckoned…and won.

Callie opened her eyes. Wavering light spilled over a hodgepodge of clothing draped across a rickety chair and table.

This isn't Mother's garden in St. Louis.

She blinked twice, pushing aside the vision, then scanned past the denim and cambric and wool. Weak flames flickered inside a stone fireplace, and wispy curlicues of smoke disappeared up the chimney.

The vaquero's shack?

Everything crashed into recall…Diego's panic, the rising water, Jackson's strong, reassuring voice filtering past her despair. The fires of awareness burned inside her. Heaviness around her waist pulled Callie back to the moment. She glanced down and identified the weight.

A man's arm.

Her gaze lanced to the garments again and her breath seized in her chest. She stared at the collection of dark colors. *Her* shirt. *Her* denims. Another pair of pants, larger—a man's. And another shirt. Which meant…

Callie swallowed and squeezed her eyes for a moment, fighting back the panic that bubbled into her throat. She didn't need anyone to blaze her a trail to the explanation.

Jackson.

She lay naked beside the man who'd stripped her and whose arm now encircled her waist. The quivering inside her grew and she waited, expecting some kind of churning indignation in her chest to heat her blood. Instead, riotous warmth coursed through her veins, pounding against her temples.

Callie closed her eyes again and allowed the truth to intensify. Life was fleeting and could be snuffed out in the flicker of an instant. Yet, miraculously she'd been given another chance. If not for Jackson's rescue, she would never know another thunderstorm or another sunny day. If not for his courage, his strength, she might never see another roundup or drive another herd of horses to Tucson.

The palpitations deepened, but not from fear. No matter how hard she tried to dismiss the facts or tamp them down, behind every exciting quiver fluttered the unrelenting wings of hope.

Frightening, elusive and exhilarating.

A kaleidoscope of memories rolled through her. The night she'd met Jackson, challenging her even as he pinned her to the ground. The day he broke the stallion in the corral, his raw masculinity astonishing her far more than even Salvaje's surrender. The weeks he'd commanded the militia, respected by so many of her neighbors and friends.

Every time she turned around, there Jackson stood, just as defiant and challenging as the magnificent stallion he now rode. He broke down every damn wall she'd ever erected. And the more she tested Jackson, the more determined he became, proving time and again his allegiance to their partnership.

Time and again his allegiance to *her*.

Heat swept Callie's face and neck and then skidded down her back, tingling every nerve-ending where his body met hers.

She bit her lower lip and pushed back the groan welling in her throat. She'd spent years denying her needs, crushing any tendrils of tenderness beneath her boot heels, thwarting trust in anyone or anything as she lost herself beneath her cloak of sadness and invincibility.

Why had she tried so hard to control this stalwart man? Her ragged sigh rose into the room. Jackson *was* right. She had propped her parents' deaths around her like a shield, holding the world at bay...until she found herself dangling at the end of a long rope, sobbing for her partner to save her.

But Jackson had saved her long before tonight.

Thunder echoed again in the distance, but the violence of the storm had ebbed into steady raindrops on the roof. Callie rolled onto her back and stared at the ceiling. Firelight gamboled across the rusty metal, drawing her gaze to the tousled cobwebs near the corner. Time had frayed the flimsy strands, just as life's ungodly journey had frayed her. Since Jackson's arrival, all her habits and beliefs had deteriorated, until finally, like the cobwebs clinging to the weathered rafters, the misconceptions that had shaped her clung by fragile threads.

Tension drifted from taut muscles as the remaining remnants of defiance faded from Callie's heart. She yearned for a new beginning filled with happiness. But more than anything, she wanted to share this breakthrough with the man who had saved her life.

Besides...he promised me he'd stay.

She glanced at Jackson to reassure herself she could trust him, but the revelation that she already did, and must have for some time, settled over her like a warm spring sun after a bitterly cold winter.

Callie swallowed and rolled to face him. Waves of dark hair tumbled about his head and neck, and a scar atop one broad shoulder had faded into a pale-colored zigzag that captured her gaze. She longed to touch the spot, wondering how he'd received the mark. Was it in war? Did it still hurt? Her hands flexed against the urgent desire and scanned further. His eyes were closed, and his lashes formed dark crescents against his skin. His mustache, a dark chevron following the curve of his upper lip, was full but well-trimmed. And a golden-brown hue, acquired during months under the territorial sun, had stained his skin. The extraordinary ache inside Callie deepened. He was handsome enough to bend iron, and she craved for only him. Craved too his constant dependability in her life.

In that moment, she realized she could never love any man but him.

The truth, hidden for so long beneath irrational fears, rippled in rivulets around her impatience. Callie moistened her lips and leaned closer, willing his eyes to open.

And they did.

Their gazes connected and heat sluiced over her cheeks. "Th-Thank you," she whispered on a shaky rush of air. "If not for you, I'd be dead."

Jackson spread his hand across her back, his palm pressing against her spine. "I'm just glad I found you in time."

His tenderness startled her, lifting a weight from her heart. Caught up in the whirling sensation setting her soul aflame, Callie issued a throaty laugh. She slipped her hand between them, and her fingers stroked the thick locks tumbling across the arm beneath his head. She lifted the sable strands, then feathered them back into place as words fell from her lips in breathless admiration. "You're so strong..." she said, hesitating as her gaze shifted back to his. "And so brave."

His eyes narrowed, but an answering smile flickered across his lips. "And you, my tough little hellion, are incredibly beautiful."

A shiver radiated from an aching void inside Callie. Her breathing quickened anew. She hungered to push past her tightly strung life, to consume him whole and to have him consume her, but she didn't know how...or where to begin. She knew so little about the dance between a man and a woman.

With each ragged inhalation, her breasts grazed his chest. Under the heat and friction, her nipples tightened into hard buds. Callie, who'd never believed in miracles, found herself believing in one tonight.

"No more beautiful than you," she said, another husky laugh slipping out. Surely amusement was wrong at such a time, but she couldn't stop herself. Not with the joyful bubbles percolating through her from the unfamiliar intimacy. She inhaled, reveling in the marvelous scent of this man. "You smell so good... like raindrops and horses and...man."

Jackson chuckled, and her heartbeat accelerated. She was unversed in so many things. When his hand on her back pressed harder, scooping her body closer, her breasts flattened against the solid wall of his chest. The compression sent her blood into a feverish race.

"And you smell good enough to eat," he whispered, a glint shimmering from the depths of his dark eyes. A long pause pulled between them and then he said, "I thought I'd lost you, Cal."

Any doubts about him really caring for her dissolved beneath his tender, compelling words. She slid a fingertip over his cheek, then down his mustache to his mouth. His lips tilted upward.

"I am so sorry I've caused you such grief," she whispered. Jackson's grin widened into a smile beneath her finger. She yearned to make him understand how she felt, but words alone could never accomplish that feat. Longing tripped through her as an idea formed. She could barely contain her own smile. "Remember when you said I'd yet to be truly kissed?" Her gaze rose, meeting his again. "You were right. Before you, I never had."

Jackson's eyes darkened and he caught her digit between his teeth in a playful nip.

The heat in her veins coursed stronger, spilling in rivulets down both legs. She traced a path to his chin, the stubble of his day-old beard rough against her fingertip. "If I promise not to scold, would you…"

"Would I what?"

"Would you show me again?"

Amusement brightened his eyes. He quirked a brow. "Are you certain? I don't want another fist in my gut." The husky chuckle that followed flowed into every lonely crevice of her heart.

Callie nodded, her face flushing hot with embarrassment. "Yes, I'm more than sure."

Jackson pushed onto one elbow, pulling the blanket's edge from beneath her. His bare leg slid over hers, and the feel of his hair-roughened flesh sent another shiver upward. She inhaled, drawing in the clean smell of his hair, the spiciness of his skin, the unique aroma of their closeness.

Firelight outlined Jackson in an amber silhouette. The breadth of his shoulders, all muscle and sinew, and his thick, tousled hair made him appear like some mighty warrior. He gazed down at her, mesmeric light reflecting in his eyes. A frisson of heat crackled through her, knowing she was the reason they shimmered.

Unable to stop herself, she trembled. Her body had a mind of its own, though she didn't quite understand what was happening. She did, however, like the unaccustomed sensations.

"Don't be afraid," he whispered.

"I'm not."

Jackson lowered his head, pausing a hair's breadth from her lips. "You sure you're not gonna punch me?"

She couldn't contain a giggle. "Keep talking and I just mi—"

He claimed her lips, lightly at first, then slanting his mouth over hers, kissed her deeply, breaking away only to catch a breath and reclaim her lips again, demanding from her as much as he gave. Callie lost herself to the taste of him, the feel of him, the rhythm of his breath against hers. But she coveted more than this teasing torment.

She wanted—no, needed—his all. Desire pumped unrestrained through her body. Jackson shifted, adjusting his weight. She gasped when his lips left hers, shuddered when he nuzzled a scalding path down her neck. The tremors deepened when his warm tongue found the pulse beating wildly in the hollow of her throat.

Beneath the caress of his calloused palms, her skin sizzled. He moved past the indent of her waist, the curve of her naked hip, smoothed his hand over her stomach. Callie slowly unraveled, and her breath caught at the back of her throat when he finally palmed her breast.

"You feel so good, Cal…" His words ended on a moan, and a wondrous burn scalded her veins. She melted beneath him and slipped her hands up and over his shoulders. Eager to be engulfed by the emotions flooding her, she allowed her exuberance to surge to the surface. Her nails dug into his muscles as she tugged him closer, rejoicing in the solid feel of this amazing man.

A nip on his shoulder brought the taste of him to her tongue.

Jackson shifted, rolling onto his hip. "Easy, hellion," he whispered against her kiss-swollen lips. "I'm not going anywhere." He pushed aside the blanket. On its drift to the floor, the wool chafed her sensitized skin.

A rush of air chilled Callie, and her skin pebbled beneath the press of his warm hands. He slid upward and again cupped her breast. A provocative tormentor, he flicked his thumb across her swollen nipple.

"Jackson," she gasped, gripping his arms, her need for him as constant as the rain's steady drumming upon the roof.

His mouth covered her breast, and any lingering inhibitions she'd felt evaporated under the heat of his tongue upon her nipple. Where his beard stubble brushed, her flesh tingled. Her breathing accelerated as waves of heat radiated across her neck and down her chest, moving past her navel and down her thighs. Between her legs, in her most intimate area, shivers tightened and throbbed. And still Jackson goaded. With each sweet suckle, each swirl of his tongue, the unbearable ache for this man deepened.

Reckless in the face of such pleasure, Callie arched her body against his, an urgency to feel his hardness banishing every thought save one.

"Please, Jackson...please," she panted, repeating his name like a prayer.

"Yes, Cal...I know," he rasped. "I want you, too." He skimmed hands down her stomach and hips, burning a path wherever he touched. "You're everything I've ever wanted."

A sob escaped her throat, frantic and raw, and she dropped the last shield from her soul and welcomed him in.

With slow, deliberate ease, he pressed lower, and lower still, until his hand nestled against her womanhood. A great, hollow need engulfed her as his bold touch ignited a hunger inside, thrilling and all-consuming. In wanton impatience, Callie spread wide her legs. When his two fingers slipped inside her cleft, she tightened her passage around them, relishing his audacious exploration.

Jackson began to stroke—easy one moment, with pressure the next—until Callie could no longer control herself. She writhed beneath him, panting his name so loudly she feared she might be crying. Joy seemed too small a word next to what she felt at the center of her being. Lost in paradise, she clung to him, their partnership now complete. Trusting Jackson hadn't made her weak; it gave her wings to fly.

And she soared toward a peak she'd never before scaled. Her heart thumped in wild staccato, and she again dug her fingers into his sweat-slickened skin. Her breathing quickened, then shallowed, and with a will of their own, every muscle inside her tensed.

And still Jackson stroked while he whispered soft words in her ear, a bewitching, hypnotic summons. Callie arched higher and higher, then finally crested...tipping over an unfathomable pinnacle. An intense white-hot fire engulfed her, and she clamped her legs together as the unfurling ecstasy expanded, surrounding her in blissful release. She convulsed into wave after tremulous wave of spasms.

Collapsing against the bed, she sobbed Jackson's name in a ragged chant that contained all the love she now felt for him.

Jackson glided his hands up, then around her hips, a demanding force now consuming him. Desire pulsed through his veins, the anticipation almost more than he could control. He allowed his need free rein and moved atop her, nudging wider apart her legs. Poised above her, Jackson pressed the length of his erection against her cleft. Slowly, he lowered, guiding himself into her slickened passage.

Even her scent embraced him, provocative and beguiling.

"I want you," he groaned, his heart hammering against his ribs. *And I love you.* Her moans answered, and with a throaty growl, Jackson surrendered to the need he'd denied for too damn long.

Callie was his paradise. And he gave himself completely to her, to the warmth between her thighs. Despite a growing euphoria, Jackson felt her fragile barrier. He hesitated, knowing he was her first. He clutched at the ends of his fraying control. *Go slow. Be gentle. I won't hurt her.*

But in her usual reckless fashion, Callie answered his pause with an edgy groan. Thrusting herself upward to break her virginal wall, she gave him her ultimate gift.

Jackson shuddered with pleasure and finally slipped *home.* He eased out, then in, again and again, building a rhythmic wave.

"Move with me," he whispered against her lips. "Yes, Cal…like that… just like that." His words, a hoarse chant, guided her onward, and his glorious nymph, bathed in firelight, somehow understood. She was a perfect fit, their bodies melting together.

He guided her long legs upward, and then around him.

Coupled together in an ageless dance, they rode heart to heart. Jackson withdrew and Callie rose, matching him in intensity and stroke. No longer separate, they moved as one with a wild and potent fury. As her fingers dug into his shoulders, Jackson fought the urge to pump faster. The soft mounds of her breasts crushed beneath him, her sweet softness molding to his chest. His body begged for release, yet he refused to yield—until Callie quickened, tightening into convulsing waves. Only then did he rear backward, slipping his hands under her hips. Only then did he give in to his need.

He intensified his strokes, driving deeper and building in speed. And then, a guttural groan ripped from his throat. He trembled, then tensed. Spasms of pleasure ripped through him and in a searing flash Jackson delivered himself unto this woman forever.

Totality slipped over him. He sunk to the bed beside her and pulled her into his arms, cradling her precious body up against his. At long last, he knew exactly where he belonged.

Chapter Twenty-Four

The rain had stopped hours before and a new day's sun shone bright around a canvas of turquoise-blue. The glare momentarily blinded Jackson when he stepped from the cabin. He needed a cup of coffee, but that'd have to wait. He blinked several times, adjusting his eyes to the intense light, then settled his Stetson. A tug on the brim helped to shade his face from the glare. Washed clean by the rain, the air was pure and invigorating and he inhaled, easing his breath out in a long sigh.

The events of last night had birthed a miracle, sweeping him away on magical wings. A euphoric completeness centered him, bouncing off the rough edges of concern. Gus and the others would be worried about their safety. And an anxious push to return to the ranch bulldogged Jackson. He'd spent far too many years being responsible to disregard the accountability sitting on his shoulders now.

They needed to head back to the ranch soon.

Jackson shoved his hands into the pair of worn gloves he'd pulled from his back pocket, flexing his fingers to work the still-damp leather into place. A low chuckle spilled from his lips as he shook his head. Gus. Hell, that ol' codger would probably figure things out the moment he caught a glimpse of Callie's pink-tinged cheeks.

The horses whickered when Jackson ducked his head and stepped inside the lean-to. Streaks of sunshine slashed through the shanty's ramshackle roof, swabbing bright stripes on the dirt floor and across the broad rumps of both animals. Two steps took him to the leathers, and he bent to lift his saddle. A moment later, he eased the McClellan onto Salvaje's back. Diego gave Jackson's shoulder a head-butt, knocking Jackson sideways.

He laughed and pushed the gelding's soft muzzle. "Sorry, pal. You're gonna stay here with our sleeping beauty 'til I get back. She needs all the rest she can get." He snugged the cinch against Salvaje's belly, unable to prevent the lingering contentment of last night from tipping his lips upward again. After her harrowing experience, Callie did need to recuperate, yet he'd kept her awake half the night.

Jackson ran a gloved hand through his hair, then resettled his hat. *What a woman my little hellion has become.* Yes, he'd let her sleep a while longer while he looked for the safest route across the creek.

"Come on, boy," he said, backing Salvaje out of the shed and sweeping into the saddle. The sun hit him full-on and hot.

Just like Callie.

His heart hammered his ribs as he fought the urge to return to her arms and bury himself inside her again. Instead, he nudged the stallion toward the Angel.

The storm had pummeled the desert. Devastation lay everywhere Jackson looked: the severed pads of prickly pear, the broken cacti and snapped willow fronds. In an embankment on his left, a saguaro jutted from the moist sand at an odd angle. On Jackson's right, desert flowers carpeted the ground in mangled clumps, their colorful blooms ripped away by the storm.

The smell of saturated soil played around Jackson's nostrils, melding with the scents of juniper and palo verde. The desert was primed to absorb soft, infrequent rain showers, not the deluge that had swallowed it whole last night.

He squinted against the refracting light filtering through a bank of snow-colored clouds. The rays fell across the carcasses of several unlucky desert cottontails not yet found by the pack of hungry coyotes who also called Dos Caballos home. Jackson plodded past, and sage sparrows fluttered from a nearby bush away from Salvaje's hooves.

Winding his way through open areas void of shrubs and perennial succulents, Jackson reached the Angel. The creek still ran deep, the water swirling reddish brown around uprooted creosote and junipers, their bark fibrous and broken and gray-brown against the rushing torrent. The saddle creaked as he shifted his weight.

They wouldn't be crossing here anytime soon.

He turned Salvaje upstream. Within a few days, the desert would burst into bloom again, invigorated by the rain's bounty. This land had an amazing ability to heal.

Like our partnership.

His relationship with Callie had shifted into a new place, and Jackson relished the intensity and discoveries yet to come. The double-quick beat of his heart concurred. Hell's fire, he'd never been in love before, and the tightness in his chest matched the tightness throbbing inside his denims.

As terrifying as the experience had been, Callie's near-drowning had forced him to realize his emptiness. Driven and determined, she possessed strengths he never expected in a woman. Her spirit completed him. He admired and respected her—most likely always had, but he'd been too stubborn to admit the truth.

Jackson revisited a glimpse of a well-satisfied Callie from last night, her skin dewy in the soft firelight. When he'd unbraided her hair, the curls had tumbled around them.

A curtain of pure silk.

Wishing he were sliding his hands through those glorious curls again, he inhaled deeply and clenched his fingers around the reins for control. When they got back to the ranch house, they'd talk about their future. Make big plans. Jackson's laugh joined the raucous shriek of a Harris hawk swirling overhead. Hell, he'd even marry her, then spend the rest of his life attempting to keep up with her reckless ways. Yes, everything had changed for them, and there was no way in hell he'd be taking that command position with the territorial militia now.

A new letter to the governor would retract his offer.

Jackson shoved aside his momentary guilt. The politician could find someone else. Jackson had finally found his purpose. But the guilt resurfaced, this time twisting his gut.

Sonofabitch.

He prided himself on being a man of his word, but now, he'd need to renege on the obligation. He'd spent a half-dozen years fighting other people's battles; he didn't want to fight anymore. More than anything else, he was damned glad he wouldn't be fighting Callie any longer. She needed him. Trusted him. He would not abandon her now. The moment he slid inside her warm and willing body, his promise to her became the only promise that mattered.

Jackson straightened in the saddle, his decision made. He'd post the necessary correspondence and withdraw his commission as soon as he returned to the ranch.

And right after that he'd take his Callie-girl to his room and make love to her again—in a proper bed this time.

Callie awoke to sunlight shining through the cabin window. Exhilaration danced through her veins. She scanned the room, but Jackson was nowhere in sight. He must've slipped away to look for a place to cross the Angel. He'd mentioned his intention last night while she lay wrapped in his embrace.

Last night.

Rolling to her back, she slipped her arms above her head and languidly stretched only to suck in her breath at the sweet, tingling awareness that claimed her. Her pulse began a slow and steady beat as Callie revisited the joy he'd brought her hours earlier.

A contented smile lifted her lips. A giggle soon followed, spilling into the room to melt with the morning sunbeams. She loved Jackson with an intensity that matched the throbbing in her veins. Never had she suspected a man's body could be so...enchanting, his arms so comforting. Indeed, Callie was pleasantly surprised to discover her broad-shouldered stallion's lovemaking was nothing like Salvaje mounting a mare.

She gingerly pushed onto her hip, then brought her legs around, dropping her feet to the floor. Callie glanced down at her naked form, expecting to see some kind of change, an outward signal, something to verify last night actually happened. But she looked the same. Only her muscles, her mind and that pleasant smolder still lingering between her legs confirmed her transformation. Sitting erect, she lowered her chin and rolled her head from side to side, concentrating on each pinch and release of the muscles along her neck and shoulders. Her ribs ached from the lifeline, but her thighs ached for a far different reason. More than a new and burning passion for Jackson Neale oozed through Callie. Hopes and dreams now searched for a place to lay down roots.

From the beginning, the man had possessed an uncanny way of crawling under her skin. Along with her clothes, last night Jackson also stripped away her protective barrier. But now she trusted him to protect her.

"Hmm," she mumbled as she stared at the warm beams of light laid across her bare feet. "The wall's down, and I didn't dissolve. In fact…" she paused and wiggled her feet in the dust motes dancing in the bright light, "…I feel pretty damn good."

In an attempt to stifle a shiver, her arms tightened around her nakedness. Before last night she'd felt sharp and brittle, the Ugly Duckling of childhood tales. Then Jackson breathed magic into her empty soul and she'd somehow been transformed—perhaps not into a beautiful swan but closer to pretty than she'd ever felt before.

The depth of her love for him aroused, yet disturbed her; the foundations of her trust lay exposed and fragile. Before Jackson, she'd thought she'd die a spinster, dried-up and unwanted, but he'd changed everything. Was this her chance for heaven on earth, a marriage filled with happiness and love like Mother and Father? Or was this thing between them destined to be a single, scandalous night?

In the aftermath of her near-death experience, turning over the reins had been easy. But now, in the light of day, she wondered if she might have given in too easily. Forevermore was a long, long time and happy endings only happened to swans and princesses in fairy tales. And nobody who loved her—well, certainly not her parents or her big brother—had ever managed to stay. To her way of thinking, there was no such thing as happily ever after.

Callie inhaled and rammed to her feet. *Stop thinking about the bad things.* She snagged her clothes from the table and dressed with a quiet calmness until the last button on her torn shirt slipped into place. Then, without warning, tears began, coursing down her cheeks in rivulets of repressed despair. Now that she'd finally admitted her love to him, Jackson would leave too.

She headed for the cabin door.

It's only a matter of time.

Ten minutes later, she had saddled Diego and was backing the gelding from the lean-to when Jackson rode up. Callie's heart lodged somewhere between its usual location and her throat. She shoved her boot into a stirrup and pulled into the saddle, then settled her hat atop her head, shoving the tangled braid over her shoulder. She avoided looking at Jackson and instead focused her gaze on a broken-armed saguaro growing at the bottom of a nearby sandy swell.

Jackson reined Salvaje to a stop beside her.

What exactly did one say to a man after making love? It didn't matter since the words wouldn't find passage past the lump in her throat anyway. Callie's cheeks blazed hotter than the rising sun.

"Good morning," he said, his saddle creaking beneath his weight.

Callie's gaze dropped to a cactus wren hopping around the remains of a nest near the base of the cactus. "Mornin'," she mumbled.

"I trust you slept well?"

His voice warmed her even more than the sunshine. She nodded, feeling as giddy as some damned school girl. "Yes. Very well. Thank you."

Thank you? Like he's just given me the time of day? Her head ached. Hell even her eyelids ached. Everything within her ached at his nearness. All she really wanted to do was climb over onto his saddle and curl up within the protective shelter of his arms again.

From the corner of her eye, Callie saw his thumb angle backward over his broad shoulder. "I've found us a safe crossing 'bout a mile upriver. Should work if we take it nice and slow."

Nice 'n' slow…like your body moved inside mine last night.

Another shiver raced through her, and her gaze ambled to his. "That's good. I'm glad you've found one." Her lips tightened as she swallowed. She owed this man so much more than distancing conversation. "Thank you again for coming to find me, and for showing me those…other things." She thought she was prepared for this moment. In fact, she'd rehearsed a speech a dozen times between crying jags and getting dressed, until nervous frustration sent her out to saddle Diego.

Yet still, she bit back a nervous giggle.

Nodding, Jackson re-settled his hat and issued a matching grin, his lips curving just a bit slower, his look more intense. He seemed to be enjoying her discomfort. Callie dipped her chin as another unaccustomed rush of giddiness tripped through her. She toyed with the reins in her hands, wrapping the leather around each finger. "Last night was—"

"Wonderful."

"Yes…wonder—"

Before she could finish the word, Jackson leaned sideways, banded her waist and nearly pulled her from the saddle as he brought her closer. "You're too far away," he whispered before his lips covered hers. Slowly, he increased the pressure, his lips parting hers until their mouths opened. Jackson increased the pressure a bit more and continued to move his lips upon hers. If not for his vise-like grip, Callie would've melted to the ground. She reveled in the warmth of his mouth, but too soon the kiss ended. A groan slipped from her when he moved away.

As easily as he'd pulled her to him, he straightened her in the saddle. "I had to have one more of those before we headed back." He lifted one devilish brow. "Hope you don't mind?"

Desire for him swept Callie's veins…their intimacy a banquet spread before her after years of isolated starvation.

"I didn't mind," she whispered. Impulsively, she leaned toward him and slid her hand across the faded denim covering his hard-muscled thigh. "In fact, I didn't mind one single bit, Mr. Neale."

Jackson's deep chuckle brought the goose bumps back to Callie. She could listen to his laughter forever. "You get any closer with your hand, hellion, and our return might be delayed."

She laughed and straightened in the saddle, gathering Diego's reins. *I could learn to be a seductress.* Her gaze locked with his. *For him.* "Well then," she said. "I suppose we'd better head back then before Gus sends out the troops."

Jackson nudged his horse alongside hers. "And the sooner we get home, the sooner I can take you back to bed."

"In that case…let's ride, partner." Again, her throaty laugh spilled between them. "And this time, I'll take the lead."

Chapter Twenty-Five

Yesterday's storm had added a stifling humidity to an already hot day and Callie couldn't wait to escape the heat. But more than that, she couldn't wait to bed Jackson again.

"Looks like we've got company," he said, spurring Salvaje into a canter.

Callie rounded the outcropping of rocks just outside the entry posts and saw horses and people filling the clearing to the side of the hacienda. She nudged Diego, and caught up. An irritated sigh slid out as she realized their plans for lovemaking would be delayed. "Guess we won't be spending the afternoon like we'd hoped," she said, staring at an elegant, black-lacquered carriage near the front steps. An impressive pair of horses pawed the sandy soil. "Never seen that rig before, have you? And there's some type of seal on the side of the door."

Her attention swept past a half-dozen soldiers, finally settling on a well-dressed man standing beside Gus near the edge of the group. Callie recognized their visitor at the same moment a ragged curse tumbled from Jackson.

Her gaze cut back to him. "I wonder why the governor's here."

Jackson didn't respond.

She stared at him as unease settled in the pit of her stomach. *He knows something.* Without waiting, she spurred Diego toward the dignitary, hollering back to Jackson over her shoulder. "I'll see what he wants."

Jackson shouted for her to hold up, but Callie kept riding. A half minute later, she reached Gus and the visiting politician and dismounted. After pulling off her gloves in stride, she shoved them into her back pocket.

"Glad to see you're not hurt," Gus said as she approached. Worry creased his weathered face. "I was just about to send the vaqueros out to find you."

"We're fine. Got caught in the floodwaters and Jackson pulled me out. Spent the night in the cabin near the Angel." She shifted her gaze to their visitor. "Afternoon, Governor. What can I do for you?"

"Nice to see you again, Miss Cutteridge." Goodwin reached into the breast pocket of his coat and pulled out a letter. He snapped it open. "I've come to escort Major Neale back to Prescott with me. With the Indian raids and all, it's not safe for anyone to ride unprotected these days."

Apprehension crept up Callie's spine. She narrowed her eyes, her heartbeat pounding in her chest. "Why does Neale need to go to Prescott with you?"

He smiled and glanced over her shoulder. The chink of Jackson's spurs hitting the ground with his dismount forced Callie to thin her lips. She willed herself to stand straighter as the approaching crunch of his boot heels echoed across her growing dread.

"Well, I've got his letter of acceptance right here." The man jiggled the correspondence in front of her, the motion generating a maddening crackle that smacked against her heart-wrenching disbelief.

Acceptance? Of what?

Callie swallowed and stared at a smudge of dirt on the lapel of the man's black serge jacket. "I was returning from El Paso anyway," he continued. "Thought I'd offer him a proper escort. I'm delighted he's moving to Prescott to take permanent command of my new territorial militia."

Callie's heart vaulted into her throat. *Oh God. No. No. No.* Her gaze cut from the governor over to Gus, but her foreman simply shrugged, eyebrows raising.

"There's obviously some mistake here," she whispered, but Jackson's *non*-reaction upon seeing the politician minutes ago had already proven otherwise. She snatched the letter from the man's well-manicured hand, agony coursing clear into her fingertips as she gripped the paper. She'd just finished reading the last line when Jackson's rich voice rumbled against her heartbreak.

"Hello, Governor," he said. Moisture flooded Callie's eyes. The bold script on the page blurred behind a growing veil of tears. Her eyes slipped shut. Inside, her heart crumbled into a million agonizing pieces.

Jackson slipped his arm around her waist and pulled her tight against him. She gasped, but the sound skidded past her lips as a brittle groan. "What brings you out this way?"

Callie's eyelids flew open. Gus, the governor, the milling soldiers faded into her peripheral vision. She pushed from Jackson's hold, staggering sideways. Turning to face him, she slammed the paper against his chest.

"Perhaps this might enlighten you," she rasped. Past the twisting misery, Callie dredged up the necessary strength to continue breathing. "H-How could you do this to me?"

Jackson secured the letter, scanned it, then dropped the correspondence to the ground. His eyes narrowed just before a sigh trailed out. "I can explain this, Cal."

"I believe it's all clearly explained right there. You've used me...nothing else needs clarification." Her temples pounded, matching her drumming pulse. Rising on tiptoes, she branded him with a glare. "Just exactly when had you planned on telling me...before or after our mounting this afternoon?"

His dark gaze bore down into hers.

And a sob pressed against her trembling lips. Only hours before he'd soothed her with his velvet-trimmed lies, his breath purling into her oh-so-trusting ears. *Don't you dare look at me with those soulful eyes, you...you insufferable liar.* The joy-filled hope she'd carried home with her severed away with the swiftness of a guillotine. Before she could stop them, blistering words propelled from the bowels of her shattered dreams. "How dare you bed me like a whore for your pleasures when you knew full well you were leaving?" The splendor of their lovemaking had now become an oozing wound.

Jackson reached out and banded her waist, jerking her up against him once more. Dark brows furrowed, and his penetrating gaze burned into hers.

His voice a husky command, he growled, "Don't do this."

"Don't do this?" Holding fast to the lifeline of her wrath, Callie flung the words back at him. The dreadful ache inside her swelled, spilling down both unsteady legs. "How ironic, since it appears to be you who has already done the *undoing?*" Since she could not make the feelings this man had birthed inside her last night go away, she'd make damn sure he did.

Barely seeing past the tears now filling her eyes, she jabbed a finger against his hard-muscled chest. "You've got ten minutes to get off this ranch. If you're not gone by then, I'll have the vaqueros tie your sorry ass to that carriage."

Jackson's lips tightened into a hard line, his gaze unwavering and intense.

She pushed from his arms and stumbled backward. Again he reached for her, but this time Callie sidestepped and spun away. His searing deceit melted her fairy tales into wretched piles of dust. If he touched her again, she'd splinter into a million teardrops. The last thing she expected the first thing this morning was for Jackson to ride out on her so soon, but she'd rather die than beg him to stay.

She swung and pointed a finger at her foreman. "You make sure he's on that rig, Gus. Do you hear me?" The man nodded and she whirled to face the governor as she pointed down the entrance lane. "And you...you've got who you came for, now get the hell off my ranch."

The hurt so heavy now she could hardly breathe, Callie turned and forced herself to put one foot in front of the other. Each step labored against a desperate need for Jackson. A dozen footfalls later, she stumbled up the risers and across the porch. Her hand closed around the front door's iron latch as the image of his body atop hers resurfaced in her mind.

God...I slept with him. How could I?

Tears finally spilled, cascading down her cheeks and seeping into the corners of her mouth. The briny tang only accentuated her foolishness.

I didn't want him here, anyway.

But the ludicrous lie impaled her heart. Callie pushed into the house, no longer able to hold back her sobs. With as much force as she could muster, she slammed the door behind her. The entry room windows rattled in their frames.

She shoved past Pilar and stormed down the long corridor toward her bedroom.

Jackson pulled his gaze from the front door and settled it upon Gus. "She didn't know about the letter."

"That'd be my guess," Gus said, bending to retrieve the correspondence from the ground. He handed it to him.

Jackson jammed the paper into his back pocket, then jerked a thumb toward the politician. "I'd written him several weeks ago, Gus, and if you'll remember, things between me and Callie were a whole lot different back then."

The wrangler scuffed a booted foot over the ground, then glanced at the house. "Looks like nothing's changed from where I'm standing, son."

Jackson stared at Gus. *How can I share the amazing details of last night with this man?* He couldn't, so he settled for saying, "You're so wrong. Everything's changed between us now." Jackson shifted his attention to the governor. "I was planning on writing you this evening, John. I've changed my mind about taking the command. I'm sorry about your wasted trip, but my life is here with Callie and—"

"Now wait just a damn minute!" Goodwin interrupted. "You can't change your mind. I need you and the people of this territory need you. Telegrams have already gone to the forts and settlements, and the militia volunteers are en route. Mustering begins at the end of the week. Hell, I've even wired Washington to let them know I've finally got my commander. We're growing, and we need to show the bureaucrats back east we can protect our citizens."

Jackson dismissed the frantic expression clouding the man's face. "Things have changed since I wrote the letter."

"Well nothing's changed as far as I'm concerned," the politician countered, his chest puffing out. "You gave me your word, Neale, and out here that means something." He lifted his hand and shook a finger in Jackson's face. "I trusted you. Hell, even extra provisions are on their way from Fort Whipple to Camp Lowell, per your request. Within a few months, we're moving the capitol down Tucson. You can't let me down now, not at a time like this. Things are only getting worse. In fact, just before I arrived, I received word there's been another attack near Dry Springs. More lives lost. We don't have the luxury of options any longer." The man shifted backward, lifted his hat and ran a palm through his thinning brown hair before resettling the Derby. "The army's doing what it can with the military resources they have, but this territorial militia is my major line of defense now. And whether you like it or not, it's too damn late to change your mind."

Jackson crossed his arms over his chest. "Find somebody else. You found me, didn't you?"

The governor shook his head, jamming his hands into his trousers pockets. "There's no one more qualified than you, at least not at this short notice. And you know it. You can't leave me in the lurch just because you'd rather bed some wench. For Christ's sake, Neale, people's lives are at stake here."

Jackson clenched his jaw, his lips tightening. And there it was again. Responsibility and all its insufferable weight. He damn well knew he couldn't abandon innocent settlers, and it was obvious the governor wouldn't listen anyway. Nor would Callie. Jackson was over a barrel of his own making… stretched good and tight.

"Sonofabitch," he hissed. "At least give me a few minutes to talk to her, try to get her to understand the situation."

Goodwin shifted his shoulders and adjusted his frockcoat. Relief etched across his features. "Take whatever time you need, but the sooner we're on our way, the better I'll like it."

Jackson glanced to Gus. "I'm not leaving like this, not without talking to her."

"I guarantee you, she ain't up to chatting," the wrangler drawled. "And I told her I'd make sure you got on that rig, which is exactly what I aim to do." He slid his gaze to the hacienda. "So you might want to use this time to pack your gear." He paused briefly and reached into his shirt pocket, retrieving a tarnished silver pocket watch, then tapped the glass face. "'Course, my timepiece ain't workin' quite right. Can't tell how many minutes are tickin' by." A wry smirk lifted the old man's face. "Well…get your ass a-movin', son. You ain't got all day."

Jackson nodded, turned on his boot heel and headed toward the house.

The cool interior enveloped him the moment he shoved the front door open and stepped across the threshold. He scanned the entryway, searching for Callie. His gaze came to rest upon a wide-eyed Pilar standing in the arched opening of the dining room. Sunbeams sifted through the bank of windows behind her, silhouetting her in a wash of morning light.

The cook lifted a shaky hand, pointing down the hallway.

Jackson nodded, then turned toward the bedrooms, his footsteps clipped and determined. Several seconds later, he stood before Callie's closed door. Heart-wrenching sobs emanated from within and carved a path to the center of his soul. Even through the wooden panel, he could feel her pain. He reached down and tried the latch.

Locked. Just as he knew it would be.

Her weeping instantly stopped.

He rapped upon the dark pine. "Let me in, Callie."

No reply.

He clenched his jaw. *Sonofabitch.* A shove with his foot would kick down the door. He could barge in. Try to make her listen. Try to make her understand what happened and why. With other women, the weaker ones he'd known before her, that might've worked. But not with this wounded hellion whose sapphire-blue eyes long ago had blazed a trail to his heart.

He swallowed and knocked again. Harder this time, his knuckles scraping the wood. "I wrote the letter weeks ago. And as soon as we got back I was going to write another to let John know I wasn't taking the position—that I'd changed my mind."

No crying. No words. No sound.

"Come on, Callie." His plea, carried on a taut breath, hit the barrier and fell. Without blinking, Jackson waited for any noise, any sign indicating she was willing to talk to him. He stared at the grain patterns in the wood, a masterpiece of textures and design.

Just like my hellion.

An aching tightness blossomed in his throat, the dryness forcing him to swallow again. He waited several more seconds before he spoke. "Please, Cal, let me in."

Still nothing.

Jackson's eyes drifted closed, and he flattened both palms on the door. He leaned his head against the wood, his stomach constricting into a hard knot.

He'd rather she curse or throw something. Tell him to get the hell away from her door. Jeezus, he'd even welcome another punch in the gut. Anything would be better than the damnable silence tangling his heartstrings now. His palms slid down the wood until his hands fell limp at his sides. She'd barely trusted him before; she'd likely never trust him again. She'd barricaded herself away from him as if last night had never happened.

And the door between them didn't matter one damn bit.

The thumping inside his chest pulsed in edgy rhythm. He'd received the only answer she would give him. *Silence.* His fingers curled into his palms. He ached to touch her again, to see her smile, to smell her skin. The sweet beginning, which had breathed such hope into his heart with their precious coupling last night, had evaporated in the mournful sound of her tears.

Bile rose into the back of Jackson's throat. He stifled gritty tears that clawed their way into his eyes. His heart ached. Hell, his whole body ached. He rolled his shoulder against the niggling reminder of where a reb's saber had nicked him at Chancelorsville.

Slowly, he turned around and leaned against the door, gulping a deep breath. He'd kick his own damn ass, if he could reach it. He couldn't undo the damage he'd done. His teeth grated together, echoing in his ears as anger with himself undulated through his veins in scalding waves. Regret followed, cleaving a path through a heart as hollow as a dried gourd. He'd finally found the woman with whom he wanted to spend the rest of his life, but ice would glaze hell's chambers before Callie would welcome him back to her arms.

The ache inside him churned as Jackson spotted Pilar at the end of the long hallway. His gaze dropped to the raven-black braids draping the cook's shoulders. The thick plaits resembled exclamation marks underscoring his futile attempts to try reaching Callie. A mournful expression creased the woman's sun-darkened face, and she shook her head. Without so much as a word, she stepped from his view, leaving him alone in his misery.

Jackson's pain grew—new and fearsome and raw. For one magical moment he'd reached paradise, found that wondrous place inside Callie where no man had ever touched. And then, he'd lost everything. Her rejection broke him when nothing else had—not the nightmare of Antietam or Fredericksburg or any of the other hellish slaughters he'd endured.

He pressed his hands against the cool pine until his fingertips became numb. The thought of begging her to open the damned door, begging her to listen, to believe in him again, coiled his gut tighter than a copperhead. He blew out an oath and then shoved from the door. He stalked to his own room, the spurs on his boot heels chinking across his misery. It took five minutes to jam his belongings into his saddlebags, another five to say goodbye to Gus, Banner and the vaqueros. Five minutes beyond that, Jackson sat beside the governor in the carriage, Salvaje saddled and hitched behind the vehicle.

As the entourage rode away from Dos Caballos, Jackson faced forward in silence, staring at the rocky buttes puncturing the horizon. Late-morning sun spilled in rusty red streaks across the peaks he'd grown to love. He had everything he would need to meet the governor's expectations: his guns, his military skills, his horse.

The only thing he left behind was his heart.

Chapter Twenty-Six

Six months later

The ever-present wind peppered Callie's face with sand the moment she stepped from the stable. Drawn outside by the clatter of an approaching wagon, she raised one hand to shelter her eyes and peered toward the road. Just as she had for weeks, she again wondered if this newest interruption in her now monotonous life meant Jackson Neale had returned to the ranch.

Of course she didn't mention this to her two companions inside the stable.

Callie pressed her lips together, remembering that painful dinner when she had all but screamed her new rules at everyone. Standing at the head of the table, she glared at them, her eyes swollen from tears. "And I don't ever again want his name mentioned in this house. Are we clear on that, too?"

Gus stared down at his half-empty coffee cup. Banner gripped a fork so tightly the knuckles on his ebony hand flushed white, and Pilar, whose coal-black eyes usually gleamed with adoration, glistened with intolerable sorrow.

In silence, they all nodded.

"He's gone. It's over. And that's the way it's gonna stay," Callie snapped. "We didn't need him before—and we sure as hell don't need him now."

They obeyed her demands, or at least while she was in earshot. And she hadn't spoken his name aloud since. Not once in the sixy months since he'd left her. Thankfully, most of the vaqueros were gone, having been dismissed during Dos Caballos' slow season. And their absence made enduring Jackson's that much easier to bear. The men had admired Jackson's skills and easy-going nature. They surely would've questioned his sudden disappearance. She wanted nothing to remind her he had left their lives as swiftly as he had entered. Only that hollow place where her heart still beat carried his imprint. With each passing day, the ache inside her grew…along with her list of regrets.

Thudding hooves and the jangle of halter chains drew Callie's thoughts back to the moment. A six-mule team rode the distant wavering haze.

"We got company," she hollered over her shoulder. Several seconds later, Gus and Banner ambled out of the stable.

Callie headed toward the side of the hacienda, then slumped against the pink adobe. Heat radiated into the shoulder she pressed against the wall. She crossed her ankles and jammed the toe of one boot into the sand. At least she could watch from the shade as the team maneuvered around the boulders near the entrance posts.

"Looks like a freighter," Gus said, shielding his eyes from the glare. Under the noonday sun, his white hair clung to his scalp like melting snow.

"We're not expecting supplies, are we?" Callie asked, glancing at Banner.

"No, ma'am." He mopped glistening sweat from his closely-cropped black hair with a blue-checked handkerchief. "We got all dat last week."

She shifted her gaze, scanning the area. Everything was brown—sucked dry by the hellish heat. *Just like me.* Callie wanted to blame her current temperament on the weather, but she damn well knew better.

She swallowed and tightened her lips. Every single day that passed, she wanted to curl up and die all over again.

Gus took another step forward as the wagon rolled past the stacked stones that marked the ranch's entrance. "Looks like Cavanaugh's freighter out of Tucson. See that lead mule on the right? The one with half his ear lopped off?" He tugged his gloves from his hands and jammed them into his pocket. "It's definitely Cavanaugh's. But he don't roll his big rig 'less they're delivering heavy goods."

Callie crossed her arms over her chest and worked to tamp down the frisson of excitement gasping for life inside her. "Either of you order something this month you ain't told me about?" As one, the men shook their heads. "Well then, the driver's probably lost. Give him something to drink, then get rid of him. We've got work to do."

She pushed away from the wall. Pivoting on her boot heel, she headed back inside the stable. She wanted the day to be cooler. She wanted the chores to go away. She wanted to be anywhere but here, facing a lifetime of loneliness created by her own asinine fears and God-awful stupidity. Snatching up a bucket of water, she headed toward Diego's stall.

"I can always count on you not to leave me, can't I, boy?" She dumped the tepid liquid into the trough. "You don't require a damn thing from me but sustenance."

Callie dropped the bucket and laid her head against the gelding. Diego's hide was cool and smelled like a grassy, rain-washed field. She raised her arms, wrapping them around the horse's neck.

Even breathing hurts.

"I should've just opened the damned door," she whispered, knowing the animal had heard the same confession a dozen times or more since Jackson's departure.

Callie pulled in a ragged breath, incredibly tired of replaying in her mind the events of that miserable morning. Phantom whispers of its previous night reached out to torture her with a reminder of Jackson's masculinity. Helplessly she gave in, her eyes slipping closed. She recalled the prickling sensation of his day-old scruff against her naked flesh…his warm, calloused palm sliding along her inner thigh…the thrusting strength of him between her—

"Might want to get out here, suga'pie." Her eyes flew open at Gus's gravelly rasp. With a display of energy she was far from feeling, she broke her embrace around Diego and turned to face her old friend.

"What's wrong now?" she asked flatly.

"Come take a look." Gus crooked his thumb over his shoulder, motioning toward the house. Callie's gaze followed. The wagon had angled up to the hacienda's back porch. A canvas tarp covered a large object tied in the center of the vehicle's bed.

"What is it?"

"Head on over." Gus nudged her shoulder as she pushed past. "It's for you."

"Me?" Her eyes widened, her forehead crinkling in the process. "What the hell is it?" Her heart tripped faster than it had in weeks.

He rustled a shipping form in his hand. "Been freighted all the way from New York."

"New York!" Callie headed across the clearing toward the wagon. Nodding to the teamster, she locked her gaze on Banner. "Go ahead," she ordered. "Pull off the cover. Let's see what it is."

Banner jumped into the wagon. He fumbled with the heavy knots. The driver slipped over the seat to help him complete the task, and together the men tossed free the cords.

Gus's footsteps crunched across the gravel, stopping at her back. Papers rustled again, and then she heard the low rumble of his chuckle.

Without turning to look at him, she asked, "Who sent this?"

Just as the canvas slipped aside, revealing polished mahogany, Gus announced in a gritty voice, "Steinway & Sons, New York City."

"Oh my God…" Callie gasped, her hands rising to her cheeks. She stared at the opulent square grand gleaming in the bright sunlight.

"Yep. Steinway & Sons," Gus repeated. More papers shuffled, and then he added, "'To my hot-tempered, little hellion for years and years of enjoyment. Jackson.'"

Banner dropped the tarp and shuffled backward. "Jumpin' Jeezus, Miz Callie…it's…a piano!"

"She knows what it is, you jackrabbit," Gus rasped, laying the paperwork on the seat beside the teamster who'd scrambled back to his perch. "Now get outta the way so she can have a better look."

Banner hopped from the wagon to stand beside him.

Callie couldn't move. Disbelief hammered inside her skull as a throat-clogging and bewildering joy snaked out to shred her breath. Her mind whirled around the memory of the day in the Talmadge parlor when Jackson had caught her playing with wild abandon.

H-He's bought me a piano?

Unable to stop herself, she slowly dropped to her knees. Her hands fell limp at her sides. She couldn't take her gaze off the breathtaking instrument, let alone move forward to see if it was real. Tears welled in her eyes so quickly she hadn't even had time to stop them. The back of her throat stung.

He's bought me a piano!

Her bottom lip began to quiver. Forbidden feelings unraveled from the darkness of denial at a startling rate. All she wanted to do was climb into Jackson's arms and tell him how sorry she was for not believing him, beg him to forgive her for not opening the door that day, thank him for this amazing gift.

He...bought...me...a...piano.

The tears she'd held at bay for so long finally spilled from her eyes, coursing in heated streaks down her face. She stared at the hand-rubbed Chippendale lacquered finish, at the dark, rich craftsmanship of the amazing instrument. Her lip quivered faster and faster, and like rain rushing down a dry gully, old wounds ripped open. Images bled out. Jackson breaking Salvaje with compassion. Jackson laughing about homemade ice cream. Jackson making love to her while the whole world beyond the little cabin fell away.

A sob erupted from her lips like a hiccup. Another followed. And another. She shook her head side to side. "It's the m-most beautiful thing I've ever s-seen," she sputtered, rubbing her hands up and down the front of her denims. The depth of her anguish warred with the thrill of owning such a treasure.

"That it is, suga'pie," Gus whispered, patting her shoulder. "That it surely is." Several seconds later, he stepped around her and heaved himself into the wagon. "Well, come on," he said, motioning to Banner and the driver. "This thing ain't gonna lift itself out." They worked to push the Steinway toward the backend of the vehicle.

Callie sniffled, wiping her hands down her face. She steadied her bottom lip. One minute turned into two amid the grumbles and cursing of the men as they lowered the piano.

"Well get off that ground, girl, and show us where you want to put this thing," Gus groused, groaning under the substantial weight of the instrument.

Callie scrambled to her feet and dashed the remaining moisture from her face. She whirled and headed for the house. Three steps took her across the back porch and she reached for the knob just as Pilar whisked open the door.

"*Qué pasa aquí?*" the cook asked, her eyes widening.

"Yes! Yes! And isn't it wonderful?" Callie said, a wobbly smile pushing up her lips. "It's a gift...from Jackson."

Pilar's dark eyebrows shot heavenward at hearing the man's name. Seconds later, a joyful smile erupted, plumping the cook's already chubby cheeks. "F-From Señor Neale?"

"*Sí*. Señor Neale." Callie giggled, holding the door and stepping aside so the cursing, groaning men could shuffle through the opening. They inched through the rooms with their burden until they reached the front parlor room.

Callie scooted through the doorway ahead of them, shoving aside chairs and tables and kicking away colorful Mexican rugs to clear a path. A few more vulgarities and the men finally positioned the Steinway against the wall between the two front windows.

Callie jammed her hand into her pocket, pulled out several coins and dropped them into the driver's hand. "Thanks for all your help."

"*De nada*," the man replied, swiping a sleeve across his sweaty brow. He turned and followed Pilar and Banner back through the house.

Callie and Gus simply stared at the Steinway.

Sunlight spilled over the wood, drawing out the deeper tones of rusty red and black. Gus nudged her with his elbow, his head angling toward the exquisite piece. "Well. Go on over and try 'er out."

She rubbed her hands down her hips. "Should we keep it?" she mumbled, looking up at him. "I mean, h-he's not here anymore."

"Hell yes we're keeping it! If Neale didn't want you to have this, dumplin', he wouldn't have sent it. Now get over there and play me something. I hate to see a good piano go to waste."

Callie hesitated. She should turn around and stomp away. This was so like Jackson to upstage her wounded... She paused. What? Pride? What exactly had he wounded?

Absolutely nothing that I didn't allow.

The little girl she'd buried beneath eons of unhappiness begged her to forgive him, but Callie wasn't ready to revisit the reason for her earlier tears. For the moment, she would just allow her feelings and obey Gus's request.

She took a deep breath and started toward the piano just as Banner dashed into the room. He clutched an elegantly carved round piano stool in one hand, a collection of sheet music in the other. "Dis all come wif da order too, Miz Callie," he announced, positioning the items where they belonged.

Shooting a broad grin in her direction, he stepped back.

A wavering smile touched Callie's lips. "Why thank you, sir." Pretending she again wore Pamela's beautiful evening gown, Callie swept up imaginary emerald material and then daintily lowered into place. A quick, impulsive spin on the stool brought laughter from all three in the room.

She slowed to a stop and smoothed her hands over the warmed-by-the-sun mahogany. Carefully, she lifted the wooden cover and smiled. All eighty-eight black and white ivory keys had made the journey across country without suffering a single chip.

Gus moved closer. "You do remember how to play this, don'cha?" he asked, folding his arms across his chest.

"I played a little bit back at the fort. The piano Colonel Talmadge had in his parlor." She couldn't contain a giggle. "Jackson caught me playing that afternoon and..." Her words trailed off. *Jackson.* She was so relieved to say his name again that her face actually warmed.

"Well, go on, then. Get to playin'." Gus leaned against the square grand, a proud smile anchored into place.

Nearby, Banner eased down upon the settee. "Dat's right, Miz Callie. Let's hear you play."

Callie took a breath, lifted her fingers and spread them across the ivories. As it had in Pamela's parlor, nervous anticipation flip-flopped in her stomach. She pressed down and a melodious chord filled the room. Although the instrument was somewhat out of tune from its trip across country, under the circumstances it sounded like a heavenly chorus.

"You play mighty fine," Banner said.

This time Callie laughed. "I just pushed on the keys, silly."

"Well push on 'em some more," Gus urged, an even bigger smile flooding his face. Pilar rushed into the room, wiping her hands on her apron. "Señorita Callie, *puedo?*" she asked, motioning to the space beside Banner on the settee.

Callie nodded. "Yes, of course. Everyone else is here. You might as well join in too."

For the remainder of the afternoon and well into the evening, Callie entertained her odd little family with classical selections as well as remembered tunes from her childhood. And together, they celebrated in the amazing gift from her absent partner.

As an exhausted Callie dragged herself off to bed that evening, she finally admitted changes needed to be made in her sad and empty life. Tomorrow, when she made her monthly visit to Father Miguel's orphanage with her donation in hand, *this time* she would require something in return.

"Dinner was delicious, Sarita," Callie said, laying the napkin across the center of her empty plate. She leaned aside as the young orphan removed the dishes and cutlery.

"*Muchas gracias,* señorita. We make meal especially for you." A coronet of raven-black braids wrapped the girl's head, but a few rebellious wisps managed to escape and dance against her cinnamon-brown cheeks. "Father Miguel says you are an angel. And we agree with him."

Callie chuckled and settled back in the chair. "Believe me, darling. I'm no angel, but it's my pleasure to help you all."

The child whisked away Father Miguel's empty plate and the priest nodded with a warm smile. "Thank you, Sarita. Remember, you and Flora are in charge of the kitchen duties today, so make certain the boys collect fresh water from the well. And have the other children help you with the dishes."

Both girls dutifully bobbed their heads, then glanced at Callie. "Please come back soon," whispered little Flora, who giggled as the two sprites scampered from the room. The rattle of dinner plates echoed behind them.

Callie laughed and relaxed into the chair.

"They're quite outspoken today," Father Miguel said, laughter warming his voice. The setting sun spilled through the long case window, laying tangerine-colored rays across his linsey wool cassock. He leaned back in his chair. "But what they say is true, Callie. Your gift this month will purchase McGuffey primers and a few additional writing slates for the children."

Callie smiled, remembering the colorful school books her mother had taught her from—spelling and vocabulary and word enunciations, all frustrating to a young girl who'd rather have been outdoors with her brother working horses. In spite of her slapdash approach to education, she realized the primers were probably her most important academic influence, although she'd sent more than one arithmetic slate sailing across the parlor during an especially vexing day.

Callie eased her breath out on a long sigh. "I love helping the children. And besides, it's what my family would've wanted me to do…since they're not here anymore, I mean." Leaning forward, she rested her arms upon the battered tabletop. The cuff on her right shirt sleeve still carried coffee stains from this morning. "But today, Father…" she paused and reached for her cup, "…I'm in need of something from you."

The priest's forehead crinkled with concern. "But of course. What is it you need, my child?"

Just tell him everything.

"Well…I need…" she slumped her shoulders in surrender, "…some honest advice. Yes, that's it. I need honest advice. And I figured, who better to ask than a man of God?"

The padre's brows pinched with worry. "Certainly, I am sworn to secrecy. What can I do to help you?"

Callie slid her fingers in and out of the porcelain handle of the mug. She bit her bottom lip, then released the tender tissue with another solemn exhale. "Yes. And I appreciate that, Father."

Clearing his throat, he straightened in the chair. His features shifted into a calming expression as he folded his hands into his lap. "Why don't you return to the beginning of what's troubling you, my dear. Perhaps that might be a good place to start."

Her gaze lifted and momentarily locked with his before falling away. "Yes," she replied, pausing again as Jackson's image filled her mind. She missed him so, and the ache of his absence tightened inside her. *Good God, I can't cry right here in front of the good padre.* She glanced out the window, pressing her lips together. Her focus settled on the boys retrieving buckets of water from the well in the center of the dusty courtyard. She swallowed, fighting to unknot her twisted heartstrings.

Her gaze slowly tracked back to the priest. "Well, Father…it's about my partner…"

I was a damned fool to leave her.

Jackson stared at the moon skimming the roof of the building across the dusty street. Behind him, music and laughter spilled from the cantina.

A double-damned fool.

In a slow, steady stream, he blew smoke upward, and then flicked the butt of his cheroot into the dirt. He'd spent the better part of the summer organizing the green volunteers into a solid fighting force. The men patrolled daily, and the number of Indian attacks had sharply declined. As a result, his responsibilities had eased, and along the way, he'd managed to garner a few commendations for heroic efforts.

A smirk dug into the corner of his mouth.

I don't feel so damned heroic. He raised his glass in a mock salute to the ivory globe squatting in the sky. Yep, things were running smoothly with the territorial militia. They'd even moved the capitol to Tucson and now things were running just fine everywhere except inside his heart. He'd been away from Callie for one-hundred and ninety-five days, and every damn one of them felt like an eternity. The image of her playing the piano that afternoon in the Talmadge parlor flashed across his mind once again.

She's probably gotten hers by now.

He wished he had seen her face when Cavanaugh's wagon pulled up with the piano he'd ordered that day after the horse race. That would've been worth every damn dollar he'd spent to buy the gift.

The aroma of fried beef carried on the breeze from somewhere down the street caused his stomach to rumble, reminding Jackson he hadn't eaten since this morning. He'd done his share of drinking, of course, but eating hadn't fit into his plans.

In fact, nothing fit into his plans anymore.

Dillon's voice wandered out to him from the other side of the cantina's batwing doors. "You're missing out on the festivities inside, my friend."

Jackson shrugged without looking back. "They'll get along without me." The squeak and thump of swinging wood told him his friend had stepped outside.

"Let's see," Dillon said, sidling up beside him, "you've been here for months, and you've yet to mention your hot-tempered partner even once." The scout folded his arms across his chest and stared at the mountain peaks. "So I'm guessin' that trying to ignore your feelings for Callie ain't working out, right?"

The clinking notes of the cantina's out-of-tune piano pounded around the tight grip of Jackson's heart. "What do you expect me to say about her?"

"Well...she was a big part of your life. And, now she's not."

Jackson tossed the last swallow of whiskey down his throat, wincing as the cheap swill hit his gut. He rolled the glass between his fingers, letting another flash of anguish subside. His point of inebriation finally pushed him to tell Dillon the damn truth. "I've made a big mistake, and I've hurt her."

The scout shifted, leaning a shoulder against the whitewashed post supporting the cantina's overhang. "I see. Well, did you two ever try talkin'?"

Jackson almost laughed aloud at the man's simplistic solution. He and Callie were way past the point of talking. Ever since that night in the cabin, when words weren't needed and few were spoken.

Closing his eyes, he remembered all over again the exquisite feel of her.

His grip around the empty tumbler tightened as his eyelids rose. Several horses ambled down the wide street, their riders nearly as inebriated as he was now. Moonlight glinted off spurs and brass bridle rosettes. Farther down the corridor, the braying resonance of mules settled into his ears like low-rolling thunder. "I tried talking to her. She wouldn't listen." Frustration oozed through Jackson, and he bit down hard on the words. "Everyone in her life has left her. One by one. They've all gone. Including me. And I'm the biggest bastard of all."

He glanced down at the tiny rainbows of light reflected in the glass he held. "After that local militia skirmish with the Apache this past spring, I sent the governor a letter telling him I'd accept his offer to train his volunteers, but then time passed and I forgot about it. And then Callie and I worked things out a bit." He hesitated, staring up at the moon again. "Then the storm came, and I nearly lost her." The knife of loneliness cleaved deeper. "And then things changed between us forever that night. But before I could let Goodwin know I was no longer interested in his command, the sonofabitch showed up at the ranch with my letter and a raving speech about home and country and God save the damn queen. Callie never gave me a chance to explain."

"But you did send the letter, right?" Dillon asked, never cracking a smile. "So she thought you were leaving her, too."

Jackson nodded, his gaze lifting upward. A thousand stars blanketed the night, but what he saw lay over twenty-eight weeks in the past.

"This is not an irreversible mistake, my friend." Dillon's words worked like a vise across Jackson's heart. The thump of the batwings again fractured the night as a pair of cowboys staggered out of the cantina. Teetering on wobbly legs, the vaqueros nearly bumped into Jackson before stumbling off down the boardwalk.

Jackson glanced at them, but his mind focused elsewhere. "You don't understand what happened that night," he whispered.

"Judging by the way you're acting, I've a pretty good idea." The scout levered away from the post, and Jackson's gaze slid back to lock with his. "Look," Dillon said, "I don't usually mess in issues of the heart, but take a hard look around you." Gone was his usual amusement. His mouth formed a straight, grim line. "This problem between you two is something you can fix. And it all comes down to whether or not you love her. The rest of the bullshit is just details." He stepped from the walkway onto the street. Dust puffed up from beneath his boot. Glancing over his shoulder, Dillon stared at Jackson for a long moment. "A good woman is hard to find out here. If it were me, and if I'd had the privilege of bedding her, I sure as hell wouldn't be standing here holding an empty glass in my hand and nursing regrets. Not when there's someone like her back home."

The scout disappeared into the shadows and Jackson listened to the crunch of his friend's boots fading into the night. The warm breeze off the desert buffeted the mournful sounds of a bugler playing taps over at Camp Lowell.

Jackson listened, the lump tightening in his throat. A moment later, he turned and entered the cantina. He had a glass that needed filling and a heart that ached for only one thing.

Callie.

Not until she stared up at the moon that night did Callie know what she was going to do. The opaque, velvety circle clung to the sky like a milky-white stone. Even the pinpricks of stars winked in agreement with her growing plans.

Sharing everything with Father Miguel earlier had helped her recognize the unresolved torment that had plagued her life since her parents' death. The conversation gave her a new understanding about how to face the new fears regarding her and Jackson.

Loving doesn't have to mean losing. Loving can mean trust.

Callie leaned against the railing, raising her face into the breeze. Though it was well past midnight, she'd already gotten out of bed twice, just to sit before her beautiful piano.

The instrument was a treasure…as was the giver. Why had she not realized this before? She sighed. Her absent partner hadn't done anything wrong. In fact, she had made the grievous mistake. Jackson deserved an apology, and she would make certain he received one.

Yes…she could make it to Tucson in less than a day if she pushed hard. She would bring him back if it was the last damn thing she ever did. Callie stared at the star-draped heavens. Fearful he might not want to leave his militia command—or even see her again for that matter—revived the anguish she'd held at bay all night.

I'm such a damn fool for letting him go.

Teardrops slipped down her cheek, tracing a cool path to her mouth. She raised her hands to swipe them away. She was finished with her spiritless existence, finished with sitting here doing nothing. She had to at least try to bring Jackson home. Raiding Apaches be damned.

She owed herself that much. She owed him even more.

Chapter Twenty-Seven

"And just where do you think you're ridin'?" Gus asked, stepping into the pre-dawn shadows of the stable. He hiked up cotton suspenders over a rumpled work shirt. "It's barely daybreak, gal."

"Tucson," she said, leading a saddled Diego past the man. She stopped at the wide-open double doors, and looked back. "And you can't stop me."

"All right," he said, shoving the ends of his shirt into the waistband of his trousers. "But how about telling me why you're really going, and don't tell me you want to see the new capitol."

A heavy sigh left Callie's mouth. She gathered the reins tighter in her hands and looked eastward from the open doors. The Catalinas held back the sun, and the mountains' tenacious hold would continue for another few minutes.

"I'm bringin' him home, Gus." Her words were barely a whisper and all she could manage, yet she knew he'd heard them.

His voice lowered to match hers. "Suppose he don't want to come back, dumplin'? Did you give that some thought?"

She shrugged. "He'll come back...or else."

"Or else what?"

I don't know...

A movement across the corral caught Callie's gaze. Pilar emerged from Gus's small pueblo and headed toward the hacienda's back door. From the furtive glances she and Gus had shared lately, Callie suspected they had become intimate. Seeing Pilar settle her clothes now as she slipped into the house only confirmed things.

Not that Callie minded. Gus and Pilar seemed suited for each other. The cook's quiet reliability balanced something inside the old wrangler. Callie's gaze shifted back to the mountains. The dwindling darkness dissipated. Daylight crept over the ridgeline and spilled a weak shaft of light across her boots.

What if Jackson doesn't want me anymore?

As quickly as she conjured the grim possibility, she shoved it aside. "I'm going regardless of the outcome." Callie hesitated, took a fortifying breath and then added, "I was dead wrong, and I owe him an apology."

"An apology?"

She nodded. "I've been nothin' but crazy, and…I…I need to tell him I'm sorry for not believing in him."

"Well, you're not going without me." Gus's words were firm and left no room for argument.

Callie planted her foot in the stirrup and pulled onto Diego's back. "You stay here with Pilar." She eased into the seat. "She needs you here. I'll be fine." Reaching behind her, she rearranged the cloth bag that held her rations, then rested her hand on the cantle.

Four steps brought Gus to the gelding's side. Before Callie could react, he yanked the reins from her hand. "There's Apache out there," he snapped, all traces of warmth and understanding gone from his voice. "And you're not going without me."

"This ain't no leisurely trip, Gus. I'm riding hard and fast."

He coiled the reins in his hand and rammed himself up against Diego's neck to glare into her face. "I'm coming along, or you ain't going. And that's my final word."

Callie had seen him angry only one other time—after her parents died. She sighed. Gus had been her only *parent* since then. And instinctively she knew she must obey him.

"Fine. But you're only gonna slow me down."

"You'll get there fast enough." Five long seconds passed before he eased back, his blue eyes softening again. "It'll be safer with two riders. 'Sides, I'm good company."

Callie angled her leg over the front of the leather swell, hooking her knee around the saddle horn. Damned if the old man didn't make sense. And besides, a day in the saddle would get tiresome all alone. She leaned forward and settled her hand across her leg, her finger spinning the rowel on the spur strapped around her boot heel. "Don't you think you'd better run all this past Pilar first? I mean, you riding off into the sunset might not sit well with her. And don't think I don't know what's going on between you two, 'cause I do."

Gus chuckled, and then, reins still in his hand, he led Diego to the back porch. Callie grabbed for the saddle horn and bobbled in the seat atop the beast.

"Pilar," he hollered. A moment later, the back door cracked open.

"*Sí?*" she asked, glancing at Callie and then back to Gus.

"Come here, punkin'," he said, his voice gentled. She smiled and stepped closer. Gus slipped his arm around her plump waist, pulling her up against him. His snow-colored head bent and he whispered in her ear. Pilar giggled and nodded. Then Gus reared back and planted a kiss smack on her lips.

A second later, blushing, the cook turned and scurried back inside.

Callie sighed. "What the hell are we doing now, Gus? Playing patty cake?" Her fingers itched to pull the reins from the man and sink her spurs into Diego. *I've got to go!*

"We're waiting." He slumped against the rough-hewed post and crossed his arms, the leather leads trailing from beneath one thick arm. "So shut your trap, and relax."

Callie bit back a retort and averted her eyes, her fingers impatiently spinning the brass rowel again. Several minutes later, Pilar re-emerged and handed Gus a satchel. The cook then stepped from the porch and headed toward the stable, dipping inside. Five minutes later, a sleepy-eyed Banner emerged, leading a fully-outfitted horse.

A beaming Pilar followed behind.

Jeezus, now everybody's up...all that's missing is a marching band.

Gus stepped to the ground, flattening a palm against Banner's rumpled shirtfront. "You take care of the place while we're gone. Stay alert, the weapons loaded, and keep my gal safe."

Banner nodded.

Gus turned, planted another kiss on Pilar's lips and then climbed into the saddle. Only after he settled did he toss Diego's reins back to Callie.

"*Now* we're ready to go," he said, grinning.

A thin smile touched Callie's lips. "You're a crazy old dolt," she mumbled, unwrapping her leg and tucking her foot in the stirrup.

"That I am." Gus laughed and his gaze slid to Callie's. "You sure you want to go through with this?"

"I'm sure."

His gaze shifted westward to the distant mountain range bathed in sunlight.

"Even with them bastard Apache hidin' behind every one of the rocks out yonder?"

Her gaze followed his. A full day of arduous riding lay between this moment and Jackson's warm embrace and the only way to right the wrong she'd done and find out if he'd come back to her was to endure the perils that lay in the middle. She loved Jackson. That was all that mattered now.

Callie straightened in the saddle. "Yes," she whispered. "I'm very sure."

Gus inhaled deeply, then pulled his battered hat low over his forehead. "Well then, since you're sure, suga'pie, what'ya say we go bring your man home?" A nudge sent his gelding forward.

Callie kicked Diego into a canter behind him.

Jackson tossed the paper on the cluttered desk in front of the governor. The small-framed man glanced at the bold writing, then bolted up from his chair and stared through wide, bespectacled eyes. "What the hell is this?"

"It's my resignation."

Goodwin opened his mouth to speak, apparently thought better of the idea, and then slowly leaned back, clasping his hands behind his back.

"Now look, Jackson," the politician all but purred. "Things are running smoothly. Cochise hasn't been seen in a month, and every señorita this side of the border is begging to warm your bed. Why in the hell do you want to go and do a damn fool thing like this?"

"Let's just say I'm done soldiering, and leave it at that."

Goodwin looked up at Jackson through squinty eyes. A full moment passed before he placed a palm flat upon the resignation paper and leaned forward. "But that doesn't quite explain why you're handing me this."

Jackson remained silent.

The governor issued a deep sigh, straightened and then walked around the desk to sit on a corner facing him. The man's expensive linen frockcoat fell to one side, revealing costly buff-colored britches. He matched the superior appointments of the plush office.

All polish and brass.

Heavy tapestry adorning the windows of the chamber held back the morning sun, darkening the room to a cozy haze. Acrid smoke coiled upward in a thin stream from a cigar burning in the crystal ashtray. The ember end of the tobacco glowed orange.

"Do you want more money? Will that keep you here?" he asked.

Jackson shook his head. "It's not about money."

"How about a drink then?" The politician motioned toward a crystal carafe sitting on a silver tray near the bookcase. Jackson declined, but Goodwin slid from the desk anyway and walked to the cluster of glasses beside the decanter. "A little something, perhaps, while we discuss this."

He poured liquid into two shot glasses and handed one to Jackson.

After raising his glass in a halfhearted salute to the statesman, Jackson brought the expensive brandy to his mouth. The first sip cut like a knife as it scraped a path to his stomach. The second emptied the amber contents and slid down his throat. He placed the glass on the desk and picked up his hat.

"The militia's running fine, John, and Major Beckman is ready to assume command. I've trained him myself, so I know he's able." Not that he owed the governor any explanations. Nor was he legally bound to the position. Jackson nonetheless skimmed across the only answer that mattered. "I'm returning to Dos Caballos after the review on Saturday, and I wanted to take this opportunity to thank you for the chance to serve the territory."

The governor downed his drink in one gulp. He coughed once, then stared at Jackson. "I assume there's no stopping you?"

"Not a chance."

John studied him for several seconds, his lips tightening in obvious defeat. Finally, he extended his hand. Their palms slid together and they shook.

"You're the best damn leader I've ever known, Neale. The volunteers respect you, the Injuns are afraid of you and that black beast you ride, and the women...hell, the women adore you." He laughed, patting Jackson on the back as he walked him to the open door. "If I was a worrying man, I'd be afraid you'd take away my future votes. So you be sure to let me know if you ever have any grand illusions of running for office, will you?"

"Rest easy, Goodwin. I'm leaving the politics to you."

The broad smile returned to the man's face. "I appreciate your hard work, Neale. I sure do."

Jackson nodded, settled his hat and strode from the office, closing the door behind him with a firm tug. A smile sunk into the corner of his mouth as his heartbeat kicked up another notch. "I'm coming home, hellion," he said out loud as he headed toward the militia headquarters. "Whether you like it or not, I'm coming home."

Chapter Twenty-Eight

The desert heat shimmered in undulating waves, settling over the Apaches like a heavy hand. Straddling their ponies, the twelve exhausted braves endured the soaring temperature in stony silence.

Taza scanned his companions as they rested their horses beneath a stand of ironwood trees. Army scouts tracked them with relentless vigor. Bows and arrows were no match for the powerful weapons of the military.

A subtle motion caught Taza's attention. He pulled himself straighter. Was that human or wildlife slipping in and out of the shifting shadows?

He leaned forward, staring past the craggy outcropping of stone, across individual clumps of sage grass and wide-armed saguaros, centering his focus on the images wavering in the heat.

Human.

Better yet, white-eyes.

The muscles in Taza's neck tightened. He searched for additional horsemen, but saw nothing.

He eased back. These were not the skillful scouts of the white man's army. These two rode alone. With amazing proficiency, they melded into their surroundings, seemingly floating across the sandy valley. But as good as they were at blending into the desert, they were not good enough to hide from his eyes.

He issued a bird-like chirp, drawing the attention of his companions. In silence, he indicated the prey.

Taza allowed a grin to shift his dry lips. Gone from their mountain home for more than two weeks on a desperate search for provisions, the hunting party seemed destined to return empty handed. *Usen* had now interceded, bringing him the gifts of saddles and horses.

He wanted so much to please Cochise.

Taza watched in silence as the riders maneuvered their mounts down a shale incline, one following in the other's tracks.

His lips shifted into a smirk. Skilled, these two. But not skilled enough to avoid him.

His gaze again swept the arid terrain. In the distance, serrated rocks jutted upward and in between, the ground rose higher. Taza turned his pony toward the swell, motioning for his comrades to follow.

He maneuvered around a cluster of saguaros, guiding his pony over several exposed roots near the base of the soaring, sixty-foot giants. Several small birds poked their heads from cavities carved into a massive arm of a nearby cactus. Taza hoped the feathered creatures would not chatter their displeasure as the group rode past. As quickly as the birds had emerged, however, they retreated, and Taza breathed a sigh of relief.

He reined his pony to a stop and waited for the two unsuspecting riders to draw closer, waited until they crossed into the shadowy silhouette cast by the ridge behind them, waited until he knew his aim would be true, then he reached over his shoulder into the leather pouch strapped across his back. Carefully, he withdrew a slender willow and notched the arrow against the taut strand of his bow.

Inhaling, he stretched high from his waist and readied his weapon of death. The rays of the late-afternoon sun warmed his skin, yet Taza paused, his patience ingrained—learned from a lifetime of watching.

His eyes narrowed with concentration.

A single bead of sweat trickled down his face, tracking over his cheekbone, and down into the spill of hair that fell over his bare shoulder. And still he waited, mimicking the bold form of his father, the warrior leader he hoped one day to become.

Just as the sun sizzled into the sand, Taza let the arrow fly, barely feeling his callused fingertips release the bowstring. Only the snap of sinew against the silence confirmed the deed.

The willow struck the front rider. The shock and impact heaved the body upward from the saddle, forcing the *ndaa's* arms into a cradling motion in a feeble attempt to hold on to life.

Another smile traced Taza's parched lips. A heartbeat later, the old white man with hair the color of snow tumbled sideways from the saddle and fell to the ground.

Yes!

The trap he'd set had been sure; the location he'd selected would offer no sanctuary to these two. He'd learned well from his elders.

He reached behind him, withdrawing another arrow. This one he would send into the smaller rider who'd bolted from the saddle to hunker beside Taza's first mark.

Raising his readied bow, he again stretched tall from the waist. His elbow rose as he angled his shot. A shaft of amber light fell across his mark, and he caught sight of the rider's long, golden plait.

Startled, he lowered his bow.

Though cleverly disguised beneath her layers of man's clothing, her shape was more rounded—her outline female. Taza's forehead creased with his momentary pause. He'd killed white women before, but never at such close range.

Taza lowered back to his horse and narrowed his eyes. He stared at her, watching as she struggled with the weight of the old man, attempting to pull him up against a cluster of rocks.

She ripped away the man's shirt to view the penetration point where the arrow had embedded. She broke the shaft. Though he could not speak their language, he recognized the distress in her garbled words, understood the hand gestures.

The wounded man wanted her to flee.

She refused to go.

Regardless, the woman would never outrun Taza. His resolve strengthened. Barbaric invaders such as these had slaughtered his family, invading his home and life, ripping away his happiness and forevermore replacing it with an unquenchable drive for revenge.

He raised his bow again, sighting down the slender willow shaft. He'd send this deep into her chest, spreading the mark of death across her breast as surely as her kind had torn his own mother from him.

"For *shima*," he whispered.

The harsh shriek of a hawk shattered the fury raging inside Taza. The sound forced his focus up. His fingers loosened their grip on the bow. In stunned silence he stared at the great soaring bird riding the air currents just above his head.

Chéek'e. Let it be?

Why had those words run through his mind? An omen? Reluctantly, he lowered his weapon.

Taza returned the arrow to the pouch and stared at the circling bird. Did the Powers know something he did not? Perhaps this woman would be of more value to him alive than dead.

He acknowledged the creature, issuing a sharp shriek in return. Seconds later, the magnificent hawk glided away.

Taza spoke to his comrades, sharing with them his plan. And several moments after that, they began their slow approach to the woman.

The circling birds caught Dillon's attention. He pulled back on the reins of his paint and issued a heavy sigh. He'd seen the telltale sign of death so often it rarely unsettled him. He knew something unpleasant waited over the rise.

The Papago Indian riding beside him muttered something along the same lines, and Dillon nodded before nudging his gelding forward. The sand made soft sucking noises beneath the animals' hooves.

What would it be this time? A dead freighter? Another destroyed homestead? Hell, the Apaches didn't give a tinker's damn whom they killed. They just killed.

Dillon had seen it all. But like a tincture, the need to continue scouting swirled inside his veins, making him hard and bitter and perfect for the job. Truth be told, deep down inside his heart, he didn't care what bodies he stumbled across because no one alive mattered all that much to him—except Jackson Neale.

Hell, the only person he could say he liked probably was making plans right now to saddle up his horse and return to his ranch.

Lucky bastard.

At least Jackson had someone to care about. As strange as she could be, Callie Cutteridge was a woman, and a beautiful one beneath all her animosity. Jackson loved her—an emotion Dillon had never quite understood or experienced.

Nor had he wanted to, for that matter. He'd been alone for so long he rather liked it that way. He preferred isolation, and that pathetic quality was what made him so damn good at his job. He only rode with a handful of scouts—all handpicked by him. Though not as skilled as he, they were nonetheless adequate. And their presence provided him the additional eyes he needed.

He passed the back of his hand over his bristled face to wipe away the sweat.

They'd been trailing this band of Apaches for nearly ten miles. A small party, no more than a dozen, but the sonsofbitches were too damn close to Tucson to allow the good citizens any comfort.

A shout pulled Dillon from his musings. He glanced up and spotted one of his outriders galloping fast toward him.

"You're a damn fool for riding like that in this heat, Ronnie," he snapped when the boy pulled up hard beside him.

"A b-b-body, Reed. J-Just over yond-der." Dillon ignored the boy's heavy stutter. Despite the affliction, the young buck could sniff out a mountain lion if he'd been asked to.

The boy gestured toward the slope of rocks behind him. "I d-don't know if h-he's still alive th-though."

Dillon nodded, easing his Colt from its holster. The sun laid a silver glint across the barrel. "What do you say we all ride over and take another look? If he's dead, then we'll drape the body behind your saddle for the ride home since you found him."

Dillon didn't wait for the reply; he simply nudged his gelding into an easy canter toward the rocks.

Jackson heard the heavy thump of the scout's footfalls before he saw the man. He wanted to buy his friend a drink since dawn would find Jackson heading for Dos Caballos.

He shoved back the chair opposite him with the toe of his boot and waited for the scout. A moment later, Dillon pushed through the saloon's batwing doors.

The man made a lean, lethal-looking silhouette against the smoking oil lamps. Another heartbeat passed before Dillon's gaze connected with Jackson's. Worry etched the wind-scraped face.

The scout headed toward him, then eased down onto the spindle-back. The chink of his Mexican spurs brushing the wooden chair rowels sounded tinny and cold.

Jackson pushed the shot glass filled with whiskey toward his friend. "How'd it go?" He knew something was wrong when Dillon refused the liquor. Jackson leaned back, raising the front legs of his own chair in the process. "What happened?" he asked, crossing his arms over his chest. As of this morning he was no longer in charge of *problems*, but his voice filled with a calm authority out of habit.

He waited while the scout drew a sustaining breath, obviously searching for words—so unlike the other times when he'd shared scouting reports with amazing glee.

"We found a rider an hour or so out," Dillon finally replied, his words falling out in a flat whisper. "West toward the Tanque Verde corridor. From what I could tell, they were skirting the ridgeline, trying to make it into Tucson before nightfall. He's with the doctor now, but he's lost a lot of blood."

Jackson waited, nodding. The physician had honed his skill on the battlefields back east and could speak five languages. Whoever the poor bastard was who needed medical treatment, at least there'd be no language barrier.

But Jackson knew Dillon well enough to know the scout was heading into unpleasant territory. Uncertainty about why he'd present bad news like this sent an uneasy chill up Jackson's spine.

Dillon slid his right hand around the drink. Dirt ringed the fingernails gripping the shot glass. He raised his head. Their gazes locked. The creases carved into the corner of the scout's eyes deepened. "We just got back a few minutes ago. The wounded man with the doc is your friend, Gus Gilbert."

The chair dropped to all fours with a slam so loud Dillon closed his eyes. He opened them in time to see Jackson unfolding his arms.

"What the hell did you say?" His friend leaned forward and stared across the scarred tabletop.

This was the worst part. The part that would hurt. The part that he didn't want to say.

Dillon dropped his gaze to his drink. "He took it low in the shoulder. Damn arrow sunk deep into his muscle, glancing off his shoulder blade. She tried to break the willow shaft, to push it out and stanch the blood. But there wasn't enough time."

"What in the hell are you talking about?" Jackson growled, climbing to his full height to tower over Dillon. The chair clattering to the floor only emphasized the horror. Nauseating fear threaded through each one of Jackson's words. "Goddammit, are you saying—"

"Callie. Yes, Callie was with him. They were riding in to find you. She wanted to bring you home, to apologize to you. At least that's what I got from Gus before he blacked out."

Dillon didn't look up. He didn't need to. He knew exactly what he would see.

He moved his hand in a tight circle, swirling the liquor in his glass, working hard to keep his own emotions in check.

When at last he raised his head, it was to see the back of Jackson's large form pushing out through the swinging doors on a frantic course toward the doctor's office.

Dillon brought the glass to his mouth and winced at the sting against his chapped lips. In one long pull, he swallowed the blistering whiskey, welcoming the stab that did a fine job of disguising the damn lump in his throat. He returned the emptied glass, upside down to the table, then pushed his chair backward.

Another reason why I'll never fall in love.

The medical office lay three doors down from Renaldo's Cantina, and as Dillon drew closer he could hear Jackson interrogating the surgeon. Heard, too, the doctor reminding in a gruff voice that his skills had been honed on the battlefields, and if anyone could save Gus Gilbert it would be him.

Dillon glanced inside as he surged past. Gas lights on the far wall illuminated the occupants within. He caught sight of his friend bending over Gus, his left hand gripping the shoulder of the old wrangler. Panic darkened Jackson's face into a mask of sheer misery.

Dillon shifted his gaze back to the street.

If there was any hope at all of finding Callie, his friend would need the best tracker available.

And that'd be me.

He stepped from the boardwalk, his spurs chinking in stride. Crossing the dusty street, Dillon headed straight toward the stable and their waiting horses.

Chapter Twenty-Nine

"She's still alive." Jackson's voice was the thinnest of whispers. "They've got her trussed up pretty good though." Two hundred yards below, a thread-thin flicker from the Apache campfire would offer little warmth to his hellion. He lowered his field glasses and demanded calm to the restlessness churning inside. The previous four hours had been a tortuous hell, not knowing what he'd find.

Fear for her safety had carved tight creases across his forehead. "I count twelve. They're armed with bows."

"And Gus and Callie's guns," Dillon added. "Looks like a food-scavenging group. They're young. Less-experienced. Set themselves up for the night ringed by mountains, and there's only one way out."

"A foolish mistake for them."

"But perfect for us."

Jackson glanced toward his friend sprawled nearby across the ledge. Darkness draped them both. At the bottom of the rocky slope milled a dozen Papago and Navajo scouts. "You all did a good job finding her. I owe you."

Dillon nodded and Jackson turned back to the Apache camp. Inhaling, he lowered his head to his forearms. His heart ached for Callie, knowing how terrified she must be. He longed to hold her, to kiss away her fears, to tell her how he loved her. The gut-wrenching longings pushed for reckless action, for him to draw his Remington and shoot every red-skinned sonofabitch in the encampment below. But an ingrained restraint birthed on the battlefields back east cut straight through Jackson's yearnings with a caution that needed no utterance.

She lived...for now that would have to be enough. His thoughts tripped one over the other as he grappled for a plan to free her—something that would place her in the least amount of danger. He raised his head. Peering through the field glasses, he again sighted his tempestuous partner.

Word of Callie's abduction had spread through Tucson like a desert storm, but he'd been surprised at the number of volunteers who'd shown up. Half the state militia was only hours behind them and eager to kill more Indians for the fifty dollar reward each male Apache scalp would bring. In their anticipation, most would forget about the precious woman caught in the middle of the communal hatred the whites and Apache bore one another.

The silence of the sleeping desert pushed against Jackson, and his heart hammered with an intensity that nearly cleaved his chest. The heat of the day had not predicted the bone-chilling night to come. Despite the frigid bite, sweat streaked Jackson's face. Callie possessed more courage than any of her captors, but her mettle was of little help in untying her bonds.

Jackson's breath steadied as a plan began to germinate. Coiling inside his brain, the idea gained merit. It was a reach by any standard, yet killing them outright might get Callie injured in the process. He allowed his plan to grow. Swallowing the lump in his throat, Jackson breathed in the calmness of the surrounding desert.

Yes, the concept might work.

Dillon's low voice broke into Jackson's thoughts. "We could wait for the militia to arrive and then spread them out along the ridge and—"

"A stray bullet could be disastrous." Jackson's reply scraped the darkness like a rusty blade. "I'm not willing to take that chance." He pointed to the right. "You agree the only way out for them is through that rocky spur?"

The scout's gaze followed. He nodded.

"Then we're not waiting for the militia to arrive." He dismissed the puzzled expression creasing his companion's face. "Come with me."

On hands and knees, Jackson pushed backward down the rocky incline, crushing brick-red petals of a honeysuckle vine that clung to the stony face.

The sweet perfume trailed him. During his descent, his coat sleeve snagged a Staghorn cactus drooping under the chill of night. One of its barbs stabbed through the wool. Jackson disregarded the irritation and continued down the slope. He jumped the last few feet to the bottom, landing with a heavy thud. Dried seed pods dropped by nearby palo verde trees crunched beneath his boots.

The horses snorted when they rejoined the scouting party. Jackson moved close to the ancient trees where Salvaje was tied. He smoothed his hand down the stallion's neck. "You're a damn good horse. The best I've ever had," he whispered. "And you helped save her life that rainy night. I'm gonna ask you to save her one more time, my friend." The animal bobbed his head in the silvery light as if already knowing what fate awaited him. Eager to put his idea into action, Jackson climbed into his saddle.

Dillon pulled up onto the paint. The Indians followed suit, climbing atop their own mounts.

And a moment later, they all headed toward the rocky opening while Jackson told them of his plans.

Callie shivered as she peered up at the canopy of sky speckled with diamond-light. One by one, the stars winked out, marking an end to the miserably long night. Her gaze shifted to the horizon brightening under a smear of violet. For a fleeting breath the sterling light hovered, the silence of daybreak oppressive because it brought a reminder of her losses.

The throbbing pain inside her chest bloomed. *Gus.* He'd filled her father's shoes and stepped in for her brother—he was her pillar of strength, and he loved her despite her odious ways. She should never have allowed him to ride with her.

Tears slid into the creases of her mouth. Her tongue slipped out to lick away the moisture, the salty taste reminding her she hadn't had a drop of water in more than ten hours. A dull ache radiated down her jaw. She stared at the pockets of blue sky filtering through the emerging lavender. The striking color held the promise of another scorching, cloudless day.

She lowered her gaze to her hands. Rawhide strips bound her wrists, and the knifelike straps cut through her skin. The blood on the bindings had dried to a purple crust. She was long past caring. Her gaze moved lower. At least her denims and boots protected her bound ankles from the wicked rawhide straps.

If only she could constrict the ache inside her heart.

For the hundredth time, Callie replayed the scenes from yesterday. What could she have done differently? How could she have saved Gus? As the Apaches circled them, she'd sighted-up her shots, only to watch her bullets disappear into useless puffs of sand.

She'd even lain across Gus to protect him, ignoring his feeble protests that she save herself instead. Like ghoulish specters in the dying light, the Apaches descended upon them. Why they hadn't scalped Gus mystified her. Regardless, by now the arrow would've already drained his lifeblood.

Her thoughts scattered along with the incipient dawn when the camp awakened behind her. She knew better than to look at the Apaches, having already discovered her insolence resulted in pain. Even cursing them in Spanish had brought blows. After repeated pummeling, Callie had stopped resisting.

She pulled her body into a tight curl beside the dead campfire. The agony she'd held at bay throughout the long night overwhelmed her. Maybe she could force herself to die, too. A life excluding her loved ones did not warrant living. Tears filled her eyes again, and she pressed her lips together to stifle a sob. Jackson would never know of her love, never hear her apology and never hold her again.

If she could do everything differently, she would start by writing her brother and thanking him for delivering such a strong man into her lonely life. In sending his best friend, Reece had shown her his love, his understanding of needs even she had never known she'd harbored.

Hollow inside, Callie shifted her gaze to the rocky opening through which they would leave this hidden place. A silver object caught the morning light, producing a glint. She blinked and refocused. So deep was her grief, perhaps she'd simply imagined the gleam.

Then she heard the sharp whistles of the lookouts posted near the entrance of the stronghold.

She eased upward, leaning on her bound hands. Blinking several more times to clear her vision, she stared at the point where the creamy light of the new day melted with the rocky opening. The glint was faint, but nonetheless visible. Callie's despair subsided another notch. She pushed herself higher onto her hip.

Then she saw the two riders, their broad-shouldered outlines hazy in the pale light. They rode purposefully toward camp. Behind her the Indians moved into elevated perches around the camp.

Narrowing her eyes, Callie focused harder on the approaching riders as the seconds crawled past. The young Apache leader rushed forward and delivered a swift kick to her hip with a moccasin-covered foot. She angled upward, struggling onto her knees. Despite the Apache's warning, her gaze remained riveted upon the riders. The Indian jerked her up by her arm, and she swayed on her bound feet.

The images set. Her parched lips cracked as they formed an *O* around her loud gasp. The rider in front astride his sleek-coated stallion carved a familiar profile. She didn't dare blink for fear the sight would dissolve into the sand. Elation grabbed hold, breathing life into Callie's dying heart.

Tears returned, slipping from her eyes to scald a path down her cheeks. The Apaches, the other rider—everything else faded from view. She tracked only the man who'd seized her emotions from the moment he'd entered her life, the man who'd broken down the walls she'd erected around her pain, who'd claimed her for his own in a cabin near Angel Creek. On a rush of love, his name fell from her mouth in a raw and throaty whisper.

"Jackson."

Chapter Thirty

Having heard the warning signals from the posted lookouts, Taza ordered his warriors to ready their weapons. Two riders emerged through a narrow cleft in the rocks and guided their mounts into the clearing that fronted his camp.

A curse fell from his mouth. For months, he'd used this secluded haven as a stopping-off point to refresh and gain strength. Now he'd be forced to find another site.

His lips compressed into a tight line.

White-eyes. He despised every one of them. And these two thought to taunt him by riding into *his* camp? Not likely. Soon they would be dead.

Taza snapped an order that sent several comrades scrambling onto rocky ledges. He tightened his grip on the woman's arm and jerked her upward. By now she'd learned not to fight him.

The *ndaa* drew closer, raising their arms to indicate they carried no weapons. Riding into an enemy's camp took courage; riding in unarmed was crazy.

Fools.

The woman gasped, then spoke a single, garbled word.

She knows them.

Taza narrowed his eyes, centering his gaze on the lead man. Tall. Broad-shouldered. Determined. The *ndaa* didn't look crazy, but still… Those who were not right in the head had been touched by the spirits. He could not take their lives until he first determined this fact. Another order to his men caused them to lower their bows and stand ready.

Dawn's golden light crept up the escarpment as each passing moment brought the interlopers closer to the camp. Taza dropped his gaze to the impressive mount the *ndaa* in front rode. The animal's ebony hide glistened under the brittle light. Recognition tightened his chest. Stories of this wild beast's capture had spread throughout the camps of Cochise.

Excitement mingled with indignation. He'd been captivated by this particular stallion for years...vowing one day to capture the mystical creature himself. Taza shoved the woman toward the closest comrade, then stepped forward, centering his attention on the man who straddled the fabled horse.

The white-eyes reined to a stop before him and dismounted. Taza did not have long to wait to hear the strange words. A heartbeat later, the second man translated the taller one's garbled sounds into the smooth tongue of the Apache.

"I recognize and respect you as the leader of this band of hunters. My name is Jackson Neale, and I, too, am a leader of warriors. But today I choose to talk instead of kill."

Heat flushed Taza's face. He narrowed his eyes. *Bold words from one without a weapon.* Curiosity nipped at him, tamping back his anger. He waited for one breath, then another, before glancing at the interpreter, then back to Jackson Neale. The man's eyes were the color of night and filled with an odd gleam.

Taza cocked his head and scanned the *ndaa* from the top of his wide-brimmed hat to the tip of his dusty boots. "I am Taza. First son of Cochise. Why are you so foolish as to ride unarmed into my camp?"

"I've come to offer you something other than your death this day."

Although the man did not look crazy, his ludicrous words indicated otherwise. Taza quirked his brow. "That is the second time you have spoken of my death, Jackson Neale, but it is you who is closer to dying." He swept his arm wide to indicate the warriors poised atop boulders, all of them eager to let fly their readied arrows. "Without weapons, your words hold no bite."

The *ndaa* stepped closer, the tenor of his voice plunging. "Listen to me carefully." He pointed westward to the purple-hued mountains. "Before the sun crests the top of those peaks, three hundred of my soldiers will arrive at this place. Even if you run from them, they will follow. They will not turn back this time. They will hunt you until they find you. And then, they will kill you and take your scalps."

A flush seared Taza's cheeks as the killing rage returned. His chin rose higher. He stepped forward, bumping against the man. "What kind of leader warns away his enemy?"

"The kind that will risk anything to save the woman he loves." The *ndaa* scanned the female behind him and then looked back. "To die is your choice, but I offer you an alternative…something to take back to your father. A trade for the woman."

"The woman?" Taza cut his gaze to the captive. Tears flowed down her face as she stared up at this reckless man. He ground his teeth and returned his attention to the *ndaa*. "What could you offer me?"

The man ran a leather-gloved hand over the muscular neck of the stallion. "I offer my horse, the great Salvaje."

Taza swallowed. He scanned the animal's strong lines. The solid build. He'd never seen the creature this close. His fingers curled into his palm as he stifled the urge to touch the beast.

He huffed out a breath. "You could have waited for your army to arrive and taken your woman back then."

"And if it was up to the others…that is what would have happened. But I did not want to chance her being injured. Trade me my woman for the stallion and you can live to share this victory over many campfires."

Full-throated laughter from his men buttressed Taza's sarcastic chuckle. Crazy or not, the *ndaa* intrigued him. "We are but two among many, and we have listened to the white man's lies far too long—"

"I speak only the truth." The *ndaa's* dark eyes narrowed. "And I offer you this opportunity out of respect. Choose to live and tell Cochise of my hope for a new beginning for our people."

"There will be no new beginning," Taza snapped, finished with the game. "Instead, I will kill you both now and take all the horses."

The *ndaa* showed no fear. He leaned sideways and spoke to his interpreter. A nod followed, and the second man cupped his hands to his mouth, then whistled.

Mumblings from Taza's warriors grew into shouts of alarm behind him, forcing his attention to the ridgeline. Morning light fell across a dozen or more Navajo and Papago Indians, hated enemies of the Apache, traitors who chose to become the eyes of the desert for the white man. These very serpents now trained their repeating rifles upon Taza's raiding party.

Taza's breath caught, his blood chilling.

Trapped.

Seconds passed like hours as the hair on the back of his neck prickled. With only one way out, he and his warriors were the ones who would die.

"I want no bloodshed," the *ndaa* continued, his voice deep and direct. "Rather, I offer you the trade. Accept it, and you and your men can ride away free."

Too late, Taza realized the *ndaa* was as crazy as a fox. But Taza also understood family devotion and love. If the roles were reversed, he would stop at nothing to save his wife from his oppressors. He tightened his lips, a queasy feeling rolling through his stomach. This had been the omen carried by the hawk yesterday. The venerated beings who dwelled inside the mountains had sent the fearsome, feathered creature as a warning of the white-eyes' appearance.

His heart pounded against his ribs as he again scanned the ridgeline. The sight of the rifles spoke even louder than the *ndaa*. Honed from years of knowing how to survive, Taza lifted his mouth into a smirk. Yes, he would choose to survive and strike back the *ndaas* another day. "I will trade with you, and I will tell my father of your words."

The interpreter nodded and waved his arm toward the traitors lining the ridge. Upon seeing them lower their weapons, Taza shouted the order for his comrades to mount their ponies.

Turning back to his enemy, he pulled a knife from inside the tall legging of his moccasin. The blade caught the emerging light and flashed like sunrays bouncing off water. His gaze bored into Jackson Neale's. Leaning down, Taza sliced through the braided strips of rawhide that secured the woman. In the blink of an eye, the weapon returned to its place.

"You have made a wise choice today, my friend," the *ndaa* replied.

The smirk across Taza's lips widened as his warriors galloped past toward the rocky opening. "The *ndaa* and the Apache will never be friends."

He snagged the stallion's reins from the man's outstretched hand, then jammed his foot into the stirrup, swung his leg over the saddle and settled into place atop the great beast.

Nudging the stallion backward several paces, he said, "I will not soon forget your name, Jackson Neale."

The man nodded, sliding his gaze to the softly sobbing female. "Nor I yours, Taza, eldest son of Cochise."

Taza snorted in disgust, then gouged the horse's flanks with his heels, sending the animal into a strong gallop. He glanced over his shoulder in time to see the *ndaa* sweep the woman into his arms.

Straightening, Taza shrieked the Apache war cry, allowing the ebony beast to thunder over the desert toward freedom.

Chapter Thirty-One

A distant plinking from the cantina's piano floated through the open window of Room 2 at the Silver Lady Hotel. Moonlight fell in a gossamer drift over Callie and Jackson's naked forms stretched across the bed. The soft breeze kissed skin still damp from their fervent coupling.

Resting in the crook of Jackson's arm, Callie gazed at her lover. He lay on his back, his solid leg still sprawled across her thigh. The back of his other wrist rested over his eyes and a satisfied smile lifted his lips.

A hot burn flushed her cheeks. Their lovemaking had helped ease the sting of their long and dreadful ride back to Tucson, the painful procedure she'd endured while the doctor bandaged her wrists, and the angst when Jackson pulled her away from Gus's bedside following multiple assurances from the physician that the old man would survive.

After securing a room for the night, Jackson led her down a darkened hallway, their boot heels scuffing on the brick-red clay tiles. She had waited while he fumbled with the key and turned the lock, then followed him over the threshold into the dark room. She'd barely had time to close out the world before she heard her name fall from Jackson's lips, as soft as the moonbeams illuminating the sparsely decorated room.

He pressed her up against the door, and then joined his mouth to hers in a desperate mating. Raw desire shot through Callie, and she wrapped herself around him. Within a minute, they'd shed their clothing and tumbled together onto the bed. The mattress sagged beneath their weight.

Their breathing matched. Rapid. Desperate. He slid his hand up her leg, over her stomach, cupping her breast with a warm palm. She gasped and flowed into him, rippling like the Angel when his thumb stroked her budded peak.

He trailed hot kisses across her face, his voice a racked whisper against her ear. "I'd thought I'd lost you forever…"

And then his mouth found hers—a sweet, hot conquest…their tongues touching, then mating. She adored the taste and essence of this man.

Callie quickened and rasped, "I'm s-so glad you saved me."

Her hands slicked over the tight muscles of his buttocks, her blood a roar in her ears. She arched against him, her shoulders straining upward from the mattress. His name, a pleading petition, escaped her mouth as his hot flesh finally found hers. Ready and eager, she burned for the fulfillment only he could give her. Few words were spoken. None were needed anyway. Their passion was a restorative drug, Jackson's strength her compass.

His hands slid beneath her hips and lifted; their breathing matched in intensity and need. And then, they merged together. Every stroke came faster. And as a whole, he healed them both.

And now they lay quiet and spent. Reconnected. Never to part again. Memorizing every line of his face, Callie traced her finger over the bristles on his cheek. The prickling sensation sent a sizzle through her, boiling her blood once more. She pushed back his long hair, tucking the thick strands behind his ear. The silken hanks slipped from her fingers as her breath stuck somewhere inside, snagging on a joyful sob that lingered in her throat. Their wedding had been quick, in front of an old priest from the church at the edge of town.

Callie had been broken. Jackson had pieced her back together—with his body, with his burning desire for her, with his promised vow to love only her. She could never thank him enough.

"I love you so much," she whispered. The words tripped over the catch in her throat. She slipped her finger over his lips, tracing his soft smile.

He nipped her slender digit. "And I you, hellion…your strength and your shoot-from-the-hip spirit." He turned his head to look at her, then added, "And your beautiful body made just for loving me."

His boldness and skill sent the flush cascading down her neck. Oh, how she cherished their intimacy. She'd never realized how lonely she'd been...until Jackson.

And now she was his wife.

Joy bubbled inside her. She wanted to laugh and learn to live again. More importantly, she wanted him to show her how. The muffled clopping of horses' hooves filtered in through the window, followed by a faint bugle call from Camp Lowell.

She released a fluttery breath and drew her hand across his chest, her palm moving in languid circles over the dark whorls that defined his solid contours. In stark contrast, moonlight bled over the white bandage wrapping her wrist. The wounds made by the Apache straps would leave scars, but they would forevermore remind her of her second chance at love and life with Jackson.

The simple gold band she wore flashed in the pale light to confirm that fact.

Jackson slipped a palm down her arm and drew her thoughts back to him. "How do your wrists feel now?" he asked, edging toward the bandage. His words tumbled into her soul, refilling the chambers of her heart.

"Better."

"I'm glad." He caressed the strip of cotton, then skimmed his fingertips lower, touching the gold band. "As long as I draw breath, Cal...you'll never hurt again."

She entwined their fingers and squeezed, relishing the waves of heat that traveled to her very core. She loved this man with a hunger that knew no bound. Gazing into his eyes, she read only adoration and abiding promise.

"I'm so sorry I didn't trust you..." Her apology hovered in the sterling light. "Please forgive me." The fragile plea tripped from her lips on a tremulous sigh.

A moment later, he pushed onto his elbow, hovering above her. "You're my world now. Forgiving is part of loving."

Bliss welled inside Callie. Never before had she known such openness. She wanted to savor all of him again, only slower…much slower this time.

The sultry night sounds beyond their marriage bed faded beneath Jackson's breathing. He slid his palm over her curves again, the husky groan of his approval nearly her undoing. And she responded, raising her hands to his shoulders, rejoicing in the way his body weighted hers. His dark eyes burned with ardent intensity for her.

He bent and caressed her ear with his lips even as his hands lovingly stroked her body. "Everything about you drives me wild."

"Me?" She giggled, skimming her palms down his sweat-slicked back. Ripples of his desire tightened his muscles. "What about you?"

"What about me?"

"I'm drowning under you," she teased.

His low laugh seared straight through her. "As I recall, hellion, you nearly drowning is what changed things between us." His hand recaptured her breast. He teased the nipple between his thumb and forefinger.

Callie gasped, enjoying the puckering sensation beneath his skillful summons. By slow degrees, Jackson lowered his head until he captured the nub in his mouth. He suckled. Flicked. Tormented. Then suckled again, drawing slow circles with his tongue. Frissons of desire radiated through Callie, then centered lower, tugging and scorching deep inside.

Her fingers dug into the rock-hard muscles of his shoulders. She pulled him closer…and closer still.

"P-Please…" she begged, not knowing the words, but knowing he'd understand.

After moving upward again, he paused, his mouth inches from hers. How easily he plucked the strings of her yearnings. "I know what you need," he crooned. "I've always known."

"I…I need you," she panted, her words a fractured groan. "Only and always you."

"And I you, Cal. Only and forever." Before her next heartbeat, Jackson covered her mouth with his. Unlike their frantic coupling of an hour before, this time he drew back and tasted again. Nibbling on her bottom lip. Savoring and suckling. Once. Twice. Teasing and tormenting, taking his time in loving her.

Shyness fled as Callie's litheness returned. Over and over she moaned her husband's name until, with an indrawn groan, she spread herself wide open for him. They moved as one in true renewal to the passionate rhythm of their hearts. And on that perfect and precious night, they saved each other, and sealed their interminable partnership within the bonds of an eternal love.

Epilogue

Dos Caballos

Twenty-six years later…

Callie smoothed her palms over the tight skirt of her peacock-blue silk dress. The full, leg-of-mutton sleeve puffs seemed absurd and she could barely see over them, but she had agreed to wear the latest fashionable design since today was an extraordinary day. She also tried to ignore the way the bustled contraption, now propped on her backside, forced her to sit even straighter. She scanned the rows of people in the room until her gaze came to rest upon the venerable form of her brother. Reece Cutteridge sat beside his precious Emaline, his arm draped across the back of his wife's parlor chair. His dark hair had turned a distinguished shade of silver, as had Emaline's previously rich raven locks. Their visits from Virginia were few and far between, and Callie was thrilled to have them here.

Her gaze shifted. Beside them, Gus Gilbert sat decked out in a new gray suit. A corded string tie gleamed against his starched linen shirt. Nearing eighty now, he moved much slower. The Apache wound he'd received that long-ago day had been slow to heal and had left his right arm useless. Since then, his responsibility at the ranch had evolved into supervising the boys' work. And, of course, offering his sage advice.

He caught Callie's gaze and sent her a quick wink.

She grinned back, her heart melting. She cherished him so. Her gaze drifted to Pilar, sitting beside Gus. A thick silver plait coiled high atop her head. She scolded him for blocking her view of the upcoming ceremony. The wrangler patted her on the hand and then eased back into his chair. Callie stifled a laugh and skimmed her gaze past their other guests..

Her attention stopped at the front of the parlor where three men stood shoulder-to-shoulder. Tall and handsome, they were the epitome of perfection. She stared at them, so proud her heart nearly burst with joy.

Cameron, her firstborn—conceived on that fateful night at the hotel in Tucson. It hardly seemed possible the precious little boy who'd tagged along after his father as Jackson worked the horses had received a law degree from Harvard last fall. Cameron now managed the business end of Dos Caballos, their well-respected breeding stable.

Callie's gaze moved to Lucas, her second son. He looked so uncomfortable in his dark woolen suit, rolling his broad shoulders against the constricting garment. She hid a grin, realizing he would much rather be stringing barbed wire in his dusty denims than standing in the parlor in such a fanciful display. He tugged at her heartstrings the most, for Lucas was their rebellious son, his hair falling well past his shoulders in thick drifts of sable. If given a choice, he far preferred the freedom of the great outdoors as he worked the horses from dawn to dark.

Then Callie's gaze came to rest upon Captain William Morrison, a friend of Cameron's from their college days. An officer now stationed at Fort Riley, Kansas, Billy had been the only one to tame their precocious Francesca. And Callie would soon call him her son-in-law.

Her joy deepened as Father Miguel hobbled forward to begin the wedding ceremony. Moments later, whispers filled the room, drawing her attention away from the old cleric and back to the doorway of the parlor.

A gasp tumbled from her lips.

Her youngest child and only daughter stood just inside the doorway. Instead of her usual attire of denims and cotton shirt, Francesca radiated elegance in a white gown that draped the corridor behind her in a flowing train.

Even though Callie vowed she would not cry…moisture flooded her eyes. When had her precious baby grown into such a magnificent woman?

A sprinkling of daisies danced like butterflies amid the golden chignon she'd fashioned of her usually riotous locks. Dashing away the tears, Callie nearly laughed aloud when she caught sight of the boots her daughter elected to wear beneath her fancy wedding dress.

Oh, Francesca...you are such a jewel. How fast the years have flown.

Callie swept her gaze to the man who waited to escort their beloved daughter down the aisle to the waiting arms of another. Her heart thundered beneath the layers of blue silk at her breast. She raised her fingers to her throat and caressed the strand of pearls Jackson had presented to her on the night of Francesca's birth.

She loved this man with a passion that knew no end.

Strands of silver now dusted Jackson's once-sable locks. And a dark suit covered the strong body that had cradled her nakedness just this morning. His gaze met hers, and his lopsided grin told her how much he loved her.

Another wave of happiness surged through her as she smiled back. Jackson walked their daughter toward her waiting groom, and as they moved past her, Callie prayed Francesca's life would be as rich and as blessed as her own had been. At Father Miguel's cue, Jackson relinquished his little girl, stepped back and then settled onto the chair next to Callie.

He clasped her hand. Their fingers entwined. "Despite our rocky start, hellion, I'd say we did pretty well."

Callie nodded, biting her lower lip to prevent a joyful sob.

"And don't worry," he whispered. "Frankie will be just fine. Fort Riley isn't that far by train. We'll go visit anytime you want. The boys can take care of things while we're gone."

"I should never have allowed you all to start calling her by that silly nickname when she was a baby."

"She's you made over, Cal...all full of sass and sparkle." He stifled a laugh. "Hell's fire, Billy's good times are just beginning." Callie shushed him before he raised her hand to his lips and pressed a warm kiss upon her fingertips.

She giggled and cupped his jaw. "We made wonderful babies, didn't we?"

she whispered, gazing at their children as the ceremony continued.

Jackson nodded. "We sure did. And you finally had a daughter you could dress up in frills and lace, only she turned out to be just like her mother after all."

"But we both play the piano well," she said, pleased with her fiftieth birthday gift from her husband. Shipped all the way from New York last fall, the elegant grand piano now occupied a place in the parlor while Callie's old one had found a new home at the orphanage.

"You look gorgeous today, by the way," Jackson added, drawing her gaze back to his. "All dressed up fancy and clean." He chuckled as she tugged at her skirt.

"Well, I hate this getup even though Pamela insisted I wear the dang thing." She glanced over his shoulder toward the smartly-dressed couple sitting behind Gus and Pilar. Even after twenty years of marriage to her soldier-dear, Pamela still radiated pure elegance.

"I'd do it all over again, Mrs. Neale," Jackson said, bringing Callie's attention back to him. "Every single bit of it." His grin shifted into the delicious smirk that stirred her most pleasurable places.

"I was hoping you'd say that," she said, bumping her shoulder against his. "And if you're nice, I'll let you show me again tonight just exactly what you mean."

His brow arched as a hot glint filled his gaze. "Again?"

She smiled and leaned against him. "Remember, you did save me from a lifetime of loneliness."

"Yes I did, hellion…and when it was all said and done, you welcomed me with open arms after all." He winked at her, squeezing her hand. "'Sides, I got me a pretty good trade for a black horse. A pretty good trade, indeed."

About the Author

Say hello to USA Today Recommended Read Historical Romance writer, CINDY NORD...who hopes you've enjoyed reading WITH OPEN ARMS, book two in her bestselling 'The Cutteridge Series', as well as a #1 bestselling western historical romance. Each novel of her four-book series is written to 'stand alone', but you won't want to miss the excitement also awaiting you in book one, NO GREATER GLORY, the #1 Civil War Romance at Amazon for over one full year, which the Library Journal proclaimed 'a stellar read'. The recent debut of book three, AN UNLIKELY HERO, also surged onto the coveted 'Top 100 Romances at Amazon' list thxs to her devoted readers. Book four, BY ANY MEANS, debuts the spring of 2018. Cindy is a member of numerous writers groups, and her work has finaled or won countless times in writing competitions—including the prestigious Romance Writers of America National Golden Heart Contest. A luscious blend of history and romance, her stories meld both genres around fast-paced action and emotionally driven characters. Indeed, true love awaits you in the writings of Cindy Nord. Please join her on Facebook at her popular Monday-thru-Friday morning "Coffee Klatch", as well as on Twitter at @cnord2. And keep up with her appearances, booksignings, and her love of sharing historical tidbits at her webpage: www.cindynord.com -- Long live historical romance! ♥

Website: www.cindynord.com
Facebook: Cindy Nord - www.facebook.com/cindy.nord.9
Twitter: www.twitter.com/cnord2

No Greater Glory
Amid the carnage of war, he commandeers far more than just her home.

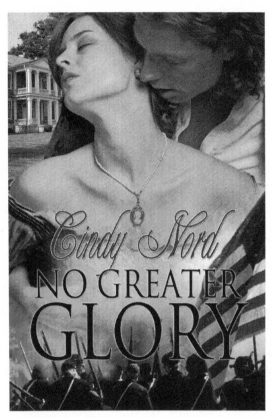

The Cutteridge Series, Book One

Widowed plantation owner Emaline McDaniels has struggled to hold on to her late husband's dreams. Despite the responsibilities resting on her slender shoulders, she'll not let anyone wrest away what's left of her way of life—particularly a Yankee officer who wants to set up winter camp on her land.

With a defiance born of desperation, she defends her home as though it were the child she never had…and no mother gives up her child without a fight.

Despite the brazen wisp of a woman pointing a gun at his head, Colonel

Reece Cutteridge has his orders. Requisition Shapinsay—and its valuable livestock—for his regiment's use, and pay her with Union vouchers. He never expected her fierce determination, then her concern for his wounded, to upend his heart—and possibly his career.

As the armies go dormant for the winter, battle lines are drawn inside the mansion. Yet just as their clash of wills shifts to forbidden passion, the tides of war sweep Reece away. And now their most desperate battle is to survive the war with their lives—and their love—intact.

Enjoy the following excerpt for No Greater Glory:

Emaline crossed the hallway and pushed open the library door.

Her eyes widened in surprise.

Reece Cutteridge sat at her desk, boldly examining the entries in her ledger.

"What are you doing?" she demanded, closing the door behind her with a firm shove. He glanced up as she strode across the rug, then continued his study of the tome. She reached across the desk and flipped the volume closed, her heartfelt resolution to be pleasant toward the man squashed beneath the intricately tooled cover. "I'll ask you again, Colonel. What are you doing in here?"

He leaned back and steepled his fingers. "I'm impressed with the horses in your stable and wanted to look over their bloodlines. They come from excellent stock." A faint smile curved his lips. "The extent of your recordkeeping is remarkable."

His compliment disturbed her. In fact, everything about him this morning disturbed her.

She straightened and locked her arms across her chest. "I've always kept excellent household records. I would've told you what you wanted to know without you snooping. In fact, I can reel off the pedigree of each animal as easily as a child can the *ABCs*."

The chair moved backward. He stood and rounded the desk, then came to a stop directly in front of her. Beneath his unbuttoned frockcoat, his white shirt lay open at his throat and a hint of dark hair teased her from the vee-shaped opening.

Emaline swallowed, squelching the preposterous urge to touch that sun-darkened spot.

Heat prickled down her spine. She averted her gaze and settled on the taut set of his shoulders. The rush of warmth spread across her belly and down her legs. She attributed the sensation to emotional and physical exhaustion.

She refused to attribute it to need.

"Men aren't the only casualties of war," he said, his silky smooth words drifting over her. "We lose good mounts in battle, too." She looked back and nearly shuddered at the coldness reflected in his eyes. "When we leave, we'll be taking your horses with us."

"W-what?" she stammered. "You can't take them. It took years for Benjamin to achieve that bloodline."

"I didn't ask for your permission."

White-hot fury poured through Emaline. All her good intentions, all her attempts to understand this man, died in the wake of his words. She didn't grieve the horses; they were another casualty of war.

What hurt most was how much he enjoyed this.

"No, Colonel, you never did ask, did you? You pilfered my supplies, mocked my character and lifestyle, filled my home with your dying, and had the audacity to lure me in with your heartbreaking loss. Then when you had me falling under your wretched spell, you boldly proclaim you're here to also steal my family's heritage." Her words tumbled out in a maddening rush. "Tell me, you…despicable heathen, do you plan on leaving me anything when you leave?"

He smiled flatly. "Vouchers."

Vouchers!

Emaline nearly buckled. "I live for the day you ride into battle and are blown straight back to hell, for that is surely where you've spawned."

"And that may well happen, Mrs. McDaniels, but when it does we'll be riding your horses."

With lightning speed, Emaline's palm connected with his jaw. The blow rocked his head to the side. The echo hardly faded before he reached out to band her waist. With a strong jerk, he brought her up against him. His belt buckle pressed into the softness of her belly. He leaned forward, dark eyes narrowing as he growled, "You will be paying me for that one."

His hold tightened and he bent her backward. His other hand slipped up to bury fingers in the base of her braid. The lower he bent, the closer he loomed. Until, in a fierce possession, he finally covered her mouth with his. Hard and demanding, he deepened the kiss. His hand freed her plait, moving down the arch in her back, then farther down over the curve of her buttocks.

With an easy sweep, he lifted her and nestled her against him.

Emaline pummeled his shoulders.

He only tightened his hold.

An incomprehensible pressure gathered deep inside her. The longer he branded her and the harder she fought, the more mesmerizing the sensations spiraled.

Unabated. Unrestrained.

Until finally her entire world tipped out of control.

Her flailing ceased. Her hands dropped back to his shoulders. She no longer could fight against his intoxicating onslaught or staunch the flow of emotions cresting over her. In fact, she could no longer remember why she needed to fight this man at all. An incredulous yearning ignited somewhere deep inside and she issued a husky, guttural groan, her lips softening beneath his just one small fraction.

An acquiescing moan followed. Abruptly, he straightened her and when his pressure lifted from her lips, Emaline's breath caught in her throat. Her eyelids shuttered open and through a shimmering veil, she watched his mouth shift sideways into a smirk. The sight slammed hard against her ragged nerves. The fragile flame of desire, so precious and new, sputtered and then flickered out.

Unable to force words past her tingling lips, she simply stared up at him. Deep inside, however, she found her fury. Like a soothing balm, she smeared it across her heart, praying all the while for God's flaming hand to strike him dead on the very spot he stood. With their gazes still locked, he reached sideways and retrieved his hat from the desk, then settled it upon his head. A heartbeat later, both he and her leather-bound ledger were gone.

An Unlikely Hero

He's a hard-as-stone scout with a broken past...and she's a reminder of all he's lost...

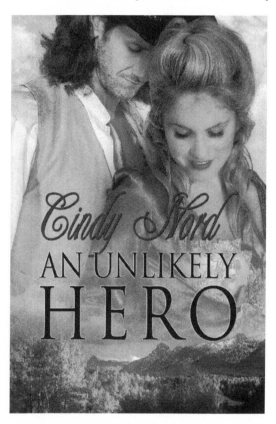

The Cutteridge Series, Book Three

Rugged army scout Dillon Reed has met his match in spoiled Boston debutante Alma Talmadge, but an unwanted assignment escorting the beauty across the wilds of America soon evolves into a journey of monumental change for them both. With killers hot on their trail, the odds of staying alive are stacked against them...and yet, falling in love was nowhere in their plans for survival.

By Any Means
Coming Spring, 2018

The Cutteridge Series, Book Four

A binding contract, five nuns, and a French beauty on the run...Riverboat gambler, Brennen Benedict has just been dealt a full hand, and his queen of hearts holds all the cards.

Made in the USA
San Bernardino, CA
28 June 2017